The *New York Times* bestselling author who brings "passion, spirit, and strength" (*Publishers Weekly*) to her unsurpassed Calder series and scores of other unforgettable novels,

JANET DAILEY

is the #1 best-selling female author in North America!

Praise for the storytelling talents of JANET DAILEY

"[Dailey] moves her story ahead so purposefully and dramatically . . . readers will be glad they've gone along for the ride."

—*Chicago Sun-Times*

"Janet Dailey's name is synonymous with romance."
—*Tulsa World* (OK)

Foxfire Light

and

For the Love of God

Books by Janet Dailey

Calder Born, Calder Bred
Stands a Calder Man
This Calder Range
This Calder Sky
The Best Way to Lose
Touch the Wind
The Glory Game
The Pride of Hannah Wade
Silver Wings, Santiago Blue
For the Love of God
Foxfire Light
The Hostage Bride
The Lancaster Men
Leftover Love
Mistletoe & Holly
The Second Time
Separate Cabins
Terms of Surrender
Western Man
Nightway
Ride the Thunder
The Rogue

Published by POCKET BOOKS

JANET DAILEY

FOXFIRE LIGHT

— AND —

FOR THE LOVE OF GOD

POCKET BOOKS
New York   London   Toronto   Sydney

POCKET BOOKS, a division of Simon & Schuster, Inc.
1230 Avenue of the Americas, New York, NY 10020

This book is a work of fiction. Names, characters, places and incidents are products of the author's imagination or are used fictitiously. Any resemblance to actual events or locales or persons living or dead is entirely coincidental.

ISBN-13: 978-1-4165-2357-4
ISBN-10:   1-4165-2357-X

This Pocket Books paperback edition February 2007

10 9 8 7 6 5 4 3 2 1

POCKET and colophon are registered trademarks of Simon & Schuster, Inc.

Manufactured in the United States of America

These titles were previously published individually by Pocket Books.

For information regarding special discounts for bulk purchases, please contact Simon & Schuster Special Sales at 1-800-456-6798 or business@simonandschuster.com.

Chapter One

*M*ost of the lime-green bedspread was hidden by the two suitcases lying open. Both were nearly filled with neatly folded summer clothes. The doors leading off the bedroom to the veranda were standing open to let in the cool night breeze off the California desert.

Joanna Morgan emerged from the spacious walk-in closet with more clothes destined for the suitcases. Her shoulder-length, ash-blonde hair was tied with a white silk scarf at the nape of her neck to keep it out of the way while she packed. Leggy and slim, she moved with an unconscious grace, her posture revealing her self-assurance and self-confidence. It was all completely natural to her, an in-born characteristic that did not need an artificial air of sophistication.

7

Preoccupied with her packing, she didn't notice the elegantly dressed woman pause outside the hall door. She was older than Joanna, but skillful makeup and the youthful style of her bleached blonde hair concealed her true age. The physical resemblance was sufficient for any on-looker to guess they were related but few suspected that Elizabeth Morgan was Joanna's mother. More often, outsiders guessed she was a young aunt.

The veneer of amiable sophistication fell away as Elizabeth surveyed the partially packed suitcases with surprise and sharpening suspicion. "Joanna, what is the meaning of this?" she demanded as she entered the room.

After sliding a brief glance at her mother, Joanna resumed her packing. There was a faint lifting of her chin to indicate her determination not to surrender to the intimidating ways of her mother.

"Uncle Reece is vacationing at his place in the Ozarks. He invited me to join him—and I've decided to accept." Her reply ended on a note of challenge.

There was a thinning of the precisely outlined carmine lips. "Why wasn't I told about this before now?"

With a pair of white slacks neatly positioned in the suitcase, Joanna turned and walked calmly to the chest of drawers. She didn't bother to immediately answer as she took out several sets of undergarments and carried them to the bed.

"In case you've forgotten, Mother, I am twenty-one. I don't exactly need your permission anymore," she stated. One shoulder was lifted in a shrug that seemed to lessen her stand of defiance. "Besides—I only decided this afternoon that I was going."

"You'll simply have to change your plans," Elizabeth Morgan announced with the airy certainty of one accustomed to having her wishes granted. "I've made arrangements for us to have lunch tomorrow with Sid Clemens. He's the head of a very prestigious advertising firm. I'm certain he can find a position for you in his agency."

Joanna stopped packing to face the woman standing at the foot of the brass bed. "I am leaving to get away from all these private job interviews you keep setting up. I haven't had a minute to call my own since I received my bachelor's degree."

With barely disguised irritation, she picked up the underclothes and began arranging them in the suitcase. Without looking, Joanna was fully aware of the affronted expression her mother was wearing. A trace of ironic humor appeared in the sudden slant of her mouth.

"We really have—'come a long way, baby,'" Joanna mockingly quoted the phrase attached to the women's lib movement. "You know there was a time when mothers paraded their daughters in front of every eligible bachelor in town. Now—we're dragged around to meet every prospective employer."

"I am only trying to help you," her mother declared stiffly.

"Well, don't," Joanna retorted sharply, then released a long breath. "I just want to get away and relax for a couple of days. There isn't any harm in that."

"But why on earth would you want to go to the Ozarks?" Elizabeth Morgan plainly showed her disapproval of the choice.

Joanna just shrugged. "It's been quite awhile since I've spent any time with Reece." She rarely referred to him as "Uncle" Reece, although he was her father's brother. She had always called him by his first name. Again, there was a half-smile when Joanna added, "And the Ozarks sound *far* away from Los Angeles." Her brown eyes cast a measuring glance at her mother. "You're just upset because Reece didn't invite you to come, too."

Her mother appeared taken aback, and more than a little flustered by the hint of an accusation that she was jealous. "I don't know what you're talking about," she protested. "Why would I be upset over that?"

Aware that her question had hit a sensitive nerve, Joanna continued with her packing, taking her time. "Daddy's been dead for almost fifteen years now. And lately, I've been getting the impression that Reece is more than just Daddy's older brother to you."

There was a wary attempt to guard her expression and hide her true feelings when Elizabeth replied, too calmly, "Over the years, Reece and I have become very good friends but if you are hinting that I want to marry him"—she paused, a little uncomfortably—"Reece has always been too much of a playboy to ever settle down." She stopped trying to explain her own attitude, diverting the topic to an explanation of his. "He isn't likely to change his spots this late in life."

But Joanna had guessed that her mother would love to be wrong. Her ego needed the excuse that it was Reece's inability to settle down that had kept him from marrying, rather than her inability to attract him to the altar.

Her mother deliberately changed the subject to revert to their original topic. "Since you insist on traveling to that hillbilly country," she began, on a faint note of contempt for Joanna's destination, "you could at least postpone your trip for a couple of days. I went to a great deal of trouble arranging our luncheon engagement with Sid Clemens tomorrow. The least you could do is keep it."

"No." Joanna closed the lid of one of the suitcases and locked it. "I've already talked to Reece and told him I have reservations on the first flight out of L.A. in the morning. I'm not changing my plans for you—or Sid Clemens."

On this issue, she could be as stubborn as her mother. She was going and she wouldn't be talked out of it.

The night air was somnolent and still, with not enough breeze to ripple the moon-shot surface of the lake. The dark sky was dusty with stars. In a nearby cove of the lake, a bullfrog sang its bass solo to the background music of *chirruping* crickets. It was a warm summer evening, the heavily wooded Ozark hills unwilling to relinquish the day's heat.

Where a hill sloped into the lake, a cabin sat in a man-made clearing, the new-fangled kind made of precut logs, modern rustic. Its covered porch faced the lake and ran the width of the cabin. A light burned inside, attracting the moths to the screened door. The soft whirr of their wings could be heard as they beat themselves against the wire mesh.

In the shadows of the porch, beyond the fall of light fanning out from the doorway, two men sat in a pair of cane-backed rockers. The run of silence between them was companionable. Yet the two men were sharply different and the differences were evident in a glance.

One was older, on one side or the other of the fifty mark. His dark hair was showing signs of graying, but his features retained the lean handsomeness of his youth, proud and strong. His eyes were dark, nearly black, lit by an unquenchable vitality. There was a worldliness about him that was not gained from this environment. His experience did not come from these hills, but outside them. Reece Morgan was the outsider, the "furriner."

The fact was reinforced by the creased finish of his khaki tan slacks and the silk-like material of his white shirt, tailored to fit his physique.

The cuffs of his shirt were precisely rolled back to reveal tanned forearms and the gold sheen of an expensive watch on his wrist. His hands were smooth, unmarked by callouses, indicating an absence of physical labor in his lifestyle. Yet, the "Ozark Mountain Country" of Missouri, raw and untamable, satisfied an inner need in Reece.

In contrast, Linc Wilder was a product of the hills, a ridgerunner as the Ozark natives called themselves. A generation younger, he was two years past thirty. His long legs were stretched in front of him, the rundown heel of a boot hooked over the arch of the other.

His faded Levis were worn smooth and soft, the material naturally molding itself to narrow hips and sinewed thighs. The plaid shirt had seen many washings. Its thinness was evident as it pulled across his wide shoulders. Clothes were not indicative of a man's status in the community. It was the quality of the man they judged, not his possessions, and his name commanded a hard-earned respect.

His long-bodied frame was relaxed in the high-backed rocker. A weather-beaten cowboy hat sat low on his forehead, shadowing his features. A ravel of smoke curled from the cigarette between his work-roughened fingers.

When he took a drag on it, the flaring glow from the cigarette cast a light on his angular features, throwing into sharp relief the hard curve of his cheekbones flattening out to the carved line of his jaw. The light briefly reflected the lustre of thick, brown hair before the hand holding the cigarette was lowered.

His brown eyes were light-colored with a dominant gold sheen. Some called them "painter's" eyes, the Ozark term for panthers or cougars. They were ever-alert, ever-alive to what went on around him, making his surface indolence deceptive.

Even now, Linc had noticed his older companion's intense interest in the thick forest of hardwoods that crowded the clearing. Without changing his relaxed position, he swung his gaze to the woods, a mixture of hickory, oak, and cedar.

A ghostly light, bluish in color, wavered in the distance at about a man's height. His glance ran back to his friend's curiously aroused expression as the corners of his mouth were pulled in, a controlled show of amusement.

"Linc, do you see that light? What is it?" Reece Morgan's voice did not contain the lazy, regional drawl of the area. Its accent came from another part of the country.

The rocker creaked as Linc pretended to look, then settled back in his chair. "Must be ghostlights, the spirit of a lost soul wandering the woods."

"Please, none of your folklore and legends." The reply was heavy with amused patience.

"It's called by a lot of names, depending on where it's seen—graveyard lights, marsh lights. In the deep woods, it's known as foxfire." He flicked his cigarette butt into the night's darkness, watching the red arc it made.

"A will o'the wisp." Reece Morgan gave it the term he was more familiar with.

"Right." Linc let his gaze wander back to the light, a phenomenon of nature. "It's caused by the decomposition of matter, giving off gases. When the conditions are right, there is an incandescent glow." The strange light appeared to move away, fading into the night and disappearing altogether.

"In all the times I've been here, I don't recall seeing it before. Is it common?" Reece asked with an intrigued frown.

"No. I've only seen it a few times myself. The first time I was just a boy and it scared the livin' daylights out of me," Linc smiled briefly at the memory. "I thought it was the ghosts of the Spanish soldiers with Cortez that were massacred by the Indians, come back to haunt the hills."

"A child's imagination is a vivid thing," Reece agreed and released a soft, contented sigh. He paused a moment as if to savor all that was around him, the sounds, the smells, the silences of the land. "I have been coming here, to this place, for the last ten years, yet I haven't tired of it. Sometimes, when my life becomes really hectic out there, it is by remembering all this that I am able to retain not only my sanity but also my perspective on what is important."

"It doesn't seem like it's been ten years," Linc mused, thoughtful for a moment.

"You have changed a great deal since that first summer we met," Reece observed and watched the dry quirk of Linc's mouth. "You were a regular hellion then. The following year, when I learned your father had died, I half-expected you to squander all the wealth and property your father had managed to accumulate in his lifetime."

"So did a lot of people," he acknowledged.

"You had to grow up fast." Reece considered that fact. "Perhaps too fast."

Only now and then did he see traces of the wild, devil-may-care youth. Responsibility at a young age had hardened the man, leaving him with a mouth less inclined to smile and a closed-in expression. Linc Wilder had become somewhat of a loner, a rogue, not without friends but with few who could appreciate the pressure associated with his responsibilities.

This was the common ground they shared, the foundation their friendship was built on. It was this insight that enabled Reece to see the restlessness that stirred beneath Linc's apparently calm surface, and had been present since Linc had arrived nearly an hour ago. He didn't know the cause for it, and nothing Linc had said enlightened him. He had been waiting for Linc to tell him, but now he decided to do a little probing.

"Have you heard from the bride and groom since they returned from their honeymoon?" Reece masked his interest in a casual question, referring to the recent marriage of Linc's baby sister, Sharon; at eighteen the youngest of the Wilder children.

"They stopped by the other evening," he admitted. "Sharon is still a giggly bride with stars in her eyes, blushing at the smallest remark." That statement led him into imparting information about the third member of the family, his younger brother, David. "David won't be coming home at all this summer. He's clerking for an attorney firm in Dallas."

"The house must seem empty." His dark gaze narrowed thoughtfully as Reece read between the lines.

After nine years of being the family breadwinner and stand-in father for his younger brother and sister, he was no longer required to fill those roles. His mother had passed away last fall; his brother was in law school; and his sister was married.

"I have some peace and quiet at last." Linc seemed to mock his own words.

"Now you are free to think of yourself," Reece reminded him. "You should find a woman, get married and raise a family before you become a crusty bachelor too set in his ways to change."

"In one breath you say I'm free, and in the next you're suggesting I should tie myself down again," Linc chided. "I notice you're still single. Why don't you get married?"

"If I could persuade a certain lady to say 'yes,' I would. But unfortunately—" There was an expressive shrug of his shoulders—"it seems the desire is all one-sided."

Linc knew the woman about whom Reece spoke. "Have you seen Rachel since you got here?" The widow, Rachel Parmelee, was in her mid-forties, proud and independent, and still attractive.

"Yes, I've seen her—and renewed my long standing invitation to dinner—and received her polite refusal." The reply was made with a faint biting edge to his voice that indicated his frustration and growing sense of hopelessness. "Is she seeing someone else? Am I trespassing?"

"I haven't heard that she's dating anyone on a regular basis. Be patient, Reece," Linc advised. "You are only here one month out of the year. It's natural for her to be wary. We ridgerunners are slow to believe the intentions of outsiders."

"Patient." There was a wealth of meaning in that single word and the raised eyebrow.

Linc had the impression that his friend's supply of patience was dwindling. He understood, but he also understood Rachel's mistrust. "If you were around all the time, it would be a different story."

"Unfortunately my business does not permit that," Reece replied with obvious regret and changed the subject. "My niece is arriving tomorrow to spend a couple of weeks with me." He paused to muse, "Joanna and I are alike in many ways. Perhaps she will find the same peace these mountains have given me."

"There's always the possibility she won't like it here. She might find it too tame after L.A.," Linc suggested.

"No." Reece shook away that thought. "She is too much like me."

"For your sake, I hope you're right." Linc gathered his feet under him to stand up. "It's getting late and I have a full day tomorrow."

"Come over tomorrow evening for dinner," Reece invited, rising too. "I want you to meet my niece."

"We'll see." Linc didn't commit himself. "I have to be over this way tomorrow afternoon to pick up the buckboard Jessie restored for me."

"Jessie Bates?" At Linc's nod, Reece laughed softly. "I think that man enjoys being a character out of the hills. I am never certain how much of what he says he really means and how much is an act put on for my benefit."

"There's no doubt he's one of a kind," Linc agreed. "I'll stop by after I leave Jessie's and let you know whether I can make it to dinner tomorrow night."

"That will be fine," Reece assured him.

"Good night." His hand lifted in a half-salute as he descended down the porch steps and walked around to the front of the cabin, facing the road.

Climbing into the four-wheel-drive pickup

parked there, he reversed it out of the driveway and onto the hard and rutted surface of a graveled road. It was narrow, twisting and winding, like nearly all the roads in the Ozark hills, especially the back roads. It was virtually without shoulders; a narrow drainage ditch separated it from the woods. Linc slowed once as an opossum scurried to escape the beam of his headlights. He slowed again where another road branched off from the one he traveled. It led to Jessie Bates's place.

Three miles further he turned into the driveway of his six hundred plus acre ranch. The yardlight was on, but no light shone from the windows of the sprawling ranch house, sitting on the crown of a bald hill overlooking the lake. Linc didn't immediately go inside, but walked around the house to stand on the patio and take in the familiar view.

Far below him and some distance away, he noticed the light shining dimly from the log cabin where Reece Morgan was staying. The cabin had once belonged to his family, as did most of the land around it. His father had built the cabin on speculation ten years ago, intending to develop and sell the lakefront property he owned. But it had turned out to be too far off the beaten path for summer tourists to want it as a vacation retreat.

In the end, his father had sold it to Reece Morgan and didn't attempt to develop the rest of the frontage. Neither had Linc since he'd taken over, although there was a market for it now.

He made a slow turn and walked to the sliding glass doors. Even as he entered the house, Linc knew he was too restless, too on edge to sleep. He went instead to the study where there was always paperwork to be done.

Chapter Two

$\mathcal{I}$t was early afternoon when Joanna Morgan's plane arrived in Springfield, Missouri. By the time she had claimed her baggage, signed all the papers to rent a car, and found where it was parked, she was almost sorry she had insisted it wasn't necessary for her uncle to pick her up at the airport.

It had sounded so simple and sensible when she'd told him her plans over the phone, especially when she'd looked at a Missouri map and seen it was roughly forty-five miles from the airport to her uncle's cabin. In Los Angeles, that was just across town.

After more than two hours in airports, waiting to leave and changing planes, plus another three hours in the air, she wasn't overjoyed by the thought her final destination was still an hour's drive away. She didn't take it too well when she discovered the little economy car she had rented didn't have air-conditioning.

She had already begun to wilt under the unrelenting heat typical of a Midwestern summer. Rolling all the car windows down gave her some relief as she traveled south on the highway. But the hot wind that blew in ruined the smoothly coiffed style of her ash-blonde hair.

The city limits of Springfield were about twenty minutes behind her when the gently rolling plateau gave way to sharply ridged hills. Her uncle had often mentioned the beauty of the Ozark Mountains, but Joanna had little time to spare to reflect on the scenery. There seemed to be more traffic than the two-lane highway could handle and she had to give her full attention to the road.

As the highway twisted up one high ridge and curved down to the next valley, Joanna found herself trapped behind a slow-moving fuel tanker truck. At twenty miles an hour, she crawled up a hill behind it, her little economy car lacking the power to accelerate past the truck in the rare narrow gaps of oncoming traffic. As soon as they reached the crest, the truck barreled down the hill trying to pick up momentum to climb the next, not giving Joanna a chance to pass. It was an exercise in utter frustration.

Between that and the baking heat of the sun,

Joanna was at the end of her patience when she reached the intersection of the state road her uncle had directed her to take. In a gesture of defiance, she thumbed her nose at the truck as she turned off.

She hadn't gone a half a mile when a farmer in a pickup truck, loaded with hogs, pulled onto the road in front of her. Again, the oncoming traffic wouldn't allow her to pass and her speed was reduced to a nerve-wracking crawl. Knotted with tension, she sat behind the wheel, her cheeks flushed with the heat, her temper seething.

Joanna wasn't sure when she first suspected that she had gone past the second turnoff. The farther she went, the more convinced she became that she had missed it. She glanced again at the directions her uncle had given her over the telephone. They sounded so straightforward and simple. How could she have possibly gotten lost?

A hundred yards ahead, there was an old service station built out of rock. A couple of old cars were parked beside the building, but it looked deserted when Joanna pulled in front of the gasoline pumps. She pushed on the horn and peered at the station, trying to see through the dusty windows. There wasn't any response to the honking of her horn but as she climbed out of the car, a man in greasy overalls ambled out of the building.

"Do ya' want reg'lar or unleaded?" he drawled and wiped his hands on an equally greasy rag.

"I don't need gas," she declared with a curt shake of her head. "I think I missed my turn—"

"You're lost, huh?" He didn't sound surprised.

Joanna bristled. "I am not lost. I only missed my turn." In her opinion, there was a definite distinction between the two.

He pushed the billed cap to the back of his head and propped his hands on his hips to shrug away the difference. "Lost or missed yore turn, you can call a cat anything you like, but it's still a cat. Where is it you are headed?"

"I was supposed to turn on Lake-road number—"

He interrupted her with a wave of his hand. "The number don't mean nothin' to me. I've been livin' here long before any of these roads had numbers on 'em. I wouldn't know one from the other. Just tell me who you want to see and I'll tell ya' how to get there."

"I'm trying to find my uncle. You probably wouldn't know him," she insisted tightly. "He owns a cabin here."

"Yore uncle gotta name?"

"Yes, he has a name, Reece Morgan," she retorted, no longer trying to contain her irritation. "If you would just tell me—"

"Is he that fella from California that bought the Wilder cabin?" His gaze narrowed as he interrupted her, studying her closely as if sizing her up. "The one I heard was sweet on the Parmelee widow?"

Joanna was taken back by his information. She didn't know who her uncle had bought the cabin from and she'd never heard of any woman named Parmelee. "He is from California," she admitted. "Los Angeles."

"Go back the way ya' come and take the second gravel road on yore left. Every time the road branches, stay to the left. Ya'll run right into it," he stated with a certainty she found difficult to question.

"How far is it?" she asked instead.

"As the crow flies, it's probably no more than four miles, but you'll have to go 'bout eleven mountain miles 'fore you get there."

As far as she was concerned, he was talking in riddles. "What is the difference between mountain miles and regular miles?" she demanded, too hot and tired to be amused by his picturesque phrases.

"A mountain mile measures the same as a regular mile. It jest takes longer to travel over it 'cause it does a lot of snakin' and twistin'." He grinned and bobbed his head. "Ya'll get the idea."

Joanna turned back to her car, muttering under her breath. "I already have."

The man had disappeared behind the building by the time Joanna drove away from the pumps and onto the road, going back the way she came. After she had made the turn onto the second gravel road on the left-hand side, she noticed the small signboard with the faded numbers of the lake road. It was no wonder she had missed it the first time.

Her car kicked up a fine, powdery dust that

drifted in through the opened windows. Joanna could feel it caking her sweat-dampened face. The only alternative was to roll up the windows. She decided she preferred the dust to the stifling heat of a closed car.

The graveled road had started out smooth enough, at least no rougher than she had expected. But within minutes after she had noticed the big ranch house sprawled on the knob of a hill, the condition of the road rapidly deteriorated. The little car bounced and bumped its way along the rough track, not wide enough to straddle the ruts.

She was forced to slow down to keep from having the teeth jolted out of her head. The trees crowded close to the road making it seem more narrow than it actually was. Their thick canopy of leaves gave shade from the sun but the thick growth also stopped the breeze and Joanna was going so slowly that the car generated little wind of its own. Her uncle had to be out of his mind to come here!

Old Jessie Bates was a wheelwright, among a handful of other things. Linc wasn't sure it was fair to call Jessie Bates "old" either. He doubted if the bony man was much past forty but everyone had called him "Old Jessie" for as long as Linc could remember. Maybe it was because the man was always spouting saws of Ozark wisdom, or maybe it was the way these Ozark hills had of aging a man before his time.

Either way, Jessie Bates was a colorful character and, like Reece, Linc suspected that the man deliberately played the part of a hillbilly. If he needed further convincing, he found it when he pulled into the yard of Jessie's cabin, a chinked log cabin, and saw Jessie hitching his pair of mules to the buckboard.

Turning off the engine, Linc climbed out of the pickup cab and walked over to where the man was hooking up the trace chains. Jessie was wearing new overalls, only they were a size too large. They made his wiry frame look scrawny— more of his costume.

"'Lo, Jessie. What do you know?" Linc stopped beside the near mule and absently slid his hand over its sleek neck.

"I don't know nothin'." The man straightened and paused for effect, a twinkle brightening his eye. "The heck of it is I didn't find that out 'til yesterday."

As he was supposed to do, Linc chuckled briefly in his throat, then questioned the man's actions. "What are you planning to do with the mules?"

"Zeb and Zeke were needin' a little exercise so I thought I'd use them to take the buckboard up to yore place," Jessie explained as if that was perfectly logical.

"There's no need. We can run it up the ramp onto the bed of my truck. It'll be quicker," Linc reasoned.

"It's too much trouble to unhitch 'em now." Jessie scratched his scraggly hair and shrugged away that logic. "You can follow me in the truck if you've a mind to."

"Then I suppose you'll want me to drive you back here." Linc eyed the man with veiled amusement.

Jessie made an exaggerated show of looking down at his feet. "I still got two legs. Reckon I can walk. Besides it's mostly all downhill. Zeke might even give in and let me ride him. Never know." He climbed into the seat of the buckboard and unwrapped the reins from around the brake handle.

Aware that he wasn't going to change Jessie's mind, Linc stepped out of the way as Jessie slapped the rumps of the mules with the flat of the reins and hollered to them. "Gee up there!"

There was the bunching of hindquarters and hooves digging in as the mules swung to the right. The buckboard groaned a brief protest before the wheels began turning. Linc waited until the team was past the pickup before he returned to it and climbed in to start the motor. It was quite a sight to travel behind the mule-drawn buckboard. If the truth were told, Linc was enjoying it just as much as Jessie.

His father had bought the old buckboard at an auction some years ago. He'd always intended to restore it but he'd always been too busy. Then he'd died and it had been left to Linc. He hadn't gotten around to it either, until this spring. There it was, rattling thirty feet ahead of him.

There was satisfaction in that, satisfaction

and just a trace of sadness. He had finished another job his father had started and not been allowed to complete. The same as he had raised his father's children; seen one of them marry and the second completing his education for a law degree—just as he'd seen to the burial of his father's wife, his mother.

The truck crept along behind the buckboard, the slow pace not requiring his undivided attention. His thoughts wandered. Linc didn't notice the buckboard had reached the fork in the road where it branched to Reece's log cabin and toward the main road. Since the intersection occurred on a relatively steep upgrade, Jessie didn't check the mules. Not expecting any traffic, he giddyuped them onto the main road.

The sudden blare of a car's horn snapped Linc out of his reverie. It was followed by a startled outcry and a thudding crunch. He braked the truck to an immediate stop and whipped out of the cab. He had enough of a view of the road to see the buckboard was halted and Jessie was setting the brake. The mules were fidgeting, on the edge of bolting, but obviously the oncoming car had taken the ditch to avoid hitting them.

Chapter Three

*P*erspiration beaded her face until Joanna felt like one big, wet dishrag. On this narrow, tree-shaded road, she didn't need the sunglasses any more so she took them off and laid them on the car seat near her purse. She opened it, looking for a tissue to wipe away some of this sticky moisture.

Her groping fingers found the usual clutter of things but didn't locate the travel box of tissues. She took her eyes off the road for only a second, locating the small container of Kleenex almost immediately.

Her glance swung back to the road as she took one out. There was an instant of disbelief. Mules hitched to a wagon! It had to be a mirage. The car was almost on top of them before she accepted that it wasn't. A second after the flat of her palm hit the horn, she wrenched the wheel sharply to the right to avoid them, slamming on the brakes at the same time.

Even at the slow pace she was traveling because of the rough road, there was still enough momentum to bounce the light car out of the narrow ditch and onto the opposite bank. The spreading, gnarled branches of a cedar tree cushioned the impact before the front bumper hit its sturdy trunk.

For several seconds after the car came to a stop and the motor died, Joanna was too shocked to move. Both hands were clenching the steering wheel. As she became aware that she was unscathed, without a bump or a bruise, the blood began to rush through her system at the absolute stupidity of the man driving that team of mules onto the road without checking for oncoming traffic. She was out of the car in a flash—hot, tired, and irritable—her patience exhausted and her temper boiling.

The slamming of the car door was a small sample of her anger. Indifferent to the rattle of harness and chains, she advanced on the skinny man in baggy overalls now standing at the head of the mule team, trying to calm them. She was too blinded with anger to notice the second man on foot approaching the scene.

"You crazy old coot!" Joanna stormed at him, her hands clenched into fists at her side as she came to a stiff-legged stop in the middle of the road. "Don't you ever look where you're go-ing?"

"Pipe down. You're scarin' ma' mules." The bony-cheeked man flashed her a hushing look and began mumbling to the edgy animals.

"*I'm* scaring *your* mules!" She couldn't be-lieve the gall of the scrawny man. "What about the fright they gave me?"

"Are you all right, Miss?"

Joanna whirled in the direction of the second voice and glared at the tall, broad-shouldered man in the western hat. "Do I look all right?!!"

She felt the swift assessment of the tawny pair of eyes. The sensation was followed by an in-stant awareness of the georgette blouse sticking damply to her skin and her travel-wrinkled skirt clinging to her sticky legs. She had perspired away all her makeup and her hair looked like a rag mop, the style blown apart by the wind and plastered to her forehead and temples by perspi-ration. She caught a fleeting glimpse of humor in his look, then it was gone. But it was like a red flag to an already angry bull.

"I wasn't hurt but it's certainly no thanks to him!" Joanna turned again on the driver of the buckboard. "You could have got somebody killed! You could have got *me* killed! You must be crazy to pull out on the road like that! Those mules are a menace! They shouldn't be allowed on public roads!"

"Now, hold on thare." The driver turned a baleful eye on her. "Don't you go blamin' my mules. They only did what they was told. It was me at the reins and it was my fault for pullin' out. I jest didn't figure anybody'd be comin'.''

Joanna wasn't mollified by his confession of guilt. "You should have looked! That's common sense! If I had been going any faster, I couldn't have avoided hitting you! You're just lucky I was going slow on this road—which doesn't even deserve to be called a road!" she added on an angry breath of contempt and was further irritated by the way the man kept soothing the mules. "In case you hadn't noticed, it happens to be my car that's damaged, not your damned mules!"

"And I'm right sorry about that, too," the man assured her curtly. "I'll pay to fix whatever damage's been done."

She looked at the man with the baggy overalls, faded shirt, and straggly dark hair. He didn't appear to have enough to keep body and soul together. Her uncle had mentioned that this area was the heart of the Ozarks and she'd heard about the poor people of these hills, barely able to scratch a living out of a soil that grew only rocks. However, at this point, her concern wasn't for his plight, but her own.

Uppermost in her mind was the fact that she was driving a rented car. If he didn't pay, she was liable, and he didn't appear to have two dollars to rub together.

"With what?" Without thinking, Joanna scoffed at the driver's offer to pay. "Some scrawny chickens?"

His head jerked as if she had slapped him. Joanna bit at the inside of her lips as she realized her thoughtless remark had hurt his pride. He shifted to face her more squarely and stood very tall and erect, his expression shuttered and cold.

"I'll pay in hard cash if it takes every cent I got," he retorted stiffly. "Ain't no one ever said yet that Jessie Bates don't pay his debts."

He made her feel like a complete ass, which didn't improve her disposition. "Just keep your money and forget it!" she muttered in angry self-disgust.

As Joanna turned to stalk back to her car, she was confronted by the second man, the younger one. His vital, rough-hewn features were cut on hostile lines, cold and forbidding.

"I can understand that you are upset because of the accident, Miss." His steady voice was low and cutting. "But you could show better manners than to insult a person by saying he doesn't have the money to pay, then refusing to accept his offer."

She was stung by his criticism and leapt to her own defense. "I'm upset and I'm hot and I'm tired. I've been driving on your wretched roads for more than two hours with a bunch of snails in front of me, no air-conditioning in the car, and in heat only the devil could tolerate. Without any warning, some jerk drives a team of mules out in front of me and my car winds up in a ditch. It isn't even my car! It's rented! I guess you could say I'm upset. Being lectured on manners is just about the last thing I'm in the mood for. I'm sorry I ever came here and I can hardly wait to leave!"

His mouth was tight and thin. "We'll be glad to help you on your way." There was a bite of sarcasm in his voice. He turned his hard glance to the driver. "Put some rocks behind those wheels and unhitch the team so we can pull her car out of the ditch."

Her attention was split between the actions of the two men, the driver as he placed chunks of rock behind the wheels so the buckboard couldn't roll backwards down the hill, then moved to unhitch the mule team from the wagon, and the tall, slightly arrogant stranger as he walked over to examine the rear of her car. When the driver began backing the harnessed mules up to her car, it suddenly became clear to Joanna what they were going to do.

"You aren't planning to use those mules to pull my car out of the ditch, are you?" she protested vigorously. "It's because of them that it's in the ditch!"

"It seems only right that they get it out, then, don't it?" the driver reasoned with defiant logic.

Joanna breathed in a deep, angry breath, and vented her disapproval on the other man, bending close to the ground to attach a chain to the frame of her car. "I told you that car is rented. Enough has happened to me already because of those mules! Get something sane and sensible—

like a truck, for heaven's sake! I've had it with these four-legged beasts!"

He paused to throw her a hard glance over his shoulder. "That makes two of us, Miss, because I've taken about all the sass I'm going to take from a woman," he snapped. "You have two choices: either shut up and stay out of the way so we can pull your car out of the ditch, or keep talking and we'll leave you here to get it out by yourself. Now, which is it to be?"

She wished she knew whether it was a short walk to her uncle's cabin or not. She'd love to tell them she didn't need their help. But she suspected it was another three or four miles—not easy, flat miles—but three or four rough and winding mountain miles. Joanna pressed her lips tightly together in a mute reply to his question, indicating with her silence the choice she made.

There wasn't any change in his expression as he turned to complete his task, not uttering a word. When the mules were hooked up to the car, he slid behind the steering wheel to assist by guiding the car. Joanna stayed well out of the way, flinching when the mules threw their weight against the car and she heard the first crunch of the tires.

The slow, steady pull of the mules began to drag the car out of the ditch without inflicting any damage on the muffler, tailpipe, or undercarriage. The combination of hundred degree temperatures, high humidity, and the air's stillness made her conscious again of the oppressive heat. She felt the uncomfortable trickle of per-spiration down her neck and into the valley formed by her breasts. A cool shower sounded like heaven at the moment.

"Whoa up thare!"

Her car was sitting squarely on the road once more. Joanna walked toward it as the man stepped out of the driver's side. He was examin-ing the front of the car when she reached it. The man in the baggy overalls was behind the car, unhooking his mules.

"Some scratches from the cedar branches on the left fender and the dent in the bumper seem to be the extent of the damages," the man announced to her.

Joanna inspected the fenders, hood, and grill for herself and arrived at the same conclusion. Not even a headlamp had been broken.

"It's a small miracle," she retorted and felt the hard pressure of his gaze on her. She lifted her gaze coolly to his face. "I suppose I should thank you for getting my car out of the ditch."

"I suppose you should," he agreed, and the uncompromising set of his features set her teeth on edge.

"Thank you." The phrase was neither sincere, warm, nor grateful.

There wasn't any satisfaction in the way his mouth tightened at her rudeness. She felt boor-ish and he was the one who was the country bumpkin.

He took a step to the side, out of her way.

"You'd better start the motor to make sure it runs."

A little irritated that she hadn't thought of that, she swept past him to climb behind the wheel. The motor kicked over on the first try and ran smoothly.

"It works," Joanna stated the obvious as the insufferable cowboy walked to the driver's door she'd left standing open. He pushed it shut for her, as though silently sending Joanna on her way. "Excuse me." Out of sheer stubbornness, she summoned him back. "My uncle has rented a cabin down this road somewhere—Reece Morgan. Would you tell me how much farther it is?"

His eyes narrowed into burnished slits. "No."

Her temper flared at his blatant refusal. She shifted the car into gear and he stepped out of the way just as she pushed her foot down on the accelerator. A glance in the rear view mirror saw him encapsulated in the dust cloud swept up by her car.

Very little of the dust actually reached Linc, but he narrowed his eyes against it to watch the car disappear around the next curve. He'd expected Reece's niece to be something better than that ill-tempered spitfire. Reece was so mannerly and courteous, but the same certainly couldn't be said for his niece. Linc was glad he hadn't gotten around to accepting that dinner invitation. This was one he was definitely going to turn down.

He turned to the buckboard and saw Jessie eyeing him with a knowing look. "T'wasn't polite *not* to tell her how far it was to the cabin."

"I give as I get," Linc reasoned, but indifferently.

"Morgan's niece, huh?" Jessie stayed with the subject of the girl.

"That's what she said." Linc changed it. "This time I'll drive ahead of you with the truck so you don't run any more cars off the road."

"Don't slow me down," Jessie advised as he hooked the last trace. "Else these mules will run right up your backside."

Linc didn't bother to respond to that boast, turning to walk to his truck.

It turned out to be closer to five miles. Joanna was just beginning to think the cowboy hadn't told her how far she had to go because she was on the wrong road. She was about ready to make up her mind to turn around when she saw the cabin.

"If this isn't Reece's cabin, it will be the last straw," she muttered to herself and turned the car into the short driveway. There was some consolation that the cabin looked civilized.

Before she was fully out of the car, a cabin door opened and her uncle appeared. "Joanna!" He greeted her with a broad smile of welcome. "I was beginning to worry about you. Didn't you say your plane was scheduled to arrive before two this afternoon?" As he came down the steps, he glanced at his watch. "It is nearly five. Was it delayed?"

"No," she swiftly corrected herself. "It was a few minutes late." He looked so cool and unruffled that she couldn't help wondering how he managed it in this heat.

"Then what took you so long to get here?" he frowned, then asked, "Did you have trouble finding the place?"

"Trouble is an understatement," she replied with an edge of remembered anger in her voice. "I do hope that cabin has indoor plumbing . . . and air-conditioning!" she added on a hopeful note.

"You are hot and tired after the trip," he realized. "Come inside and have a cool drink, then you can tell me all about your trouble." He curved his arm affectionately around her shoulders as he guided her to the cabin door. "And we do have indoor plumbing, but no air-conditioning. However, there is a cool breeze coming in from the lake."

"Do you mean they do have breezes in the Ozarks?" she murmured sardonically. "I was beginning to wonder."

The interior of the cabin seemed dark and cool after the brilliance of the afternoon that not even the shade of the trees had alleviated. She exhaled a relieved sigh, suddenly too tired and travel-worn to take in the furnishings of the rooms her uncle guided her through.

He led her straight through the cabin to a

screen door that opened onto a wide porch. Joanna collapsed into a cane-backed rocker while her uncle poured a glass of iced tea from a perspiring pitcher.

She took a long swallow from the glass he gave her and leaned her head against the chair back. "I swear if this hadn't been your cabin, Reece"—Joanna paused to shake her head—"I would have turned around and gone back to California." She sat up. "I left the suitcases in the car."

"We can get them later," he assured her.

Joanna settled back into the chair. "I just don't understand what you see in this godforsaken place," she sighed, remembering all she had gone through to get here.

"Godforsaken?" He frowned narrowly at her choice of adjectives. "It is far from 'godforsaken,' Joanna. Just look at the beauty around you," he demanded.

It was rare for those dark eyes to look at her with disapproval. It wasn't a comfortable feeling. His scolding tone forced her to look beyond the porch. The rocky clearing sloped down to the shimmering waters of a lake, the source of the breeze cooling her skin.

On the opposite shore, there was another ridge of mountains, cloaked in a myriad of green shades and contrasted by a milk-blue sky. A flash of scarlet in the trees near the cabin caught her eye. She turned to see a black-beaked cardinal flitting among the tree limbs. A squirrel chattered angrily at the bird's intrusion.

"Godforsaken was perhaps the wrong word," Joanna conceded, because there was the rustic beauty of nature around her, relatively untouched by civilization and untamed. "But you have to admit it's far from anywhere—and next to impossible to reach."

"That is a part of its charm," he smiled and settled into the matching rocking chair next to hers. "Its isolation. Its distance from large metropolitan centers. Getting here isn't easy but once you are here—" He lifted his shoulders to indicate how little the hardships mattered.

"You can say that but I'll bet you didn't drive twenty miles behind a fuel truck, then get stuck behind some farmer poking along to market, miss the turn to this road—which by any sane person's standards doesn't deserve to called a road." She paused to cast a wary glance at her uncle. "I suppose that *road* is the only way out of this place."

"It is," he admitted. "The spring rains eroded it badly. It is worse this year than it has ever been." Then Reece Morgan picked up on what she had said. "You got lost."

"As far as I'm concerned, I wasn't really lost. I just missed the turn. Of course, the man at the gas station who gave me directions felt that was a moot point," Joanna inserted dryly. "Then when I did find the road, I almost ran into a pair of mules pulling a wagon. I ended up going into the ditch."

"You weren't hurt, were you?" He studied her more closely, leaning forward with concern.

"No. I didn't get a scratch or a bruise. Lucki-ly." She was able to smile about it now as she took another drink of cold tea, her sense of humor slowly returning. "I thought I was seeing things when the mules and wagon suddenly pulled onto the road ahead of me," she laughed briefly. "I want you to know that's quite a shock for this California girl."

"I can imagine." He chuckled with her. "It must have been Jessie Bates. He's a marvelous character that lives in an old cabin up the road."

"Character is right, if it's the same man."

"He was thin with overalls a size too big and hair that had probably never seen a comb," her uncle described the man who had been driving the mules.

"That's him," she nodded.

"You should hear some of the stories he tells about these hills," he said. "He is a natural storyteller. His tales are colored with regional phrases. He plays the fiddle, too, and the dulci-mer, banjo. An extremely talented man. I'm convinced he dresses and acts the way he does to draw attention to himself—the way an actor would. But you'll find that out for yourself."

"I doubt it," Joanna grimaced. "After I landed in the ditch, I got a little upset and lost my temper. He took offense at some things I said."

"What did you say?" He eyed her, well aware that she occasionally lost control of her tongue.

"After he admitted that he was at fault, he offered to pay for any damages to the car. To look at him, a person would think he didn't have a dime to his name. I said as much." She was still irritated with herself for talking without thinking about what she was saying. "I hurt his pride. So, I very much doubt that he'll be interested in seeing me again." Joanna shrugged, trying to pretend it didn't matter, but she wasn't normally unkind to people—not deliberately. "Of course, I won't be here that long so there isn't much chance of running into him again." She winced. "That was a bad pun."

"I was hoping to persuade you to spend the rest of my month here," Reece stated. "I have some work that, unfortunately, can't wait until I get back. I thought it would be good practice for you to stay and help me with it."

"I don't know." Joanna hesitated. "Mother is expecting me back the day after tomorrow."

"You are twenty-one. You don't need her permission." He dismissed that excuse. "Besides, I want to correct your impression of these Ozark Mountains and the people." Inside the cabin, a telephone rang. "Excuse me." He rose from his chair and entered the cabin to answer it.

Joanna took another drink from her iced tea and leaned back in her chair to close her eyes and dream about the shower she was going to take just as soon as she got some energy.

He answered the phone on the fourth ring. "Reece Morgan speaking," he identified himself.

"Reece, this is Linc," came the reply.

"Linc, I'm glad you called. My niece just arrived a few minutes ago. Will you be able to

45

come to dinner tonight?" Linc Wilder had become a good friend, someone Reece took special interest in, as he did in his niece.

He was looking forward to Linc and Joanna meeting. Naturally, since he had affection for both of them, he expected them to like each other. Beyond that, he didn't plan. If anything developed, it would happen on its own. But it was a wish he subconsciously made.

There was a pause that seemed heavy. It drew the jet-dark brows together as Reece tried to guess at the reason. Linc wasn't usually a taciturn man.

"Sorry, I won't be able to make it this time." Linc's voice sounded casual, natural. Reece briefly shook his head, deciding he had imagined it. "I'll have to take a raincheck."

"You are always welcome here, Linc. If you're not busy, stop by tomorrow night—if not for dinner, then later in the evening," Reece invited.

"I'll see," was all Linc would promise. "Thanks for the invitation."

A few seconds later, Reece hung up the telephone. Perhaps it was just as well Linc didn't come tonight. Joanna was tired after traveling all day. She would probably welcome a quiet evening. He returned to the porch where his niece was relaxing. She lazily opened her eyes to look at him.

"Business?" she asked.

"No, social," he replied. "I had invited Linc Wilder for dinner this evening. I bought this cabin from the Wilders. They own most of the land around it. He just called to say he couldn't make it."

"It's probably just as well," Joanna declared wryly. "I probably would have stuck my foot in my mouth again and said something embarrassing."

"I wouldn't worry about what happened this afternoon." He moved toward the door. "I'll bring your luggage in so you can shower and clean up before dinner."

"Thanks," she said. "I'm not sure I can move."

Chapter Four

A morning sun had already burned away the swirling layers of mist from the lake's surface when a woodpecker flew to an oak tree growing close to the cabin. It hammered at the bark and the sound carried through the wire mesh of the opened bedroom window. Joanna stirred beneath the lightweight coverlet at the prodding noise.

As it persisted, she dragged open her sleep-heavy eyelids, becoming aware of the daylight pouring through the window. Initially, she was disoriented by the strangeness of the room until she remembered where she was.

With a yawn, she folded back the covers and slid out of bed. Her cotton robe was lying on a chair. She slipped into it before leaving the loft bedroom for the second floor bath.

Fifteen minutes later, with the sleep washed from her face and her teeth brushed, Joanna descended the rustic log staircase. Her uncle was seated at the breakfast table by the window that looked out over the lake. He turned in his chair when she entered the spacious kitchen.

"Good morning," he greeted her with a brightness that Joanna doubted she could match. "Did you sleep well?"

"Ask me that question after I've had my orange juice and coffee." Her smile showed traces of tiredness as she walked to the refrigerator to help herself to the container of orange juice inside.

"What would you like for breakfast this morning?"

"Nothing." She carried the glass of orange juice to the table and pulled out a chair opposite him. "I'm not hungry when I first get up in the morning," Joanna explained. Reece poured a cup of coffee for her from the insulated pot on the table. "Thanks. What's on the agenda today?"

"I thought we could drive to the post office in Branson after you've had a chance to enjoy your morning coffee and dress." There was a brief flash of white as he smiled. "I will drive so you can enjoy the scenery and not worry about running into any mules."

Joanna smiled with a wry pull of her mouth.

There continued to be a nagging regret that she hadn't seen the inherent amusement in yesterday's incident at the time. She wasn't very proud of the way she had reacted—regardless of the causes for her ill-humor. It wasn't any justification for the way she had behaved.

An hour later, Joanna was riding over the narrow lake road again, this time in the plush comfort of her uncle's Chrysler New Yorker, its shocks absorbing the roughness of the lane. It didn't seem to take them any time to reach the place where she'd had her accident.

"There should be a sign posted that says Mule Crossing," she suggested, pointing out the spot to her uncle as they approached it.

He smiled in acknowledgment of her joking remark. "Jessie Bates has his cabin just down the road," he explained.

"Does he have a family?" she asked, suddenly wondering if the tall cowboy had been his son, even though there wasn't any resemblance.

It occurred to her that she hadn't mentioned the presence of a second man to her uncle, but it hardly seemed important now. Remembering the censure that had been in the man's hard, golden-brown eyes stirred some of the previous day's antagonism to life.

It didn't matter that her behavior had warranted his criticism. Since her resentment of the cowboy was at odds with her regret, that was an additional reason not to mention to her uncle the presence of a third party at the accident.

"No. To my knowledge, Jess has never been married," Reece replied to her question as they passed the spot where her car had gone into the ditch without slowing.

Settling back in the richly upholstered car seat, she mused aloud, "I suppose there are a lot of hillbillies around here." She wasn't conscious that there had been anything derogatory in her use of the word.

"I don't doubt that there are many, but don't make the mistake of believing that simply because they live in the *backwoods* that they are *backwards*." He stressed the two words to be certain she was forming an incorrect perception of Ozark natives. "In their own way, these natives are extremely worldly—as intelligent and shrewd as any corporate executive."

"I won't make the mistake," Joanna promised with a smile.

After covering a few more miles of the lake road, a white board fence ran parallel with them. Cattle grazed in the grassy tree-studded meadow it enclosed. Joanna noticed again the ranch house sitting back from the road on the mountain knoll.

"That's a beautiful home," she remarked to her uncle. "Who lives there?"

"Linc Wilder." His sideways glance was slightly mocking. "He happens to be fourth generation hillbilly." And Joanna knew this was an example to prove his statement that hillbillies were not backward. "Very few describe themselves as hillbillies," he explained. "They use the term ridgerunner. I'm sure you must have noticed that most of the roads here run along the mountain ridges, hence the name."

As they turned onto the main road, Joanna gazed out the window at this ancient mountain country. Since she wasn't driving, she could ignore the traffic and admire the scenery instead.

From the higher elevations of the winding road, she could see the rippling effect as the land spilled away in wave after wave of tree-covered mountain ridges and the diamond glitter of the lake in the nearby valley. She was beginning to revise her opinion about the wild land—and the people who lived here. She was almost sorry when the buildings of town came into view.

It was mid-morning but the day was already beginning to feel hot when they reached the resort town of Branson.

"Have you been awake long enough to be hungry?" he asked. "We can stop at a local cafe if you feel like eating.'"

"Thanks, but I'm not really hungry. I'll wait until lunch."

"Do you remember that Kewpie doll I gave you six years ago?" Reece waited for the traffic to pass before turning onto the street.

"Yes. As a matter of fact, I still have it." She

had been sixteen at the time and crushed that her uncle had brought her a doll when she was trying to be so grown up. Then Joanna remembered vaguely, "You had just come back from vacationing here, hadn't you? Is this where you bought the doll?"

"Yes, from a quaint little shop down the street. We'll stop there and you can look around. I'm sure you don't remember, since it was long before your time, but Kewpie dolls were very popular in the forties. Rose O'Neil, the woman who created the original Kewpie doll, was from this area."

"I have the feeling there is a great deal to learn about the Ozarks and its people," Joanna stated and sent him a twinkling glance. "And I also have the feeling that you are planning to teach me about it."

Her uncle neither confirmed nor denied her suspicion. "I think you will grow to appreciate and enjoy the culture of this region as much as I do." He parked the car in the lot next to the doll shop.

The picturesque building looked as though it had been converted from a two-story home for commercial use. Its stucco exterior was painted baby pink and an assortment of dolls crowded the displays at its curtained windows. It looked enchanted rather than out of step with its surroundings.

As the nearly full parking lot had indicated, there were plenty of shoppers inside when Joanna entered the doll store with her uncle.

She was drawn first to the artfully arranged shelves of Kewpie dolls for sale. The mischievous-looking cupids came in a variety of sizes and poses, bright-eyed imps that had timeless appeal.

Wandering further into the shop, Joanna realized that nearly every kind of doll imaginable was there—rag dolls, corn-shuck dolls, china dolls. They were all represented. It was a little girl's dream world, and an adult's fantasy of toyland.

Absorbed by the collection of dolls, she wasn't aware she had become separated from her uncle until she noticed him standing at a counter ahead of her. He was just greeting one of the store clerks, an attractive and mature woman with light brown hair. The woman's slimness and her erect carriage gave the impression of height although she wasn't as tall as Reece. Her uncle turned, his gaze quickly locating her.

"Joanna, come here," he summoned her with a smile and a motioning wave of his hand. "I'd like you to meet the proprietor of this shop."

The information renewed Joanna's interest in the woman, since she was so impressed with the quality of the shop. Age had begun to etch the lines of maturity about the woman's mouth and blue eyes, but not unattractively. Her smile was warm, yet polite, friendly yet with a trace of reserve. Joanna liked the air of quiet dignity the woman possessed.

"This is my niece, Joanna Morgan." Reece

introduced her first to the woman. "Joanna, I'd like you to meet Mrs. Rachel Parmelee."

"Welcome to the Ozarks, Miss Morgan." The hand she extended to Joanna was slim and smooth.

"Thank you." She smiled, liking the woman immediately. "I know you have probably heard it before but you have a lovely shop, Mrs. Parmelee." Where had she heard that name before? It sounded so familiar to her.

"You're very kind." The woman returned the smile, then inquired, "Is this your first visit to our area?"

"Yes," Joanna admitted.

"Joanna only arrived yesterday," her uncle elaborated on her answer. "I'm afraid her first impression of the Ozarks wasn't very favorable. Now I have the task of correcting it."

"I hope you enjoy your stay," Rachel Parmelee murmured.

Something had happened to change the woman's attitude. Joanna could sense it. There was a coolness in her voice and her expression that hadn't been there before. She was puzzled by it because it seemed to have happened when Reece joined the conversation, and he had said nothing offensive, nothing remotely personal that could have been misinterpreted. She glanced at her uncle and realized that he had noticed it, too. His expression had altered, a certain stiffness entering it that wasn't natural for him.

"We are keeping you from your customers." His remark appeared to offer an excuse for her sudden coolness toward them. "We won't take any more of your time."

There was a disturbing darkness to his gaze, an intensity that could almost be measured. Joanna watched the woman drop her glance to avoid it.

She took her lead from Reece. "It was a pleasure meeting you, Mrs. Parmelee."

The instant she said the woman's name a second time, she recalled where she had first heard it. The man at the service station had mentioned it. What was it he had said? Something about her uncle being sweet on the Widow Parmelee, she remembered. With new eyes, she studied her uncle and the woman.

"Have a good day." Rachel included both of them in the comment.

"Perhaps we'll see each other again soon," her uncle said. It was almost a question but it received no answer as the woman smiled politely and moved along the counter to a customer looking at a selection of dolls in a glass case.

Reece turned to Joanna. "Did you wish to look around a little longer?" he inquired.

"Another time, perhaps," she said, because she guessed that he wanted to leave.

"Yes, another time." The phrase seemed to hold another meaning for him as his glance strayed to Rachel Parmelee with a certain wistfulness.

As they exited the store and started toward the car parked in the lot, Joanna murmured, loud enough for her uncle to hear, "So that is the Widow Parmelee."

Her sidelong glance caught his startled look. "What do you know about her?" He recovered quickly and sounded only mildly curious.

"Do you remember I told you that I stopped at a gas station yesterday to ask directions?" she said.

"Yes," he nodded slowly, not following what that had to do with Mrs. Parmelee.

"When I told him that I was trying to reach the cabin owned by my uncle, Reece Morgan, he knew you right away," Joanna explained. "He asked if it was the same Morgan who was sweet on the Widow Parmelee. Are you the same Morgan?" she asked, already guessing the answer after what she had witnessed inside.

Her question appeared to make him vaguely uncomfortable. Faint lines creased his forehead. "Yes, I suppose I am that man."

"And is the Widow Parmelee sweet on you?" she prompted.

A heavy sigh came from him as he stopped beside the car's passenger door to open it for her. "I don't know. Sometimes I think she finds me attractive. Yet every time I ask her to have dinner with me, I get the cold shoulder. Linc advises me to be patient. I'm an outsider. So—" There was an expressive lift of his shoulders. "I am patient."

"Personally, I think she needs her head examined for not snapping you up," Joanna declared.

"Now, do you see why I want you to spend the rest of the month here?" he laughed at her strident defense of his attractiveness. "It's your moral support I require."

Chapter Five

Outside the cabin, the shadows were lengthening as sundown approached. Joanna wiped the last of the cooking pans dry and stacked it in a lower cupboard with the rest of the pots and pans. Folding the damp dishtowel, she neatly hung it on a wallrack to dry.

"We're all finished." Joanna turned to her uncle and halted briefly to study the picture he made, so maturely handsome and well-dressed, except for the plain white apron around his waist to protect his dark slacks. It struck an incongruous note. "I wish I had a picture of you in that apron." A bemused smile deepened the corners of her mouth.

"Why?" His out-reaching glance was curious as he untied the bow in back to take it off.

"Somehow you just don't seem the domestic type to me," she shrugged.

"Just what is the domestic type?" Reece challenged with an amused look.

Joanna was without an answer to that. She was saved from a reply by the sound of a vehicle turning into the cabin's drive. "I think you have company," she said to her uncle.

"Perhaps it is Linc. I have been wanting you to meet him," he stated as he moved past her into the living room.

Joanna was slow to follow him, taking time to hang up the apron he'd left on the countertop. The vehicle's motor had already stopped and a door had been slammed when she started for the living room. She heard the creaking hinges of the screen door as her uncle opened it to admit the visitor.

"Linc. I'm so glad you came by." The delight was evident in her uncle's greeting.

"Hello, Reece. How have you been?" There was the heavy thud of footsteps ascending the steps of the front entrance.

But it was the familiar sound of the man's voice that caused Joanna to falter in her stride a foot short of the opening to the living room. It couldn't be the cowboy. From the little Reece had told her about Linc Wilder, she had gained the impression that he and her uncle were the same age, contemporaries.

"Fine. Come in. Come in." Her uncle's voice urged the man into the house.

Joanna continued into the living room, less

certainly than before. Alarm bells went off in her head when she recognized the tall, broad shouldered man crossing the threshold. Instead of the faded Levis and workshirt, he was wearing a white shirt with pearl snaps and slim-fitting, western cut slacks of tan drill.

It wasn't his casual attire that held her attention, but the rugged planes of his tanned features—sun-hardened and strong. The brim of his cowboy hat shadowed his eyes but Joanna had no difficulty remembering the hard amber flecks in the light brown irises that glittered their message of caution.

She watched the straight, firm line of his mouth curve in a smile that gentled the hard contours of his face as he shook hands with her uncle. It was an expression that didn't last long, fading when his glance traveled beyond her uncle to notice her.

"Joanna, come meet Linc Wilder." Her uncle seemed oblivious to the subtle undercurrents impregnating the air as he invited her to come forward.

With a stiffness to her carriage, she started across the room. All her nerve ends were tingling under the study of those eyes. She knew her appearance was a definite improvement on the way she had looked the first time he'd seen her. The smooth style of her ash-blonde hair flattered her features, features that were enhanced by the light application of makeup—a hint of mascara to darken her lashes, a touch of green shadow to bring out the warm brown of her eyes, and a lingering trace of brown-rose gloss to define the curve of her lips.

There was no artificial cause for the color in her cheeks as his re-assessing gaze traveled the length of her body, taking note of the slim-fitting designer jeans that hugged her hips, and of the clinging fabric of her red knit top that outlined the swell of her young breasts.

There was a definite shimmer of defiance in her eyes when she met his glance. All her defenses were raised against him. Joanna didn't fully understand this inner need to protect herself from him. It seemed purely instinctive, a reaction beyond her control. When she stopped beside her uncle, she was rigid with tension.

"Linc, I want you to meet my niece, Joanna Morgan," her uncle finished the introduction.

The strong mouth slanted its line but it never made the full transition into a smile. His glance locked with hers, his heavy with irony.

"Your niece and I have already met, although we didn't bother to introduce ourselves at the time." He held out his hand to her, the gesture in the way of a challenge.

Joanna longed to ignore it but it would have meant a gross display of bad manners to a guest of her uncle's. She forced herself to shake his hand. His grip seemed to swallow her, the contact sending tingles up her arm.

"You have met?" Her uncle reacted to Linc Wilder's statement, the frowning arch of a dark brow directing a silent query to Joanna for confirmation.

"Yes, we have," she admitted and withdrew her hand from his grasp the instant he relaxed it. She faked an air of innocent oversight when she met her uncle's puzzled glance. "Didn't I mention that there was another man present yesterday when my car landed in the ditch?"

"No, I don't recall that you did," Reece frowned in an effort to remember what she had said.

"I must have forgotten." She made light of the omission with a dismissing shrug.

Reece accepted her explanation that it had been an oversight and moved away from the door, inviting them to follow by his action. "Joanna told me about the incident on the road yesterday," he admitted to Linc.

"Did she?" The mocking lilt of his voice dryly intimated that Joanna had colored the story so she wouldn't be seen in a bad light.

Her retort was quick. "Yes, I did. Reece knows me very well—and my embarrassing habit of saying the wrong thing at the wrong time."

"Yes, Joanna felt badly about some of the things she said to Jessie." Her uncle corroborated her assertion that she had been candid about her role in the events that transpired after her car landed in the ditch. Reece paused near the chintz-covered sofa positioned in front of the brick fireplace. "May I bring you some coffee, Linc?"

"Please," he accepted.

"I'll get it," Joanna volunteered, welcoming an excuse to leave the room.

"No." Her uncle firmly rejected the offer. "You stay here. I want you and Linc to get acquainted."

Joanna was left with little choice except to agree. As her uncle departed for the kitchen, she let her gaze swing to Linc Wilder. He was standing near the couch, watching her lazily with his cat's eyes.

Relegated to the role of hostess, she made a stiff gesture to invite him to sit down. "Make yourself comfortable."

"Thank you." Dryness quirked the corners of his mouth as he folded his long body onto the couch.

He removed his hat, setting it on the adjoining sofa cushion, and combed his fingers through the brown thickness of his hair to unflatten it. His glance ran back to her in a prodding reminder that she was still standing. Joanna sat down in the nearest chair, too nervous to relax against the seat back.

"So you were embarrassed yesterday?" It was a baiting question. "You didn't appear to be."

"No one likes to feel embarrassed. They usually try to cover it up with a show of indifference or bravado." She relied on those ploys now and attempted to put him on the defensive by questioning his actions the previous day. "You knew who I was. You probably even guessed Reece was my uncle before I mentioned it. Yet you didn't acknowledge that you knew him. Don't you think that was rude not to let me know how much farther it was to the cabin?"

"That wasn't rude. It was rural."

"Which means?" she bristled.

"Which means we aren't in the habit of turning the other cheek," he replied, his level gaze on her. "You didn't appreciate the help we gave you getting the car out of the ditch. So why should I help you again?"

"I did appreciate your help," Joanna insisted.

"You didn't show it," Linc Wilder countered. "Or were you trying to supposedly cover up your true feelings again?"

"Maybe I didn't sound properly grateful," she conceded stiffly. "But you weren't exactly a model of tact yourself. You can't say that you behaved like a gentleman."

"No, but I didn't see any lady in the vicinity either." His smooth reply was almost a slap in the face.

Joanna whitened. "I hope you don't expect me to apologize for yesterday."

"I expect nothing."

"Good, because Mr. Bates is the only one who deserves an apology from me," she stated with a cold glare.

An eyebrow was briefly lifted. "At least you recognize that," he murmured.

"I recognize a lot of things, Mr. Wilder." She was angry, controlling her temper and the volume of her voice with an effort. "I have already admitted that I'm not proud of the way I behaved yesterday, but that isn't good enough for you. I pity your wife for being married to such a hard, unforgiving man."

"You can save your pity. I'm not married," he replied.

"I can see why," Joanna declared.

Her uncle returned from the kitchen, carrying a tray with three coffee mugs on it. He set it down on the short cypress table in front of the sofa, not noticing the sudden silence that dominated the room. After he had handed each of them a mug, he sat on the couch with Linc.

"It is a lovely evening," Reece stated on a contented note. "Did you hear the whippoorwills outside a few minutes ago?"

"No. I must not have been listening," Linc's drawled reply indicated a lack of interest. Joanna didn't answer at all.

For the first time, Reece noticed the closed expressions both of them were wearing and began to suspect that all was not right. He also sensed there would be no conversation unless he carried it. "Joanna admired your home when we drove by it today, Linc," he offered as a gambit to draw both of them into the discussion.

"Did she? I'm flattered." But a strong thread of mockery ran through the reply.

Reece saw the way Joanna's lips tightened in a thin line, a sure sign of temper. "His house commands quite a fantastic view. You can see for miles. We will have to stop sometime so you can see it."

"It sounds lovely. I can hardly wait." She was equally taunting, cloaking it behind false politeness. As if this front of pleasantness was too difficult to maintain, she abruptly set her cup down and rose from the chair. "Excuse me, will you? If I want to reach my mother before she goes out for the evening, I need to phone her now. I have some things I want her to send." The last was added to Reece as an explanation for the phone call.

"Use the phone in the study so you can have some privacy." Reece straightened, out of deference to her sex, but Linc remained seated as she left the room and closed the door. Resuming his seat, Reece let the silence run between them before he finally spoke his thoughts, needing to know what was wrong. "There is friction between you and my niece. What has caused it?"

Linc's gaze swung to the study door, narrowing slightly, then he attempted a smile. "Maybe it would be better if we talked about something else."

"Is it something that happened yesterday?" Reece persisted with the subject, anxious to smooth out any differences between the two. "Joanna admitted to me that she had said some pretty unforgivable things. She is young and her temper is quick."

"And her tongue is sharp," Linc added. "And she's a little too big for her britches." His glance ran sideways to Reece. "Sorry, but you asked for my opinion."

"From the time Joanna was small, her mother —my sister-in-law—has attempted to run every minute of her life. It's natural that Joanna began to resent that and learn to stand up for herself." Reece sketched in a little of his niece's background so Linc could understand her present behavior. "She doesn't like being told what to do," he paused to eye Linc with a knowing look. "And you are used to telling people what to do."

"Message received," Linc acknowledged with a wry twist of his mouth. "But I still think she needs to be pushed on her backside. It takes falling on your rear end a few times before you appreciate landing on your feet."

"You may have a point," Reece chuckled at the piece of Ozark wisdom. "But you also have to admit she is an attractive girl."

"A very attractive woman," Linc agreed on a thoughtful note, then appeared restless, a little irritated. He drained his cup and set it on the tray. "Thanks for the coffee, Reece."

"You aren't leaving already," he protested as Linc pushed to his feet.

"Yes. Give my goodbyes to your niece. I've done enough damage for one night," he said.

"Come by again," Reece issued the long standing invitation again.

"Thanks, I will." Taking his hat, he carried it with him to the door and put it on as he walked out.

When the truck motor started up, Reece saw the doorknob to the study turning slowly. "It's safe to come out now, Joanna," he called to his niece, a faint light gleaming in his dark eyes. "He's gone."

It was several seconds before the door actually opened and Joanna emerged. Reece pretended not to notice the way her glance went immediately to the place where Linc had been sitting. "Linc said to pass along his goodbye. He wasn't able to stay longer. By the way, did you reach Elizabeth?"

"No." Actually she hadn't tried, but she didn't tell her uncle that. It would be akin to admitting cowardice. "It's just as well. It would take too long to mail the things to me anyway. I'll go shopping tomorrow in town and pick up the few things I'll need while I'm here."

"That sounds sensible," he agreed.

"Why did you tell me it was safe to come out just because Linc Wilder was gone?" She wanted to know.

"It was obvious the two of you had been exchanging blows," he stated. "You wanted to avoid him. That's why you decided to call your mother."

"I couldn't help it. I know you like him and if I had stayed in the room—" she began tightly.

"Yes, I was aware of the sparks flying," he smiled gently. "What happened yesterday?"

"He started giving me a lecture on my manners."

"Which you needed?" Reece suggested with a raised eyebrow.

"Even if I did, he had no right to tell me about it, and I told him so," she retorted.

"Joanna." He shook his head at her with affection. "Hasn't it occurred to you that you aren't the only one with a lot of pride?"

"Yes, a couple of times," she admitted grudgingly, then smiled. "How about a game of back-gammon?"

"Get the board and I'll pour some more coffee."

They played until nearly midnight with neither one winding up a clear-cut winner although Reece did have the advantage.

Upstairs in the loft, Joanna undressed for bed. A cool breeze was whispering through the trees outside her window where a whippoorwill was making its plaintive call. After pulling on a nightgown, she folded down the bed's coverlet and used only the sheet. She switched off the bedside lamp to send the room into darkness.

Her thoughts roamed over the evening's events, spending too much time on Linc Wilder and the way his presence had unnerved her. Joanna turned on her side and punched the pillow beneath her head. She couldn't seem to get comfortable. Maybe it was her conscience that was troubling her. On that thought, she closed her eyes.

Chapter Six

*J*oanna leaned her head out of the opened car window to call to her uncle. "Are you sure you don't want to come with me? It might not be smart to trust me with this car. I could run into a mule."

"I trust you." Reece laughed from the doorway of the cabin. "I have some notes to go over. Later on this afternoon I plan to do a little fishing."

"You just don't want to be dragged around from store to store while I try on clothes," she accused.

"You're right." He waved to her and she waved back before shifting the luxury car into reverse to back out of the driveway. "Enjoy yourself!"

The big car made better going over the rough

road. As she neared the fork in the road where a lane turned off to Jessie Bates's cabin, she chewed her lip thoughtfully. It had been at the back of her mind since last night that she really should apologize to the man. She slowed the car and made the sharp turn onto the track leading to his cabin.

It was set a quarter of a mile back, deep in the woods that grew thickly all the way to the lake. All the buildings looked ancient—the log cabin, a shed, and a small barnlike structure, yet there was an absence of litter in the yard. It had a tidy and neat appearance, not at all what she had expected.

The two mules were standing head to tail inside an enclosure fenced with rough cedar posts. One turned its head to look at her, its big ears flopping at the flies, but it lost interest when she stepped out of the car. She was about to decide the owner wasn't home. Just then the barn door squealed open and the man emerged.

Nothing about him had changed. He appeared to be wearing the same pair of baggy overalls— or a pair just like them—and a faded blue work shirt. His dark hair was just as straggly and in need of a combing, yet he looked clean. When he saw her standing there, his bony face assumed a closed expression.

"I would have come to pay you for the repairs to your car," he declared tightly. "There was no call to come collectin'. I told you I pay ma' debts."

She had offended him again. "I didn't stop

because of that," she said quickly. "I always pay my debts, too, and I owe you an apology." When she paused, he tipped his head back and gave her a long, considering look.

"I'm sorry for the things I said about you and your mules the other day. I wish I could take them all back, but I can't change the fact that I said them. But I am sorry."

"I reckon I can overlook it. 'Course I can't speak for my mules," he said but there appeared to be a suggestion of a twinkle in his eyes even though his stern expression didn't change.

"Thank you." She smiled, a little relieved. "I want you to know that my uncle speaks very highly of you." She realized that she hadn't introduced herself, not formally. "My name is Joanna Morgan." She extended her hand to him.

He self-consciously wiped his on the back of his overalls before pumping her hand. "Pleased to meet you, Miss Morgan."

"You have a very nice place here—quiet and secluded." Joanna felt she should say something favorable about his place as she let her glance sweep around the surroundings once more.

"Well, it's home," he drawled. "I ain't interested in the luxuries of life but I shore wouldn't mind havin' some of the necessities, like indoor plumbin'. I'm getting tired of takin' a bath in the spring behind the house. That water gets awful blasted cold at times."

Her eyes widened slightly, noticing that his hair was damp and there was the smell of pine-soap clinging to his skin. He had just come from taking his bath. She was a little dazed to discover he was serious about not having running water. In these modern times, it sounded so unlikely that she had to ask.

"Do you mean you really don't have indoor plumbing?" Unconsciously her gaze swept the buildings again. She noticed the path worn through the trees leading behind the cabin. To an outhouse?

"No," he confirmed her suspicion. "I been thinkin' about gettin' some electricity. But I get to thinkin' that after that I'd be wantin' a stove, a refrigerator, and a television. Right now I don't want none of those things 'cause I don't have electricity. I decided I'm probably happier without it, 'cause I'm not wantin' those other things that I can't afford."

"How do you keep your food from spoiling?"

"I gotta springhouse. It keeps everythin' chilled just right an' you don't have to defrost it. Folks have been keepin' food in a springhouse for years," he explained.

"Oh." She had thought they had vanished with the advent of television. It was becoming clear what Reece had meant when he'd said Jessie Bates enjoyed being eccentric.

"Excuse me a minute, while I go in the house and get the money I owe ya'." He started to turn away to walk to the porch steps.

"Wait." Joanna caught at his arm, feeling the tensile strength of his wiry muscles beneath the thin fabric of his shirt sleeve. "I really would rather that you didn't pay it because I feel so badly about the way I behaved. Besides, there virtually wasn't any damage to the car—just the paint scratched in a few places. It doesn't amount to anything."

"It was my fault for pulling out on the road like that. I gotta pay," he insisted.

She was about to argue when she remembered her uncle's comment last night that other people had pride, too. "All right," she gave in. "Ten dollars should cover the damage."

"It won't take me but a minute to fetch it," he said. His spindly legs carried him swiftly over the ground and up the steps to the cabin's door.

Alone in the yard, Joanna studied the clearing and its primitive buildings. The rocky ground was scattered with clumps of grass stubbornly forcing their way through the inhospitable earth. Most were thin, spindly blades, but some grew tall and defiant.

There was a quiet here that wasn't really silent. The buzz of the flies and the stomping of a mule's hoof, the soft swish of its tail intermixed with the distant chatter of a squirrel in the woods and the trilling calls of birds. But all of them were subtle sounds, in harmony with the surroundings. Therefore, it was the quiet solitude of the place that made the strongest impression on Joanna, rather than its many inhabitants.

The slam of the screen door hit a strident note and her glance swung to the cabin and the scrawny man descending the porch steps. She noticed the several bills clasped between his long, bony fingers.

"Here you go." He handed the money to her. "Now we're square."

"Yes." Joanna wasn't about to insult him by counting it. So she folded the curling and age-worn bills and slipped them in the side pocket of her slacks, trying not to think about where it might have been stashed in his cabin. No doubt he had some secure and obscure hidey-hole for his valuables. "It's very quiet here. Doesn't it bother you not to have any neighbors living close by?"

"If I wanted people livin' on top of me, I'd have a place in town." He seemed to find her question a little foolish.

"How much land do you have here?" As soon as she asked, Joanna wondered if she was being too nosy, but her curiosity was quite innocent.

"Thare's no way of tellin' just how much land I got," he explained with a serious frown. "The homestead papers say I got forty acres. But forty acres of this hill land ain't like forty acres of any other land. If you was to roll it out flat, I might have three, four times as much land."

She tried to hold back a smile until she noticed the definite twinkle in his eyes. He had meant the remark to be amusing. The line of her mouth curved in obliging response.

"You do have a point," she agreed, the smile broadening. "I wouldn't want to walk it."

His head was tilted to the side in a gesture of

disagreement. "Now thare's advantages to walkin' in these hills. Walkin' on flat land would be just plumb borin', not to mention how tirin' it would be without a downhill to spell ya'."

Joanna laughed openly this time at his pearl of Ozark wit. "I hadn't thought of that," she admitted.

"It's hard for some people to look and see at the same time," Jessie Bates stated.

Joanna sobered, because she knew she was guilty of that. The other day on the road, she had looked at Jessie Bates and judged him to be poor and ignorant without taking the time to *see* his worth as a man.

"Yes, it is." She didn't add more because they both understood what was meant. Instead, Joanna made the initial move to take her leave. "I'm on my way into town. Is there anything I could pick up for you?"

There was silent approval in his look. "That's right neighborly of you to offer but I got all I need to hold me for a spell."

"I'd better be leaving. Thanks for being so understanding, Mr. Bates." Joanna spoke as she began to turn to walk to the Chrysler.

He walked along side her. "Like I said, we're all squared."

A cardinal swooped out of the trees, flying directly in front of Joanna. The sudden flash of red startled her. She took a half-step backward, laughing at herself when she realized it had only been a bird. Continuing toward the car, she glanced sideways at her companion.

"These woods seemed to be filled with cardinals," she remarked.

"Thare's a few," he nodded. There was the smallest pause before he continued. "Some hill-folks believe that when a redbird flies across a girl's path, it means she's gonna be kissed twice before nightfall."

She turned her head to look at him, wondering if he was pulling her leg. "Why would they believe that?"

"They tend to be a superstitious lot." He shrugged. "'Course, it's foolishness. I don't put any stock in such things myself."

"Neither do I," she agreed on a more decisive note, then lightly mocked the belief. "Besides, I don't even have a boyfriend here." Or elsewhere, at the moment.

"The superstition just says you're gonna be kissed twice. It don't say who's gonna do the kissin'. 'Could be someone you know, or someone you don't."

She paused as she opened the car door to look at him closely, a tiny frown creeping across her forehead. He had disclaimed any belief in the superstition, yet he was defending it. It seemed very contradictory to her. A little confused, she laughed it off and slipped behind the steering wheel.

"I'm supposed to be kissed twice before nightfall, huh?" Her wry smile was taunting with skepticism. "I'll let you know what happens."

There was a trace of a smile in his expression

as he shut her car door—an expression that appeared to contain some secret knowledge. She shook her head slightly as she started the car, unsure what to believe about the man. She turned the car around in the yard to drive out the lane, waving to the man.

All the way to town her mind kept wandering back to the conversation. It was certainly something she would have to remember to tell her uncle. She knew he'd find it amusing, and interesting.

With the unscheduled stop at Jessie Bates's cabin and the traffic on the highway, it was nearly eleven by the time she reached town. She found a place to park on the main street. There were several nice dress shops within the block and Joanna entered the closest one first to look over their selection.

Despite her growing hunger, she shopped through the lunch hour while the stores were less crowded. At half-past one, she went in search of a restaurant. Two of the small cafes in town were filled with people waiting to be seated. At the third one, there was no one waiting in line although all the tables and booths were filled.

Since she wasn't sure if she'd have better luck elsewhere, Joanna decided to wait until there was a place. As she shifted the packages under her arm, her glance absently swept the room.

A woman was seated alone at a table for four. It was Rachel Parmelee. As Joanna recognized her, the woman happened to look up straight at Joanna. Joanna smiled in acknowledgment but the widow looked right through her.

Although it was possible Rachel Parmelee was too preoccupied with her own thoughts to notice Joanna or else she honestly didn't recognize her, it was also possible she was deliberately ignoring her. Remembering how cool and unfriendly the widow had become toward her uncle prompted Joanna to force the issue. She walked to the table for four where the woman was seated.

"Good afternoon, Mrs. Parmelee." There was a slight challenge in her smile as she stopped beside one of the empty chairs at the table.

The woman looked up, a little too blank. "Good afternoon." Again there was a surface pleasantness that didn't truly welcome.

"I'm Joanna Morgan. We met yesterday in your shop," she reminded the woman of their previous introduction.

"Yes, of course. How are you, Miss Morgan?" The polite inquiry was just that and nothing more.

"Fine, thank you." The less welcome she was made to feel, the more determined Joanna became to stay. "The rest of the tables are full. Would you mind if I sat with you?"

Without waiting for an invitation, Joanna deposited her packages on the empty seat of a chair and sat down in the one opposite the widow. Not even Rachel Parmelee could be so rude as to refuse the request and Joanna knew it.

"Please do," the woman murmured after the fact.

The waitress stopped at their table with a glass of water and a menu for Joanna and a diet plate consisting of tomato slices, cottage cheese, and a hamburger patty for Rachel Parmelee. The waitress left, promising to be back to take Joanna's order. She opened the menu and pretended to study the bill of fare.

"Do you eat here regularly, Mrs. Parmelee?" Joanna inquired as she continued to peruse the menu.

"Yes."

"I suppose it takes too much time to run home every day and fix lunch for yourself when you have a business to run," she suggested.

"Yes."

"Myself, I never eat breakfast in the morning so by noontime, I'm starving," Joanna chattered away, deliberately keeping the conversation going in opposition to the woman's one-word answers. "Everything on the menu looks good. What would you recommend?"

"All restaurant food has begun to taste alike for me." Rachel Parmelee disqualified herself as the person to ask. "The restaurant has a good reputation in the area so I'm sure anything you choose would be satisfactory."

"That's good to know." Joanna contained a smug smile at the longer reply she had forced from the widow. The waitress returned to the table to take her order, diverting Joanna's attention for the moment. "I'll have the beef and noodles, and a glass of iced tea, please." When the waitress left, Joanna let a rueful smile touch her mouth. "I'll probably regret eating so much later on when I start trying on clothes again."

"Really?" Rachel murmured, displaying little interest.

"Yes. It's been a long time since I've been on a shopping spree. I'm really enjoying it," she explained. "Reece decided he'd rather stay at the cabin than follow me around while I shop."

"I'm sure."

Joanna couldn't help noticing the way the widow seemed to freeze up when she mentioned Reece's name. "The stores here seem to carry a quality brand of clothes. Now I know why you always look so well dressed. Where do you shop locally?" Joanna knew few members of her own sex who were not willing to talk about clothes.

"Several places. I don't patronize any one store. As a rule, I make my own," Rachel stated, removing herself from any discussion about the relative merits of one shop over another.

"As busy as you are, I'm surprised you find the time to sew," Joanna murmured dryly.

"After a long day, it helps me to relax although the bulk of my sewing I do in the winter when business is slower," she admitted.

Joanna ran an appraising eye over the smartly tailored suit of cool mint seersucker. "That's an attractive outfit you're wearing. Did you make it?"

"Yes."

"With a business to run, I don't imagine you have a chance to go out much—socially." She surmised the reason Rachel had turned down Reece's invitations.

"No. It keeps me very busy." Again there was a stiffness in the reply. "I don't mind it a bit. I prefer to be independent rather than to rely on someone else to support me."

Joanna had the vague impression there was some kind of a dig in the last statement. "I must admit I agree with your philosophy."

This time Rachel didn't make any comment at all to Joanna's remark. Again she sensed that it was the mention of Reece. But why? If only she could get the woman to open up, maybe she would learn something. With an inner sigh, Joanna returned to the only safe topic she knew —the woman's pride in her business.

"From what I saw the other day, your shop seems to be very successful. That can't happen without a good deal of time and effort."

"It has taken several years to establish a reputation and acquire a clientele that keeps coming back," Rachel agreed that it had required an effort.

"How long have you had the store?" she asked. "I know it's been more than six years, because Reece bought me a Kewpie doll. At the time, I wasn't overly enthused about it. I was trying so hard to be accepted as an adult and here was my uncle bringing me a child's gift—or so I thought at the time."

"He is your uncle?" The question appeared to be startled from Rachel, a wary and surprised look in her eyes.

"Of course, he's my uncle," Joanna laughed with some surprise at the question and noticed the sudden flush that colored the woman's cheeks. "Who did you think he was?"

"I'm sorry. Of course I knew he was your uncle." Rachel insisted forcefully and did an excellent job of recovering her poise.

It was beginning to register what the widow had thought. "You didn't believe I was his niece, did you?" she accused thoughtfully. "You had convinced yourself I was his lover masquerading as his niece for the sake of propriety."

"Is it so illogical?" Rachel no longer attempted to deny it. "Your uncle is an extraordinarily charming man, wealthy—sophisticated. It isn't that unlikely he would have a young mistress, is it?"

"It isn't unlikely," Joanna admitted. "But it doesn't happen to be true either. And I doubt very much if Reece would try to hide the fact. If he cared enough about a woman to have an affair with her, he certainly wouldn't treat her with the disrespect of a false claim that they were related. He simply isn't made that way."

"I don't know your uncle all that well," Rachel asserted in defense of her wrong conclusion.

"From what I can gather, it's your fault that the two of you haven't become better acquainted," Joanna murmured.

She lowered her gaze, losing her air of self-containment. Joanna was startled to see how unsure the widow seemed, almost vulnerable. But her voice was steady when she replied to Joanna's subtle jibe.

"Considering the circumstances, there has hardly been time to become acquainted with your uncle. Running my business requires most of my hours and the summer is my busiest season. I barely have time for close friends and your uncle is only here one month of the year. That is hardly the basis for a stable relationship, even discounting the fact that we have nothing in common."

"Nothing in common," Joanna repeated, a little puzzled. "It would seem to me that you have several things in common, not the least among them would be that you both own and manage your own company."

"Please, Miss Morgan," the widow protested in a scathing tone. "Let's not pretend that my little store in any way compares to the large organization Reece runs. He lives in a sophisticated world of high finance and I'm just a little shopkeeper. We hardly travel in the same circles."

"I don't think we're talking about the same person," Joanna said with a vaguely amused look. "The man you are describing would be vacationing in the South of France, not the Ozark Mountains of Missouri."

Rachel Parmelee was plainly at a loss to argue

that point although her mouth opened on several attempts. "Perhaps," she said finally and appeared discomfitted by the admission.

Letting instinct guide her, Joanna asked a question that seemed to be off the subject, but the inner workings of her mind were already plotting a use for the answer. "You surely don't work seven days a week at the store, do you? I should think it would be impossible to keep up a pace like that."

It took a second for the widow to adjust to the apparent change of subject. "No. Since the weekends are generally our busiest time, I take off on Friday to rest up for them."

"You mentioned that you'd lost your taste for restaurant food. Why don't you have dinner with us Friday night and enjoy a home-cooked meal for a change?" The invitation bordered on a challenge. Rachel's initial reaction was what Joanna had expected—refusal.

"No." She seemed to struggle to find an acceptable excuse. "I'll be too busy. It's the only time I have to wash clothes and clean. I—"

"This way you won't have to worry about fixing a meal," Joanna reasoned.

Rachel abandoned her pretence. "I know what you're trying to do and it just won't work," she insisted. "After five minutes with your uncle, I run out of things to say."

The remark confirmed Joanna's suspicions that the widow's coolness was an attempt to conceal she felt awkward and self-conscious with Reece. "So?" She made light of it. "If that happens, you can talk to me instead. Will you come?" She watched the hesitation and indecision in the woman's face. "You have nothing to lose—and, maybe, everything to gain," she prodded softly.

A very human expression took over Rachel's features as she yielded to the temptation. "All right, I'll come," she agreed and smiled a little foolishly. "I'm probably making a big mistake."

Satisfaction swelled inside Joanna until she thought she would burst, but she managed to contain most of it. "Look on the bright side," she reasoned. "You can always blame me and say I told you so."

The waitress came to the table with Joanna's order. She glanced at the widow. "Was there anything else you wanted, Rachel?"

The query seemed to prompt Rachel Parmelee to glance at her watch. "No." She was surprised at the time that had passed. "I have to get back to the store. It's much later than I realized."

"Do you know where we're staying?" Joanna asked as the woman gathered up her purse and her luncheon check.

"Yes, I do." She still didn't look positive that she had been right in accepting the invitation.

"Dinner will be ready at seven on Friday. You can come at six or six-thirty—any time you like," Joanna said. "We'll be expecting you."

"Friday at seven." There was a responding nod.

As Rachel walked to the cashier, Joanna couldn't help feeling very pleased with herself.

The sheer fact that Rachel had accepted the invitation indicated that she was attracted to Reece. Joanna really hadn't needed to twist her arm that much. She could hardly wait to see Reece's face when she told him Rachel was coming to dinner.

Chapter Seven

$\mathcal{I}$t was late afternoon by the time Joanna had finished her shopping and returned to the cabin by the lake. Her uncle wasn't on hand to greet her. A note on the table reminded her that he had gone fishing. In her excitement to relay the day's momentous events to him, it had slipped her mind that he'd mentioned his fishing plans when she'd left in the morning.

It was a letdown to have to wait to tell him about what had happened. She carried her packages up the stairs to the loft bedroom where she removed the price tags from the garments she'd purchased.

The windows were opened to admit any breeze but there wasn't a breath of air stirring. All the afternoon heat seemed to have gathered in the second floor of the cabin, stifling in its staleness and humidity. Perspiration trickled down her neck as she hung the new clothes in the closet.

By the time she was through, she was hot and sticky. She was considering a shower when she glanced out the bedroom window and saw the beckoning waters of the lake. Splashing around in it sounded infinitely more refreshing than a cool shower. In five minutes, Joanna had changed into her turquoise green swimsuit and grabbed a terrycloth beach jacket and towel.

She didn't bother with sandals, which she regretted seconds after stepping off the back porch onto the gravel-based earth. Unable to face the thought of climbing those stairs back to the stifling heat of the second floor for the sandals, Joanna minced her way across the stony ground barefoot to the lake shore.

Leaving her jacket and towel on a limestone ledge, she waded into the water, its coolness almost shocking her hot skin. When the water reached her waist, she pushed off to begin a leisurely crawl.

Linc climbed out of the cab of his truck and paused to stare at the log cabin. He wasn't entirely sure of his motive for stopping, except that he'd been drawn here after Jessie's revelation to him that Joanna had stopped to apologize. It didn't make a lot of sense why that mattered and the prospect of delving too deeply into the reason why it did made him uncomfortable.

The cabin looked quiet and unoccupied. His glance went again to the New Yorker parked near his truck. Its presence confirmed the cabin's inhabitants had not left. With a little shrug to rid himself of his brief indecision, Linc walked to the door and knocked. The screen door rattled in its frame at the pounding while the wire mesh kept him from seeing anything more than shadowy forms inside the cabin.

No sounds came from inside to indicate his knock had been heard. He started to knock again, then changed his mind, opening the door instead.

"Hello! Anybody home!" His voice seemed to echo through the empty house as silence answered him. Linc walked in, letting the door close behind him. "Reece?"

Nothing. He crossed the living room to the screened door leading onto the back porch. His gaze, always alert to his surroundings, moved absently about the room. It ran automatically to the large window that overlooked the lake and its shore, since that was where he suspected the occupants of this home were. Linc paused when he noticed the boat wasn't beached on the shore, reaching the conclusion that Reece had obviously gone fishing and probably taken Joanna with him.

He would have turned around and left if he hadn't glimpsed some movement in his side vision. When he looked to see what it was, he forgot all about leaving. Joanna was wading ashore, her sun-golden limbs glistening.

The jewel-colored swimsuit was molded to her figure like a second skin, boldly outlining the jutting swell of her breasts and the curve of her firm hips. He was conscious of the quickening rush that disturbed his senses, proving he was vulnerable to the attractions of a shapely body— if he had any doubts.

She picked her way along the rocky shoreline to a ledge of rock. Linc watched from the window while she toweled dry and rubbed the dampness from her honey-dark hair. There was a supple grace to her movements, a natural earthiness that was innocently sexy.

It didn't occur to him to go to the porch door and alert her to his presence. He was content to leave her unaware that she was being observed while his mind played back its impressions of their previous meetings and coupled them with the facts he'd learned about her from Reece. She had aroused his interest as few women had these past years.

When she slipped on her beach jacket without bothering to tie the front closed and started toward the cabin, Linc reached in his pocket for a cigarette, lighting it and shaking out the match although he continued to hold it between his fingers.

Everything about him—his stance, his posture —indicated disinterest toward the blonde girl approaching the cabin—everything except his eyes. They were alive to her, watching as she picked her way, barefoot, over the rough ground.

In spite of himself—it seemed—Linc was stirred by the freshness of her beauty and the intelligence that was such an integral part of her features. Although she had the face, the figure, and the coloring for it, there was nothing about her that suggested a dumb blonde. The more he learned about her, the more she seemed to challenge him.

When she climbed the steps to the porch, Linc half-turned so he would be facing the door when she entered the cabin. Her lips lay against each other in a relaxed curve of contentment as she crossed the threshold and paused to close the screen door, the towel swinging in one hand.

Joanna didn't immediately see him standing there. Something warned her of his presence before her eyes made the adjustment from bright sunlight to shade. Perhaps it was the smell of cigarette smoke or a faint sound. It might have been some sixth sense that alerted her to him.

When she saw him standing there, so motionless and catlike in his quiet study of her, her heart did a somersault and never properly regained its former location. This failure was concealed by the quick erection of her defenses. Joanna had long ago learned that sometimes the best way to defend herself was to attack.

"How did you get in here?" Her voice was husky.

"Sorry, I didn't mean to startle you. I knocked

but no one answered," Linc Wilder explained somewhat casually. Joanna watched him toss a burned-out match into an ashtray.

"No one answered the door and you walked in anyway?" She made it a challenge, conscious of the uneven hammering of her pulse under the steady regard of his tawny eyes.

They gleamed with amusement and the corners of his mouth lifted. "Since the car was outside, I presumed someone was here. I figured you or Reece were down by the lake so I took the liberty of taking a shortcut through the cabin instead of walking around it. I happened to see you from the window when you were walking up from the lake so I waited here."

He made it all sound very plausible, which Joanna supposed it was. It was just that she felt so awkward and self-conscious whenever she was around him, probably because she hadn't made a very good first impression. But she didn't want to admit that it mattered, especially not to him.

"Why are you here?" she demanded. "If you came to see Reece, he's fishing. You can come back later or leave a message for him."

"I didn't stop to see Reece."

The statement caught her off guard. Her hand crept up to close the front of her jacket. She was suddenly conscious of her scanty attire and wasn't sure whether it had been caused by the lick of his downward glance or the touch of a light breeze from outside.

"I can't think why you would want to see me. I

don't want to see you," she said with an attempt at callous indifference and turned away to walk to the kitchen. She could hear the even tread of his footsteps above the silent patter of her own bare feet as he followed her as far as the doorway and stopped.

"Jessie Bates mentioned you stopped to see him this morning." His statement seemed to contain a request for an explanation.

"So?" Joanna opened the refrigerator door to take out the pitcher of lemonade. Since he showed no signs of leaving, it would have been rude not to offer him some refreshment. "Would you like a glass?" She threw him a glance over her shoulder.

"Yes, thank you." He waited until she had poured a glass for each of them and was crossing the kitchen to the doorway where he stood. "He also told me that you apologized to him."

"I did." Joanna held out a glass to him. He took it, then turned aside so she could pass. "I told you I owed him an apology. Didn't you believe that I actually meant to tell him?" Her senses reacted to the brief seconds of closeness when she moved by him.

"I guess I was wondering whether you went on your own or if Reece suggested it," Linc replied.

Joanna pivoted a little sharply, the lemonade sloshing in her glass. "I didn't get around to telling Reece my intentions. He doesn't even know about it yet, so you can stop wondering," she retorted.

It was difficult to hold his look, so she sought a

chair. Sitting down, Joanna crossed her long legs and struggled for that cool sophistication her mother had worked so hard to instill in her. On the surface, she appeared to achieve it. Linc crushed out his cigarette in an ashtray and continued to stand.

"I decided it was better to ask the question than to arrive at any more hasty conclusions," he said.

"Are you having doubts that I might not be the spoiled, ill-mannered brat you thought I was?" she mocked him.

"It's possible you might even be human." The devilish light in his eyes taunted her.

"The next thing you know you'll be admitting I have feelings," Joanna warned him lightly.

"I might even concede there were extenuating circumstances for your behavior," Linc suggested.

"I don't know if I could take the shock," she countered.

"Then let's just say you've improved my opinion of you." A half-smile slanted his mouth, crooking it in an attractive manner.

She was stiffened by the feeling that she had to guard against liking him or end up being hurt. It brought a dryness to her voice. "I'd ask what that opinion is, but I don't think I would like it."

"Why?" Her reply sharpened his interest.

"Probably because you strike me as the type who believes women belong in the home." She gave him a cool look. "Isn't it the motto of the hills to keep them barefoot and pregnant?"

"Are you for it or against it?"

"Against it, of course," she flashed. "It's old-fashioned and ridiculous. Why?" She was suddenly suspicious of the apparent innocence of his question.

"I thought you might be planning to go native. I notice you're barefoot but I didn't know if you were pregnant, too." The golden flecks in his eyes were dancing with pure mockery.

Her stomach was churning with a violent emotion, which she believed was akin to anger. She pushed to her feet, discarding the lemonade glass on a side table, not trusting her hand to hold it and not throw it in his face.

"I'm not going native and I'm not pregnant. I was swimming as you very well know." She was on the verge of losing her temper, and was shaking with the effort to keep it under control. "I'm not going to turn myself into a baby factory for any man."

Linc tipped his head to one side. "Has someone asked?"

Joanna realized that she had allowed his remarks to grow out of all proportion. She was suddenly embarrassed and at a loss for words. Aware of her reddening cheeks, she held her head a little higher.

"I don't see any point in continuing this conversation," she declared on a note of pride, and would have swept past him in a grand exit, but his hand caught her arm.

Joanna stopped at the contact, before any pressure had been exerted to halt her. As a result, she was positioned to one side of him. She didn't turn her head to look at him, but merely swung her gaze, elevating its angle the necessary degrees to center on his rough-hewn features.

"Did you lose your sense of humor again?" His low voice was rich and smooth with amusement. "You are very sensitive, aren't you? Your pride is easily pricked even though you pretend to have a thick skin."

She had been accused of a lot of things by various men friends but none had ever suggested she was sensitive or easily hurt. Her gaze wavered under the probing inspection of his eyes. Joanna let it fall to the hand on her bare forearm, sun-tanned and strong. Its easy touch managed to hint at the potential of power in his grip. A warmth radiated from it, sensitizing her skin.

"Do you know what your problem is, Joanna?" Linc's all-knowing tone provoked a response.

"No, but I'm sure you're going to tell me whether I want to hear it or not," she retorted acidly.

When she lifted her gaze to his face, she saw that her remark had transmitted very little of its sting. The fanning lines at the corners of his eyes were crinkled in silent laughter.

"You always want to have the upper hand in a conversation. The minute you lose control, you run." A trace of wryness flitted across his expression. "You can dish it out but you can't take it."

"Is that right?" Joanna attempted to mock him but it sounded weak even to her.

She was nervous and on edge, trembling from an inner turmoil she couldn't define. She wanted to escape this conversation, but how could she after what Linc had just said? A little desperately, she tore her gaze from his face to search the room as if something in it would provide an excuse.

"Why are you frightened?" Linc asked with a steadiness that started a flood of panic.

"That's ridiculous! I'm not frightened of anything," Joanna denied and started to twist away from the loose grip of his hand.

But he shifted his hold, changing it from her arm to the curve of her waist and turning her as he turned so they were squarely facing each other. When that was accomplished, he cupped a large hand to the side of her neck where her pulse was visibly throbbing.

"Aren't you?" he challenged quietly. "Then why are you trembling?"

"I'm not," she lied.

Her hands were braced against his waistline to maintain the space between them, but he was so close that she could see the individual flecks of gold in his light brown eyes and the masculine texture of his skin stretched across his angular features, shadowed slightly by the shaven growth of his beard.

She was conscious of his flatly muscled stomach and the width of his shoulders and chest. With each breath, she was inhaling the tang of tobacco smoke that blended with the natural odor of his body, a combination that seemed to stimulate her senses. Joanna wasn't comfortable with the way he was affecting her.

"Are you afraid of sex?" His seemingly idle question skyrocketed her pulse, turning her thoughts in a direction she didn't want them to take.

The hand on her neck moved, showing disinterest in the rapid escalation of her pulse as his fingers absently traced the underside of her jaw and paused to let his thumb rub the point of her chin.

"Sex is a normal, biological function. Every living thing is designed to reproduce through one method or another. The birds and the bees do it. The human species is gifted with the capacity to enjoy it."

She was distracted by his reference to birds, the single word triggering her memory. When he lowered his mouth onto hers, her lips parted in surprise. There was nothing hesitant about his kiss, nothing tentative or uncertain. Yet neither was there force. The pressure of his mouth was warm and firm against hers, moving over her lips and tasting their natural softness.

His fingers tunneled into her hair to support the back of her neck. Brute strength she could have fought, but not this tantalizing possession that seemed to seek no more than a mutual enjoyment of the experience.

Was that true? Or was she subconsciously being influenced by primitive superstition into believing this kiss was inevitable because it had been foretold by an omen? His mouth eased from her lips and began to graze slowly along her smooth cheek.

"Did Jessie Bates put you up to this?" There was a disturbed level to her voice that proved she wasn't unaffected by this kiss. The stirring warmth of his breath against her lashes kept her eyes closed.

"Jessie?" He lifted his head an inch or two, a puzzled frown arching a dark brow. Joanna risked a glance at him and saw the vague bemusement in his eyes. "What has he got to do with this?"

"He arranged this with you so I would be kissed before nightfall and fulfill his silly prophecy because that bird flew in front of me," she accused in a none too steady voice.

There was a brief, negative movement of his head. "Jessie didn't mention anything to me about birds or kisses but if that's what he said, I don't want to make a liar out of him," Linc murmured huskily.

His mouth took hers again with familiar ease. There was a subtle difference in its possession, a quality of probing hunger in his kiss that seemed to test her ability to satisfy him. Her response to the silent challenge was almost involuntary as a melting warmth spread over her body.

His arms were around her, his hands gliding along her spine and applying casual pressure to arch her to his length. Her own fingers were splayed across the back of his ribcage, feeling the hard sinewed flesh and the body heat that flowed through the material of his shirt.

There was a traitorous excitement building in her system. Her hold on reality was weakening under the dizzying rush of emotion aroused by his experienced advance. Joanna became conscious of the scrape of rough denim against the bareness of her thighs and legs as she leaned against the solid support of his hips. The western buckle of his belt was poking her ribs and she realized her beach jacket was hanging open.

She was frightened by the part of her that wanted this intimacy to continue and grow, yet she lacked the determination and willpower to end the kiss. It was up to Linc to bring it to a gradual conclusion, which he did.

The instant her mouth was free of his possession, Joanna lowered her chin. There seemed to be so little air in her lungs. She struggled not to drink it in in gulps, not wanting Linc to know how breathless his kiss had left her. She brought her hands around to rest against his chest and establish space between them while still taking advantage of his support.

"Now you can tell Jessie that his prediction came true." With a slight toss of her head, Joanna met his heavily lidded gaze and attempted to show her indifference of him.

But she had the uneasy feeling those eyes saw right through her pretence. When his head began to descend toward her, she turned her face aside to avoid another kiss and stiffened her arms. Linc didn't try to hold her when she pushed out of his embrace and took a couple of steps to put distance between them.

"No more, Linc." She forced out a short laugh as she tried to treat the incident as a humorous experiment. "Jessie predicted I would only be kissed twice. As you said, we don't want to make a liar out of him."

When she turned around to look at him, his narrowed gaze slowly traveled down the length of her body, lingering on the exposed swell of her breasts revealed by the daring cut of her bathing suit and on the tanned bareness of her long legs. The boldness of his look brought a draining rush of heat through her body.

Her hands were shaking as she quickly wrapped the front of her terrycloth jacket closed and tied its sash in a tight knot. Flustered by the physical effect he was having on her, Joanna half-turned away. Purely by chance, she faced the screen door to the back porch. Through its dark mesh, she saw a figure approaching the cabin.

"Joanna—" Linc spoke her name, a summons in its pitch.

"Here comes Reece." She leaped on the excuse to ignore him and took long, swift steps to reach the screen door. She pushed it open and called to her uncle. "Hi! Did you catch any fish?"

"None." There was little disappointment in either his voice or his expression as he climbed the steps to the porch. "I had a few nibbles, but that's all. They'll probably start biting closer to evening."

Reece paused to set his fishing rod and reel against the outside of the cabin along with his tackle box before he moved to the door she was holding open for him. His glance took in the beach jacket she was wearing and the bareness of her legs.

"You've been swimming, I see," he observed as he crossed the threshold. Almost immediately he noticed their visitor. "Well, hello, Linc." His quick smile revealed his pleasure at seeing the man. "Have you been here long?"

"He arrived a few minutes ago," Joanna answered before Linc could.

"Yes." Linc went along with her answer and added a comment of his own. "Joanna has been entertaining me."

She knew precisely what he meant by his mocking insinuation and was glad it escaped her uncle. As she became aware of sudden quiet that had fallen, she noticed Reece dart her a sharp glance before his gaze returned to Linc. That's when she saw what had caught her uncle's eyes. The front of Linc's shirt was damp where it had absorbed the moisture from her wet swimsuit. Fortunately her uncle was too tactful to mention it.

"Was there something special you wanted to see me about?" he asked Linc.

"No. I just stopped to say hello." Linc assured him there was no other purpose behind his visit other than a friendly one.

"Since you're here, why don't you stay for dinner?" Reece invited.

"No thanks."

"That reminds me," Joanna inserted quickly before her uncle could pursue that topic and possibly change Linc's mind. "I had lunch with Rachel Parmelee today."

It was a subject guaranteed to attract her uncle's undivided attention. She saw the quick eagerness leap into his expression and light his dark eyes. The mere mention of her name brought an added warmth to his smile.

"Did you? How was she?" He tried to disguise his avid interest, but wasn't too successful.

"Fine." Joanna paused to add impetus to her next statement. "I invited her to dinner Friday night." She waited for the rush of elation in his expression but it never came. Instead he became guarded.

"Did she accept?" he questioned.

"Yes," she assured him, pleased with her success. "It took a little persuading, but she finally agreed to come."

It was several seconds before Reece said a rather bland, "Good." It left her slightly stunned. She had expected him to rejoice at the news but he had practically no positive reaction at all. She was too confused to protest when he turned to Linc and asked, "Will you join us for dinner Friday evening to even out the numbers?"

"It would be my pleasure," Linc accepted.

"What time did you tell Rachel?" he inquired with a glance at Joanna.

"I said dinner would be at seven and for her to

come any time before that," she replied as confusion drew lines in her expression. "I thought you would prefer to contact her and make arrangements to pick her up."

"Would you object to bringing Mrs. Parmelee, Linc?" Reece asked.

Like Joanna, Linc appeared slightly puzzled by the request, too. "If that's what you want," he agreed to it.

"Thank you."

There appeared to be a great many unanswered questions in Linc's eyes when he studied his friend but he didn't ask one of them. Instead he made his excuse to leave. "I'd better be getting back to the place."

"It was good to see you, Linc." For once her uncle didn't attempt to persuade him to stay or protest that it was early.

A fact that didn't escape Linc's notice either. "I'll see you on Friday." His glance held hers for an instant. "Joanna," he nodded in her direction before moving toward the front door.

When it closed behind him, she looked back at her uncle, still puzzled by his behavior. He seemed to deliberately avoid her eyes and assumed a preoccupation that indicated he had a great many important matters on his mind.

"Would you mind fixing the meal tonight, Joanna?" It was more in the order of a request than a question. "I have some things I must do. I'll be in the study."

As he started to walk away without waiting for a response, she frowned and shook her head. "I don't understand you," she declared on a heavy breath of exasperation.

"Is something wrong?" His arched glance was too smooth.

"Something is, but I don't know what," she admitted and went to the heart of the matter. "Aren't you *glad* Rachel is coming for dinner?"

"Of course." Again there was an unnatural ease to his reply that completely lacked expression. "Are you upset because I invited Linc? Haven't the two of you patched up your differences yet?" His tone made it plain that he believed they had.

Joanna wouldn't be sidetracked from the real issue. "I don't care if he comes but I thought you'd welcome the chance to be alone with Rachel."

"It was your invitation she accepted, not mine," he stated.

That was the crux of the matter. Her mouth dropped open at this discovery her uncle was jealous that she had succeeded where he had failed. He disappeared into the study while she was still trying to find her voice.

Chapter Eight

$\mathcal{L}$ater on that evening, Joanna had the opportunity to explain to her uncle how the dinner invitation had come about and the reason she had been successful in persuading Rachel Parmelee to come. It had been a very one-sided conversation with Reece offering no comment and asking no questions. When it was over, she wasn't entirely sure that she had convinced him Rachel Parmelee's sole reason for accepting was based on a desire to spend the evening with him.

Ever since, he had been moody and preoccupied most of the time. He wasn't himself at all. Everything was left up to Joanna. He didn't offer any suggestions for the menu or help in any of the advance preparations for the meal.

The spinach salad was in the refrigerator

along with the trout in its broiling pan, ready to be slipped under the broiler. The potatoes were baking in the oven and the broccoli sat in its steaming pan on the range, while the peach cobbler cooled on a wire rack. Joanna checked it all one last time before entering the living room where she had set the table, complete with a white linen cloth, candles, and the best glass and silverware she could find.

The living room was too well lit, so she began a circuit of the room shutting off unnecessary lamps and leaving a strategic few on to create a more intimate atmosphere. The porch door opened and closed. Aware it was her uncle, Joanna didn't bother to look around.

"What are you doing?" he asked.

"There were too many lights on." She stopped beside the fireplace and a trace of regret flitted across her expression. "It's a pity it's July. It would be nice to have a fire blazing away." Then she turned and smiled quickly. "You look very handsome tonight."

Which he did. There was a casual sophistication to his simple attire of a plain silk shirt and dark slacks. It enhanced the silvered darkness of his hair and eyes, the leanness of his build.

He returned the compliment. "You look very lovely in that dress. Is it new?"

Reflex caused her to glance at the china blue tunic-style dress of crepe de chine, belted at the waist. It had an understated elegance to its basic style. She smoothed a hand over the practically wrinkle-free material.

"It's one I brought with me," she explained.

When she looked up, she saw that he had once again become preoccupied. His attention was away from her as his glance skimmed the table set for four.

"You shouldn't have gone to so much trouble," he said flatly.

"Why not? It's a special occasion," Joanna insisted.

He glanced briefly at his gold watch. "She isn't coming."

Reece sounded so positive that, for an instant, Joanna thought Rachel might have telephoned to cancel the invitation, but she hadn't heard the phone ring. She glanced at the wall clock above the kitchen cupboards, just visible through the archway, and saw it was half past six.

"The traffic is probably holding them up." She found an excuse to explain why Rachel Parmelee and Linc hadn't arrived yet.

"She won't come," he repeated. "You'll see." He walked to the window to gaze at the lake, the lowering rays of the sun reflecting off its mirror surface.

Joanna sighed, but didn't try to argue with him.

The car traveled at a reduced speed over the rutted gravel road. Rachel Parmelee sat as stiff as a statue in the passenger seat, rarely looking to the right or left. Her hands were clasped tightly on the clutch purse in her lap, the knuckles of her fingers showing white. Tension was written all over her expression.

"It's less than a mile now," Linc informed her.

On the drive here, they had talked about everything but their destination. The weather had been discussed at great length; this summer's trade had been compared to last year's.

"I shouldn't have come," Rachel blurted out the thought that had been on her mind ever since Linc had picked her up. She was embarrassed to discover she'd said it aloud.

"It's too late to turn back now," he replied evenly.

"I'm sorry," she apologized for her lack of poise. "I must sound like a silly schoolgirl on her first date." That was the way she felt, painfully nervous and awkward, her stomach churning. It was absurd to be so close to tears.

"There's no reason to be nervous." There was gentle humor in the warm look Linc Wilder gave her. "Reece won't bite—at least not on the first date."

In her present agitation, the remark was hardly laughable. "I can't help feeling that I'm out of my league," she sighed. "Here I am in a dress I made myself when he's used to taking out fashion models in designer clothes."

"I have known Reece for ten years. He isn't the kind of man who judges a person's worth by the label on their clothes." He applied the brake and made the turn into the cabin's driveway.

Stopping the car, he switched off the engine

and glanced at his passenger. She sat frozen in her seat while he climbed out of the car and walked around to open her door. Her hands were like ice when he helped her out of the car and closed the door.

Inside the cabin, Joanna had heard the car drive in and the first door being slammed shut. She unconsciously held her breath until she heard the second, half-afraid Reece might be right and Rachel Parmelee would back out at the last minute.

"They have arrived." She stressed the plural slightly and glanced at her uncle to see his reaction.

But he continued to stare out the window at the lake. Joanna sighed, wanting to shake him. At the rap on the door, she crossed the room to admit their guests. She pushed open the screen door and smiled warmly.

"Come in. I see Linc managed to get you here safely," she said addressing her comments to Rachel and ignoring Linc—on the surface. An inner radar was completely sensitive to his presence. "Was the traffic very heavy?"

"No." Even as the widow entered the cabin, her gaze was racing past Joanna.

A hint of pink appeared in the woman's cheeks, almost a match to the pale pink dress she was wearing. Joanna stole a look over her shoulder, already guessing the cause for the widow's faint blush.

Reece was standing near the center of the living room, waiting to greet their guests. Joanna wished he would smile and get rid of that proudly courteous look.

"Hello, Reece," Rachel greeted him in a stilted fashion.

"Good evening, Rachel," he responded in a like manner.

They both sounded so formal that Joanna wouldn't have been surprised if he'd made a stiff and courtly bow over the widow's hand. Her mouth tightened.

"I think it's going to be cool tonight," Linc murmured as he paused beside her.

She flashed him a glance that said she knew exactly what he meant. Although when his hand moved to the hollow of her back to guide her into the room with the others, she felt anything but cool. She shifted away from his touch at the first opportunity.

"Make yourselves comfortable," she urged and excused herself. "I have to check on dinner. Why don't you offer them a drink, Reece?"

"What would you like?" her uncle inquired of his guests while Joanna retreated to the kitchen and left them to break the ice—literally. "A glass of sherry? Wine?"

"A glass of sherry, please," Rachel requested because she'd read in books that's what real ladies ordered.

"I'll have a beer," Linc said.

A liquor tray was sitting on one of the tables, complete with decanters, glasses, and an ice bucket. But it included no beer, which Linc had already noted.

"Fix Rachel's drink. I know where the beer is kept." He crossed to the kitchen archway, leaving the two of them alone in the room.

After pouring the glass of sherry, Reece handed it to Rachel. His dark gaze probed her expression, but it was locked against him—as it always, was.

"You have turned down all of my invitations to dinner. My niece must be more persuasive than I am," he murmured.

What could she say? That she had been wrong to accept this one? That would have been too rude. "She is a very lovely girl," Rachel said as if that explained it and sipped at the sherry.

Its dryness seemed to cake her tongue, leaving a strong after-taste. It had been a mistake to order it. She should have asked for something she knew she would like instead of attempting to impress Reece. She watched him splash whiskey into a tumbler of ice cubes and wished she could trade with him.

"Please sit down." He gestured toward the seat cushion of the sofa while he chose the armchair on its left. There was an aura of worldly authority about him that seemed so natural.

Rachel tried to emulate his aloof composure as she sank gracefully—or so she hoped—onto the couch. She couldn't help noticing how well the silk shirt fit the cut of his shoulders. He was so trim and manly that she couldn't look at him without feeling that wild fluttering in her stomach.

She had never believed such men truly existed, which was why she couldn't believe someone like Reece was really interested in her. For all intents and purposes, she had never been out of the Ozarks in her life except for that one trip to Chicago twenty years ago.

She took another sip of the sherry and almost couldn't swallow it. She tried to be very casual when she set the glass on the coffee table.

"Is the sherry too dry?" Reece inquired.

"It's fine," she lied.

Joanna was slipping a bibbed apron over her head when Linc walked into the kitchen. She glanced at him, sharply curious and suspicious. The lazy flick of his glance sent a rippling warning along her nerve ends. She felt raw and exposed, on edge in his presence.

"Do you want a beer?" he asked and walked straight to the refrigerator.

"No thanks." She tied the apron's bow at the back of her waist. The pop-top of an aluminum can sounded behind her as she turned on the burner under the pan of broccoli.

"Rachel made the dress she's wearing. You might want to compliment her on it," Linc suggested.

Joanna glanced to the side where he was standing, a hip leaning against the counter and a can of beer in his hand. His shirt was half-unbuttoned, showing more of his bronzed torso than she felt safe to see.

"I'll remember that," she said stiffly.

As she removed the potatoes from the oven, she switched the setting to broil for the trout. She was conscious of his eyes following her every move, tracking her like a cat sighting its prey.

"I never would have guessed you had domestic talents," Linc remarked.

"I had a very good teacher," she tried to keep the irritation out of her voice.

Tonight was too important for Reece. She didn't want to ruin it by losing her temper with Linc. It wouldn't be easy since he had the knack of rubbing her the wrong way. Completely unbidden, the thought came that he also knew how to rub her the right way; his kiss had been proof of that.

"Who? Your mother?"

"No—Reece. My mother has difficulty boiling water," Joanna admitted on a rebellious note.

Linc made no comment on that, as he straightened from the counter. "It's getting awfully quiet in the living room. I suggest you serve dinner as soon as possible. It might make up for the lack of conversation."

As he left the kitchen to rejoin the couple alone in the living room, Joanna conceded that he did have a point. Silence could become an insurmountable barrier. She remembered too well that Rachel had told her that she ran out of things to say after five minutes and Reece was showing no inclination to use his considerable charm to draw the woman into a conversation.

If that trend continued, it would be a long evening.

Removing the salad plates from the refrigerator, Joanna carried them out to the table. She glanced briefly into the living room where Linc seemed to be carrying the conversation. Her uncle didn't appear to be following the talk, his gaze continuously roaming over Rachel Parmelee who didn't look at him at all. When each of the place settings had a salad, Joanna slipped the broiler pan into the oven and took off her apron.

She entered the living room and paused near the table. "If you would come to the table, we can sit down for dinner." The seating arrangements were simple, the men and women sitting opposite each other. "That's a very lovely dress," she remarked and prompted her uncle, "Isn't it, Reece?"

"Yes, it is very lovely. Very becoming on you, Rachel," he agreed with a display of his old charm.

The compliment was rewarded by the softening of the woman's features and the sparkle that brightened her eyes. Joanna thought that at last they were getting somewhere.

"Did you make it yourself, Rachel?" she asked.

The widow lowered her gaze to the table as she picked up her salad fork. "Yes, I did."

Joanna interpreted the lowered eyes and quiet reply as a display of modesty. A knee nudged her right leg under the table. Since Linc was seated on her right, it had to have been him. But she wasn't sure if it had been accidental or on purpose. Joanna slid him a glance and was confused by the hard look he was giving her.

Annoyed, she ignored him to concentrate on Rachel. "You certainly are an excellent seamstress. I wish you had time to give me some sewing lessons."

There was an uncomfortable silence for several seconds during which Joanna instinctively glanced at Linc. His mouth was pulled down at the corners in dry exasperation.

"Sewing is a matter of practice," Rachel replied at last. "A skill that is generally learned out of necessity."

"But once it is learned, it would be a shame not to use it," Reece inserted.

"Have you seen Jessie Bates lately?" Linc directed his question at Joanna, bringing about a complete change of topic.

"Not lately, no." She eyed him warily. "Why?"

"I thought he might have regaled you with more tales and superstitions of the Ozarks," he shrugged. "He is a walking encyclopedia of folklore."

"Well, he hasn't." Joanna was just as glad, too. She was still half convinced that she had made his superstition about the redbird flying across her path a self-fulfilling prophecy.

"I can remember one of my first meetings with Jessie," Reece recalled with a smile. "He explained to me about the 'law of the hills.'"

"What is the law of the hills?" Joanna was the

only one at the table who didn't smile at his comment.

"Ridgerunners—hill-folks—don't look favorably on the so-called outside authorities whether it's a sheriff, state, or federal agents. They prefer to handle their own problems," Linc explained. "It's commonly known as hill 'just-us.'"

At first, she thought he had said justice, then she caught his pun and smiled. "I won't ask how it works." She finished her salad and noticed that her uncle had also. "Excuse me while I check on the trout."

"Let me carry these plates out for you and help dish the food," Rachel volunteered as Joanna pushed her chair away from the table.

Before she stood up, she felt the toe of Linc's boot nudge her foot. She smothered the burst of irritation. She was well aware of how to act with guests. She certainly didn't need any sideline coaching from him.

"No, you stay here," Joanna refused the offer. "We didn't invite you here to put you to work. This is your day off."

With the salad plates stacked in her hand, she carried them to the kitchen and set them in the sink. It only took a few minutes to dish up the broccoli and arrange the broiled trout on a platter. This only left the baked potatoes and the cheese sauce. When they were served, she rejoined them at the table.

"This cheese sauce is delicious, Joanna. So smooth. Did you make it?" Rachel asked.

"Yes, but I can't take the credit. The recipe is a

family secret," she explained. "Actually I shouldn't say that because it belongs to Reece. He is a marvelous cook."

"I didn't know that." Rachel looked at him anew.

"Yes, I once considered training to be a master chef," he admitted and shrugged. "Now it is merely a hobby."

"With your hours, I doubt if you have much time to cook, do you, Rachel?" Joanna remarked sympathetically and was kicked in the shin by Linc. She breathed in sharply at the pain but he was already talking, covering her small sound.

"I don't know about you, Rachel, but I can fix a mean batch of scrambled egss," he declared, mocking their culinary feats.

"That's more in my line," Rachel admitted with a wan smile.

Through the rest of the main course and into dessert and coffee, the conversation vacillated over various subjects without ever becoming truly lively. On two other occasions, Joanna was prodded by Linc's foot. She no more understood the cause for it then than she did the other times.

Rachel finished her coffee and replaced the cup on its saucer. "I enjoyed the meal, Joanna, and I insist that you let me help with the clean-up."

"Sorry." Her smile was bright as she refused Rachel's offer again. "But Linc has already volunteered for kitchen duty tonight. This time you can relax after dinner and chat with Reece."

Joanna noticed how ill at ease the woman looked at the prospect, but it couldn't be helped. The object of this evening was to get the two together. Joanna carried some of the remaining dishes into the kitchen and Linc brought the rest.

"Did I *volunteer* to wash the dishes or dry them?" Linc mocked.

"Dry." The dishes clattered loudly as she stacked them in the sink with an impatient disregard for their breakability. "And would you mind explaining why you kept kicking me all night? It's a miracle I'm not limping."

"I was trying to keep you from putting your foot in your mouth, but I'm now convinced that's impossible," he said dryly.

"Why? What did I do?" Joanna stopped to stare at him incredulously.

"Do you want that answered point by point or just the highlights?" He lifted a dark brow in mocking inquiry.

"The highlights will do." She jammed the stopper in the sink drain and wished it was his face.

"A candlelight dinner isn't exactly subtle. You should have barbequed steaks outside so it could have been less formal and more relaxed. The only thing missing tonight was the violin music in the background."

"And?" She tightly prompted him to continue, irritated by the common sense of his answer.

"And—you should have complimented her on the dress and let it go at that. That's partly my

fault since I told you she had made it herself.
What I failed to mention was how self-conscious
she felt because it didn't carry a fancy label,
therefore it was unworthy and not up to Reece's
standards."

"Now, that is ridiculous." She resented that
attitude. "Reece isn't a snob."

"You know that, and I know that, but Rachel
doesn't," Linc reasoned calmly as she turned on
the taps to fill the sink with water.

Recognizing the inherent truth of his observation, Joanna sighed. "What else?"

"If you wanted her to feel comfortable, you
should have allowed her to help serve. She isn't
used to being waited on, not in this kind of
situation," he stated.

"I wanted to show her that she was important,
a guest," she defended her action.

"I'm not questioning your intentions, Joanna."
There was a faint smile curving his mouth.
"Unfortunately, you only succeeded in making
her feel awkward."

"I see." The line of her mouth was tight. She
pushed the faucet over to fill the other half of the
double sink with rinse water. "Is there anything
else?"

"Just one."

"That figures," she grumbled.

"If you wanted them to meet on common
ground, they should be here in the kitchen doing
the dishes instead of us. Maybe if Rachel saw
Reece up to his elbows in dishsoap, she would

realize he doesn't exist on some elevated plane," Linc concluded.

She attacked the dirty dishes, angry with herself for not seeing the things that had been so obvious to Linc. It didn't help that he had been the one to point out her shortcomings. That was salt on the wound.

"I have to admit," Linc went on as he lifted the dishes out of the rinse water and stacked them on the drainboard, "you do have a talent for saying and doing the wrong things at the wrong time."

"Thanks a lot," she murmured sarcastically. "I really needed that vote of confidence."

"I wouldn't worry about it." He began drying the dishes she washed. "After all, it's something they have to work out themselves. All you could have accomplished would have been to smooth the path a little but it's still up to them to walk down it."

"I suppose it is," Joanna sighed, but she did feel a little better.

He crooked a finger under her chin, startling her with his touch. Her widened gaze flew to his face, pleasantly rugged and lean. His mouth slanted in a half-smile. He rubbed a thumb over her cheek and explained, "You had some dishsoap on your face."

Unaware he'd already wiped it away, she lifted a wet hand to her cheek, trailing more soap bubbles across it. "Is it gone?"

He chuckled in his throat. "Not at that rate."

This time he used a corner of the dishtowel to wipe away the suds. "There. It's all gone."

Unexpectedly her gaze became locked by his. There was an uneven patter to her heartbeat, an unsteady rhythm to her breathing. A sudden, inexplicable tension knotted her stomach. She had an urge to smooth the springing thickness of his dark hair. With an effort, Joanna dragged her gaze away from him and tried to concentrate on the dirty dishes in the sink.

"Did any birds fly in front of you today?" Linc murmured the question.

She swallowed in an attempt to ease the sudden constriction in her throat. "No."

"That's funny."

At his cryptic reply, she glanced at him. Linc reached out and turned her away from the sink and into his arms, his mouth coming down to cover hers. Heat flared in her veins as she strained toward him, yet careful not to touch him with her wet hands. She pressed herself against the hard strength of his body.

His caressing hands became tangled in the ties of her apron. It brought them both back to the present. He released her slowly, breathing in deeply, a light continuing to smolder in his tawny eyes.

"You have to be the most exasperating female I've met," he said, the remark stinging her. "You get under a man's skin whether it's what he wants or not."

"Do you want me to get under your skin?"

Joanna didn't intend for her question to be as provocative as it sounded.

"Not as much as I want to get into yours," Linc replied with so much desire in his look that she had to turn back to the sink to quiet her own lusting thoughts.

Chapter Nine

$\mathcal{T}$he terrible pangs of self-consciousness returned in full force the minute Rachel left the dinner table and lost the buffer of Linc and Joanna. She was tongue-tied, helpless to find a subject to discuss with Reece. Her knees were weak as she walked to the couch where she had been sitting before dinner.

"Would you care for an after-dinner liqueur?" Reece paused in front of the fireplace. "Perhaps a brandy or Drambuie?"

"No, thank you." After the fiasco with the sherry, Rachel didn't intend to repeat the mistake by requesting something she had never tasted.

Then she noticed that Reece was turning away from the liquor tray to walk to the armchair he'd previously occupied on her right. She panicked a little when she thought he wasn't having a drink because she had refused one.

"Aren't you going to fix yourself something?" she asked.

"No, I don't care for alcohol that well," he explained and allowed a smile to pull at the corners of his mouth. "Except on occasions when I sometimes seek the dutch courage that's in the bottle."

It was difficult to imagine he would ever need that. He always seemed to be in command of any situation. Rachel wondered if he'd meant that because the remark implied he had needed the false courage of liquor before dinner. But she couldn't ask him about it.

"This cabin is very nice, isn't it?" She filled the silence with an empty remark and wished she had said something witty and intelligent.

"Yes," Reece agreed and looked around the room with quiet satisfaction. "I think of it as my second home. It is much more comfortable than my place in California. Sometimes I wish I could move the cabin there."

"It would be out of place." Just as she would be in Los Angeles. "Your home in California must be very grand."

Rachel could easily picture him in such a setting and was a little surprised to discover how well he blended into this rustic surrounding.

"It is quite large," he admitted then raised his downcast glance to look at her. "It is also quite empty."

"I'm sure you have many friends to fill it," she insisted.

There was a wry lift of his mouth. "A man in my position has a great many acquaintances, Rachel, but very few friends."

"I suppose." But she had difficulty believing that.

He seemed to sense it. "Are there not times when you are lonely?"

"Of course." She tried to make light of the admission with an indifferent smile but there were many times when loneliness weighed down her spirit.

"I used to think the night times were the worst," Reece mused. "Now I know it is the mornings—with no one sitting across the breakfast table and no one to wave goodbye to you when you leave for work."

There was a tight constriction in her chest at the apt way he described the emptiness that yawned at the start of each new day, with nothing to look forward to at the end of it except more of the same. Yet Rachel wasn't able to voice it as readily as he had. Her glance strayed to the window. Beyond its glass panes, crimson and gold banners were streaking the sky.

"Look at the sunset." She called Reece's attention to the window, relieved to change the subject. Rising from the couch, she walked to the window for a better view. "Isn't it beautiful?"

She marveled at the brilliant colors shading the clouds and coloring the hills. Hearing his approach, she glanced over her shoulder. He stopped behind her and a little to one side. The disturbing darkness of his gaze stayed on her for several seconds before swinging to the window.

"It is very beautiful," he agreed with a nod of his head.

His nearness started little tremors of excitement that she couldn't control. A strong sense of self-preservation insisted that she deny herself the pleasure she found in his company or suffer the consequences.

"I can't stay late," Rachel said and stared out the window.

Out of the corner of her eyes, she saw the sharp frown of displeasure Reece directed at her. She fought down the thrill that he didn't want her to leave yet.

"I have to be at the shop bright and early tomorrow morning," she justified her reason.

"You work too hard and too many hours," he criticized.

"It can't be helped," she shrugged.

"You should hire a qualified assistant who can operate the store in your absence so you can have more free time," Reece advised.

"That is easier said than done." Her sidelong glance was both amused and resigned to the situation.

"Do you know why I say that?" The lilting inflection of his voice put a question mark at the end of the sentence. "There is so little time left. I want to spend every possible minute that I can with you. I am selfish. I want you to have more free hours so you can be with me."

She was thrown by the vibrating pitch of his voice that spoke with such intensity. It left her shaken and unnerved, unable to combat this undermining of her defenses.

"It . . . isn't possible." She faltered over her reply.

"When will I see you again?" When his direct question was met with silence, a smile twisted his mouth. "Or should I have Joanna ask that question for me? She seems to be more successful at obtaining an affirmative reply than I am. I shall have to learn her secret."

"There isn't any secret." Rachel assured him quickly. "It just worked out this way. Summer is my busy season and I—" She had used the shop as an excuse so many times that it sounded tired even to her. She abandoned it altogether. "There are dozens of ladies who would be more than delighted to spend time with you."

"It wouldn't matter if there were a million," Reece declared as he turned to face her. The warm firm touch of his hands catapulted her heart into her throat. "It is still *you* I'm asking, Rachel. Linc argues that I must be patient because you don't know me, but how patient must I be? Ask me what it is you want to know and I'll tell you. I want to be with *you*, Rachel, and I think—" He paused to lightly cup her cheek in his hand and tilt her face up. Although she tried, she couldn't resist the magnetic force of his charm and felt all her carefully guarded defenses melt away under his possessive look. "—you want to be with me."

Rachel couldn't say it. "Yes, but—" There were too many differences, too many obstacles.

"Sssh." He pressed his thumb to her lips before she could add more. "For now, it is enough that you have said 'yes' to me." She was incapable of arguing the point. "You close your shop early on Sunday, don't you? You don't keep it open in the evenings?"

"I generally close around six," she admitted.

"Then I will pick you up at six. Bring some old clothes and we'll go fishing," Reece stated.

"Fishing?" It was the last thing Rachel had expected him to suggest. A movie, dinner, a show perhaps—but not fishing. She couldn't keep the stunned reaction out of her expression.

"Yes, fishing." He frowned at her failure to endorse his suggestion. "Don't you like to fish? I thought you might enjoy the chance to be outside. You spend so much of your time indoors."

"I like to fish," she assured him, then qualified the answer, "At least I did. It's been years since I went fishing."

"Would you like to go Sunday?" This time he asked.

"Yes." It sounded novel and fun. "I'll have to get a license," she remembered.

"That's easily handled," Reece said and began to outline his plans for the evening. "I'll pick you up at six and get your license. We'll fish until dark and cook whatever we catch for a late supper."

"What if we don't catch anything?" She raised the possibility, not fully aware how easily she was joking with him, how naturally she was reacting.

"Then we will come back here and you can scramble me some eggs. And I will love it." His light tone became progressively serious until he ended on a husky note.

Under the burning darkness of his gaze, she stopped breathing. Her senses quivered in anticipation as his hand tightened on her shoulder, impelling her forward. His kiss was warm and firm, his needs controlled. It was all too brief to satisfy either of them, but it held an exciting promise that quickened her blood.

"I'll drive you home," Reece stated.

Rachel nodded, then remembered belatedly, "Linc—"

"Wait here," he interrupted, "and I'll tell them we're going."

"Okay," she smiled a contented agreement and watched him cross the room to the kitchen.

She felt as giddy and gay as a teenager who had just accepted an invitation from a boy she'd had a crush on for years. It was a sensation a mature forty-year-old woman didn't expect to experience again.

When Reece entered the kitchen, there weren't any more dirty dishes to be washed. Linc was drying the last pan while Joanna wiped off the range top.

Linc glanced over his shoulder. "If you've come to see if we need any help, Reece, your timing is excellent. We have just finished the dishes."

Reece's laugh drew Joanna's gaze. He was practically beaming. "No, I came to tell you that I'm driving Rachel home," he explained the reason for his presence. "She has to work tomorrow."

"Are you leaving now?" Joanna wondered.

"Yes. I'll be back later," her uncle promised and retraced his steps to the living room.

Joanna stared thoughtfully at the archway where he had disappeared while she folded the wet dishcloth and draped it over the sink divider. Linc was hanging up his towel on the rack. She cast him a sideways glance.

"It seems the dinner was a success after all," she murmured and reached behind her back to untie the apron bow. When she pulled the tie, it knotted. "Damn," she swore softly and struggled with the knot before giving up. "Will you untie this for me, Linc?" she demanded in irritation. "I can't see what I'm doing."

"Sure." He came up behind her.

Joanna faced the sink, her hands resting on the counter so they wouldn't be in his way. As he worked to free the knot, the touch of his hands along the small of her back caused a disturbing sensation that tingled up her spine. She heard her uncle's car drive out of the yard.

"Haven't you got it untied yet?" she demanded impatiently.

"Patience," he counseled. "By the way, the dinner was very good tonight. With a little practice, you might make some man a good wife."

"With a little more practice, you could become

a good wife, too," Joanna retorted, twisting and throwing back his sexist remark.

The knot was freed, loosening the apron around her waist. She slipped the haltered neckline over her head and stopped in the middle of folding the apron as his hands settled on her shoulders, rubbing them in an intimate fashion.

"You could have beautiful shoulders if you didn't carry that big chip on them all the time," Linc commented.

"If it wasn't for men like you, it wouldn't be there." She twisted away from his hands with a shrugging turn of her shoulders and moved a pace away. She could feel his narrowed gaze.

"You like being a deliberately aggravating female, don't you?" Linc challenged.

She gave him a wide-eyed look of mock innocence. "Because I make you itch?"

"I've decided it's a heat rash. Nothing a cold shower won't cure." The natural curve of his mouth deepened with dryness as topaz lights glittered in his brown eyes.

The double meaning wasn't lost on her. Heat warmed her cheeks, but she didn't know if it was caused by his insinuation of sex or his off-hand dismissal that she could arouse any lasting passion. She glared at him silently.

A satisfied smile spread slowly across his expression. "This is the first time I've ever seen you at a loss for words—especially sharp ones. Maybe there's hope for you yet," Linc suggested.

"Very funny." She found her sarcasm.

"The battle of the sexes is usually fought with words. Didn't you know that?" he mocked.

"Who said I was fighting?" Joanna challenged.

"You are. Do you know why?" he asked.

"You seem to know everything. Why don't you tell me?" Her jaw was tightly clenched.

"You don't respect anyone you can push around. By the same token, every time you're pushed, you push back. Somewhere, sometime, you're going to have to work out a compromise," Linc advised.

There was the sting of tears at the back of her eyes, but she kept her head held high and proud and showed no expression. A weariness passed over his face and he turned from her.

"Thanks for dinner," he said. "Tell Reece I'll see him."

Joanna stared as he walked out of the kitchen, shocked that he was actually leaving. She realized she didn't want him to go. She took a step after him and heard the front door slam. Halting, she listened and heard the start of a car's engine. When its roar faded into the night, there was only silence in the cabin, a silence broken by the ticking of the clock.

Chapter Ten

$\mathcal{I}$t was well over an hour before Reece returned from driving Rachel Parmelee home. When he walked in the door, his dark eyes shining and his handsome features radiating an inner happiness, Joanna felt a twinge of envy.

"You certainly took Rachel on the long way home," she observed with a glance at the clock, teasing him with her smile.

"We began talking and lost track of time." Reece was in too good a mood to take offense at her affectionate ribbing.

"Talking, huh?" Joanna moved closer and inspected the pink smudge on his white collar. "Is that how this lipstick got on your shirt?"

He glanced down, briefly self-conscious, then

laughed in his throat. The sound held a note of triumph, a battle long-fought and finally won.

"There are other, equally satisfactory methods of communication besides talking, as you already know," he stated.

She was pleased to see him so happy and contented. "When are you seeing her again?"

"Sunday," Reece answered without hesitation. "We're going fishing together."

"Fishing?" Joanna showed her surprise at his questionable choice for a romantic outing.

"That's exactly what Rachel said." A tiny crease showed on his forehead.

"I can understand why," Joanna replied. "Going fishing isn't exactly a romantic thing to do." Then she remembered Linc had indicated Rachel was uncomfortable with a staged, romantic setting. She quickly changed her opinion of his plans. "But I think it's a great idea. It's much easier for a person to relax and be themselves when they're fishing."

Her explanation erased his last doubts and he turned his mind to other things. "When did Linc leave?"

"Shortly after you did," she admitted and felt the quiet scrutiny of his eyes.

"I thought he would stay later than that," he remarked.

Joanna shrugged her lack of an explanation for his decision, uncomfortable with the subject. She went back to one that was safer. "Do you want me to make myself scarce Sunday night?"

"It isn't necessary as far as I'm concerned," he assured her. "Naturally you are free to make whatever plans you wish."

Late on Sunday afternoon, Reece was preparing to leave the cabin to pick up Rachel. Joanna was curled up in an armchair with a book that she pretended to be interested in, because she didn't want Reece to think she was at loose ends for something to do. The telephone rang. She started to uncoil her legs to answer it but he waved her back into the chair.

"I'll answer it." He walked to the phone and picked up the receiver. "Reece Morgan speaking."

Absently curious, Joanna watched recognition register in his expression as the caller obviously identified himself as someone her uncle knew. Then Reece was glancing her way.

"Yes, she's here. Just a minute." His hand covered the mouthpiece. "It's Linc. He wants to speak to you."

Surprise flickered across her face. Her heartbeat quickened as she pushed out of the chair and crossed the room to take the receiver from her uncle's hand. A little nervous, she took the phone and lifted it to her ear.

"Hello?"

"Joanna." Linc's voice quietly drawled her name in greeting. "Do you know how to ride a horse?"

She was too startled by the question to do more than give a simple answer. "Yes."

"Change into some jeans and we'll go riding," he instructed.

"When?" she asked blankly.

"Now. It'll probably take me about twenty minutes to ride down to the cabin. Can you be ready by then?"

"Yes." It wouldn't take that long to change clothes.

"Okay, I'll see you then."

There was a click and the buzz of a dial tone in her ear. She kept the phone in her hand an instant longer then hung it up. When she looked up, Reece was watching her with a bemused look.

"That was a very brief conversation," he remarked.

"Linc's coming down," she explained the reason for his call. "We're going horseback riding." Suddenly realizing her twenty minutes was being used up, she moved toward the stairs. "I have to change yet."

"I'll be leaving. Have a good time." He raised a hand in farewell as he retreated toward the door.

As she raced up the stairs, Joanna heard the car pulling out of the drive. Changing out of her shorts and suntop, she tugged on a pair of brushed denims and a pin-striped blouse. After running a brush through her ash-blonde hair, she dabbed on some lipgloss. Since she didn't have a pair of riding boots with her, she slipped on a pair of canvas sneakers and tied the laces.

She had barely reached the bottom of the

stairs when she heard the clip-clopping of horses' hooves out on the road, followed by the rolling snort of a horse. As she crossed the living room to the front door, she could see Linc riding into the driveway astride a dappled buckskin and leading a saddled, blaze-faced bay. By the time she reached the door and had walked outside, he had halted the horses.

Joanna paused a little uncertainly. "Hello," she said. After the way he had left so abruptly the other night, she didn't know what his attitude would be toward her now.

"Hello, yourself." His smile was lazy as his glance ran over her in quiet approval.

"Are we ready?" Relief relaxed her features into a bright smile.

The saddle groaned as he leaned forward to pass her the reins of the second horse. "Do you need some help mounting?" The brim of his western hat shadowed his eyes, but she was conscious of their warmth and interest.

"I think I can manage." She looped the reins over the horse's neck as Linc maneuvered his horse out of her way.

It was a long stretch to the stirrup. Joanna had to hop a couple of times to keep her balance before she got a toe in it. Gripping the saddlehorn, she swung into the seat. She adjusted the length of the reins in her hand, aware of the swiveling ears of her alert mount. She patted its sleek neck and crooned a few words to the horse so it would know her voice.

"All set?" Linc asked.

She gave an affirmative nod. "Where are we going?"

A touch of the rein turned her horse alongside of his buckskin. Both animals moved out at a walk, eager yet obedient.

"I thought we'd ride over to Jessie's and cut through his place to the lake," Linc answered. "Is that all right with you?"

Joanna darted a quick look at him to see if he was mocking her, but the expression on his rugged features was bland. "That's fine." She let her attention swing back to her horse and the road ahead.

"You're not a bad rider," he observed.

There was an impulse to make a quick retort at the back-handed compliment, but Joanna smothered it. "It's a good horse."

"Coffee is my sister's favorite. She used to ride him all the time."

She noticed the way the horse's ears pricked at the mention of its name. "Coffee. Is that what they call you, fella?" Joanna murmured to it, then glanced self-consciously at Linc who didn't seem to find anything wrong with talking to the horse. "Doesn't your sister ride her anymore?"

"Not since she got married and moved to her own home," he replied.

"Oh." She fell silent, listening to the steady clop of hooves, the jingle of bridle chains, and squeaking leather. "Why haven't you gotten married?"

"Too busy, I guess." He shifted in the saddle, his head lifted as he idly looked around.

"Do you mean you're not a confirmed bachelor?" she teased.

"Nope." Again there was a dry and lazy smile. "How about you?"

"I'm not sure that I want to get married," Joanna admitted, unexpectedly serious. A wry grimace tugged at her expression. "I haven't seen many 'happy' marriages in California. Of course, I look at Reece and then I want to believe—for his sake."

"Rachel?"

"Yes. I've never seen him so relaxed and carefree. He's practically walking on air." She smiled. "He's seeing her tonight. They're going fishing—of all things." Her side glance caught his look. "I know," she nodded. "They'll meet on the same level."

"You are quite a contradiction, Joanna." He shook his head in mild amazement. "Here you are match-making, yet you claim not to believe in the 'happily ever after' part."

"It doesn't make sense, does it?" she admitted with a faint laugh.

"No," he agreed and kneed his horse into a reaching trot.

Joanna urged her mount to keep pace. The jarring gait eliminated more conversation as they followed the rough and twisting road. The heat of the afternoon was fading, the sun's rays slanted against the earth. The shadows cast by the trees were lengthened across the road. Joanna turned her face to the cooling breeze their pace generated.

Where the road smoothed out, Linc spurred his horse into a rocking lope and Joanna followed suit. They stayed in a slow canter until they neared the turn-off to Jessie Bates's cabin. Checking their horses to a blowing walk, they turned down the narrow lane and followed it back to the log cabin. A mule brayed, announcing their arrival. Her horse snorted and turned its head to study its hybrid cousin.

"Hello! Anybody home!" Linc called.

There was a stirring inside the cabin. The hinges on the screen door squealed a protest as the door was pushed open and Jessie stepped out, yawning and scratching his head, ruffling hair that was already rumpled.

"Ya' caught me nappin'," he said and blinked his eyes. "What d'ya want?"

"We thought we'd ride down to the lake," Linc explained.

"Oh," Jessie grunted. "I thought ya mighta come to visit."

Joanna caught the trace of disappointment in his voice and glanced at Linc. He'd heard it, too, and lifted an eyebrow in silent question. She answered with a slight nod.

"We did," she told Jessie and kicked her foot out of the off-stirrup to dismount. "Unless you have other plans, of course."

"None at all," he said, brightening a little.

Linc had stepped to the ground and reached to take the reins of her horse so he could tie them both to the corral post. "What have you been up to, Jess?"

"Nothin'." He shook his head. "You know that's a real problem, too."

"Why?" Joanna frowned in concern.

"'Cause if a fella's doin' nothin', how can he stop to rest?" His hands were outstretched, palm upward, in a beseeching gesture.

It took a second for his witticism to register, then she laughed. "Jessie, I'm never sure when you're serious or pulling my leg."

He recoiled in mock offense. "I'm serious. It is a problem." But she could see the laughing twinkle in his eye.

"Let me know when you come up with a solution." She walked to the porch where he was standing. Linc's angle intercepted her path as she reached her destination.

"Grab a step and sit yourself down." Jessie waved a hand to the porch steps. He claimed the top one while Joanna and Linc sat down on the second. "Going ridin', eh?"

"Yes, it should be a pleasant evening for it," Linc replied, tipping his hat to the back of his head.

"If'n I was you, I'd make a point of gettin' back afore dark," he nodded sagely.

"Why?" Joanna shifted her position to sit sideways on the step so she could see the slightly eccentric character.

"It's a night for 'haints.'"

"Haints? What is that?" She'd never heard the word.

"Haunts. Ghosts," Linc translated.

Her leg was being pulled again, she realized. "You aren't trying to tell me that you believe in ghosts?" she laughed uncertainly.

"Ain't sayin' I do, an' I ain't sayin' I don't," Jessie hedged. "But thare's folks that claim to have seen some things that would stand your hair on end."

Joanna couldn't help being skeptical. "Such as?"

"Have ya' ever heard tell of Breadtray Mountain?" he challenged.

"No." She shook her head and glanced at Linc. He was lighting a cigarette, his hand cupping the flame. She couldn't see his face. "What about it?"

"It's a mountain over in Stone County. There's been a lot of stories told about that place but one thing is a fact—hill-folks don't go around there after dark."

"Why not?"

"It's haunted, that's why not." He gave her a look that questioned her intelligence for asking such a thing.

"How do you know it's haunted?" Joanna persisted.

"I never said *I* knew it. I'm just tellin' you what I've heard," he explained patiently, neither claiming to believe it or disbelieve it. "The stories say that Spaniards buried a bunch of gold there years ago. Right after that, they was attacked by Indians and all of 'em were killed. If you go to Breadtray Mountain at night, you can

hear the sobs and screams of those dying men."
His voice became low and theatrical as he bent
closer to Joanna, his eyes widening.

Despite her common sense, she felt a little
shiver run down her spine. "Why would they
want to haunt the mountain?"

"Some say them ghosts will stay 'til somebody
finds that gold they buried. Those Spanish soldiers can't rest 'til it's dug up and recovered."

"And nobody's found it?" She already guessed
the answer.

"Nope." He shook his head sadly. "Tho' plenty
a'people has looked."

"There probably isn't any gold or any ghosts,"
Joanna doubted.

"I s'pose you don't believe in ghosts just 'cause
you've never seen one," Jessie challenged. All
the while, Linc sat quietly smoking his cigarette
and watching the two of them with indulgent
interest. "Just 'cause you ain't seen one, don't
mean there ain't none."

"I know it doesn't, but—"

"Ghosts are spirits. Most of the time, they're
invisible. But there is a way you can see 'em," he
declared.

"How?"

"A rider can see a ghost—even if it's invisible
—by looking at it from behind his horse's ears,"
Jessie stated with complete certainty. "Jest
sight down that horse's nose like it was a rifle."

"What!" Joanna exclaimed in disbelief at the
wild claim.

"Why's that so hard to believe?" Jessie protested. "Animals—horses and dogs—can see things we can't. If there's a ghost around, your horse will be pointing his head at it. Why do you think folks say that a horse 'spooks' when he shies from somethin' that his rider can't see. You try it sometime. Just look between his ears when you're sittin' a'straddle him."

"I'll do it," she stated to put an end to all this superstitious nonsense.

"You wouldn't happen to have a pitcher of that cold spring water in the house, Jessie? I'm a little thirsty," Linc said. "How about you, Joanna?"

"If you have some, yes," she nodded, remembering that he didn't have running water in the old cabin.

"It'll just take me a minute to fetch it." He rose with a turn and walked into the house.

Joanna looked at Linc and lowered her voice. "Does he really believe all that nonsense about the ghosts?"

"You should be here when he really gets wound up. Of course, it's best when it's dark and you're sitting around the flickering light of a campfire. He can scare you silly with some of his tales." Linc paused. "Storytelling is almost a lost art. Radio, television, movies, they have taken it over."

"I guess that's true," Joanna agreed.

When Jessie returned, he was carrying two mismatched glasses of water. It was cool and sweet. She drank every drop of hers. Jessie nodded his approval.

"Best water around," he stated with pride.

"Mmm, delicious." She wiped a droplet of water from her chin and handed him back the glass. "Thanks."

"Ready to start out?" Linc asked and pushed to his feet.

"Sure." She stood to walk with him to the horses.

"Keep an eye out for them haints," Jessie advised.

Chapter Eleven

$\mathscr{T}$he boat was a simple runabout, powered by an outboard motor. A pair of flotation cushions offered some relief from the hardness of the board seats. Any change of position in the small boat almost required logistic planning even though there were only two people. With all their fishing paraphernalia—tacklebox, bait, nets, and rods—there wasn't much room for their feet.

In a quiet cove, the boat drifted on the still waters of the lake. The skeletons of trees poked their white limbs above the surface close to shore, long ago drowned by the damming of White River that had formed the lake.

The striated layers of a limestone bluff were drenched by the rays of the setting sun. Hugging the shoreline, a mallard hen kept counting heads and quacking to make sure her brood of ducklings stayed together. High overhead, a hawk soared in a lazy circle, gliding effortlessly on the air currents.

The boat rocked gently as Rachel shifted her position slightly and cast her line into the deep water. Her first few attempts had been uncoordinated and inaccurate, but she had since regained the knack of casting so the line sailed out smoothly and on target.

"Very good," Reece nodded in smiling approval.

His dark eyes noticed the way she beamed proudly at his compliment. They noticed a lot of things about her, from her appearance to the unmasking of her personality. A cloth hat covered her light brown hair, its shapeless brim protecting her pale complexion from the burning rays of the sun.

Over a modest tanktop of yellow knit she was wearing an old blue blouse with long sleeves as a light jacket. At Reece's insistence, there was a life belt around her trim waist. Splotches of white paint on her faded jeans indicated they had long ago been relegated to less than everyday clothes. The worn material softly hugged her hips and legs in a way that was decidedly attractive.

Dressed as she was, there was a gamin charm about her. A complete abandonment of pretence that she was any more than what he saw. Proud, spirited . . . vulnerable, she was naturally woman. Her eyes no longer tried to keep him from seeing inside.

Rachel was all the things he had thought her to be and more, much more. A heady excitement swelled inside him until he wanted to shout his happiness to the world.

"What are you smiling about?" Rachel studied him with a look that was wary yet openly warm.

"You." His smile deepened with incredible inner pleasure.

"I must look a mess," she admitted without embarrassment.

"A beautiful mess," Reece corrected in a vibrant tone of undisguised adoration.

Her attention shifted to her fishing rod as she tested the tautness of the line. "One of the first signs of age is failing eyesight. I think you need yours tested." She was deliberately provocative.

With a small, negative movement of his head, Reece dismissed her reasoning. "I have contracted a malady that attacks all ages," he explained. "It is a widely known fact that love is blind."

Rachel faltered, unable to look at him, afraid to breathe, afraid to hope that it wasn't an empty phrase. Her fingers closed tightly around the handle of the fishing rod. For several seconds, there was only the quiet lapping of the water against the sides of the boat.

"I promised myself I wouldn't rush you." His sigh was heavy with irritation. "That I would wait until—" He stopped in midsentence then abruptly refused to retract his admission. "Love is a beautiful word. It is what I feel, and I don't regret saying it."

When she finally looked at him, she was fighting the happiness that misted his image. "Do you know what I feel like right now, Reece?" Her voice was husky with emotion. "I can't seem to act my age. My legs are like rubber and, I swear, I'd swoon if you touched me."

The grimness was erased from his expression as he leaned forward, absently setting his pole aside. His eyes were dark with longing, possessive in their study of her face. He brought up his hand to caress her cheek. There was a fluttering of her lashes but she didn't swoon.

"It isn't too soon?" He needed to verify that she didn't object to this quantum leap in their relationship.

"It probably is," she replied. "There hasn't been enough time to be sure. It could all be a mistake."

"It isn't. Don't ask me how I know but it isn't," he insisted. "We are not young any more, Rachel, and I'm glad. We have the experience to see and appreciate the worth of what we share, and the wisdom to treasure it."

The smallest smile touched her mouth. "You sound so wise and experienced. You must be a lot older than I am, because there isn't a single sane or sensible thought in my head," she declared with the faintest trace of humor.

His soft laugh was barely audible. The warmth of his breath caressed her skin as he brought his mouth against her lips. They strained toward each other across the distance between their seats, bridging it with their kiss yet unable to close the gap.

The kiss burned with the passion of the young, its fire sealing the promises of their words. There was a certain savoring quality about the embrace, a sense of rapturous wonder that must be tasted slowly to be enjoyed.

When the feast was brought to a reluctant end, Rachel sighed in partial satisfaction. They continued to gaze at one another as if assuring themselves that it all was real, and their contentment was mutual.

A passing speedboat sent its wake into the cove where the runabout bobbed on its rippling waves. Reece let his gaze slide to their surroundings and return to her.

"Here we are in a small boat in the middle of the lake with smelly fish bait at our feet." There was regret in his bemused expression. "It is hardly a romantic setting. I can't even properly hold you in my arms. Shall we go back to the cabin?"

She straightened to sit erectly, mocking him with a reproving look. "Without catching our supper?" she chided. "I don't know about you, but I'd like something more substantial than scrambled eggs."

Reece chuckled. "It is amazing how hungry I suddenly feel."

The reel began to spin on Rachel's rod as a fish

took the baited hook on her line. The sudden sound startled her until she realized what it was.

Then she cried out in triumph, "I've got one!"

Her fingers became all thumbs as she clumsily began to reel it in. Reece laughed heartily at her uncoordinated efforts.

"It's probably a minnow," he teased.

"That's more than you've caught," she responded to his challenging remark. Just at that second, the fish broke the surface of the water. Rachel stared at the size of it and forgot to keep reeling in the line. "Did you see that?"

Reece was already whistling in surprise. "It's a big one. Don't lose it." He reached for her pole. "You'd better let me land it."

"Oh, no." She moved the pole out of his reach. "This one's mine. I'm not going to let you take credit for catching it."

His glance of surprise became one of approval. He liked the spark of competition in her eyes and that assertion of self-reliance. He sat back and let his help take the form of encouragement and advice.

A worn trail wandered away from Jessie's cabin and eventually wound its way to the lake. The way was narrow and they were forced to ride single file with Linc taking the lead astride the dappled buckskin. When they reached the shore, the forest gave way to a natural clearing and Joanna urged her horse to ride up alongside of the buckskin.

"Where do you suppose Reece took Rachel

fishing?" She could see several boats out on the lake but they were all too far away.

"It's hard to tell. It's a big lake," Linc didn't hazard a guess.

Something rustled in the brush near the edge of the trees. Her horse turned its head toward the area, snorting and pricking its ears. Joanna looked, too, but saw nothing.

"Aren't you going to test out Jessie's theory?" Linc asked with an amused, sideways glance.

She reddened slightly, because it had been on her mind to lean forward in the saddle so she could look between her horse's ears and possibly sight a spectre.

"There are no such things as ghosts," she stated emphatically and settled deeper in the saddle seat.

"But you were going to look, weren't you?" he guessed.

She started to vigorously deny it but the laughter in his eyes was completely without malice. A slightly sheepish look crossed her face.

"For a split second, I was," Joanna admitted. "I really don't know why. I don't believe for a minute that I would see anything."

"But, just in case—" Linc added the qualification that had prompted her initial reaction.

"Yes, just in case," she agreed on a note of amused self-derision.

"You're not alone. Everyone who has ever heard that story has tested it out to see if it's true. It's human nature to be curious and skeptical at the same time," he grinned, then changed the subject to point to the top of the hill. "There's a great view from that knob. Do you want to ride up and take a look?"

"Sure."

This time there was no trail to follow and Linc had to blaze a new path. It was long and twisting, dictated by the course of least resistance. Even then, Joanna still found herself dodging and ducking low-hanging tree limbs. Occasionally their progress was punctuated by the strike of metal against stone as the shod horses scrambled over rocky stretches.

As they neared the top of the hill, the ground became barren of trees and undergrowth. The slope became steep and the horses lunged the last few feet to the crest. Joanna reined in her horse beside Linc's and let it blow.

He stepped out of his saddle in a single, coordinated move and held the bridle of her horse while she dismounted to join him on the ground. The muscles in her legs quivered slightly, showing the strain of the ride.

"I have the feeling I'm going to be stiff tomorrow," she said.

"A long soak in the tub tonight should ease most of the soreness." Linc released the reins to both bridles, letting the ends trail loose.

The horses were trained to stand when the reins dragged the ground. They lowered their heads to graze on the tufts of sun-yellowed grass on the knoll.

His hand rested on her shoulder near the base of her neck, its slight pressure guiding her away from the horses. Joanna took her first look at the panoramic view from the high knob. The western horizon was turning yellow as the fiery gold orb of the sun sank lower in the sky. In all directions, there was the roll of high-ridged hills that seemed without end, their slopes thick with trees. The vantage point gave her a view of the many-armed lake, its surface shimmering like glass.

"I promised you a view," Linc said.

Joanna realized they had stopped. "You were right." It was an understatement but there weren't any words to do it justice.

"The Ozark Mountains are one of the oldest mountain ranges in the country, possibly the world. You're looking at what is probably the last hardwood forest we have," he explained.

She became conscious of the weight of his hand on her shoulder and the touch of his fingers against the sensitive skin on her neck. Through her clothes, she could feel the warmth of his body heat as he stood close beside her. It rippled through her like the spreading heat of a warm fire.

"The mountain men trapped their furs here and the Indians hunted the game of the forests, but this area wasn't really settled until the start of the nineteenth century. Most of the early pioneers came from the Southern Appalachians. They brought with them their stories, superstitions, and sure-cure remedies. The very roughness of the land isolated them from the rest of the world and gave birth to their culture."

"Where did they learn all their superstitions?" Joanna wondered. "From the Indian? The Negro?"

"As I said, they came from the Appalachians, which was settled mainly by the English. I guess there are areas where even the accent is decidedly English. So are the songs and stories."

"And the English claim to have an abundance of ghosts haunting their many castles," she remembered. A scattering of clouds were turning orange as the sun began to settle behind them. "Look at the sunset," she murmured.

"Let's settle back and watch it," Linc stated and pressed his hand on her shoulder to push her to the ground.

While she sat cross-legged, Linc stretched out on his side, propping himself up with an elbow. He tore off a long blade of grass and chewed on one end. The cloud-haze turned the sun into a crimson red ball that spread its stain across the sky. Joanna watched the hues change from gold to coral and red.

"People aren't going to believe me about this place," she declared.

"Why?"

"Back in California, they will laugh when I tell them about nearly running into a wagon pulled by a team of mules. They'll think I made it up. You have to admit it does sound farfetched," she pointed out with a wry shake of her head. "Then there's Jessie."

"He does have to be seen to be believed," Linc agreed.

"They'd think I was crazy if I told them how Jessie predicted I would be kissed twice before nightfall just because that cardinal flew across my path. And the ghost stories, and looking between a horse's ears to see one." It stretched the imagination too far.

"And how will you describe me to your friends?" He watched while he twirled the blade of grass between his fingers.

"You?" Joanna repeated, momentarily at a loss for a reply. "Oh, well"—she stalled—"that's easy. I'll just describe this bossy man, always throwing his weight around and telling people how to behave. You are the only blight on an otherwise perfect vacation." She deliberately baited him.

"Is that a fact?" Linc rose to the challenge.

With a laugh, Joanna attempted to elude his reaching hand, but he caught the loose fold of her blouse near the waist. It checked her escape long enough for him to grab an arm with his other hand. Her laughing shriek didn't faze him as he dragged her backward onto the ground.

She struggled briefly, trying to get free, but his superior strength was too much for her. She stopped fighting him and lay passively under his grip, her head resting on the ground while silent laughter dominated her expression. She looked up at him, out of breath.

"I was only kidding," she insisted, unable to sound totally serious. "I'm sorry, really."

"How sorry?" Linc demanded.

Something in the tawny gleam of his eyes

changed the mood from playful to one that was filled with a sexual tension. Her heart hammered wildly against her ribs as she felt the weight of his body pressing down on hers, holding her to the ground.

His hands pinned her wrists and his face was inches above hers. There was a raw ache inside her that seemed to spring from nowhere. Her gaze strayed to his mouth, its firm, well-cut line hovering above her.

"Linc," she murmured in unconscious longing.

He lowered his mouth onto hers in hard possession and all of her resistance went up in flames. Her lips parted as he kissed her deeply. She wasn't conscious of slipping her hands free of his grip, but somehow she had managed it because her fingers were threading through the springing thickness of his hair, rough and sensual against her palms.

She felt light and boneless, putty in his hands, hands that were caressing her with a sureness and ease. It was all very earthy and natural. When his fingers tugged her blouse free from the waistband of her jeans, it seemed right. Her nerve ends thrilled at the touch of his hand against her flesh, so warm and gently evocative, arousing and exploring.

She seemed filled with the golden fire of sundown, all radiant and glowing. It was a wild, new sensation that hinted at something greater. Needles of sexual excitement pierced her, stabbing at her loins with the need to know that fulfillment.

When he pulled his mouth from hers, it was to explore the curve of her throat and descend to the high, warm swell of her breasts. The front of her blouse was opened to expose the creamy gold flesh of her braless torso.

Delicious shudders quivered through her when Linc mouthed the taut peak of her breast. His hands were stroking down her body, inviting the rhythmic movement of her hips against them. Their caress offered a vague satisfaction but not the complete kind that Joanna desired.

Her fingers tightened in the virile thickness of his hair, applying pressure in an attempt to express the urgent needs of her flesh. Tiny sounds were coming from her throat, sounds that Joanna wasn't conscious of making. His body weight shifted as he raised his head as if he intended to withdraw.

"Please." Her voice wavered above a whisper, wanting him in the rawest sense. "Don't stop now, Linc." She was practically begging him to make love to her but she didn't care.

The dark blaze of the setting sun cast a burnished light on his stark, powerful features. They held only one expression, the same one she was feeling.

"Why?" He wanted her to verbalize her reason, to admit to the passion consuming her bones.

But that required an honest examination of

her emotions. All she wanted was to enjoy these sensations. Words seemed totally unnecessary at a time like this. A much more satisfactory communication could be achieved through physical expression.

"What difference does it make?" Her fingers linked together behind his neck to pull him down to her once more. "Just let it be something to tell my friends."

She closed her eyes in anticipation when Linc started to give in to the pressure of her hands. A second later, his fingers were gripping her wrists and pulling her arms from around his neck. In dazed confusion, she opened her eyes and blinked at the harshness of his features.

As he stood up, Linc pulled her to her feet. Joanna staggered against him, her sense of balance slow to return. There was a controlled roughness to his touch when he steadied her.

"What is it?" She didn't understand what was the matter with him. Why was he so angry?

"The sun's almost down. We have to start back or else we'll be riding in the dark." He let go of her and covered the distance to the horses with long, impatient strides.

Joanna followed him, stumbling as she tried to hurry. While part of her mind conceded that there was a legitimacy to the reason he'd given her, she knew instinctively that it wasn't the real one. When she reached him, he had gathered the reins to both horses.

"What did I do wrong, Linc?" Joanna persisted in her determined search for an explanation.

"Do I have to spell it out for you?" His mouth was grim. "You'd like to go back to that patch of grass and finish what we started, wouldn't you?" Her cheeks reddened at his bluntness. It sounded so crude and animalistic put that way. "Well, I don't," he snapped.

"Why?" She was stung into challenging him. "You seemed anxious enough a few minutes ago."

"Maybe I just don't like the idea of being a vacation fling—someone to brag to your friends about back in California." He threw the words in her face.

"As if *you* wouldn't brag about it to *your* friends," Joanna retorted with sarcasm. "Or are you a saint?"

"I'm no saint." There was a flatness to his voice as Linc worked to bring his anger under control—and succeeded. "Indiscriminate sex was all right when I was young and wild. If the girl was willing, so was I." In the slight pause, his gaze raked her. "Now I want her to be ready, too."

"What makes you think I was willing?" Joanna thoughtlessly snapped at his presumptive statement.

His look became dry and mocking. "You were the one who said—don't stop now." He let the simple statement speak for itself as his hand cupped her elbow and pushed her toward the bay horse. "Mount up."

Her cheeks were flame red as Joanna realized how brazen and immoral that sounded. With an angry little flounce, she spun away and stripped the reins from his hand. The muscles in her leg cramped when she attempted to lift her foot into the stirrup.

She had to grit her teeth against the soreness, but she was determined not to ask Linc for assistance. He was already astride the buckskin by the time she was able to pull herself into the bay's saddle.

She fired him an angry look and turned her horse, pointing it down the hill the same way they had come. "We're going this way," Linc stated. She glanced over her shoulder to see that he was heading in another direction. "It's a shortcut back to the road. We should be able to make it that far before we lose all the light." He explained why they were using a different route.

"Why didn't you say so?" she retorted and reined her horse in a semicircle to join up with him.

"You didn't ask," he said calmly and started his horse out at a brisk walk.

They traveled several yards before Joanna gave in to the need to defend her reputation. "For your information, I don't sleep around."

"I don't remember saying that you did," Linc replied with a brief glance.

"You seemed to have the impression that—"

He reined his horse to an abrupt halt and reached across to grab the reins of her mount, stopping it and leaning toward her. His level gaze seemed to bore into her.

"I don't see the point in conducting a post mortem. Nothing happened and nothing is likely to happen, so why don't we leave it at that."

She wanted to argue with him but he had removed any grounds for continuing the subject. His logic was irrefutable. She lowered her chin in a silent acknowledgment of the fact, signaling her agreement to his suggestion.

"Why do you have to make an issue out of everything, Joanna?" he sighed and released her horse's reins.

"I don't," she denied that as her horse started forward the instant the buckskin strided out.

"Yes, you do." There was a half-smile on his mouth and amusement in his glance. "In another two seconds, you're going to prove it by opening your mouth to argue that you don't argue over everything."

His statement forced her to keep silent, because it was precisely what she had been going to do. Only now she couldn't. His low chuckle indicated that he knew it.

"You think you're so smart, Linc Wilder," Joanna muttered in irritation. "But you're really not."

"I'm smart enough to know if we don't hurry it will be dark before we reach the road." He prodded his horse into a canter.

The bald knob of the mountain was still bathed in the golden light of the setting sun but the woods were casting longer and longer shadows. Joanna realized how quickly the twilight was encroaching when they rode into the trees. Allowing Linc to take the lead, she pulled her horse back and pointed its nose at the dappled hindquarters of the buckskin.

The deeper they went into the woods, the darker it became. What light there was in the forest seemed to be a pinkish gray. There was rustling of undergrowth and the rattling of tree limbs. An owl hooted, its eerie cry not sounding far away. Joanna admitted to being a little nervous.

They seemed to have traveled a long way. She was about to ask Linc how far it was to the road when she noticed the trees thinning out ahead of them. She breathed an unconscious sigh of relief when she saw the pale stretch of graveled road.

She checked her horse while Linc put the buckskin down the slight embankment to the road then let the bay gelding choose its own path. Once out of the trees, it didn't seem as dark as it had.

"Where are we?" she asked.

"Don't you recognize it?" He waved a hand down the road. "That's where you drove your car into the ditch to avoid Jessie."

"It doesn't look the same in this light," she said.

"The lane to his cabin is by that break in the trees." He pointed to it in his effort to orient her.

"I see it," she nodded.

Linc tipped his head back to look at the sky.

"It's a shame we don't have a moon tonight, but this half light should hold until we reach the cabin." He brought his chin down to look at her. "Now that we're on the road, it doesn't matter whether we have light. There will be enough for us to see. There isn't any reason to hurry unless you're anxious to get back."

"No. Not now that we're out of the woods," she replied.

By silent agreement, they kept their horses at a walk. The buckskin had a longer stride than Joanna's more closely coupled bay mount so it naturally stayed a little ahead of her all the time. She was less bothered by the nightsounds that came from the woods flanking the road.

The first stars were beginning to twinkle in the blue-gray sky. But the road continued to be a pale ribbon unwinding ahead of them. She became conscious of a cool draft against her skin and realized she hadn't tucked her blouse inside her jeans.

Letting the horse have its head, she wrapped the reins around the protruding horn of the saddle so her hands would be free. As she pushed her blouse inside the waistband, she became aware of the lengthening distance between her horse and the buckskin.

She was about to grab the reins when the bay jerked its head up and seemed to shudder beneath her. It snorted loudly and rolled a white eye toward the side of the woods just ahead of them. Her first glance only noticed the culvert but as her horse swung its head directly at it, she stared between the horse's ears. An eerie white cloud drifted gossamer-thin alongside the road by the culvert.

Terror gripped her throat. She blinked, certain her vivid imagination was playing tricks on her. But the funny bluish-white light remained and even wavered. She screamed and her horse bolted in panic, lunging straight at the buckskin.

"Linc!" Joanna called his name in panic.

Somehow he swung his horse to the side, avoiding a collision and reaching out for her at the same time. She grabbed for his neck and managed to kick her feet out of the stirrups as the bay horse ran out from under her. The buckskin danced nervously while she sobbed in frightened breaths and hung on tightly until his strong arms were able to sit her across the front of the saddle.

"It's a ghost! We've got to get out of here!" She buried her face in his shirt, digging her fingers into his shoulders.

"Joanna, what in heaven's name are you talking about?" His voice sounded caught between being amused and confused.

"Over there by the culvert," she whispered into the cloth of his shirt. "When my horse spooked, I looked between its ears and I saw it! Oh, let's get out of here!"

There was a moment of stillness, followed by the rumble of laughter deep in his chest. "Look. Is that what you saw, Joanna?" He tried very hard to keep the laughter inside.

His complete lack of concern forced her to peer toward the culvert. The light wavered and grew brighter. Her heart tumbled to her throat.

"Oh, my God, it's still there," she whispered, because she had expected it to be gone.

"That's foxfire."

Chapter Twelve

$\mathcal{H}$is hand gripped the upper part of her arm and held her away from him, forcing Joanna to stop hiding her eyes. Shaken out of her wits by the experience, she was slow to register his words. Her eyes stayed closed and her teeth tightly clenched, her fingers curling into the hard flesh of his shoulders.

"Hey, did you hear me?" His chiding voice was low, rich with amusement. "It's only foxfire." Linc made it sound very harmless.

Braving the worst, she dragged her lashes open and rigidly focused her gaze on his face, still too frightened to look around. His hard features were gentled by contained humor and his eyes were warm with indulgent forbearance.

"Foxfire?" Her voice was a thin, wavering whisper.

"Marsh lights. It's a natural phenomenon—as opposed to the supernatural," he explained with a faint twinkle in his look.

By degrees, she inched her head around to slide an apprehensive peek at the mysterious glow. It seemed fainter, less ominous and frightening. It floated about waist high above the ditch, drifting toward the woods.

As she watched, the wispy phosphorescence grew smaller and gradually dissolved. A shudder went through her at its passing. She lowered her head and breathed in a shaky breath.

"I've never been so scared in all my life." The low admission germinated a seed of anger. It sprouted quickly and spread through her raw nerves. "Damn that Jessie Bates and his ghost-talk. Thanks to him, I've made a complete fool of myself again."

"You should be used to that," Linc suggested dryly.

His ready concurrence ran through her like a hot knife. Indignation swelled from the wound. "You really know how to make a person feel rotten, don't you?" Joanna charged.

He tipped back his head to let the laughter roll from his throat. It faded into a chuckle as he shifted her in his hold so that she was sitting crosswise in front of him. His head was tilted down, toward hers, a wide smile curving the line of his mouth. Her anger degenerated into a mild form of irritation and hurt pride.

171

"I don't think it's funny," she protested on a low, injured note.

"My momma always said a kiss makes the hurt go away," he murmured and bent his head, bringing his mouth against her lips. The pressure of his mouth was warm and mobile but all too brief. "Feel better?" Linc studied her with a laziness that said he knew well that she wanted more.

For that very reason, she wouldn't give him the satisfaction of admitting it. "Some." But her voice was shaky and she wondered if he could hear or feel the thudding of her pulse.

Her nerves were beginning to react to the hard contact with his muscled build. His left arm supported her back, the hand holding the reins pressed hard against the side of her hip. The palm and fingers of his right hand were curved to the outer portion of her thigh.

She could feel the strong rhythm of his heartbeat against her breast as she was molded sideways to his flatly muscled frame. It was a heady position with her hand resting on his shoulderbone to link fingers with the hand draped around his neck. There was a fleeting wish that she could stay this way for a little while longer.

Then she remembered, "My horse? It bolted." Instinctively her gaze swung to the road in search of her mount.

At a signal from its rider, the buckskin moved out at a walk, mincing a little at its double burden. "He's probably half-way to the barn by now," Linc answered. "We'll have to ride double. It isn't far to the cabin though."

The motion of the horse jabbed the saddlehorn into the tender flesh of her rump. Joanna winced and shifted her center of balance to avoid the prod of the horn. His strong hands assisted in the weight shift which brought her more fully against his body.

"Comfortable?" His downward glance was three-quarters lidded.

"Yes," Joanna assured him the problem had been solved.

In fact, she was quite comfortable. She silently reveled in this contact with his powerful build. She had never encountered any man who possessed this combination of keen intelligence and brute strength. She studied the rawly masculine features of his face. In her position, it would have required an effort not to look at him since she was squarely facing his profile.

When Linc noticed the way she contemplated him, Joanna felt the need to break the silence. "What causes foxfire?"

The situation was reversed and now she was the object of his steady regard. "It's a case of spontaneous combustion. Two elements can exist in the same environment with nothing happening until a spark sets them off—a catalyst of sorts." The run of his gaze over her face seemed to give another dimension to his explanation, something to do with their personal chemistries. "It's an elusive thing that is either there or it isn't," he finished.

It all became clear to her. The friction that was always between them, the physical attraction that kept pulling her to him, and the fire that was kindled within her when they came in contact, they all made sense.

As incredible as it seemed, she was falling in love with him, a man who could irritate her beyond belief yet could arouse a response that was more than mere passion. The dawning light of discovery shone in her eyes.

The air seemed to sizzle as his gaze locked with hers. His chest lifted with a breath that wasn't released. Then he was kissing her, roughly, possessively, crushing her hard to his body. An incredulous joy swept through her, heating her blood at this blatant demonstration of his desires after he had previously denied hers. It was strictly a reflex action that tightened the pressure on the bit to stop the horse.

The buckskin wasn't pleased with its double burden and impatient with its master who couldn't seem to make up his mind whether to stop or go. The animal tossed its head in agitation and pulled at the bit, snorting and shifting sideways in protest to the pressure.

As the horse began to act up, Linc was forced to break off the kiss and bring his fractious mount under control. His arm tightened protectively around Joanna until the horse settled down. He relaxed the pressure on the reins and the buckskin moved forward at a brisk walk.

"Do you suppose he was jealous?" Linc mocked.

"Maybe." Joanna contentedly nestled her head on his shoulder, enjoying the closeness.

"The next time I take you out we'll ride in a car," he stated.

A dreamy smile curved her mouth. "That sounds nice," she sighed.

They were nearly to the cabin when a flashlight beam swept the road in front of them. A second later, it was squarely in their eyes. Joanna turned her face into his shoulder to escape the blinding glare of light.

"Linc. Joanna. Are you all right?" Reece's voice came from the darkness behind the light. "Rachel and I heard a scream. A few minutes later a horse galloped by the cabin and through the pasture gate to your place. Was Joanna thrown? Is she hurt?"

"She's fine. She wasn't thrown," Linc assured him on that score. "She just had a little scare, that's all."

The focus of the beam was lowered to the road. "What a relief. We were coming out to find you and see if you needed any help," Reece explained as he approached the horse, accompanied by Rachel Parmelee. "What happened?"

"It's a long story. Joanna thought she saw a ghost," Linc explained with an underlying thread of amusement in his voice. "She screamed. Her horse spooked and nearly collided with mine. She sorta dived at me and I sorta grabbed." He swung out of the saddle and stepped to the ground, reaching up to lift Joanna down.

"You thought you saw a ghost?" There was the amusement of disbelief in her uncle's voice.

"Jessie Bates is to blame for that." Her hands were reluctant to leave Linc's shoulders. She had to force them down to her sides where she self-consciously smoothed them over her jeans.

"Jessie Bates?" Reece frowned in absolute confusion and looked from one to the other for an explanation.

"We stopped by his place while we were out riding." Linc collected the reins to lead his horse and walk along with the others. "Jessie told her a couple ghost stories and her imagination took over after that."

"It wasn't strictly my imagination," Joanna protested. "I did see something."

"What did you see?" Rachel's question prompted Joanna to notice that she and her uncle were holding hands.

It struck her as being a youthful display of affection, yet it also made her cognizant that she didn't possess the same easy confidence to display her affection for Linc so openly.

"There was some foxfire along the ditch, although I didn't know it was foxfire," she admitted her ignorance. "It was just an eerie light." She left out the part about looking between her horse's ears. It still made her feel silly when she thought about it. "After all the nonsense Jessie told us about ghosts, I thought that I was seeing one. That's when I screamed and the horse bolted and—" She let the explanation trail off and shrugged away her foolishness. She changed the subject. "How was the fishing?"

"We caught four nice bass for dinner," Reece answered.

"That 'we' happened to be 'me,'" Rachel corrected him in mock reproval.

"Didn't you catch any, Reece?" Joanna asked.

"I seemed to have trouble keeping my mind on fishing," he admitted and the look he gave Rachel identified the source of his distraction. "But we still made it a team effort. She caught them and I cooked them."

"And ate them all, I suppose?" Joanna teased.

"Yes," he admitted. "But we do have a fresh pot of coffee made. After your experience, you could probably do with a cup."

They had reached the driveway to the cabin and Linc stopped, the others automatically coming to a halt, too. "This is where I leave you," he announced casually.

"Aren't you coming in for coffee?" Joanna protested.

His head moved to the side in a single, negative shake. "There's a horse at the barn, waiting to be unsaddled."

She didn't want to say goodbye to him with Rachel and her uncle looking on, so she gently prompted them into leaving. "You go ahead. I'll be along directly."

After an exchange of good nights with Linc, her uncle and Rachel walked toward the lights of the cabin. Joanna watched them until they were out of hearing, then turned to Linc. He held her glance for an instant, then swung idly away to move to the left side of the buckskin and gather the reins in front of the pommel, preparing to mount. A sense of awkwardness had kept her silent but his action forced her to take the initiative.

"Will you be coming by tomorrow?" She tried to sound very light and casual.

"No, I'll be busy." Linc paused long enough to slide a glance over her, then stepped a foot into the stirrup and swung aboard. "You may be on vacation, but I've got a ranch to run," he reminded her.

"But—" She took a step toward him, her hand reaching out to touch his knee. The twilight was darkening, making it difficult to see his face.

"There are times when things happen so fast that you aren't sure what did happen—or why," Linc stated. "Think about it, Joanna, and be damned sure you know what you want."

"What if I said I was?" she protested.

"Then a couple of days won't change it," he reasoned. "You have a tendency to say things on the spur of the moment and regret them later. I don't want that to be the case this time." With a turn of his wrist, Linc reined his horse around Joanna. "Good night."

"Good night." She was a second slow in answering him, his comment about her impulsiveness hitting a little too close to home.

She watched until he had disappeared into the darkness, then turned to walk toward the cabin. She felt frustrated and denied, if only temporarily.

Chapter Thirteen

_W_ith the telephone receiver held tightly against her ear, Joanna chewed nervously at her lower lip and listened to the echo of the third ring on the other end of the line. Maybe it wasn't done in the Ozarks for a woman to call a man, but three days had gone by without a word from Linc. She simply couldn't wait any longer.

In the middle of the fourth ring, a woman's voice came on the line. "Hello?"

Startled by the female voice, Joanna hesitated, wondering if she had dialed the wrong number. "Is this . . . the Wilder ranch?"

"Yes, it is."

"May I speak to Linc Wilder, please?" she requested. Tension made her voice brisk to conceal her inner turmoil.

"I'm sorry, he isn't here right now," the woman's voice answered.

"Do you know where he is or when he'll be back?" Frustration scraped at her nerves as she tried not to let her disappointment show through her voice.

"He's got a sick calf. I think he went into the vet's to get some medicine for it. He didn't mention when he'd be back but I would imagine it will be sometime this morning yet," the woman answered a little vaguely.

"I see," Joanna murmured and absently glanced around the study, trying to decide what she should do.

"Did you want to leave your phone number? I can have him call you later," the woman suggested.

"Just . . . Just tell him Joanna called," she said finally.

"Joanna." The woman repeated her name. "I'll tell him."

"Thank you." She continued to hold the receiver after the line went dead, then hesitantly returned it to its cradle.

When footsteps approached the study, she heard them, but gave them little notice. It was her uncle's voice that finally penetrated her silent contemplation.

"There you are. Good morning." His greeting was bright and cheerful as he entered the room with a jaunty stride, a wide smile curving his mouth.

"Good morning." She breathed in deeply and

tried to shake free from the grayness of her spirit in the face of Reece's sunshine. Stirring from the chair behind the desk, she managed a smile. "I thought you would sleep in this morning."

"It's a beautiful day—much too beautiful to stay in bed," he insisted.

"Alone, you mean," Joanna teased, then shook her head. "How do you manage to look so rested when you haven't gotten home until after midnight three nights running?"

"Love is a wondrous tonic," he laughed.

The remark had been meant as a joke, but looking at him, Joanna was inclined to believe it was true. At least, it appeared to be true once the doubts were erased and that love was returned.

"At a glance, I'd say you discovered the fountain of youth," she smiled.

Reece laughed and his glance strayed to the telephone on the desk. "Were you on the phone just now?"

Her reaction was almost guilty. "Yes . . . I was," she admitted.

"You look upset. Was it your mother?" His expression became serious, etched with a fine trace of concern.

"No." She hesitated an instant. "Linc hasn't been around for a couple of days so I thought I'd call and invite him to dinner this evening. You don't mind, do you?"

"Of course not." His astute gaze read more into the response. "Is he coming?"

"He wasn't there. A woman answered and

said he'd gone to the veterinarian. A calf is sick, I guess," she admitted her failure to reach Linc.

Reece also read the silent question that was in her mind. "It probably was the lady who keeps house for him. He has someone come in twice a week to do the cleaning and laundry since his sister married." He casually passed on the information and watched her uncertainty fade.

"I left word that I called. He'll probably call later on," she said.

"I hope you didn't have anything planned for this morning," Reece stated. "I wanted you to go into town with me."

"There wasn't anything special I was going to do," she assured him. "I can come with you," although she hoped Linc didn't call while she was gone.

"Good." There was something very decisive about his voice and his smile. "Because I want you to help me choose a ring for Rachel."

"A ring," she repeated and eyed him uncertainly. "Do you mean a diamond ring—an engagement ring?"

"Yes."

Joanna smothered a laugh of surprise and delight. "Does Rachel know? Have you asked her?"

"Not yet," he admitted but without any sign of doubt about her answer. "First I want to buy the ring. You will come with me?"

"Wild horses couldn't stop me!" This was an event!

* * *

As they looked over the rings in the jeweler's case, they had a difference of opinion about the size and style of ring that would please Rachel. A week ago Joanna would have gone along with Reece's choice but Linc had influenced her thinking to a great extent.

"That one is beautiful," Reece conceded as Joanna held the diamond solitaire to the light, "but it is too plain, too simple. Look at the setting of this one." He drew her attention back to his choice. The center stone of the ring was approximately the same size as the single gem in the ring Joanna liked, but it was surrounded by a cluster of smaller diamonds. "It has such fire."

Aware of the jeweler patiently looking on, Joanna sighed. "Why don't you wait until the two of you can pick out the ring together?"

"No." Reece shook his head in a very definite rejection of that thought. "She would pick something simple and less expensive."

Joanna stared at him, a tiny smile creeping around the corners of her mouth. "Do you realize what you just said?" she murmured. Amusement danced in her eyes when he met her look.

"But I want to buy her something—" He stopped to consider the problem.

Joanna put the problem into words. "You have to decide whether you are going to buy a ring that *you* want or one that *she* wants."

He hesitated, sighed, and cast a resigned glance at the jeweler. "I will take the solitaire."

"She'll love it." Joanna smiled her approval as the jeweler moved away from the glass case to write up the sales ticket. "And she is the one who has to wear it."

When the transaction was completed and they were walking out of the jewelry store, Joanna asked, "When are you going to propose to her? Tonight?"

"Yes." It was a somewhat clipped answer.

She studied him with a sidelong glance, surprised to see the lines of tension around his mouth and eyes. It was the first time she had ever seen Reece appear nervous. It was touching in a man usually so confident of himself.

"Where to, now?" She changed the subject in an effort to relax him. "What about some lunch? It's a little early but we'll miss the noon crowd."

He came to an abrupt stop on the sidewalk, his hesitancy vanishing as he came to a decision. "No. I can't wait until tonight. I'm going to ask her now."

"But . . . isn't she working?" Joanna was thrown by his sudden change of plans.

"Yes." With a quick, purposeful stride, he started for the car parked at the curb. "We'll drive to her shop."

"Wouldn't it be better to wait until she takes her lunch break?" Joanna suggested and had to hurry to keep up with him. He was already sliding behind the wheel before she had the passenger door open. "She'll probably be busy with customers and all," Joanna reasoned.

"The store is always competing with me for her time. I am not going to allow it to dictate when it would be convenient for a proposal of marriage."

The engine was started and Reece was shifting in reverse when she closed her car door. The determined set of his jaw left her in no doubt that his mind had been made up.

"Aren't you rushing things just a little, Reece?" she wondered.

"When I leave the Ozarks at the end of the month, Rachel is going to come with me as my wife," he stated. "That doesn't allow much time to find a competent manager to take over the store. I have no intention of leaving without her and I know Rachel won't go unless she is assured it is running smoothly. And she won't begin to look for someone until I have proposed."

"Wouldn't it be simpler if she sold it?" It seemed the logical solution to Joanna. In the long run, there would be fewer headaches.

"It would be simpler, yes," Reece agreed. "But it represents security and independence to Rachel. I don't expect her to give it up for me."

When he explained it, Joanna could see that he was right. Eventually Rachel would feel lost if she didn't remain involved with the store's operation, even if it had to be at a distance. It had occupied too much of her life for it to be suddenly cut out of it without leaving a void that not even Reece's love could fill.

Slowing the car, he turned into the parking lot by the shop. He parked it in an empty space and switched off the engine. "Are you coming in?" He paused with the door open to glance at Joanna.

She smiled faintly. "No, I think you'll have plenty of witnesses without me along." It broke the tension in his expression and he returned the smile. "Good luck," she called to him as he climbed out of the car.

There were more than a dozen customers in the store when Reece entered. Nervously he turned the ring box around in his hand and glanced around the store. He saw her standing behind the counter near the cash register and experienced that rush of sweet pleasure lift him. For the run of several seconds, he was content just to look at her.

As if feeling his eyes on her, Rachel looked up and noticed him on the opposite side of the room. He watched her expression change, the special warmth that entered her gaze and the smile that was reserved just for him. He crossed to the counter.

"Hello. How are you today?" Her look and tone of voice made the trite phrase sound much more meaningful and intimate.

"Fine." He was conscious of the people around them and wished, not for the first time, that he could order them out and have this woman all to himself.

"Was there something you wanted?" Again the inquiry appeared very innocent, a clerk to a customer.

Reece smiled widely. "Yes, there is but for the time being, I'll be satisfied with five minutes of your time."

She laughed a little self-consciously, and he enjoyed the warm sound of it. There was a freshness to her that had nothing to do with age. Her gaze made an appraising sweep of the shop and its customers. A dark-haired woman was studying a group of Kewpie dolls in a display case.

"Excuse me just a minute," Rachel apologized to Reece and moved down the counter. "Was there something you'd like to see?"

"Yes, please. The second doll from the left." The woman pointed to the one she meant. "I have three nieces who collect dolls," the woman explained as Rachel opened the case and brought out the doll to show her. "I want to bring them back something to add to their collection."

"This one is very popular," Rachel assured the brunette, but her gaze strayed to Reece standing by the cash register, showing where her attention was truly focused at the moment.

"I'll definitely take that one," the woman decided. "Why don't you just give me three?" She held up three fingers.

"Certainly. Is there anything else?"

"I'd like to look around a little more," the woman smiled.

"Go right ahead," Rachel encouraged her to browse. "The dolls will be at the cash register."

While she was taking the three dolls from the stock below the counter, Reece inobtrusively opened the ring box and set it on the glass shelf near the cash register. She didn't glance in that direction when she walked back to box the three dolls. "I can't promise you five minutes all at one time. Will you settle for a minute here and there?" she asked with a smile.

"I bought something for you." Reece went straight to the point, gesturing toward the ring with a nod of his head. Her eyes widened when she saw it. They became misty as they swung to him, her lips parted in wordless surprise. "Don't ring up a 'No Sale.'"

Her laugh was slightly choked by emotion. "Is this a proposal?" Her hand pushed at the side of her hair, but she made no move to reach for the ring.

"It very definitely is." He could stand it no longer and removed the ring from the velvet case. Her hand was shaking as she extended it toward him. "Does that mean you are accepting?"

"Yes," she said in a breathless voice. He slipped it on her finger, then held her hand tightly, his gaze burrowing into her. "Oh, Reece, you do pick the darnedest places. First the boat, with me looking a sight, and now here."

The ache in her voice told him that she wanted

to be in his arms, that she wanted to be kissed by him. She wasn't alone in her frustration.

"I was going to wait until tonight and do it properly with candlelight and wine and beautiful music in the background," Reece admitted. "I had a very romantic setting all planned. But I wanted you to say 'yes' because I asked you and not because you were caught up in the mood of the moment."

Her response to that was a vague shake of her head, then she was leaning across the counter, her hand curving behind the back of his neck. She kissed him without reserve, erasing any doubt about the reason behind her acceptance.

There was absolute silence in the shop when their kiss ended. All attention was obliquely focused on them. Reece turned, beaming proudly as he surveyed the customers. "It is all perfectly respectable," he informed them. "The lady has just consented to marry me."

A murmur ran through the store, rippling like a happy wave. There were smiles of understanding and silent wishes of happiness in their eyes.

Chapter Fourteen

Outside the doll shop, the suspense was building. Waiting in the car with the windows rolled down, Joanna watched the store entrance. Time passed slowly, its weight heavy on her hands. Her thoughts wandered in and around the subject of love and marriage. She tried to imagine her mother's reaction to someone like Linc without success, but it was easy to visualize her skepticism at the thought of Reece finally settling down. She wouldn't take the news well.

With the constant flow of summer traffic on the busy street, the crunching sound of tires on the graveled parking lot attracted minimal attention from Joanna. There was vague recognition that a vehicle had driven up to park next to the car. Her glance strayed to the side when a door was opened. An electric shock tingled through her system at the sight of Linc's rangy build filling her vision.

"Hello." Resting a hand on top of the car, he bent to look in the opened window and treated her to one of his crooked smiles.

Her heart seemed to tumble over her ribs with reckless abandon. "Hello." There was a slightly breathless quality to her voice.

"I was driving by and recognized the car. I thought I noticed someone sitting in it." He looked briefly toward the shop. "I take it Reece is inside."

"Yes." It seemed much longer than three days since she had seen him. An inexplicable kind of hunger filled her and she feasted her eyes on his virile features carved in bronze.

His glance returned to her, his golden-brown eyes inspecting her in a way that threw her senses into chaos. "Have you managed to stay out of trouble lately? No more run-ins with any mules or ghosts?" He was mocking her, yet with a warmth and subtle humor that made it something special.

"Things like that only seem to happen to me when you're around," Joanna replied. "My life is relatively sane otherwise."

"Implying that I make you a little crazy?" Linc rephrased the statement.

It did seem to explain the wild, wonderful feeling raging inside her—crazy in love. "Yes."

She agreed with him without elaborating on the source of this glorious madness.

"Is that good or bad?" His searching gaze probed her expression in an attempt to uncover the ulterior meaning he seemed to sense existed.

"I think it could be good," Joanna admitted but it depended so much on how he felt.

A lazy gleam of satisfaction appeared in his gaze before his attention was distracted. "Here comes Reece with Rachel," he announced as he straightened to stand erect.

One look at the beaming couple told Joanna what Rachel's answer had been. Each had an arm around the other's waist as they approached the parked car. As Joanna opened the door and stepped out, Linc moved to one side to give her room.

"She said 'yes,' didn't she?" Joanna directed the unnecessary question to her uncle, already positive of the answer.

"She did," Reece stated proudly, then informed Linc of their engagement. "Rachel has agreed to marry me."

"Welcome to the family." Joanna hugged her aunt-to-be, while Linc shook hands with Reece.

"Congratulations."

For the next couple of minutes, it was a jumble of voices as they talked over each other until none of it made sense. They all seemed to realize it simultaneously and stopped talking. The abrupt silence brought a round of shared laughter.

"This calls for a party to celebrate the occasion," Linc stated when it stopped.

"Linc is right," Joanna agreed. "Dinner, champagne, everything."

"Actually, I had in mind an old-fashioned barbeque at my place," he corrected her with an amused glance. "I'll invite a bunch of friends and neighbors over Sunday afternoon."

"There's no need to go to such trouble," Reece protested.

"If I thought it would be too much trouble, I wouldn't have suggested it," Linc replied. "I'll arrange it for Sunday . . . unless the two of you plan to keep the engagement a secret for a while."

"It would be extremely difficult." A smile dimpled Rachel's mouth. "Everyone in the store knows about it. By this afternoon, it will be all over town."

"I wouldn't have cared if the whole world had been there," Reece insisted.

Linc slid a glance at his watch. "I need to be leaving," he said indicating there was somewhere else he had to be. His glance rested on Joanna. "Would you give me a hand planning the menu for Sunday?"

"Sure," she agreed without hesitation.

"I'll stop by this evening sometime," he told her and turned his attention to the engaged couple. "Congratulations again."

"Come for dinner," Joanna invited, betraying some of her eagerness for his company.

Linc shook his head as he opened the door to

the pickup cab. "I can't make it tonight but I'll see you later in the evening."

His departure signaled the close of the gathering. Rachel reluctantly heeded the silent summons of the shop, calling her back to work. All three of them were looking forward to the coming night, but not all for the same reasons.

When Linc arrived that night, Reece had already left the cabin to meet Rachel. Their initial conversation centered on the engagement of her uncle who was his best friend and their shared approval of it. It naturally led into his plans for the Sunday barbeque and a discussion of the menu. As he made notes, Joanna was beginning to think it was the sole reason he was there, that it hadn't been an excuse to see her as she had first hoped.

She hardly paid attention when Linc read the list back to her. "If that isn't enough variety to satisfy everyone's likes and dislikes, they can just go hungry," he concluded on a mock threat. "Wouldn't you say so?"

"What?" The blankness left her expression as she remembered what he'd said. "Yes, that's right."

His gaze traveled over her, then he set his notes aside and combed his fingers through his hair. Flexing his shoulder muscles, he rolled leisurely to his feet and took a step away from the couch. Curled in an armchair, Joanna looked up in bewildered protest.

"Are you leaving?" she questioned.

"Why? Do you want me to go?" With an eyebrow raised he halted near her chair. The subdued glitter in his look said he already knew the answer.

She was irritated into pretending an indifference that she didn't feel. "No, but naturally, if you have somewhere else to go, I don't expect you to stay just to keep me company." She shrugged and challenged him. "Do you?"

"No." A smile showed briefly.

She never knew how to act with him. He kept changing the pace and course of their relationship until she didn't know what to expect next. Since she wasn't able to second-guess him, she stopped trying.

"There's iced tea in the kitchen. Would you like some?" She'd get a crick in her neck if she had to keep looking up at him so Joanna uncrossed her legs and rose from the chair.

"I'm glad you did that," Linc said.

His remark made no sense at all. "Did what?" she frowned, because to her knowledge, she had done nothing except offer him a cold drink.

"Stood up." The span of a foot separated them.

"Why?" Joanna still didn't understand. If anything, she was more confused.

"There is an old Ozark superstition," his hands found her waist and shortened some of that distance, "—that says a man shouldn't kiss a girl while he's standing and she's sitting in a chair."

The nearness of him was starting those funny

little pitter-patters of her heart. With an absent fascination, she studied the way her hands rested on the wall of his chest.

"Why not?" The upward sweep of her glance met his steady look and all sorts of crazy sensations started leaping inside.

"According to superstition, that would cause an immediate quarrel," Linc explained.

"Who told you that?" She laughed out the words.

"I have it on the best authority," he assured her.

"Let me guess. Jessie Bates." She tipped her head to one side, provocative and challenging.

"Right, and arguing is not one of the things I want to do with you tonight," Linc stated and increased the pressure to bring her fully against him.

It was all the invitation Joanna needed as she stretched to meet him halfway. His mouth seared its claim on hers in a long, drugging kiss. Arching against him, she was aware of his hard, muscular thighs and the sinewed steel of his encircling arms molding her to him. Her hands curled themselves around his neck, her anchor in this raging storm of emotions.

When they finally came up for air, Joanna was too dazzled by the heat lightning flashing through her to move an inch away from him. The brush of his lips closed her eyes, flirting with her lashes before it ran over the rest of her face. The emotion running through her was so fierce that she trembled from it.

She wanted him so much that when she spoke, it was almost a groan. "Linc, you can't believe any more that I'm not ready." It was a protest at his lack of initiative to let the embrace go beyond mere kisses.

"By God, you'd better mean that," he muttered against her throat. "I'm not interested in casual sex, Joanna. If that's all you want, you're picking the wrong man."

"I think I have the right one," she said and felt a brief stirring of surprise that she could be so positive. "I barely know you at all, yet I seem to know all that's important."

His hand covered her breast in a physical demonstration of the rights she was giving him. "Patience is not one of my strong suits," Linc warned. "If you think I'm going to be like Reece and court you for nearly six years, you're wrong. It isn't going to be like that."

"I don't want it like that," Joanna admitted huskily. "I couldn't stand it."

She felt she would go crazy now if he didn't do more than hold her. Her breast seemed to swell to fill the palm of his hand, straining to achieve a greater intimacy. All of her ached with the same need.

"I'm not going to carry on any love affair long distance—with you in California and me here." He continued to spell out his conditions, insisting that Joanna be aware of what he expected.

"What is the alternative to long distance?" She was arching against him in deliberate provocation. Her teeth teased at his earlobe, nipping at it in sexual play. "Is it this? You're from Missouri, Linc. Show me."

"It won't be a temporary coupling." Linc drew his head back to look at her while he emphasized his message. "The linkage will be a lasting one."

Her lips lay against each other in an inviting line, sensual and full. "Ever since I arrived in the Ozarks, everyone has been telling me how instinctively intelligent you hillpeople are. But I'm beginning to think I'll have to send you an engraved invitation to make love to me." She didn't try to hide any of her feelings from him, letting him see all the fires that burned inside. "I thought you were a man of action. But, maybe you act as slow as you talk."

"Are you trying to get a rise out of me?" Linc drawled and eyed her with a complacent look.

"Now, you're getting the idea, " she murmured.

His mouth began its movement toward her. "I'll give you all you can handle—and more," he taunted.

The piercing crush of his arms was sweet agony, that unique mixture of pleasure and pain. There was no holding back in this embrace. Joanna wanted to give as she got, and Linc was inflaming her with his needs.

The shrill ring of the telephone was a piercing interruption. Joanna shuddered a protest when Linc lifted his head, dragging his mouth across her temple. Leaning against him, she tried to close her hearing to the sound, but it kept repeating itself.

His arm stayed around her waist, supporting her and drawing her along with him as he turned to pick up the receiver. With her head tipped to rest against his shoulder, Joanna watched him carry the phone to his ear and answer it.

"No, it isn't. Reece isn't here at the moment," Linc said in an obvious response to a question by the caller.

During the subsequent pause, Joanna was conscious of the firm possession of the arm curved around her. She liked the feel of it, the implication of belonging to him.

"Yes, Joanna is here." Linc passed the receiver to her.

She took it with every intention of quickly getting rid of the caller. "Hello." Her tone was aloof, designed to discourage conversation.

"Joanna, what is going on there? Who was that man who answered the phone?" her mother's voice demanded.

She went rigid with surprise, stiffening self-consciously in Linc's possessive hold. "Mother! I wasn't expecting you to call." It had been the farthest thing from her mind when the phone had rung.

"I had that impression when the man answered the phone." There was a quality of disdain in her voice. "You haven't told me who he is yet?"

"That was Linc. Linc Wilder." Joanna quickly added his full name and shifted out of the loose hold of his arm. Even though her mother couldn't see the casually intimate embrace, she had been influenced by other times when her mother had come along on similar scenes.

"I'm sure Reece probably has mentioned him to you," Joanna continued and felt a sudden chill in the air. Her side glance caught the coolness of Linc's expression as he quietly studied her.

Turning aside, he wandered to the fireplace and lit a cigarette. Her glance followed him, then fell when he looked back. He was making her feel small for not claiming any personal relationship with him. It wasn't a comfortable sensation.

"I swear I will never understand why Reece vacations in such a godforsaken spot, so removed from all the conveniences," her mother decried her brother-in-law's choice. "That drawling hillbilly can't provide the kind of stimulating company Reece can find here in L.A.—or anywhere else for that matter."

Joanna bristled in defense of the Ozarks, the cabin, and Linc. "You can't know that. You've never met him, Mother. And Linc is here so we could plan the menu for Sunday's barbeque we're having for Reece and Rachel."

"Who is Rachel?" The question was quick and immediate.

"Haven't you heard?" Joanna asked with false innocence, fully aware there hadn't been time for her mother to be informed about the engagement.

"Heard what?" There was impatience in the voice on the line.

"I think I should let Reece tell you himself," Joanna replied.

"Tell me what? Joanna, will you please stop being so mysterious and tell me what is going on out there?" her mother demanded.

"Reece is engaged." She knew she was dropping a bombshell so she wasn't surprised by the explosion.

"Engaged? That's absurd! To whom?" There was a mixture of doubt and challenge.

"To Rachel Parmelee."

"Who is Rachel Parmelee?" It sounded like a request for her pedigree.

"She owns a retail store here in the area," Joanna explained. "I think you'll like her, Mother. She is a lovely, intelligent woman—a widow." The last was added in all seriousness.

"She is from the Ozarks?"

"Yes."

"Why on earth is Reece marrying her?" Her mother still didn't quite believe it. "He's been a bachelor all these years. Why should he get married now?"

"Mother, when you see them together, you won't have to ask that question," Joanna assured her.

"I have known Reece considerably longer than you have, Joanna," her mother retorted dryly. "There have been countless affairs over the years. The instant the newness wears off, Reece casts them aside. He has never been so foolish as to become engaged before." She altered her tactic to inquire, "When is this supposed marriage to take place?"

"I don't remember a date being mentioned." Which was true, but something kept her from relating to her mother how soon Reece intended to marry Rachel. "You'll have to ask Reece."

"I will." It was a very definite reply. "Where is he?"

"With Rachel. I'm not sure what time he'll be back," Joanna admitted. "Why did you call, Mother? You never have said."

"I haven't heard from you. You haven't written or called. Naturally I wanted to find out what was going on there. There seems to be a great deal more than I expected," she replied, more than a little miffed that she hadn't been kept more closely informed.

Joanna slid a glance at Linc and watched him take a drag on the cigarette, then toss the butt in the charred-black hearth of the fireplace. As he turned his head to look at her, she dropped her gaze.

"I don't mean to seem rude, Mother, but I can't talk any longer. I do have company," she reminded her. "I'm sure Reece will be calling you in the next day or two anyway."

"Your message is very clear. I won't keep you from entertaining your guest." There was an acid trace of sarcasm in her reply. "Goodbye, Joanna."

"Goodbye." Her hand was wrapped tightly around the receiver, her knuckles showing white as she hung up the phone.

Why did she let her mother do this to her? She glanced toward the fireplace and encountered Linc's steady gaze. Hooking her thumbs in the loops of her jeans, Joanna wandered in that direction.

"That was my mother on the phone," she explained.

"So I gathered," he murmured dryly. "I had the impression she wasn't pleased to hear about the engagement."

"Yes, well, it came as quite a surprise to her," she admitted, a little defensive about her mother's reaction. "Naturally she was a little stunned."

"What's your mother like?" Linc studied her with a vaguely absent look.

That wasn't an easy question to answer. "She's . . . sophisticated, beautiful . . . very self-confident . . . and"—Joanna paused, one corner of her mouth lifting at a wry angle—"and determined to have her own way in nearly everything." She looked at him. "Why?"

But Linc didn't directly respond to her question, remarking instead, "I imagine she celebrates special occasions with champagne dinners."

"She does," Joanna admitted and defended it. "Barbeques are fun, but you have to admit they aren't exactly romantic."

An eyebrow lifted in silent skepticism. "I

guess that depends on whether you are the barbeque or champagne type." He picked up his hat.

Joanna gave him a startled look. "Are you leaving now?"

"Yes."

"But—" How could he?

"You need to give some thought to which type you are—barbeque or champagne." Linc stated quietly and adjusted the hat low on his forehead. "Good night, Joanna."

Chapter Fifteen

*H*er sandaled feet lightly skimmed over the steps as Joanna hurried downstairs. There was no sign of Reece in the living room. She scanned the doorways for a clue to his whereabouts.

"Reece! Are you ready to pick up Rachel?" she called and started across the living room to expand her search for him. "Not yet," he answered, but Joanna couldn't place the direction of his voice. "I'm on the porch, having a cup of coffee. Come join me."

With that information, she altered her course to walk to the screen door facing the lake. As she pushed it open, she saw him seated in one of the wicker chairs. A water-cooled breeze drifted in from the lake, but the late morning was turning warm and somnolent.

She let the screen door shut and advanced toward her uncle. The white slacks and knit shirt of navy blue enhanced his dark good looks and his trimly masculine build.

"When are you leaving to pick up Rachel?" she asked.

"I didn't plan to leave for another twenty minutes. Why?" His glance was mildly curious.

"I told Linc we'd be there a little early," she explained.

"Certainly." He nodded and would have added more but a noise intruded on nature's stillness. They exchanged questioning looks.

"It sounds like a car just drove in. I'll go see who it is," Joanna said and turned to the screen door.

There was a vaguely puzzled frown in her expression as she entered the cabin. Since the road came to a dead end a quarter mile further, they didn't get passing traffic or the idle sight-seer stopping to ask for directions.

As she crossed the room, she heard the idling of a car motor out front and the slam of a door. The front door was open to allow cross-ventilation but the dark mesh of its screen door didn't give Joanna a clear view outside until she was all the way to the door.

Her eyes widened in surprised shock at the sight of the slimly elegant woman approaching the cabin. Dressed in an expensive beige suit and a brightly striped silk blouse, she was the epitome of breezy sophistication. Her artfully bleached blonde hair was a shade lighter than

Joanna's sun-streaked hair and styled in a loose coil. She was tanned to a golden color that took years off her age.

"Mother!" Joanna finally found her voice and the strength to open the screen door. "How did you get here?" It was a ridiculous question since the taxi was just now reversing out of the drive.

"After that ride, a pack train couldn't have been more uncomfortable." There was a stinging acidity to her dry answer.

"What are you doing here?" Joanna was still trying to recover from the astonishment of her mother's unexpected appearance. "Why didn't you let us know you were coming?"

"Isn't it obvious that I came to see you and find out for myself just what's going on here?" her mother challenged and handed Joanna the camel-brown weekender bag she was carrying. As she entered the cabin, her disdainful glance made a sweep of the surroundings. "I must admit I'm finding it difficult to see what it is you find to like about this place. After two weeks, I would be bored to tears. There's nothing but hills and trees; the roads were wretched—"

Her bronze-tinted lips were parted to add more disparaging remarks, but she stopped, distracted by something she saw. As her expression slowly changed to an aloof and challenging smile, Joanna looked around to see the "something" was Reece.

"Hello, Reece." There was a silken smoothness to her mother's greeting. "Surprised to see me?"

A brittle tension crackled through the room as the pair faced each other, familiar antagonists meeting again. There was a silent weighing of each other before Reece smoothly crossed the room to greet her.

"I wasn't expecting you but I truly can't say that I'm surprised to see you." He kissed the smooth cheek she offered him.

"Joanna tells me that congratulations are in order." She arched him a look of amusement. "I always thought you were too clever to be caught. Who would have thought a hillbilly would succeed in snaring you when so many have tried? I'm definitely looking forward to meeting your 'Daisy Mae' while I'm here."

Joanna stiffened at her mother's thinly disguised insults of Reece's choice for a wife, masked only by a taunting smile and the amusement in her softly cultured voice. Except for the hardening line of his smile, Reece gave no other outward indication that her mother's barbed references to Rachel had inflicted any damage.

"I have the feeling Rachel will find it as much of a pleasure as you do." He easily parried her remarks with a jibe of his own. Joanna saw the flash of irritation in her mother's eyes that he hadn't risen to the bait, but the fire was quickly banked. "As a matter of fact, I have to leave shortly to pick up Rachel. A friend of ours is having a party for us this afternoon to celebrate our engagement."

"I believe Joanna made some reference to that when I talked to her on the phone the other evening." Her mother pretended to vaguely recall the reference to the barbeque. "I suppose it will be one of those homespun affairs with all the grannies and the kissin' cousins there. Do you suppose they'll mind if I attend? I wouldn't want to miss it."

"Linc would not object at all," Reece assured her without blinking an eye.

"I suppose that was a silly question. After all, country people are known for their hospitality." Instead of making that a trait to be admired, she managed to imply it was quaintly stupid.

Joanna was finding it difficult to keep her temper in the face of all these snide references to the questionable worth of the Ozark natives. Aware that her attitude had been initially the same, regarding them as country bumpkins, she held her silence.

"When did you arrive, Mother?" Joanna couldn't recall that there had been an early flight scheduled from California.

"Late last night. I'm certainly glad I spent the night in a hotel instead of coming directly here. The taxi would never have been able to find this place in the dark. He charged me extra just for traveling over these roads in the daylight." She again implied her disdain for the location.

"You should have phoned from the airport. We would have picked you up," Joanna replied, "and saved you from paying a taxi to come all this way."

"And spoil my surprise?" she countered. "That would have taken the fun out of it." She brought her attention back to Reece. "I have to confess I was curious why you have kept coming here year after year. Now that I've seen it, I'm still baffled over what attracts you to this place."

"Perhaps because there is nothing artificial here," Reece suggested. "Not the scenery or the people."

Joanna flashed a quick glance at her mother to see her reaction to his insinuation that she was phony. There was the faintest crack in her mother's smiling expression, a whisper of indication in the softly indrawn breath.

Then Reece was inclining his head in mock deference to her mother and excusing himself. "I must let Rachel know I have been delayed a few minutes."

"She has you jumping through hoops already, doesn't she?" her mother mocked at his retreating back as Reece walked toward the study. With Reece gone from the room, she stopped trying to hide her intense displeasure behind the mask of a false smile. "He may have gotten himself engaged to this country yokel, but he'll never marry her."

"Mother, you aren't being fair. You haven't even met Rachel," Joanna protested impatiently with her mother's superior attitude.

"Rachel. Even her name sounds common," her mother declared in contempt. Aware the remark had spurred Joanna's temper, her mother pressed a hand to her forehead as if in pain. "Please, Joanna, I'm not in the mood to argue. After bouncing all over that road, my head is pounding. Does this rustic little hideaway possess a bathroom where I could freshen up after that dusty drive? God, how I dread traveling over that again. My nerves are shot."

Smothering her anger, Joanna turned toward the stairs. "I'll show you to my room in the loft. It has a private bath." She passed on the information in a curt voice. "We'll be leaving soon for the party. Would you rather stay here and rest? We can always send someone to get you later on."

"I wouldn't dream of causing Reece any inconvenience," she stated. "I'll ride along with him to save him the extra trip. Besides, I'd rather meet this Rachel when there aren't a lot of other people around."

Joanna didn't find that to be a very heartening statement but Reece took it in stride when he learned about it as if he had guessed it all along. Every remark seemed to have a sharp side.

When Reece stopped the car in front of a small bungalow on a tree-shaded residential street, Rachel must have been watching for him because she was out the front door before Reece stepped out of the car.

"Is this where she lives?" Elizabeth eyed the small dwelling with a trace of contempt.

Reece paused long enough to reply. "Yes, until we are married. Then she will live where I do."

Joanna observed the rigidness of her mother's features as she watched the couple meet on the sidewalk, the radiance that seemed to envelop both of them. Rachel's unerring clothes sense had chosen a sundress that was summery and mature in design. It was navy blue with white polkadots, a dark shade that complimented her creamy complexion.

"Rachel isn't what you expected is she, Mother? Joanna murmured. "I mean, she isn't exactly a hick."

"She isn't exactly worldly or sophisticated either, which is the type of wife Reece needs," her mother retorted in an equally low voice.

Once both were in the car, Reece made the introductions. Rachel seemed oblivious to the veiled hostility that laced the tone of Joanna's mother.

As Reece drove away from the curb, Elizabeth leaned forward. "After meeting you, Rachel, I wonder if you realize how extremely lucky you are?"

"I think I do." Rachel cast a warm glance at Reece and smiled.

Joanna watched her mother stiffen with jealousy, then control. "I do hope you let me help with the wedding plans," she addressed both of them, managing to sound very pleasant. "Have you two set the date?"

"Next week," Reece answered.

Elizabeth blanched at the answer, and Joanna felt sorry for her. It couldn't be easy for her. Yet, she recovered with remarkable aplomb.

"It's going to be very simple," Rachel elaborated on their plans. "Just the minister and two witnesses."

"Reece," her mother directed her protest at

him. "That isn't fair to cheat all your friends and family out of a wedding after we've waited so long." She directed a false smile at Rachel. "Not to mention your bride. I'm sure Rachel would like something a little more elaborate."

"Not me," Rachel declared with a faint laugh. "It's too much wear and tear on the nerves."

"Oh, speaking of wear and tear on the nerves—" Elizabeth switched the subject, talking to Reece and ignoring Rachel altogether. "I saw Grace Whittington the other day, Reece. She and Alex are having their annual summer party next month. You know, the usual black tie affair."

Joanna was astounded. She had never known her mother to be so flagrantly rude before. She was trying to put Rachel in the position of being the outsider, talking about people and events she was unfamiliar with, and a kind of life she'd never known.

"Naturally the Governor will be there. Sylvia was telling me that—" Elizabeth continued to rattle on, dropping names and titles, sounding disgustingly snobbish.

Joanna glanced at her uncle behind the wheel, wondering why he didn't say something. His handsome features were grim, but Reece remained silent. Joanna marveled at the control he exercised over his temper. She guessed that Rachel was the reason he said nothing. They were on their way to their engagement party. Reece didn't want any harsh words to mar the event.

Her mother's monopoly of the conversation made it a long drive to the Wilder ranch. Joanna was relieved when it came into view.

There were already more than a dozen vehicles parked in the ranch yard when they arrived, and more guests driving in behind them. Music and happy voices were coming from the rear patio area of the sprawling house. Circling around the building, they joined the party in progress.

A tent canopy was set up on the lawn to offer shade from the sun, but most of the guests had gathered on the redwood sundeck of the patio where the beer and cold drinks were located. The patio gave a hundred and eighty degree view of the lake below and the blue line of hills.

"This is quite a place," her mother murmured in an aside to Joanna.

Irritated by her previously condescending attitude toward the Ozarks and its inhabitants, Joanna couldn't resist scoring one for the other side. "It's just a typical hillbilly shack, Mother." She saw Linc engaged in a conversation with one of the guests and quickened her pace, moving ahead of her mother to greet him. "Hello! How come you started the party without the guests of honor?"

She had to force the light banter into her greeting, because she wasn't anxious for the moment when she would have to introduce Linc to her mother. But it couldn't be avoided.

"I was beginning to think you weren't going to

make it." Linc separated himself from the other guests and crossed the lawn to meet the four of them.

Although the comment was addressed to all of them, his gaze singled Joanna out. His arm curved itself quite naturally around her waist as he shook hands to welcome Reece and Rachel and turned expectantly toward the fourth member of the group.

Aware that her mother had taken due note of the familiar possession by Linc, Joanna began the introductions. "This is our host, Linc Wilder." Tension made her smile stiff. "I'd like you to meet my mother, Elizabeth Morgan. She arrived unexpectedly this morning to surprise us."

Although nothing changed in Linc's expression, she sensed an added alertness about him. "Welcome to the Ozarks, Mrs. Morgan. I believe we talked briefly the other evening."

"Yes, you answered the phone the night I talked to Joanna." Her mother made a show of recalling the incident as if it had been hardly worthy of her notice.

"I have been waiting to meet you," Linc said, "but I didn't think the opportunity would come so soon."

"Oh, really?" She was none too pleased by the comment and Joanna mentally braced herself for the scathing remarks that would come.

But Linc didn't give her a chance to reply further, nor satisfy her curiosity as to his reason. "Perhaps we'll have a chance to talk later. Right now, I think we should join the others. I know they're anxious to offer their congratulations to Reece and Rachel."

He kept Joanna firmly at his side while they walked to the patio. Reece and Rachel were quickly engulfed in a tide of well-wishers. Standing next to Linc with her mother to one side, Joanna couldn't shake the feeling of alarm over his proposed conversation with her mother.

"This is quite a gathering, Mr. Wilder," her mother remarked.

"Linc," he corrected. "We aren't formal in the Ozarks."

Her glance made a disparaging sweep of the casually dressed crowd. "So I've noticed," she murmured dryly.

But Linc didn't take any notice of the veiled contempt in her mother's reply. He glanced instead at Joanna. "There's some people I'd like you to meet." Her mother was included in the statement. The hand on her waist guided her in the direction of two couples standing nearby. "This is my sister, Sharon, and her husband, Dick Scott."

He introduced them first to the young, dark-haired couple. Joanna was a little surprised that his sister was such a petite thing. The resemblance to her brother was very slight. The second couple was older, closer to Linc's age.

"—and Tanya and Jake Lassiter," Linc continued the introduction, concluding with, "Meet Mrs. Morgan and her daughter, Joanna."

There was a murmur of exchanged greetings, then his sister, Sharon, focused a sparkling look on Joanna. "Linc has mentioned you a couple of times. I'm glad I've finally gotten to meet you."

"Thank you—I think," Joanna qualified her answer, unsure what Linc might have said about her.

"Oh, it was all good," Sharon assured her and cast a sly glance at her older brother. "Very interesting, in fact."

The others smiled, all except for her mother who looked anything but pleased at the innuendo. Linc changed the subject.

"Where are the children, Tanya?" he asked the attractive, tawny-haired woman. "Did you leave them home?"

"Yes. Grandpa and Grandma are babysitting," she answered his question and turned to Joanna to explain, "We have three boys. John is eleven, and a set of four-year-old twins."

"Proud and headstrong—just like their momma," Jake Lassiter declared with a warmly affectionate glance at his wife.

"Like their daddy, you mean," she corrected and arched him a provocative look.

Conscious of Linc's eyes on her, Joanna looked up. There was a mocking gleam in their brown depths. "Only three kids," he murmured. "I guess that proves a ridgerunner doesn't keep his wife barefoot and pregnant all the time." Her pulse skittered under his gaze. "We're a little more civilized than that."

"Don't listen to him, Joanna," Tanya inserted. "Ridgerunners are born cat-wild. You'll never tame one. But you might be able to housebreak him."

Chuckling laughter followed her comment, then the conversation became generalized. When Joanna glanced around to locate Reece and Rachel, her attention was distracted by the view from the sundeck. The blue ridges of the hills seemed to go on forever while the afternoon sun glistened on the lake curling and stretching over the valley.

"Reece was right when he said the view from your house was fantastic," she murmured to Linc.

"You like it, huh?"

"Who wouldn't?" she countered.

"Your mother, maybe," he suggested.

Agreement flickered reluctantly to darken her eyes. Joanna knew her mother wasn't impressed by this view of the countryside. Earlier, she had indicated she had found all the rocks and trees boring.

On the far side of the patio, someone played a few experimental bars of music on a fiddle. Linc turned to look in the direction of the sound.

"Jessie must have arrived," he guessed.

"Who is Jessie?" her mother inquired with an expression of supreme tolerance.

"Jessie Bates lives in a cabin down the road," Joanna explained briefly. She remembered Reece telling her what a good musician Jessie was. "Is he going to play?" she asked Linc.

"With an audience of this size? You bet he

will," he smiled lazily. "Do you want to go over and listen?"

"Yes," Joanna was quick to agree, then hesitated when she glanced at her mother. "Do you want to come?"

"Of course." But the sweet smile of agreement was plainly forced.

With Linc leading the way, they threaded through the gathering crowd until they reached the corner of the sundeck where Jessie was tuning his fiddle. Some of the other guests at the party had brought their instruments as well. Two men had guitars; another had a banjo. There was also a bass and another fiddle.

Joanna was quick to notice, though, that Jessie had dressed for the special occasion. Gone were the baggy overalls. He was wearing a snow-white shirt with a pair of red suspenders holding up his loose pants. With his chin tucked tightly on the violin, he ran the bow over the strings, then stopped to glance over his shoulder at the other musicians.

"How's that sound?" he asked.

The other man with a fiddle shook his head. "Mine has never sounded *that* good." His fellow musicians laughed.

"What ya' need is a set of rattlers to put inside it," Jessie advised his fellow fiddler. "They give it that special tone."

"Rattlers?" he repeated. "What kind of rattlers are you talking about?" The man eyed Jessie with more than a little skepticism. Joanna knew the feeling. Her leg had been pulled many times, too.

"Why, rattlers from a rattlesnake. What else?" Jessie replied with a straight face. "Next time you find a timber rattler out in the woods, stomp on him, an' cut off his rattlers. When you git home, put 'em in your fiddle and it'll sound just like mine."

"Bet it won't," the bass man laughed.

"Are you fellers gonna jaw all day—or are we gonna play something?" Jessie paused to crane his neck, searching the crowd. "Where's the bride and groom-to-be?" Someone pushed Rachel and Reece to the front of the circle. Rachel was blushing a little, but looking very happy. "We're gonna play a song for you," Jessie declared. "Orange blossoms got something to do with weddin's, don't they?" The man with the guitar nodded in answer. "Then, let's play a little Orange Blossom Special," Jessie suggested.

Jessie started the song out and the others joined in. Soon, the guests were clapping hands and tapping their feet in time with the music. It seemed to Joanna that the faster the tempo went, the wider the smiles became on everyone's face.

When the song ended, the next selection was more sedate in comparison. Crowded together by the throng of guests, Joanna unconsciously leaned closer to Linc, not wanting to be accidentally separated from him.

"Happy?" His voice murmured the question almost into her ear.

"Mmhum." It was an agreeing sound. She added softly, "I think I'm falling in love with the Ozarks."

"Only with the Ozarks?" Linc challenged quietly.

Her head turned on the pillow of his shoulder so she could look at him. For a second, nothing else existed as their gazes locked. The burst of applause around them signaled the end of the song, and reminded them they weren't alone. His mouth curved in a rueful smile. The bubble of elation didn't go away when Joanna let her attention be drawn back to the small band.

The loud clang of a dinner bell interrupted the country concert before they began another tune. "Time to eat," Linc stated.

Chapter Sixteen

$\mathcal{B}$y the time Joanna finished everything on her plate, she was so stuffed she could barely move. All the other guests seemed to be suffering similar conditions—except her mother who had barely taken more than a small spoonful of food from the long buffet table.

Joanna glanced around and noticed her mother sitting with another group, enduring a conversation with one of them. Her fingers gripped the edge of the empty plate balanced on her legs.

Jessie Bates leaned back in his folding chair that faced Joanna and Linc. He rubbed his protruding stomach with his hand. "You did yourself proud on that feast, Linc."

"It was delicious, wasn't it?" Joanna agreed, letting her attention be brought back to their small circle. "I've never been to a barbeque like this before—with a roasted pig and everything. In California, we turn on a transistor radio and charcoal steaks on a grill and call that a barbeque."

"We do it up right in the country," Jessie declared.

"I guess you do," Joanna laughed, but it faded when she saw her mother approaching.

Elizabeth Morgan paused by their chairs to ask, "Have you seen Reece?"

"He's sitting with Rachel by the deck railing." Linc pointed in their direction.

"They make a nice looking couple, don't they?" Jessie remarked.

"How long has he known her?" Elizabeth continued to study the pair seated by themselves.

"Five—six years," Linc replied and her mother looked at him with surprise.

"I hadn't realized that," she admitted on a thoughtful note, and sent a sharp glance at Joanna. "Has be been seeing her all this time?"

"Not exactly," she hedged. "It all happened just recently."

"I think they are being too hasty to marry so soon," Elizabeth stated, letting her opinion be known. "They hardly know each other. I think they should wait. As the old saying goes—marry in haste, repent at leisure."

"Now, we look at it differently in the hills," Jessie disagreed with her. "We think it's a case of—the shorter the wooing, the longer the doing."

"How quaint," her mother murmured with a cloying smile. "If you will excuse me, I think I'll go over and join them."

As she moved gracefully away from their chairs, Jessie watched her with a considering look. "She reminds me of a hen I once had—always jealously guardin' her nest." There was a slight pause before he added, "Only trouble was —she never had no eggs in it."

It was an accurate, yet sad, commentary of her mother's position.

Reece had just left her to take their dirty plates back when Rachel noticed his sister-in-law approaching her. She mentally braced herself for the meeting. She had already made a few guesses about Elizabeth Morgan and had a fair idea of the woman's motives.

"Hello, Mrs. Morgan," she greeted her politely. "Are you enjoying the party?"

"Please call me Elizabeth," she insisted. "After you and Reece are married, it will be terribly confusing if we call each other Mrs. Morgan." As she sat on the redwood bench next to Rachel, she glanced in the direction Reece had taken. "I see Reece has abandoned you already."

Rachel pretended to be unaware of the jibe. "He's taking our plates back."

"Men," Elizabeth murmured in an expressive tone. "They can be so attentive before you're married, then take you for granted afterward, can't they?"

"Sometimes." She didn't disagree. Her gaze followed Reece as he paused to speak to an attractive young woman.

"You'll get used to that eventually," Elizabeth murmured. "The Morgan men have always been known for their roving eye." She smiled at Rachel, as if they shared a common experience. "Of course, they are experts at sweeping women off their feet. I should know. I was married to one."

"You were married to Reece's brother, weren't you?" Rachel pretended to recall the face, fully aware Elizabeth's interest wasn't directed at her late husband.

"His younger brother, yes," she nodded. "He was a great deal like Reece—in looks and temperament." She studied Rachel for a long second. "I must say that I admire you."

"Oh?" She found that difficult to believe.

"Yes. There aren't many women who would tackle a new husband and plunge into a new lifestyle all in one leap—without even testing the water," Elizabeth explained her compliment —a backhanded one.

"I suppose not." It was going to be a big adjustment.

"I do hope you'll like living in California. It will take some getting used to, I'm sure," Elizabeth remarked with feigned sympathy. "I don't suppose you've had much experience dealing with a housekeeping staff. Reece has a beautiful home, very luxurious." She was not too subtly pointing out their background differences. "Of course, he has to. His business requires him to do so much entertaining—formal parties—things like that."

"Of course," Rachel murmured.

"If you would ever need any help, I hope you'll call on me." She assumed an air of false modesty. "I've given thousands of dinner parties so—arranging all the fine details is practically second nature to me."

"Thank you. It's kind of you to offer." She'd call the devil's wife before she'd ask Elizabeth.

"We're practically family," Elizabeth reminded her. "Reece and I have always been very close." But not as close as Elizabeth had wanted them to be, Rachel guessed. She was being studied with a critical eye. "And clothes. I'll take you to some of my favorite shops where we can buy you a whole new wardrobe so you won't be embarrassed when you're with the other wives."

The comment had struck a vulnerable nerve, making Rachel very self-conscious of the polka-dot dress she'd made herself. She glanced at it, silently comparing it with the elegant outfit Elizabeth was wearing.

"I hadn't thought about that." Probably none of her clothes were suitable for her new lifestyle in California.

"I doubt if Reece has given you a chance to think about anything," Elizabeth declared. "I need to have a talk with him. Marriage is difficult under the best of circumstances. I'd hate to see the two of you start out on the wrong foot."

"Yes." It was just a reply, meaning nothing.

"I'm so glad we've had this chance to chat." Elizabeth pressed her hand on top of Rachel's in a falsely affectionate gesture. "I'd like to think that we'll be friends."

"Yes, it would be nice." Even if she doubted it could ever happen.

"I'm monopolizing your time and I didn't intend to do that." She had cast a few doubts in Rachel's mind. Her mission was accomplished. "You have a lot of friends here and I'm sure you want to spend some time with them. Since you and Reece are getting married so soon, it might be your last opportunity to do so before you're uprooted." She planted one last seed before departing with a self-satisfied gleam in her eye.

As Reece attempted to tactfully excuse himself from the company of a native Californian who had recently migrated to the Ozark hills, his glance strayed to the railing where he'd left Rachel. He stiffened when he saw Elizabeth sitting with her, his jaw hardening into a grim line.

"Excuse me." He abruptly took his leave of the man without waiting for a polite opening.

Elizabeth was already walking away as he crossed the deck to rejoin Rachel. She had turned away to view the panorama of the hills, but not before Reece had noticed the troubled look in her thoughtful expression. He had known the minute Elizabeth had arrived that she would try to make some kind of trouble. After all he'd gone through, he wasn't going to lose Rachel now.

He came up beside her. "That's a long face to be wearing at your engagement party," he remarked with deliberate lightness.

Rachel turned to smile at him. "I was thinking."

"About what?" Reece prompted.

"Us."

"What about us?" He gently prodded the information from her.

"I was just wondering whether we are doing the right thing—getting married so quickly and all," she admitted with a certain hesitation, aware he had no doubts.

"Elizabeth had something to do with your second thoughts, didn't she?" Reece was certain of the source.

"Indirectly," Rachel avoided putting all the blame on his sister-in-law. "Our lives have been so different, Reece. What do I know about dinner parties and entertaining important clients? Maybe I won't fit in."

"You will."

She shook her head, disagreeing. "I'm not at all like Elizabeth."

His smile was amused. "Thank God."

"Please," she protested his attempt to make

light of the situation. "I'm trying to discuss this with you."

"After you have already discussed it with Elizabeth," he replied with vague impatience. "Why did you listen to her, Rachel? Don't you realize she is jealous?"

"I'm not blind, Reece. I know she's in love with you." Rachel recognized the signs. "But that doesn't mean the points she raised are not valid. They are. Maybe we shouldn't rush into this."

"There is only one valid reason that matters," he insisted. "I love you, Rachel, and I want you for my wife. Anything else Elizabeth may have said means nothing. Yes, there will be many adjustments to make," Reece conceded. "But we'll make them together. *Together*, Rachel. Do you understand?"

"Yes." Nothing seemed impossible with the strength of their love on their side.

Bending his head, Reece kissed her lightly, but warmly. "Wait here while I find Elizabeth," he requested. "It's time I had a little talk with her."

"Don't do that," Rachel protested, not wanting to make trouble.

"I must," Reece insisted. "She has to understand that I won't allow her to come between us." His hand caressed her cheek. "I know what I'm doing, Rachel. If I don't end this now, she will keep trying. And I won't take the risk that next time she might succeed."

Rachel couldn't argue against the wisdom of his decision. She guessed that he knew his sister-in-law much better than she did. When he walked away, she didn't attempt to stop him.

It was several minutes before Reece finally located Elizabeth in the party crowd. She was with Linc and Joanna, looking faintly bored. When she saw him walking toward her, she brightened visibly. Reece wasn't taken in by that artificial charm.

"I'd like a word with you, Elizabeth," he stated, taking her arm to lead her away after nodding briefly to Linc. He ignored Joanna's curious glance, not wanting to involve his niece in this dispute.

When they were off by themselves, Elizabeth viewed his hard expression with an innocent look. "Is something wrong?"

"I knew when you arrived this morning, you would try to make trouble," he stated.

"Trouble?" She blinked. "I don't know what you mean."

"You have been trying to convince Rachel that we should postpone the wedding," Reece accused smoothly.

"Now, that is nonsense. I did nothing of the kind," Elizabeth denied his charge. "We discussed living in California and I offered to help in any way I could to—"

Reece wasn't interested in her version of the conversation. "It doesn't matter what you discussed. Rachel and I are getting married next week—as planned," he emphasized. "There is nothing you can say or do to change that."

"I wouldn't *presume* to try," she replied with wounded dignity.

"You would *presume* a great deal if you thought you could succeed."

"How can you say that when I was only trying to be helpful?" she protested.

"We don't need your kind of help. Not now—and not later."

"Well, if that's the way you feel about it—" Elizabeth began with an exaggerated air of pride.

"I'll tell you exactly the way I feel about it." Reece cut through the niceties. "You weren't invited here. Of course, that's never stopped you. You barge in whether you're welcome or not. If it wasn't for Joanna, I would have told you to get lost a long time ago. But she is my brother's daughter, so I have tolerated you. But no more." He was hardened against the pallor that spread over her face. "Make whatever excuse you wish but take the next plane back to L.A. Is that clear?" he challenged.

Elizabeth held herself stiffly, proudly fighting back tears. "Very."

"Good," he stated. "I will tell Rachel you're leaving. There will be no need for you to speak to her again."

An exchange of goodbyes would have been hypocritical at this point. Without saying another word, Reece turned on his heel and walked away. Elizabeth stood rigidly, staring after him.

When Joanna noticed her mother slowly returning, her gaze sharpened. Although her mother was trying to appear calm and composed, Joanna observed the fine tension that put a strain in her expression and the pallor beneath her rouged complexion.

"Is something wrong, Mother?" she asked the instant she joined them.

"It's this sun," Elizabeth replied tightly. "It's given me a terrible headache. Would you mind very much if we left the party? All this heat and noise is just making it worse."

Joanna hesitated, then glanced at Linc. "Could you drive us back to the cabin?"

"Of course," he agreed, making his own assessment of her mother.

The party was regaining its former level of gaiety. Hardly anyone noticed them leave as they walked around the house to Linc's car. In the passenger seat, her mother reclined against the headrest and closed her eyes. Her attitude silenced any conversation that might have been made during the short drive to the cabin.

They entered the log home by the front door, which had been left unlocked. "Why don't you sit on the sofa, Mother?" Joanna suggested. "I'll get you some aspirin and a glass of water."

"Thank you." It was a very subdued Elizabeth who sat on the cushioned sofa.

"I'll get them for you, Joanna," Linc volunteered. "You make your mother comfortable."

"Okay." She was grateful for his offer, but at

the moment she was too concerned about her mother to express it.

Picking up a decorative pillow, Joanna plumped it to put behind her mother's head. The offer was waved aside with an autocratic hand.

"Would you telephone the airline for me?" her mother requested.

"The airline?" Joanna stared, then realized her mother was probably intending to book return passage. "We can do that later. Just sit back and rest—"

"Stop fussing over me," she protested when Joanna attempted again to put the pillow behind her head. "I don't have a headache. I only used that as an excuse to leave the party." Joanna straightened, irritated at the way she had been fooled. "Call the airline," her mother ordered. "I want to make reservations on the first flight back to Los Angeles."

"Mother, you just got here," Joanna argued the necessity for doing it this minute.

"And Reece has ordered me to leave," Elizabeth replied. She didn't have to fake the hurt look that wavered in her eyes.

"I can't believe that," Joanna frowned in stunned doubt. "Why would he do such a thing?"

Her chin quivered. "He doesn't want me here. He thinks I'm trying to come between him and Rachel. All I did was offer to help and he accused me of interfering."

"Were you, Mother?" She wouldn't put it past her.

"No," she denied it. "I think Reece is making

a foolish mistake by marrying that woman. They have absolutely nothing in common. But I *was* making an effort to be nice. And he repays me by practically throwing me out. After all the years I've—"

The sentence was left unfinished as Linc returned to the living room, carrying a glass of water and an aspirin bottle. He brought it to the sofa.

"Here you are, Mrs. Morgan." He handed them to her.

"Thank you," she murmured.

Linc waited until she had taken them, then glanced at Joanna. "We'd better be getting back to the party."

Hesitating, Joanna glanced at her mother. She didn't know what was going on, or how much of her mother's story was truth. She couldn't have completely fabricated such a tale.

"You go ahead without me," Joanna advised him reluctantly. "I'm going to stay with Mother a little while."

"Is it necessary?" he frowned in sharp question.

"Something's come up." Joanna couldn't tell him about it, not yet. "I can't explain."

"All right." But it was a grudging acceptance of her decision. "I'll see you later."

Her teeth bit at the inside of her lip. Joanna knew he didn't understand why her mother needed her. She could read it in the impatient stride that carried him to the front door.

"There have been times in the past, Joanna,"

her mother sighed when the door had closed behind Linc, "when we haven't always agreed with each other but I'm so glad you're here with me. I've never felt so abandoned."

It was the assurance Joanna needed to convince her she had made the right choice. She sat down on the sofa next to her mother.

"I still don't understand why Reece would do such a thing," Joanna stated her confusion.

"Neither do I," she admitted with a bewildered shake of her artfully bleached hair.

"But he must have given some other explanation," Joanna persisted in her search for the rest of the story.

"Reece claimed he . . . he only tolerated me because of you." She lifted her tear-bright eyes to gaze at Joanna. "That hurt."

She had never witnessed this display of vulnerability in her mother before. It touched her, moving her to a deep sympathy.

"Momma, I'm sorry," she whispered.

"You will fly home with me, won't you?" Elizabeth reached out to tightly grasp her daughter's hand in an earnest appeal.

"Do you mean today? Now?" Joanna was startled, reluctant.

"Reece said he didn't want me here," she reminded. "I have to leave now."

"But—" Her troubled brown eyes glanced toward the front door that Linc had went out a few minutes ago.

"How can you hesitate?" There was a kind of desperation in her mother's question.

Her shoulders drooped in resignation. "I'll go with you," Joanna agreed. "But I have to call Linc and let him know."

"Linc?" She took her hand away from Joanna's. "Why should you tell him anything?"

"He's expecting to see me again and I—" She tried to explain.

There was a mixture of pain and scorn in her mother's expression. "Reece has his 'Daisy Mae.' Don't tell me you think you've found your Lil' Abner?" The acid sting was back in her mother's voice, if not at full strength. Joanna darted her an angry look. "Oh, I grant you he's a handsome man, if you go for the earthy type. But, Joanna, you barely know him." Elizabeth tempered her criticism of Linc.

"That doesn't change the way I feel," she insisted.

"No doubt you are attracted to him," her mother conceded. "But, love? In a month, you'll forget what he looks like. That's the way it always happens with these holiday romances."

It wasn't a holiday romance but there was nothing to be gained by arguing that point with her mother. She kept silent as her mother stood up.

"We haven't much time," Elizabeth prodded at her. "You'd better go upstairs and start packing. I'll call the airline." When Joanna continued to remain seated, impatience raced through Elizabeth's expression. "If you feel you have to call this . . . Linc Wilder, you can do it from the airport."

* * *

With the car turned into the rental agency, Joanna slipped the receipt in her purse and hurried into the main lobby of the airport terminal. Her mother stood impatiently beside a display case.

"I have the tickets." She handed Joanna hers. "They'll be boarding the plane in a few minutes."

"You go ahead to the gate," Joanna urged. "I'll be there in a minute."

"Where are you going?" Elizabeth frowned.

"To call Linc." She was already backing away in the direction of the phone booths. "It won't take long."

"Be quick about it."

The more she tried to hurry, the longer it seemed to take. Joanna rummaged through her purse for the change for the pay telephone, then waited impatiently while the phone rang. The housekeeper answered, and she had to wait again while the woman went to fetch Linc from the party. She almost sighed in relief when she heard his voice on the other end of the line.

"Linc. It's Joanna," she identified herself quickly.

"Hello." Warmth was injected into his second greeting. "Are you ready to come back to the party? I'll come pick you up."

"No. That is—" She was interrupted by the announcement of an arriving flight over the airport's public address system.

"Where are you?" Linc questioned.

"At the airport."

"The airport? What are you doing there?" There was sharp confusion in his voice.

"Mother's flying back to California"—Joanna paused and closed her eyes—"and I'm going with her."

"What?" It was a stunned reply. "Why?"

"Mother and Reece had a falling out and—" She didn't have time to explain. "It's a long story, Linc, and I don't have time to go into it." She waited for him to say something, but there was only silence. "I just wanted to call and tell you goodbye before I left," she added lamely.

"That's it, huh?" Linc challenged. "Just goodbye and it's been nice knowing you?"

"No." She was half-angry. "Try to understand, Linc. Under the circumstances, I can't stay."

"I understand all right," he replied. "The message is loud and clear. You go ahead and enjoy your champagne flight back to L.A. I have guests and a barbeque waiting for me."

Joanna knew what he was saying but she refused to acknowledge it. "If that's the way you feel—" she began indignantly.

"What do you expect me to say?" he cut in angrily. "You said it all, Joanna, when you said goodbye."

The line went dead. Her fingers tightened on the receiver as she realized Linc had hung up on her. He hadn't even tried to understand her situation.

Slowly, she returned the receiver to its hook

and gathered up her purse and tickets. Tears were spilling down her lashes. Joanna wiped them away as she walked to the gate area.

The flight was already boarding when Joanna arrived at the gate where her mother was waiting for her. "Did you talk to Reece?" Elizabeth asked before Joanna could say anything.

"Reece? No, I didn't." She shook her head, numbed by the pain inside.

Disappointment clouded her mother's face. "I thought . . . He might have . . ." There was a dispirited shake of her head. "It doesn't matter. We'd better go. They've already begun boarding."

The party was still going strong at the Wilder ranch but Linc had isolated himself from it. He stood alone at the deck railing. His gaze wasn't admiring the view of the lake and hills. It was fastened to the western sky. A half-empty drink was in his hand. He didn't hear Reece and Rachel walk up to him.

"Where's Joanna?" Reece inquired with curious concern.

It was the use of her name that penetrated Linc's mind. He turned to look blankly at his friend for an instant. Then his gaze lowered to the drink he was holding.

"She's gone." His voice was flat—unemotional. "She called a little while ago to say she was flying back to California with her mother." Linc downed a swallow of watered-down whiskey, unaware of the glance Rachel and Reece exchanged. "Do you remember the talk we had awhile back, Reece—about all the responsibility that was suddenly mine after my dad died?"

"Yes." Reece frowned, unsure what that had to do with his niece.

"All that's over with now," he declared and exhaled a long breath. "Mom is with Dad, Sharon's married, and David is out on his own." His gaze swept the ranchland. "This place practically runs by itself now. I don't have anyone to worry about except myself." He looked at the glass again and shook his head. A wry slant of amusement lifted a corner of his mouth when Linc raised his glance to Reece. "I was wild as a young'un." There was something absent, almost brooding that claimed his features. "It's been a long time since I've been on a good drunk."

Chapter Seventeen

 $\mathcal{A}$ ll the furniture in the log home was covered with sheets, giving the place a ghostly air. Linc paused in the middle of the living room and glanced around. His features were drawn unnaturally taut, because for him, it was haunted with Joanna's ghost.

"Is that you in thare, Linc?" Jessie Bates pressed his face to the wire mesh of the screen door, cupping his hands around his eyes to peer inside.

"Yeah, it's me." The reply was rough and unfriendly, showing the edges of a short temper.

Jessie didn't wait on an invitation, just opened the screen door and came in. "I heard the truck go by my place. I didn't know whether it was you or somebody snoopin' around so I thought I'd better check." He glanced around the house. "Is everything all right here?"

"Yeah," Linc nodded curtly. "I promised Reece I'd check to see that it was all locked up."

"I guess the newlyweds got off to Californy okay," Jessie surmised.

"Yep."

Jessie peered at him closely, partially lowering one eyelid. "You still grumpin' over Joanna, ain't cha?"

"Why don't you mind your own damned business, Jessie?" Linc snapped, not liking the personal observation. He stalked toward the door, not wanting to hear any more of Jessie's comments.

"I always figured you to be the kind of a man to take the bull by the horns." Jessie followed him, baggy overalls and all.

"Is that a fact?" His reply was abrupt and loaded with sarcasm. Once outside, Linc waited until Jessie was on the stoop, then locked the door.

"I never guessed you'd turn out to be one of those tame fellas that let's a gal tell ya' how things is gonna be," Jessie didn't let up. "You want her, don't ya?"

"Lay off, Jessie." It was a tautly issued order.

"You jest don't understand women." The Ozark character shook his head. "When they say 'no,' they mean 'yes.' And when they wanta stay, they go," he explained, then paused to suggest, "If'n I was you, I'd go bring her back."

Linc stared at him, irritated and tense, but he said nothing in reply.

The living room of the Morgans' California home was a cool green and white, furnished with an understated elegance. Looking very radiant and proud, Rachel sat on the armrest of a jade-green chair where Reece was sitting. Her arm was around his shoulder in a natural display of affection while his was curved around her waist in light possession.

A wistful quality crept into Joanna's smile as she looked at the couple. "Marriage certainly agrees with you two," she said the obvious. "I don't even need to ask if you're happy."

"Ecstatic," Rachel declared. "I have you to thank for that, Joanna. If you hadn't shamed me into that dinner invitation, I probably would still be running from him."

"Sooner or later, I would have caught you," Reece stated.

"He was running out of patience," Joanna remembered from her seat on the edge of the ivory couch.

"I wish you had been able to fly back for the wedding." There was regret in Rachel's glance. "I understand why you couldn't, but—"

"I'd like to have been there," she admitted, and paused to mentally brace herself to speak his name. "Linc was best man, wasn't he?" She tried to sound happy and uncaring, interested only by the aspect of their wedding party.

"Yes, he was." Reece wasn't fooled.

Joanna tried to fake an idle curiosity. "How is Linc?"

"Fine," he nodded and closely watched his niece.

The doorbell rang, and Rachel slipped off the arm of the chair. "I'll answer it." She laid a hand on his shoulder to keep Reece in his seat, then walked toward the foyer off the living room.

It was a natural gesture of belonging that Joanna couldn't help noticing. "Rachel is already regarding this as her home, isn't she?" she remarked to her uncle.

"It is her home . . . *our* home," he corrected himself with a smile. Then he casually brought the subject back to Linc. "I was under the impression that you were becoming serious about Linc before you left."

She lowered her gaze, agitated by the direct comment. "I'd rather not discuss it." Immediately Joanna contradicted herself by saying, "Linc didn't give me a chance to explain why I had to leave."

There were muffled voices in the foyer as Rachel greeted the caller at the door. Joanna paid no attention to them. Her back was to the entry area, so she didn't see the tall, dark-haired man pause at the living room opening.

"I never guessed Elizabeth would insist that you leave with her," Reece stated. "It's ultimately my fault you had to leave at all." His startled gaze noticed Linc Wilder standing there. He started to say something to Joanna, but Linc motioned him to keep quiet.

"Linc should have listened," Joanna insisted. "I don't blame you, Reece. There are times when I'd like to slap Mother's face. But . . . with all her faults, she's still my mother. What kind of daughter would I have been if I hadn't stood beside her?"

"I know," Reece murmured.

"Linc should have understood that," Joanna rephrased her earlier statement, with a little more anger in her voice this time. "He's impossible, Reece. I mean, there he was telling *me* that I was telling *him* goodbye! And I was doing nothing of the kind!"

"Why didn't you tell me to shut up and listen?" Linc asked quietly.

His voice quivered through her, shocking her into stillness. For a split second, Joanna thought she was losing her mind. She half-turned to look behind her. Her heart stopped beating when she saw Linc standing there.

Her gaze ran in disbelief over his well-muscled, long-bodied frame. His face seemed leaner, the rugged planes of his features more pronounced. Joanna was conscious that Linc was looking her over, too, almost devouring her wth his eyes. That did nothing to calm the erratic behavior of her pulse.

"What are you doing here, Linc?" Joanna stood up slowly to face him, afraid she might be guessing wrong about his reason.

She was only partially aware of Rachel and Reece slipping quietly out of the room to leave her alone with Linc. When he walked forward to enter the room, Joanna noticed the bottle of champagne in his hand.

"Why does any man leave the hills?" Linc countered her question with one of his own, then supplied the answer. "To find himself a woman."

Linc didn't stop until he was squarely in front of her. His earthy virility reached out, disturbing her senses. It would have been easy to take the last step into his arms, but Joanna waited, breathlessly, unable to speak.

"In my case," Linc went on, "I had to fly half way across the country to find the right one." The dark glow of gold fire was in his eyes when he looked at her, searching her expression. When he spoke again, his voice was husky with intense longing. "It's lonely back there without you, Joanna."

Her breath caught in her throat. For an instant, she wasn't able to reply. "I've been lonely here, too," she admitted.

He appeared to lean toward her, as if to sweep her into his arms, then stopped. "There's one way to end our misery."

Inside, she was straining toward him, but some invisible force held her in check, too. "What's that?" Joanna whispered.

"Marry me," Linc said simply.

A smile began to curve its line along her lips. "I'll marry you," she accepted and added her own conditions to the proposal. "But—only if you promise to keep me barefoot and pregnant."

His arms were around her and it was the only

place in the world she wanted to be. Joanna closed her eyes, loving him more than she had ever believed it was possible to love a man.

His mouth came down to bruise her lips in a hungry kiss, but Joanna had been without the particular satisfaction only he could give just as long as he had. This was a feasting time. Both of them were trembling long before they had their fill.

His heart was beating so loudly, Joanna could hear it above the drumming of her own. She leaned weakly against the wide wall of his chest, momentarily satisfied just to be in his arms.

"I guess I didn't need this after all," Linc stated thickly.

One arm was withdrawn from around her. Its loss, as much as his cryptic statement, prompted Joanna to glance around. The champagne bottle was still in his hand. She had been so absorbed in loving him, she hadn't been conscious of the bottle's alien shape against her body.

It took her a second to understand why Linc had brought the champagne. It was so obvious when she realized it. He had believed she preferred champagne dinners to barbeques. The gesture of bringing champagne proved the lengths he would go to have her.

"If you had bothered to ask me," Joanna murmured, "I would have told you that I don't like champagne."

"There are times when you can be as stubborn

as a Missouri mule, Joanna," Linc declared on a vibrantly possessive note. "But I have the feeling I'll make a ridgerunner's wife out of you yet."

She partially withdrew from his embrace, but continued to rely on his steadying support as she bent to slip off her heels.

"What are you doing?" he frowned despite the hint of amusement in his voice.

"A proper ridgerunner's wife is supposed to be barefoot," Joanna reminded him. "I can handle that part of it, but I'll need your participation for the rest of it."

He laughed and pulled her back into his arms. "I'll handle it—in my own good time," Linc promised, tossing the champagne bottle onto the couch cushions. "I'm not sure that I fancy the idea of your momma marching me down the aisle with a shotgun at my back."

The reference to her mother sobered Joanna, reminding her of the reason for the separation. "You do understand why I had to come back with her, don't you?" she asked.

"Now, I do," Linc assured her. "At the time you left, I didn't. I thought she had influenced you into changing your mind about me." A wry smile crooked his mouth, a very handsome mouth. "It would be safe to say that I'm not your mother's first choice as a son-in-law."

"But I'm not marrying you so she can have a son." Joanna would have liked her mother's approval, but it wouldn't change anything if she didn't have it. In all fairness to her mother, she had to say, "She has changed a little—since that incident with Reece. When our first baby is born, I wouldn't be surprised if she came to the hills to see it."

"Let's do some practicing first before we get down to the serious business of making a baby," Linc suggested.

"Anytime," Joanna murmured provocatively.

FOR THE
LOVE OF GOD

Chapter One

The wind blowing through the opened car window held all the heat and humidity of a July day. It lifted the auburn-gold hair that lay thickly about Abbie Scott's neck, creating a cooling effect. A pair of sunglasses sat on the dashboard, looking at her with their wide, oval lenses. She had removed them earlier, not wanting the view artificially tinted.

A morning shower had brought a sharpness and clarity to the landscape of the Arkansas Ozarks. There was a vividness to the many shades of green in the trees and bushes crowding close to the highway. The air was washed clean of its dust, intensifying the lushness of the Ozark Mountain greenery.

Her hazel eyes kept stealing glances away from the winding roadway to admire the ever-changing vista of rock and tree-covered hills. The flecks of green in her eyes almost seemed like a reflection of the verdant countryside.

There was a time when Abbie hadn't appreciated the beauty around her, when she had complained about the twisting, turning double-lane roads that snaked through the Ozark hills and the lack of entertainment and shopping facilities found in cities, and the limited job opportunities in an area where the major industry was tourism.

Out of high school, Abbie had left the serenity of the rugged hills for the excitement of Kansas City. She thought she'd found it in the beginning, but the glitter had eventually faded. A year ago, Abbie had returned to her hometown of Eureka Springs after four years away.

A lot of people, her parents included, hadn't understood why she had given up a promising career with Trans World Airlines, headquartered in Kansas City, with its many travel and fringe benefits. Abbie's response, if anyone asked, and few did, was a declaration of homesickness. But that was only partially true.

She guessed that her mother suspected a man was at the root of her decision to return, but Abbie had too much pride to admit the romance she thought would lead to the altar had ended up going nowhere. Initially she had come home to lick her wounds, but a year's distance had enabled her to see it had only been the final straw and not the ultimate cause.

Now, instead of a lucrative job with a large corporation, she was her father's legal secretary, paid only a small salary compared to her previous wages. By watching her pennies, Abbie managed fairly well with some adjustments from her prior life-style. She "semilived" with her parents, which meant that she had taken her savings and fixed up the loft above the garage, once a carriage house, into a small efficiency apartment. It provided privacy, as well as low rent.

And there was Mabel—her car. She had traded in her speedy little Porsche sports car for a cheaper and older automobile. Mabel, as Abbie had dubbed the car, wasn't much to look at. Her body was showing signs of rust and dented fenders. She was accidentally two-toned blue, since the hood and the passenger door didn't match the sun-faded robin color of the rest of the car. If it was possible for vehicles to have a personality, Mabel certainly did. She was grumpy, did a lot of coughing and complaining like an old woman, but there wasn't a sick piston or plug in her body.

As the road began an uphill climb, Abbie shifted the standard-transmission car into second gear. The motor made a small grunting sound of protest but Mabel didn't hesitate. Abbie's lips curved with a faint smile.

Although July marked the height of the Ozark tourist season, there was relatively little traffic on the state highway leading into Eureka Springs. Most of the tourists used the major highways, so Abbie only had local traffic to contend with. Plus, it was the middle of a Saturday afternoon, which meant most of the tourists were at the various area attractions and few were on the road.

After experiencing city rush-hour traffic, Abbie didn't let crowded Ozark roads stop her from visiting her grandmother on the weekends. Grandmother Klein continued to live on the rocky farm she and her late husband had worked, although the acreage itself was now leased to a neighbor.

Abbie's grandmother on her mother's side still raised chickens, had a milk cow and a big garden, and canned more food than she could eat, totally ignoring the fact she was seventy years old and should slow down. No one ever visited Grandmother Klein without being loaded down with foodstuffs when they left, and no amount of protesting changed that.

On the floorboard in front of the passenger seat, Abbie had jars of pickles—sweet, dill, bread-and-butter, and cherry—as well as an assortment of homemade preserves and jellies. Plus there were two sacks on the seat. One contained tomatoes, cucumbers, and sweet corn from Grandmother Klein's garden; the other was filled with ripe peaches freshly picked from the tree, their fruity smell filling the car.

The temptation was too much to resist and Abbie reached into the sack for just one more peach as the car neared the crest of the hill. The fruit was still warm from the sun, its juice spurting with the first bite Abbie took. She had to use the side of her hand to keep it from running down her chin.

When she started to sink her teeth into the fuzzy skin for another bite, she saw the red warning light gleaming on the dashboard panel. She lowered the peach from her mouth and frowned slightly. It was rare for Mabel to overheat on these up-and-down roads.

"Don't lose your cool now, Mabel," she murmured to the car. "We're nearly to the top."

But the light stayed on even after they started the downhill run. When Abbie saw the wisps of steam rising from the hood, she knew there was trouble, and started looking for a place to pull off the road. It was another half-mile before she found a shoulder wide enough to accommodate Mabel. By then, there were more than wisps of steam coming from the hood.

Once the car was parked, Abbie made a quick glance to be sure her lane of the highway was clear of traffic before climbing out to check under Mabel's hood. She forgot she had the peach in her hand until she needed both of them to unlatch the hood. She held it in her mouth, ignoring the juice that dripped onto her blue plaid blouse.

The tails of her blouse were tied at the midriff in an attempt to beat the summer heat. When Abbie started to lift the hood, drops of scalding hot water were sprayed over the band of bare stomach between her blouse and faded Levi's. She jumped back, nearly dropping the peach, and just managing to save it while she wiped the hot water from her stomach with her other hand.

"How could you spit on me like that, Mabel?" she unconsciously scolded the car.

The upraised hood unleashed a billow of steam that quickly dissipated. Abbie moved cautiously closer to peer inside and find the cause of the spitting hot water. There was a hole in the radiator hose. Her shoulders sagged with dismay.

Abbie turned to look up the road, trying to remember how far it was to the nearest farmhouse. It was another four miles yet to the edge of town, she knew. She wasn't enthused about walking even half a mile in this heat.

A semi tractor-trailer rig zoomed by, its draft sucking at her. Abbie looked hopefully at the oncoming traffic. She knew nearly everyone in the area. Maybe someone would drive by that she knew and she could get a ride into town. Not under any circumstances would she accept a lift from a stranger.

More than a dozen vehicles passed but Abbie didn't recognize any of the drivers. A small handful slowed down when they went by her stalled car, but none stopped. And Abbie made no attempt to flag anyone down either. She took an absent bite of the peach while she debated whether to start walking until she reached the nearest house, where she could telephone her parents, or to wait a little longer.

A low-slung, dark green sports car came zipping around the curve in the road, approaching her parked car from the rear. It immediately slowed down at the sight of the upraised hood. The convertible model car had its top down, but its windshield prevented Abbie from getting a clear view of the man behind the wheel. As it edged onto the shoulder to park behind her car, she noticed the out-of-state license plates and tensed a little. Four years of living in a city had made her slightly leery of strangers.

The driver didn't bother to open the door. Instead, he lightly vaulted over the low side to walk toward Abbie's car. The man was tall, easily reaching the six-foot mark. In this land of the summer tourist, there was nothing unusual about the way he was dressed—a mottled gray T-shirt and faded cutoffs with white sneakers. It exposed an awful lot of hard, sinewy flesh, tanned to a golden brown. His hair was a toasty gold color, attractively rumpled by the wind.

Abbie couldn't see his eyes behind the mirror-like finish of his sunglasses, but she liked the strong angles and planes of his male features. She felt that instant pull of attraction to the opposite sex and experienced a twinge of regret that the man was no more than a passing stranger. There wasn't exactly a surfeit of good-looking, single men in Eureka Springs.

"Hello." His lips parted in a brief but friendly smile that showed an even row of strong white teeth. "It looks like you have some car trouble."

"'Fraid so," Abbie admitted.

In spite of the futility of it, her interest in the man mounted as he lifted a hand to remove the sunglasses. She found herself gazing into a pair of arresting blue eyes. Their depths held a warm gleam that had a dancing charm all its own. Awareness of his sexual magnetism quivered pleasantly along her nerve ends. It had been a long time since any man had fully aroused her mating interests. The few times she had gone out on a date since her return, the desire had been mainly for companionship.

"What seems to be the problem?" As the stranger bent to look under the hood, Abbie observed the flexing muscles in his tanned arms.

Even though the busted hose had stopped spitting hot water, Abbie still advised, "Be careful. Mabel sprang a leak." The curious glance he slanted at her made Abbie realize she had referred to the car by its pet name. "That's what I call her," she explained lamely, and felt slightly foolish about it.

An interest that had not been present before entered his look as he briefly skimmed Abbie from head to foot. She was tall, nearly five foot seven, with a model's slimness—except she had curves in all the right places, although no one would ever describe her as voluptuous. Her light red hair had a gold sheen to it—strawberry blond her mother called it. Abbie would have been less than honest if she didn't acknowledge she was more than reasonably attractive. A country freshness kept her from being striking.

The stranger seemed to like what he saw without being offensive about it. Then his attention was swinging easily back to the split in the radiator hose. He tested the hose, bending it a little to discover the extent of the rupture.

"I might be able to patch 'Mabel' up." He used

her pet name for the car. The faint smile that edged the corners of his mouth seemed to share —or at least understand—her personification of the car. "Would you happen to have a rag—or an old towel?"

"Sure. I have one under the front seat," Abbie admitted. "Just a second and I'll get it for you."

Rather than use the driver's side with the road traffic to watch for, Abbie walked through the tall grass along the shoulder of the highway and opened the passenger door. It was a long stretch to reach the piece of old flannel tucked under the drivers' seat. Her elbow bumped some of the jars on the floor, rattling them together. Like a row of dominoes, they began toppling over just as her groping fingers found the rag under the seat. Abbie closed her eyes, expecting to hear one of the jars break and bracing herself for the sound, but it didn't come.

The rag was in her hand and she was half lying on the seat, preparing to push out of the car when Abbie heard the swish of footsteps in the grass. There wasn't much room on the seat for maneuvering with the two sacks of vegetables and peaches. Abbie was forced to crane her neck around in an effort to see behind her.

"Are you all right?" The man was standing on the inside of the opened car door, eyeing her with concern.

She was conscious of being in a vulnerable and ungainly position with no graceful way to alter it. "Yes. I just knocked over some jars." She pushed backward off the seat and out of the

15

car. Her face felt red but it could have been caused by the blood rushing to her head when she had been half hanging over the seat to reach the rag.

When Abbie turned to give him the old cloth, she discovered how close she was standing to him. The cotton fabric of the mottled gray T-shirt was cleaved to his wide shoulders and lean, muscled chest. His maleness became a potent force Abbie had to reckon with, especially since she was standing nearly eye level with his mouth. Her pulse just wouldn't behave at all.

"Did you break anything?"

She watched his lips form the words but it was a full second before his question registered. Abbie pulled herself up sharply. What was the matter with her? She was reacting like a love-starved old maid who hadn't been near a man in years. A little voice argued that she hadn't—at least not with a man the caliber of this one.

Her hazel-green eyes darted a guilty look upward to meet his gaze. There seemed to be an awareness in his blue eyes of what she was thinking and feeling. It really wasn't so surprising. Experience with life—and women—was etched into the male lines in his face.

"Nothing was broken." Abbie remembered to answer his question. Her crooked smile held a measure of resignation. "Grandmother Klein loaded me down with her homemade jams and pickles before I left."

His shoulder brushed her forearm as he bent to set the jars upright. With his large hand, he was able to right them two at a time, sometimes with a thumb on the third to push it up. In next to no time, all the jars were standing again.

"Thank you. You really didn't have to do that," Abbie said when he had finished.

He raised his eyebrows in a kind of shrugging gesture. "I remember my grandmother used to make the best wild-raspberry jam. She knew it was my favorite and always made sure to have a couple of jars for me whenever I visited her. Grandmothers are like that. They either try to fatten you up or marry you off."

"That's true," Abbie agreed dryly, and resisted the impulse to look at his left hand to see if his grandmother had succeeded in the latter. "Here's the rag you wanted." She gave it to him and followed when he walked around the opened passenger door to the front of the car. "What are you going to do?" she asked. "Wrap the rag around the hose and use it as a bandage?"

"No." He appeared amused by her suggestion, but not in a ridiculing way. "I doubt if it would hold. I have some electrical tape in my car. Once I get the hose dried off, I'll wrap a few lengths of that around it. It's only a few miles to Eureka Springs, and the tape should hold until you get that far."

Abbie bit her lower lip, remembering. "Except most of the water boiled out of the radiator."

Using the rag as a protective pad, he un-screwed the radiator cap. "I always carry a gallon jug of drinking water with me. Between it and a gallon of antifreeze-coolant in my trunk,

17

we should be able to get you temporarily fixed up."

She shook her head in a gesture of bewildered amazement at how smoothly he was handling the breakdown. "I'm certainly glad you came along," Abbie declared openly. "I thought I was going to have to walk to a phone, and this isn't exactly the coolest day for walking, not to mention the tow charges you're saving me. Thank you for stopping."

"Just being a Good Samaritan," he replied, that easy smile coming again to his mouth.

With the coolant, water, and tape from his car, he patched the hose and partially filled Mabel's radiator. "The old gal ought to make it now," he said as he closed the hood and made sure it was tightly latched.

"It isn't enough to say 'thank you,'" Abbie insisted. "You not only fixed it but you used your tape and water and everything. Let me pay you for it."

He opened his mouth to refuse, then suddenly smiled. It seemed to take her breath away as her heart started thudding crazily. Love wasn't something that happened at first sight but physical attraction could. It was often equally potent, however, and Abbie knew she was suffering from a severe case of it.

"Were those fresh peaches I smelled in the sack on the car seat?" he asked instead.

"Yes." Abbie nodded while she studied the way the afternoon sun intensified the burnished gold color of his hair, antiquing it.

"If you insist on paying me, I'll take a couple of those peaches. Homegrown fruit has a taste all its own," he said.

"Okay, it's a deal." She laughed and walked to the passenger side to retrieve the sack through the opened car window. "Help yourself. You can have the whole sack. Grandmother Klein will just give me more next weekend."

"Two's plenty." He randomly picked two from the sack. "I'll follow you into Eureka Springs to make sure you don't have any more trouble with Mabel. I'll be stopping there, and I advise that you stop at the first garage and get a new hose put on."

"I will." It was a somewhat absentminded agreement, because her attention had been caught by his statement that he'd be stopping at Eureka Springs. "Eureka Springs is a quaint town. Will you be staying there awhile?"

"Yes, I plan to," he admitted, and she was conscious of his gaze running over her again.

"You'll like it," she rushed, only half-aware that he had been going to say something else. As a rule, she didn't socialize with summer tourists. A holiday romance was even more of a dead end than any other kind. But there was no doubt in her mind that she wanted to see this man again. "By the way, my name's Abbie Scott. You've already met Mabel."

"Abbie? Short for Abra?" He arched an eyebrow.

Abbie was dumbfounded. "How did you know that? Most people think my name is Abigail."

One muscled shoulder was lifted in an expressive shrug. "It just seemed appropriate. Abra was the favorite of Solomon in the Bible. A lucky guess." He extended a hand to complete the introductions. "My name's Talbot. Seth Talbot."

"That's a biblical name, too." Abbie was reluctant to admit she hadn't known anything about her namesake. Since he seemed so knowledgeable about it, she didn't want to reveal her ignorance.

"Seth was the third son of Adam," he informed her. "Not quite as well known as his older brothers, Cain and Abel."

"That's true." She smiled. Her hand tingled pleasantly in his firm clasp. He had very strong, capable hands, but they were relatively smooth, without the calluses of someone who made his living with them. It didn't really surprise her. Despite his hard physique and craggy good looks, there was the definite impression of a man who relied on his mental prowess and innate air of command for his living.

Then he was releasing her hand to gather up his empty jugs and roll of black tape. "If you start to have any trouble, just honk twice. I'll be right behind you," Seth Talbot assured her.

"Okay." She watched him walk along the grassy verge to his car and stow the things in the backseat.

Oncoming traffic permitted her to observe him as he swung over the low passenger door and into the driver's seat. Abbie waited until the road was clear to walk to the driver's side of her car and open the door. She set the sack of peaches on the seat and pushed it over to slide behind the wheel.

Mabel's motor grumbled to life at the turn of the ignition key. As Abbie turned the car onto the highway she waved to the driver of the sports car. Within seconds, she saw the reflection of the dark green sports car in her rearview mirror, following a safe distance behind her.

It was an older model car, but Abbie suspected it had been an expensive one. She tried to guess what kind of work he did, speculating that he could be a lawyer or maybe a doctor. If he was a salesman, he could sell her anything, she thought with a little laugh.

The four miles to Eureka Springs seemed to flash by. Not once did Mabel even wink her red warning light. Abbie couldn't make up her mind whether she was glad or sorry about that. Mechanical trouble would have given her an opportunity to find out more about Seth Talbot—essentials like where he was staying in Eureka Springs and some of the places he had planned to see while he was here.

Abbie couldn't believe the way she was thinking. She was actually considering chasing a man. There was nothing shy about her, but she didn't classify herself as the aggressive type either. Still, she couldn't help wondering what it would be like if he kissed her. Seth Talbot had certainly captured her fancy in a short time. Or maybe it was simply a sign that she was finally cured of her distrust for men after that disappointing romance in Kansas City. That was probably closer to the truth.

When Abbie turned her car into the service station-garage she patronized, there was a honk and a wave from the sports car before it sped on by. Abbie couldn't contain the sigh of regret that slipped out. It would be sheer chance if she ever saw him again and she knew it.

A portly, coverall clad man emerged from the service bay of the station and walked toward her car with an ambling gait. It was Kermit Applebaum, the owner of the establishment. He had serviced her parents' vehicles ever since she was a freckle-faced toddler. Thankfully, the freckles had faded with the onset of maturity, but Kermit Applebaum still called her Freckles, a nickname no one else had picked up—and Abbie was eternally grateful for that.

"Well, hello, Freckles," he greeted her as she had expected, and Abbie tried not to wince. "How's old Gladys doing?"

"Her name is Mabel," she corrected patiently, and stepped out of the car. "And Mabel has busted a radiator hose. I hope you have a spare one to fit her."

"I'll rustle up something." He wiped his greasy hands on a rag before he lifted the hood to have a look. "You didn't do a bad job of patchin' this."

"I can't take the credit for that," Abbie replied. "A tourist stopped when he saw I was broken-down and fixed it up for me, then followed me into town to be sure I made it."

"That fella that just honked at you?" the owner-mechanic asked with some surprise. When she nodded affirmatively his expression became thoughtful. "I thought it was just some guy tryin' to make time with you. I guess I did him a disservice." He closed the hood with a decisive shove and turned to Abbie. "Drive your car over to that empty bay, and I'll see what I've got for hoses to fit it."

In all, it took the better part of two hours before he had it fixed with interruptions from customers and phone calls. It was nearly suppertime when Abbie turned her trusty car onto a winding street for home.

Her hometown of Eureka Springs was filled with quaint charm. The restored and refurbished Victorian structures clinging to the steep hills gave the city an ambience of the past, a nostalgic flavor. Some visitors considered it an oddity in the middle of the Ozarks, but Abbie had always regarded it as home. It had been dubbed "The Little Switzerland of America" because of the combination of its architecture and steep terrain and had been a highly popular vacation resort since the turn of the century. Then, its appeal had been as a spa. Now, it was the town itself and its many gift, antique, and craft shops. There was even a trolley car to ease the weary feet of those unprepared for the endlessly winding streets.

And during the tourist season, people came by the thousands to see The Great Passion Play, an outdoor drama of Christ's last days, and to view

23

the seven-story statue of Christ of the Ozarks. There were other religious attractions, too, including the Bible Museum, the Christ Only Art Gallery, and the New Holy Land with its life-size recreations of scenes from the Bible.

As much as Abbie loved her hometown and its picturesque buildings and Ozark Mountain setting, living in a town that had essentially changed little since the turn of the century had its disadvantages. Abbie became as irritated as the next motorist on city streets that were not designed to handle a lot of modern vehicle traffic. And there weren't any traffic lights, which meant relying on the courtesy of another driver in the case of making turns onto main thoroughfares or off of them.

In the summer, when the visitors came by the hundreds, she griped along with everyone else at the traffic tie-ups, but she still loved it. Maybe it was because she was like the town—a little out-of-date and out-of-step with the times—proud and old-fashioned.

All her girl friends were married, and most of them had children. She had given up a promising career and come back to—what? To fantasize about a stranger who stopped to help?

Climbing roses spilled over the fan-shaped trellises that marked the driveway of her parents' home with its gingerbread trim. The old carriage-house-turned-garage sat at the side, literally built into the hill. Her father's car was already inside the garage. Since there was only room for one and the weather couldn't hurt

Mabel's appearance, Abbie always parked outside.

This time she stopped near the back door of the two-and-a-half story white house. Her cupboards were already filled with jars of goods from Grandmother Klein. She knew the elderly woman wouldn't mind if her granddaughter gave some of the food and home-canned goods to the woman's daughter and son-in-law. It certainly made more sense to divide it now than carry it all up a flight of stairs to her apartment, then back down to the house.

Without bothering to knock at the back door, Abbie walked into the kitchen with an armload of jars. The rush of air-conditioned coolness hit her, and she paused to savor the relief from the outside heat.

A tall, auburn-haired woman turned away from the stove where the evening meal was cooking to look at Abbie. There was a definite resemblance between mother and daughter with minor differences. Alice Scott was pencil-thin, with eyes that were more green than hazel. "You and Mother must have had quite a visit today," she remarked. "She isn't ill or anything?"

"No." Abbie walked to the breakfast table and carefully set the jars down. "I busted a radiator hose on the way home. I've been over at Kermit's for the last two hours getting it repaired."

"I don't see what keeps that car together at all," her mother replied with a wry shake of her head.

The unmistakable sound of her father running

down the steps and whistling a tuneless song echoed into the kitchen. In a few things, her father was very predictable. One of them was his routine after a day at the office. He immediately changed into a pair of khaki pants and either a cotton plaid shirt in the summer or a bedraggled maroon pullover sweater in the winter upon coming home from the office.

True to his pattern, he entered the kitchen in the plaid shirt and khaki pants. He sniffed at the food cooking on the stove. "Smells good, honey." He kissed his wife on the cheek and walked to the refrigerator for a beer. "When do we eat?" Then he saw Abbie standing by the table. "I thought we pushed that one out of the nest. Here she is back at mealtime with her mouth open."

"There's plenty," her mother assured her as she turned the sizzling pork chops in the skillet. "Why don't you have supper with us?"

"Not tonight, Mom. Thanks just the same." Abbie refused because it would be too easy to fall into the habit of eating her meals at home. She had become used to living on her own and liked the measure of independence the small apartment above the garage gave her.

"You're too stubborn," her father accused, but he grudgingly admired her streak of independence, too.

"I get it from you," she retorted.

"You can have Sunday dinner with us tomorrow." It wasn't an invitation from her mother; it was a statement. "It will be nice for all three of us to attend church together again."

26

Her father cleared his throat and looked uncomfortable. "Abe said something about going fishing tomorrow. I meant to mention that to you the other day."

"Drew Fitzgerald Scott, you are going to church." Her mother shook a fork at him. "It's the last time Reverend Augustus will be conducting the services. He's retiring."

"Hallelujah!" Her father raised a hand in the air in mock rejoicing.

"Drew." Her mother's voice held a warning note.

"I never did like the man," he reminded her. "I'm not going to be sorry to see him retire. If I go to church with you tomorrow, you can be sure I'll be sitting in that pew rejoicing."

"Not 'if,'" Alice Scott corrected. "You *are* going. And you're going to attend the farewell tea our ladies' club is giving him and Mrs. Augustus tomorrow afternoon."

His glance slid to Abbie, an impish light dancing in his brown eyes. "Are you going?"

"Yes, she's going." Her mother answered for her.

Abbie lifted her shoulders in a shrug that said the decision had been taken out of her hands. "You heard her, Dad." A smile widened her mouth. "I'm going."

"I guess I don't have a choice either," he replied affably, then took a deep, sighing breath. "I just hope we don't get another 'hell and damnation' minister. I like to go to church and be inspired, not threatened." He leaned a hip

27

against the butcher-block table in the middle of the sunny yellow kitchen. "What about it, Mother? What's the word on our new minister?"

Her mother switched off the burner under the skillet and paused. "I don't remember anyone discussing him in specifics, except that he's supposed to be highly qualified." She seemed surprised that her information was so scanty. "But we'll meet him and his family tomorrow. Reverend Augustus will be introducing them to the congregation, and I'm sure they'll attend the tea. You'll be able to draw your own conclusions."

With that subject apparently closed, Abbie had the chance to ask the question that had been buzzing around in her mind since this afternoon. "Mom, what made you choose the name Abra for me? Does it have any special meaning?"

"That's a strange question to ask after all these years," her mother declared with a faint laugh. "One of my girl friends had an aunt by that name and I liked it. Why?"

"I just found out Abra was the name of Solomon's favorite wife in the Bible. I guess I wondered if you had known that." Abbie shrugged.

"How interesting." Her mother looked pleasantly surprised. "Who told you this?"

"A tourist who stopped to help me when Mabel broke down—" Abbie didn't have a chance to complete the sentence in its entirety.

"What's this about Mabel breaking down?" her father interrupted.

And Abbie explained again about the busted radiator hose and her delay getting it fixed at the garage. By the time she had finished answering —or trying to answer—all his mechanical questions, her mother was dishing up their evening meal. Abbie refused a second invitation to join them and left the house to carry the bounty from her grandmother up to her apartment.

Chapter Two

The incessant pounding roused Abbie from her sleep. She rolled over with a groan and buried her head under the pillow, but she couldn't drown it out. Whoever was doing all that hammering should be put in jail for making so much noise on a Sunday morning, she thought.

Sunday morning. There wasn't anyone hammering, she realized. Someone was knocking on her door. Abbie threw aside the pillow and tossed back the covers to sit up in the single bed. The grogginess of sleep blurred her eyes as she grabbed for the robe draped over the foot of the bed.

"I'm coming!" she called while she hurriedly tried to pull on her robe, but she wasn't too coordinated.

Her alarm clock sat on the oak dresser, far enough from the bed so she would be forced to get up to turn it off. Abbie peered at it. The hour hand pointed to one. Sunshine was streaming through the bedroom window. It surely didn't mean it was one o'clock in the afternoon! With a groan she realized the clock had stopped. She must have forgotten to wind it last night.

It was obviously late, but Abbie had no idea what time it was. She hurried through the main room of her loft apartment, which included a living room, dining room, and kitchen, to the staircase door. As she opened it she lifted the weighty mass of auburn-gold hair away from her face.

Her father stood outside, dressed in a suit and tie. His gaze wandered over her while a smile deepened the corners of his mouth. "I don't think that's exactly the proper attire for church," he observed.

"My clock stopped." Abbie didn't mention that she had forgotten to wind it. "What time is it?" Her voice still contained the husky thickness of sleep.

"There's about ten minutes before the church service starts. Is that any help?" he asked with an amused slant to his mouth.

"I can't get ready in five minutes," Abbie groaned. "You and Mother will just have to go without me."

A rueful expression added lines to his face. "She isn't going to be too happy about that," he warned Abbie but not without understanding. "Too bad *I* didn't think of it." A boyish grin showed.

"Mom is your alarm clock," she reminded him. "She would have gotten you up in plenty of time."

A horn honked an impatient summons from the driveway. Her father glanced in the direction of the sound. "Your mother hates to be late. What shall I tell her?" he asked. "Will you be coming later on?"

"The service will be half over by the time I could make it there." Abbie shook her head to indicate she wouldn't be attending church that morning. "You'll have to convey my apologies to Reverend Augustus and assure him that I'll be at the afternoon tea."

"I think I'll let your mother have that pleasure." He began moving away from the door to the white-painted staircase. "See you after church."

With no reason for haste, Abbie took her time in the shower while coffee perked in the kitchen. The warm spray awakened her senses and eliminated the last traces of sleep and she stepped out of the shower feeling refreshed and invigorated. With a towel wrapped around her wet hair, she donned the yellow cotton robe again and ventured into the kitchen area of the apartment.

A counter bar separated the kitchen area from the rest of the room. Although there was a small wooden table and chairs, Abbie usually ate most of her meals at the counter, using the table only when she had friends over for a meal.

It was too close to dinnertime for breakfast, so Abbie settled for a glass of orange juice and a cup of freshly perked coffee, sitting on a tall, rattan-backed stool at the counter-bar. By the time she had drunk a second cup, the towel had absorbed most of the moisture from her hair. It took only a few minutes to finish drying it with the blow dryer. Its natural-bodied thickness assumed a casually loose and free style that curled softly about her neck. Choosing a dress to wear that would be both suitable for the minister's farewell party and comfortable in the July heat was relatively easy, because she had so few choices. Abbie picked out a sundress designed with classic simplicity, a white material with small, navy-blue polka dots. Its neckline was modest, while the close-fitting bodice flattered the thrusting curves of her breasts. A wide leather belt in navy-blue accented her slender waist, with the skirt flaring out to near fullness. Abbie had a pair of navy-blue sandals with stacked, wooden heels to complete the outfit. She had a three-banded bracelet and matching hooped earrings to wear with it for the finishing touch, but Reverend Augustus frowned on jewelry. After debating silently with herself for several minutes, Abbie wore them anyway.

The only clock with the right time was in the kitchen. It warned her that it was nearly time for church to be let out. She crossed the driveway to the house. Unlike Abbie, her parents had never acquired the habit of locking their doors. In this small community, there had never been any reason to worry about it.

Her mother was a terribly organized person. All the preparations for Sunday dinner were completed, from the meat and vegetables baking in the oven to the relish tray and salad sitting in the refrigerator. Abbie went ahead and put the latter on the table, already covered with their best linen tablecloth, china and silverware. There was even a bouquet of freshly cut flowers adorning the center.

When she heard her parents' car turn into the driveway, Abbie tied an apron around her waist and took the roaster from the oven. She was forking the tender roast onto the meat platter when her parents walked in the back door. Abbie sent a smile in their direction.

"How was the service?" she asked brightly, already warned by the disapproving glint in her mother's eye that she was still upset with her for missing church.

"Reverend Augustus gave an excellent farewell sermon. You should have been there, Abbie," her mother stated. Her tone held more disappointment than anger.

"She means it was brief," her father inserted in a teasing fashion. "For once he didn't rant and rave until he was drowned out by growling stomachs."

Her mother took another apron from the drawer and tied it around her middle to help Abbie dish up the food. "His sermon was quite poignant."

"Maudlin," her father declared with a wink at Abbie.

"He did wander a bit," her mother admitted. "But I thought it was just all the more touching."

34

Abbie turned to her father, going off the subject for an instant. "Are you going to carve the roast?" At his nod, she laid the carving knife and fork across the meat platter. "What is the new minister like?"

"Old Augustus got so choked up with sentimentality he forgot to introduce him." Her father laughed. "I guess he was sitting in one of the front pews but the church was so crowded I never got a look at him. I had the impression that the reverend didn't totally approve of his replacement though."

"Oh?" Abbie gave him a curious look. "Why?"

"I don't know." He admitted his uncertainty. "It was something in his tone of voice when he talked about the church having young blood in its ministry."

"I'm sure that he only meant to imply that the new minister and his family were young people," Alice Scott insisted. "It was merely an oversight that he forgot to introduce the new reverend to the congregation."

"Oversight or not, if Reverend Augustus disapproves of him, I think I'll like him," her father stated.

"You really should show more forbearance, Drew," her mother admonished as she passed him the platter of meat. "Take this into the dining room."

The tea was set for four o'clock in the church basement. Since it was Alice Scott's ladies' club that was giving it for the retiring minister, she had to be there early to help get everything set up. Somehow, Abbie and her father were persuaded to offer their assistance in setting up the rows of folding chairs and the long serving tables.

Abbie was busy setting out the trays of fancy-cut sandwiches when the guests of honor, Reverend Augustus and his wife, arrived in the company of a dozen or so of their closest friends in the church. With the napkins and silverware still to be laid out in a fanning display, Abbie hadn't the time to leave her work to greet them and managed only a brief glance in their direction. After their arrival, people seemed to flood into the large room. Abbie hurried to finish before someone approached the refreshment table.

She was still holding a handful of spoons when she heard footsteps behind her. There was no quick way to arrange so many, so she continued to place them one by one and hoped the person would be patient for a minute or two longer.

"Well, hello, Miss Scott," a man's voice greeted her with warm pleasure. The familiarity of it seemed to tingle through her as her lips parted in a silent breath of delight.

Abbie was so taken by surprise when she recognized the voice of the man, Seth Talbot, who had stopped to help her yesterday, that she didn't even wonder what he was doing at the tea. She swung around to face him.

"Hello, Mr. Talbot." At first her gaze went no farther than his magnetically blue eyes. They seemed sexier than she remembered, so blue against his darkly bronzed features.

Just what drew her attention to his attire, Abbie couldn't have said, because dumb shock set in immediately afterward. She couldn't seem to tear her gaze away from the narrow strip of a white collar that circled his neck, the symbolic garb of an ordained minister.

"Did you get a new hose for Mabel?" he asked.

Abbie heard him but her vocal chords were frozen. All she could do was nod, but his question did succeed in lifting her rounded gaze to his face. Looking at his ruggedly handsome face and darkly gold hair made it seem all the more incredible. There was nothing benign about his countenance, nothing to lead a person to suspect he was a man of God. There was too much virility, too much hard masculinity, too much that suggested male passions.

Something flickered over his expression. "Is something wrong?"

"Yes. No. That is . . ." She stumbled over the words, realizing how rudely she had been gaping at him. Finally, honesty won out. "I never guessed that you were a minister. You don't look like one."

"I see." The corner of his mouth deepened with amusement, attractive lines fanning out from the corners of his eyes.

"I meant . . . yesterday, on the road, you didn't

look like one." She was making a terrible mess of the explanation. "It's obvious by what you're wearing today that you are but . . ." Abbie paused to gather her scattered wits. "I'm sorry."

"For what?" he challenged lightly. "It was a natural reaction. I hadn't realized that you lived in Eureka Springs, or I would have mentioned my transfer to this church."

"But . . ." As her mind played back their previous day's meeting, Abbie discovered that she hadn't mentioned that she lived here. ". . . I guess I didn't tell you."

"I'm glad you're a member of my new congregation." That tantalizing half-smile seemed permanently affixed to his mouth. "I was beginning to think no one under forty belonged to this church."

There was so much potent male charm in that look, Abbie had to glance at his collar to remind herself of his profession. It would be so easy to forget.

"With summer and all, a lot of the members my age have other plans," she said tactfully, rather than criticizing the outgoing pastor for not doing more to encourage the attendance of younger members.

"Maybe you can help me persuade some of them to include Sunday-morning church service in their plans," Reverend Seth Talbot suggested.

All her impulses were to leap on the suggestion, but Abbie seriously questioned whether she was motivated by a desire to help the church or wanted to accept because she was physically attracted to him. She strongly suspected it was the latter. All her responses to him at the moment were purely feminine.

"I'm afraid I'm not a very active church member myself . . . Reverend." Abbie had trouble getting his professional title out. It seemed at such odds with his compelling manhood. She was conscious of the little vein pulsing in her neck.

If he noticed her hesitancy in addressing him, he tactfully ignored it. "Then I'll have to make you my first sheep to win back to the fold." His smile deepened with a heady force.

Abbie lowered her gaze to resist his undeniable appeal. Charisma, that's what it is, she told herself. He would attract anybody's attention—not just hers.

"Abbie, are you finished yet?" Her mother's voice broke into their conversation.

She turned with a guilty start, just as if she were a little girl again getting caught redhanded doing something naughty. It was an expression her mother recognized and it narrowed her gaze. There were still a half-dozen spoons in Abbie's hand. She glanced quickly at them, her task forgotten until that moment. "I'm almost done," she told her mother.

But Alice Scott's attention had already strayed to the man standing next to Abbie. Her eyes widened slightly at the black frock and white collar.

"I don't believe we've met." Seth took the initiative to correct that. "I'm Reverend Talbot, your new pastor."

"I'm sorry." Abbie realized she had forgotten her manners. "This is my mother, Alice Scott."

"I noticed the resemblance," he said, directing that warm, male smile at her mother. "It's easy to see that your daughter inherited her looks from you, Mrs. Scott."

The remark could have sounded so polite and commonplace, a meaningless response, but the way he said it seemed sincere, a glowing compliment. Abbie was a little astounded at the way her mother seemed to blossom under his spell, shedding years and acquiring a youthful beauty. Just for a minute, she was irritated with her mother.

"My father is here somewhere," Abbie informed Seth and glanced around the room in search of him. "But I don't see him this minute." The remark was offered in an unconscious attempt to remind her mother that she was married.

"My husband has been looking forward to meeting you, Reverend Talbot," her mother explained, then inquired, "Is your family here?"

Abbie was suddenly crushed by the idea that Seth already had a wife and children. Seth. She was thinking of him by his first name. That had to stop.

"My family?" An eyebrow quirked, then straightened to its normal line. "You mean my wife? I'm one of the rare ones, Mrs. Scott, an unmarried minister."

"You're a bachelor?" Her mother's tone of voice made it a question, as if she needed more confirmation of his single status.

"Yes." His straightforward answer didn't leave any room for doubts, and Abbie felt a tremble of relief. It was bad enough being so strongly attracted to a minister. It would have been worse if he were married on top of it.

"I wasn't trying to pry, Reverend Talbot," her mother assured him. "But as you said, it is unusual."

"I guess I'm something of a bad boy." He included Abbie in his sweeping glance. "I should be busy choosing a proper minister's wife, but I prefer to wait until I can find the right woman for me—not my job."

"I suspect you are unorthodox in a number of different ways," Abbie murmured, remembering the way he had been dressed the previous day, and the racy sports car he'd been driving.

"So I've been told." There was a wicked light dancing in his eyes. It seemed totally inappropriate for a man of God. There was more than a trace of rebel in him, Abbie realized.

"What do you do when someone tells you that?" she asked.

"I pray on it." Then he addressed himself to her mother. "My way of doing things is sometimes regarded as unconventional, but it doesn't necessarily make it wrong." He seemed to be

41

quietly warning her that his methods wouldn't be the same as those of their previous pastor.

"I'm sure we all have some adjustments to make," her mother conceded smoothly, but there appeared to be reluctant admiration in her look. "I guess we can start out by being thankful that you don't have long hair and a beard."

"You mean like Jesus," he murmured.

Her mother breathed in sharply, then smiled. "You have me there, Reverend Talbot."

"I prefer to have you at church on Sunday mornings," he replied with a silent laugh that slashed grooves in his lean cheeks.

"Our family will be there," her mother promised as her glance strayed beyond him. "Abbie, you'd better finish putting those spoons out. We want to start serving." She seemed to suddenly remember her initial purpose in coming to the refreshment table.

"Excuse me, ladies." He inclined his bronze head in their direction and withdrew.

As Abbie watched him walk away to mingle with the growing crowd, she tried not to notice how becoming he looked in black, and the way the cut of his suit showed off the tapering width of his chest and shoulders. It seemed wrong to be observing those things about him.

"Abbie." Her mother's prompting voice pulled her gaze from his compelling male figure. "Put the spoons out."

"I will." Then she asked, "What do you think of him?"

42

There was a long pause while her mother's gaze traveled across the room to where he was standing. "I haven't made up my mind," she answered finally.

People were starting to drift toward the refreshment table as Abbie laid the last few spoons out. She helped herself to two cups of coffee from the urn and went in search of her father. One of the cups was for him and the other for herself. Like a magnet, her gaze was drawn to Seth. She forced it to move onward until she spied her father in the far corner of the room, talking to one of his fishing buddies.

It wasn't easy to work her way through the throng of people, carrying two cups of hot coffee, but she made it. Engrossed in his conversation, her father looked startled when she extended the cup within range of his vision. He glanced up.

"Is that for me?" he asked.

"I thought you might have talked yourself dry with all your fish tales," Abbie said.

"There are fish *tales* and there are *fish* tails, get it?" His friend, Ben Cooper, chuckled at his own pun.

Abbie groaned in mock dismay at the poor humor. Ben Cooper had his insurance office next door to her father's law offices, so he was a frequent visitor, dropping in regularly for coffee.

"I'd offer you this cup of coffee, Ben, but it's black and I know you prefer yours drowned in milk," she explained.

"That's all right. I'll get my own." He hitched

the waistband of his suit pants higher around his middle as he stood up. "Save my chair for me, will you, Abbie?"

"Sure." She obligingly sat in it when he moved out of the way.

"That Ben is a character," her father murmured with a shake of his head.

"Mmmm." Abbie made an agreeing sound as she took a sip of coffee from her cup. Her gaze wandered idly over the crowd of people and stopped when it found Seth Talbot. She felt again that quiver of purely sexual reaction to his rough good looks.

"Penny for your thoughts?" Her father tipped his head curiously at her. "Who are you staring at?"

"Our new pastor," she admitted, and this time managed to keep her poise. "Have you met him yet?"

"No. Which one is he?" He turned to survey the crowd.

"That tall man over there, talking to Mrs. Smith." Abbie pointed him out with one finger, not wanting to be too obvious.

"Him?" There was vague surprise. "He doesn't look like a minister."

Laughter bubbled in her throat. "That's what I said, too," she admitted. "Unfortunately, I was talking to him at the time."

"That isn't like you," he said, smiling along with her. "You're usually more tactful."

"Everyone's entitled to stick their foot in their mouth once in a while." Abbie shrugged. "Besides, he's the motorist I told you about—the one who patched up Mabel so I could make it into town. He drives a sports car. And he was dressed in cutoffs and a T-shirt. Believe me, he didn't look like a minister then, either."

"No wonder you were surprised," he agreed, and turned his attention back to the more immediate subject of their conversation. "What does his wife look like?"

"He's a bachelor." Abbie pretended not to hear the soft whistle of surprise from her father as she took another sip of coffee. But it was difficult to ignore him when he turned a speculating look on her.

"Do I detect a note of interest?" he asked.

"Daddy, I just met him," she protested.

"So?" he challenged.

"So, I hardly know him. Besides, he's a minister," she reasoned.

"A minister—not a priest," he reminded her.

The conversation was taking an uncomfortable turn. Abbie was glad when she saw Ben Cooper sliding through the crowd with a cup of coffee and a napkinful of tea cakes and sandwiches. She quickly rose from the chair next to her father.

"You can have your seat back, Ben," she declared brightly, and pretended to eye the blueberry tart balanced on top of the small sandwiches. "I think I'll check out the sweets."

One blueberry tart and a cup of coffee later, Abbie found herself trapped in a conversation with the Coltrain sisters, two delightful ladies in their eighties who could ramble on for hours, reminiscing about the past. She'd heard nearly all their stories at least twice. It was inevitable that her attention wandered.

She seemed to have only one interest—Seth Talbot. Voluntarily or involuntarily, she had spent most of her time observing the way he casually mingled, getting acquainted with the members of his new congregation attending the tea. It wasn't just the women who seemed to take to him, but the men as well. The room seemed to buzz with conversations with the new minister as their main topic.

It might have been a farewell tea for Reverend Augustus, but Seth Talbot was stealing the man's thunder. Or was it only her imagination? Just because she was practically obsessed with him did not necessarily mean that everyone else was. Abbie sighed, pulling her attention back to the moment as she took a drink of coffee and discovered it had grown cold.

"Would you?" Isabel Coltrain turned an unblinking pair of blue eyes to Abbie.

"I . . ." She realized she hadn't heard a word of the recent conversation. "I'm sorry." Abbie pretended there were too many other people talking. "What did you say?"

"Would you type the manuscript Esther and I are writing when we're finished?" The older of the two sisters repeated the question. "We'll pay you . . . if it's not too much."

"Yes, I'd be happy to type it for you." Abbie relaxed a little, now that she knew exactly what she was committing herself to do. "I can do it in the evenings."

"I'm so glad that young man suggested that we should write a book, aren't you, Esther?" Isabel Coltrain practically sparkled with zest and energy.

"Young man?" Abbie murmured in vague confusion. She had been under the impression that the manuscript was already in progress.

"Yes, the new reverend." Esther showed equal excitement. "He was so fascinated by some of the stories we told him that he said we should write them down."

"My, but he's a handsome man, isn't he?" Isabel rolled her eyes and clutched a hand to her heart. "He makes me wish I was young again."

"Act your age," her younger sister scolded.

From past experience, Abbie knew the pair could become quite spiteful with sibling jealousy and quickly intervened. "It's a wonderful idea about the book. When do you plan to start on it?"

"Oh, right away," Esther assured her. "We're going to start by jotting down our ideas, then decide who's going to write what."

"That sounds practical," Abbie agreed, even though it could be the basis for a lot of arguments. Before she became embroiled in the mid-

47

dle of one, she thought it best to excuse herself. "I think I'll warm up my coffee."

"Don't drink too much. It isn't good for you," Isabel warned.

"I won't," Abbie promised while she backed away.

Chapter Three

The old Roman-numeraled clock on the office wall indicated the time was five minutes before twelve noon. Abbie opened the bottom drawer of her desk and removed her purse, a large shoulder-bag affair. Lifting the flap, she took a slightly oversized compact mirror out of a side compartment and a tube of bronzed pink lipstick.

The overhead light didn't provide the best conditions for the application of makeup but it was infinitely better than the bare light bulb in the rest room. Abbie turned in her swivel chair so she was facing the full play of light while she freshened the color of her lips and inspected the results in the mirror. She used her fingertips to fluff the ends of her copper hair, then snapped the compact mirror closed in satisfaction.

She was just replacing it in its zippered compartment in her purse when her father stepped out of his private office. His suit jacket was off and the sleeves of his white shirt were rolled back. He had a cup in his hand. It didn't require any clever deduction for Abbie to figure out he was heading to the coffee urn for more coffee. He'd been up to his elbows in law books for the last hour. Case research always seemed to go hand in hand with increased coffee consumption.

His absentminded glance at her desk took in her purse sitting atop it, which seemed to prompt a look at the antique wall clock. "It's that time already, is it?" He sighed his disbelief that the morning could have gone so quickly and walked on, then stopped. "Don't forget to make that bank deposit."

"I've got it right here." Abbie picked up the envelope from her desk top. "I plan to stop at the bank first. Are you going out for lunch, or would you like me to bring you something?"

Her father paused in the act of filling his cup to send her a frowning look. "Is Ed coming in at one or one-thirty?"

Abbie checked the appointment book. "One."

"Better bring me a sandwich then," he decided.

Standing up, Abbie slipped the long strap to her purse over her shoulder and kept the envelope with the bank deposit in her hand. "I'll be back in an hour or soooner," she said, and received an acknowledging nod from her father.

With a hot sun overhead, Abbie kept to the shady side of the street. There was a good breeze, which kept the summer heat from becoming stifling. It billowed the ice-blue material of her loose, tentlike dress, cinched at the waist with a wide white elastic belt.

The streets and sidewalks were bustling with summer traffic as Abbie walked to the bank. There were so many strangers about that she stopped looking for familiar faces. When she reached to open the door to the bank, a man's hand was there ahead of her. She half turned to absently smile a polite thanks for the gentlemanly gesture. But the man leaning forward was Seth Talbot, not a stranger.

The air seemed to leave her lungs in a sudden rush. Abbie wasn't prepared for this exposure to his virile brand of sexuality. For the last three days, she'd made a determined attempt to block him out of her mind and stop weaving romantic fantasies about a minister of the church.

"How are you today, Miss Scott?" Seth greeted her with a natural friendly warmth.

It took a tremendous force of will to pull her gaze from his roughly hewn features and the arresting indigo of his eyes, but Abbie succeeded in doing so. "Fine, thank you, Reverend." She was irritated by how prim she sounded and made a stilted attempt to correct it. "And you?"

There was a hint of amusement in his gaze when Abbie dared to glance at him again. "Very well." But there was nothing in his voice to mock her as he held the door to the bank open, then followed her inside.

Her stomach felt like a quivering ball of nerves. The summer season had brought its usual mixture of sightseers and customers to the bank. Its reconstruction as a Victorian-era institution made it one of the town's attractions.

Believing the conversation was over, Abbie skirted the high-backed chairs that were arranged around a polished potbellied stove, a brass cuspidor near one foot, and headed for the brass teller cages. Then she realized he was walking beside her. Again he was dressed in an unorthodox fashion for a minister—a pair of Levi's that hugged his narrow hips and long, muscular legs, and a white sport shirt that was unbuttoned at the throat. His shoes looked suspiciously like cowboy boots.

It was one thing for him to travel in casual clothes, but Abbie was astounded that he was going around town minus his frock and white collar. This was the community he was to serve as minister, but how would anyone know it when he dressed like everyone else?

His gaze had finished its sweep of the bank's unusual interior and stopped on her. "It really carries out the town's theme, doesn't it?" he remarked.

"Yes. They have quite a display of original business machines, too," Abbie replied, feeling the tension return with the attention he was paying her.

"I looked at them when I was in here Monday." He nodded, his burnished gold hair reflecting the light from the overhead chandeliers. "Are you downtown shopping or is this your lunch break?"

The personal query caught her off guard. "My

lunch break," Abbie admitted, then felt she needed an excuse for being in the bank. She nervously lifted the hand with the envelope. "I have a deposit to make first, though."

"Where do you work?" His question appeared to contain only idle interest.

"I'm a legal secretary—for my father." It was hardly a secret.

"There's nothing like nepotism to keep out of the unemployment lines," he declared with the flash of a white smile.

Abbie stiffened, taking offense even though she knew none had been intended. "I happen to be very qualified for the job."

An eyebrow was arched briefly, his look gentling at her sensitivity. "I'm not throwing stones, Miss Scott. After all, I work for my Father." A teasing light sparkled in his blue eyes and Abbie smiled at the comparison of their respective employers. "That's better." Seth smiled too. "Would you excuse me? I have to talk to one of the officers."

"Of course." She hadn't meant to keep him from his errand, and her smile slid away. "I need to make this deposit, too." It was a defensive reply, an insistence that she had things to do as well.

The nearest teller also happened to be the one with the shortest waiting line. Abbie walked to it, aware of Seth Talbot approaching the desk of a bank officer. The two customers ahead of her had only minor transactions to make, so it was quickly Abbie's turn at the window.

"Hello, Roberta," Abbie greeted the plump, young woman teller, and slid the deposit across the counter.

"Is it as hot outside as it looks?" the teller asked as she checked to verify that there were signatures and deposit-only stamps on all the checks.

"Hotter, but there's a nice breeze," Abbie replied.

A bleached blonde crowded close to Roberta and leaned toward Abbie to whisper eagerly. "We're all just dying to find out who that gorgeous hunk of man is that you're with?" Fran was a former classmate of Abbie's, who was married and had two children, but she'd always been a little man-crazy.

"What man?" As soon as Abbie asked she realized Fran was talking about Seth—Reverend Talbot.

"What man she says." Fran gave Roberta a knowing look.

"I guess you're referring to Reverend Talbot," Abbie admitted. "He's the new pastor of our church now that Reverend Augustus has retired."

"That is the new pastor!" Fran's stage whisper seemed alarmingly loud. "Oh, Roberta, I think I've just been saved," she declared on a giggle.

"I don't blame you," Roberta murmured, and cast a longing eye across the bank—no doubt at Seth, but Abbie refused to turn around and look. "He's the sexiest-looking man to come to this town in a long time."

"I guess," Fran agreed effusively. "I'm going to have to buy myself a new Sunday dress to wear to church."

"Do you belong to our church?" Abbie questioned with a blank look. She couldn't recall ever seeing Fran and her husband attend Sunday services.

"I haven't been there in years—not since Butch and I got married," Fran admitted indifferently, then grinned coyly. "But I think I'm going to be among the faithful from now on."

"Heck, I think I'm going to convert." Roberta smiled impishly.

"Oh, God," Fran murmured excitedly. "He's coming over here. Oh, Abbie, you've just got to introduce us."

She was disgusted at the way the two of them were carrying on about him. One glance at the other female employees behind the cages informed her that Roberta and Fran weren't the only ones avidly eyeing the man walking up, and whispering among themselves. They were only echoing her own reaction to him, but that didn't make it any less distasteful.

Roberta passed Abbie the receipt for her deposit and spoke loudly, "Here you are, Abbie."

"Thank you." She was holding her neck almost rigidly still to avoid turning her head to look at Seth Talbot when he stopped beside her. But she had to move to put the receipt in her purse.

"Are you finished?" he asked.

"Yes." Her glance bounced away before it

squarely met his eyes. Too many sensations were clawing at her because of his presence.

"Hi, I'm Fran Bigsby." The blonde introduced herself when Abbie failed to do it immediately. "Abbie was just telling us that you're the new pastor. Welcome to Eureka Springs."

"Seth Talbot's the name and I'm glad to be here." Again, that warm smiling look was on his visage.

"I'm Roberta Flack, no relation to the singer." Roberta beamed, looking very pretty, despite the unflattering pounds she carried.

"I'm happy to meet you both," he said. When Abbie started to move away from the teller's window so Roberta could wait on the next customer, Seth started to leave with her. "Maybe I'll see you in church some Sunday," he added as a farewell remark.

"You can be sure of it," Fran called after them.

Abbie couldn't walk away from the window fast enough, embarrassed without being sure why. But Seth was undeterred by her haste, easily striding at her side.

"Was there anyplace special you were going to have lunch?" he asked.

His query startled a glance from her. "No. Why?" There were others leaving the bank, and Abbie was forced to slow her pace as she scanned his expression.

"I was on my way to lunch. You're on your way to lunch. So why don't we have it together?" Seth reasoned smoothly. "There's a restaurant just down the street. Shall we go there?"

Her acceptance of his plan seemed to be taken for granted. Actually, Abbie couldn't think of a single reason why she should refuse. "Sounds good," she agreed.

The combination of noon hour and the influx of summer visitors resulted in a crowded restaurant. Luckily, Abbie and Seth had to wait only a few minutes before they were seated at a small table, hardly big enough for two. Her knees kept bumping against his under the table no matter how she tried to angle them in the close quarters. There was another man seated in a chair directly behind her, so she couldn't even edge her chair away from the table.

"Sorry," she apologized when her knee rubbed against the side of his for the fourth time. She hoped he didn't think she was doing it deliberately.

"It's close quarters in here." Seth offered the excuse, but the light glinting in his blue eyes made her feel hot.

"Yes, it is." Abbie opened her menu to study it intently. Maybe if she sat perfectly still and didn't move, it wouldn't be so bad.

"What are you going to have?" he asked as he spread open his menu.

"A chef's salad, I think." Her stomach wasn't behaving too well. She didn't want to put a lot of food into it. "How about you?"

But when she looked up, his gaze was making a leisurely survey of her upper body and appearing to take particular note of the hint of maturely rounded breasts under the loose-fitting dress. It was the look of a man, and a hundred alarm bells rang in her ears.

"Are you on a diet?" Seth finally lifted his gaze to her face. "It's just one man's opinion, but I don't see how you can improve on your figure."

In the first place, she wasn't sure if he should notice such things, and she definitely felt he shouldn't comment on them if he did. But how on earth did you reprimand a minister? Abbie preferred to believe she had misinterpreted his glance. Maybe it had been more analytical and less intimate.

"I don't like to eat a lot of food on a hot day like today." She chose to explain away her lack of appetite.

"That's probably very wise," he agreed. When the waitress came, Seth ordered for both of them. At the last minute, Abbie remembered she had promised to bring her father a sandwich.

"I'll need a cold roast-beef sandwich to go, too, please," she added hastily, then explained to Seth when the waitress left, "My father was tied up and couldn't get away for lunch."

"He's an attorney here?"

"Yes. It's just a small practice. He keeps talking about retiring but he won't. He loves what he's doing too much." It seemed easier to talk about her father than the other choice of subjects open to her—like the weather. "Although he does complain that his practice interferes with his fishing," she added with a laughing smile.

"He's an avid fisherman, I take it." Seth smiled.

"Very avid," Abbie agreed, and couldn't help thinking that Seth was a "Fisher of Men."

"I didn't have a chance to meet him last Sunday at the tea. I'm looking forward to it, though," he said. "How long have you worked for him?"

"About a year now." Abbie leaned back in her chair when the waitress returned to set a glass of iced tea in front of her and milk for Seth. The action accidentally pressed more of her leg against his.

"Don't worry," he murmured on a seductively low-pitched note. "I'm not going to think you're playing footsy with me under the table." Abbie was positive she had never blushed in her life, but her cheeks were on fire at the moment. Her mind was absolutely blank of anything to say. Seth seemed to guess and asked, "What did you do before that? Attend college?"

"No, I worked for TWA in Kansas City." She was relieved to have the subject changed.

"As a stewardess?"

"No, I was in management, in the corporate offices."

His attention deepened. Abbie braced herself for the next question, fully anticipating that he was going to ask why she had left, but it never came. There was only the quiet study of his keen eyes.

"Thomas Wolfe was obviously wrong. It is

possible to go home again," was the only comment he made.

"I'm just a small-town girl at heart," she admitted.

Just as the waitress came with their luncheon order, a local judge paused by their table. Abbie had known Judge Sessions since she was a small child, so she wasn't surprised by his greeting when he noticed her.

"Hi there, little girl. How are you doing today?" He grabbed a lock of copper hair and tugged at it affectionately.

"I'm doing just fine, Judge." She smiled up at him.

His glance went to Seth, sitting opposite from her. "Who's this with you? A new man friend?" His teasing demand was accompanied by a broad wink.

"No, of course not." Abbie denied this quickly, conscious that Seth was already rising to be introduced. "This is the new minister of our church, Reverend Seth Talbot. Reverend, I'd like you to meet Judge Sessions, a family friend."

"Reverend?" The judge almost did a double take, then shook Seth's hand and laughed. "You could have fooled me!"

"I seem to fool a lot of people," Seth admitted with a brief glance at Abbie.

"You do look more like a man of the flesh than a man of the cloth," the judge stated.

"I'm the usual combination of both," Seth replied, not at all bothered by the remark.

Abbie thought the judge's description was very accurate. Seth was made of flesh and blood, all hard, male sinew and bone. Not even the cloth could conceal that.

"I'm glad to hear it." The judge nodded. "We need a change from sanctimonious old fogies, too old to sin anymore." He laid a hand on Abbie's shoulder. "Be nice to this little girl here. They don't come any better than Abbie." Then he was moving away from their table with a farewell wave of his hand.

This time it was Seth who brushed his knee against hers when he sat down. Abbie wondered if she wouldn't feel more relaxed if it weren't for this constant physical contact with him. Her skirt had inched up above her knees, but it was impossible to pull it down without touching him. He couldn't see it, not with the table in the way, so she made no attempt to adjust it downward.

"Have you known the judge long?" Seth asked as he picked up his silverware to begin eating his chicken-fried steak with gravy smothered over it and the mound of mashed potatoes.

"Practically all my life." She stabbed a piece of lettuce and sliced ham with her fork. "It's not surprising that people are taken aback when they find out you're a minister. You really should wear your collar, so they'll at least have some advance warning."

If he'd been wearing it, the judge wouldn't have assumed he was her boyfriend, and the girls at the bank wouldn't have been lusting over him—and maybe she would feel a little safer.

The last seemed silly, yet Abbie felt the collar would provide some sort of protection for her.

"Do you have any idea how those stiff collars chafe your neck on a hot day like this?" Seth appeared amused by her comment.

"I'm sorry. I didn't mean to criticize the way you're dressed." It had been a very rude thing to do—as well as presumptuous.

"It doesn't matter." His wide shoulders were lifted in a careless shrug. There was a dancing light in his eyes when he looked at her. "I promise you that I do wear it when I make my rounds at the hospital or call on a member of the congregation in their home."

"In some ways, this is a very conservative community. I guess that's what I'm trying to say," Abbie murmured. And he seemed liberal and at the age to know about sin, as the judge had suggested.

"Right in the heart of the Bible Belt area, I know." He nodded.

She glanced at him sharply to see if there was any mockery in his expression, but it was impossible to tell. Her gaze wandered downward to the white of his shirt. With the top three buttons unfastened, she had a glimpse of curly gold chest hairs, another example of his blatant masculinity. There was a chain of some sort around his neck, too.

"Something wrong?" Seth caught her staring, and amusement deepened the edges of his mouth without materializing into a smile.

Her pulse did a quick acceleration as Abbie

dived her fork into the salad again. "You just don't look like a minister." She sighed the admission. His latent sensuality was too unnerving for her.

His low chuckle vibrated over her tingling nerve ends. "Let's see . . . what would laymen expect a minister to look like?" he mused. "I imagine there are different categories. The intensely pious should be pale, ascetically slender, with deep-set eyes, hollow cheeks, and a fervid voice. There'd be the benevolent father figure— white hair, a round face, and a kindly air. And you have the thunderer, preaching about the wrath of God and pointing out the sinners with a long accusing finger. He'd have a beard, be very tall, with beetle brows." Seth paused to send a mocking glance across the table. "How am I doing so far?"

"I guess I've been guilty of type-casting," Abbie admitted with a faint smile.

"Everyone does it," he assured her. "Now, my idea of a legal secretary is a woman in her forties with her hair pulled back in a severe bun. She'd wear wire-rimmed glasses and tailored business suits." His glance skimmed her again. "Funny, you don't look like a legal secretary."

She laughed naturally for the first time. "I promise I won't say it again, Reverend." Inside, Abbie knew she'd think it each time she referred to him by his professional title.

"I've finally made you laugh." His gaze focused on the parted curve of her lips. She felt them tremble from the look that was oddly physical. "We've cleared the first hurdle," Seth murmured enigmatically.

"To what?" Her voice sounded breathless.

"To becoming friends," he replied.

"Oh." For some reason, Abbie was disappointed by his answer. She ate a few more mouthfuls of salad but found it tasteless. She couldn't stop being conscious of the warmth of his leg against hers, and the rough texture of the denim material brushing the bareness of her calf. It became imperative to keep a conversation going. "Are you all moved in to the parsonage?"

"More or less. I still have a lot of boxes of books to unpack." There was a rueful slant to his mouth as he glanced at her. "Have you ever been in it?"

"No." The slight shake of her head swayed the ends of her pale copper hair.

"It's a rambling monstrosity. There's more rooms there than I'll ever use. I'll probably close up half of the house."

"I imagine it was intended for a family to live in rather than a single man," Abbie suggested.

"It's practically an unwritten rule. A man is supposed to have his wife picked out *before* he graduates from the seminary and is assigned to his first church." Seth didn't appear troubled that he hadn't followed the rule.

"But you didn't." She stated the obvious.

"No, I didn't," he agreed, and let his gaze lock on to hers.

Her throat muscles tightened. "I guess it is the expected thing—for a minister to be married, I mean," Abbie finally managed to get the words out. "How long have you been in the ministry?" She guessed his age to be somewhere in the range of thirty-five.

"Thirteen years. I spent four of those years as an air-force chaplain." He dropped his gaze and began slicing off a piece of steak.

"Where was your first church?" She gave in to her curiosity and began delving into his background.

"This is my first church," he admitted.

"You mean, you were always an assistant pastor before?" A slight frown of confusion creased her forehead.

"No. I worked in the national offices of the church. My work was more business-oriented than anything else." There was a sardonic curve to his mouth. "For a variety of reasons, I requested to be assigned a church in some quiet little community. I guess I'm taking something like a sabbatical."

"I see," she murmured.

"I doubt it." He showed a bit of cynical skepticism, then hid it. "But it isn't important." His glance suddenly challenged her. "Why is it that *you* aren't married, Miss Scott?"

Her mouth opened and closed twice before she could think of a safe answer. She laughed shortly to conceal her hesitation. "Grandmother Klein says it's because I haven't looked hard enough."

"Or maybe you've been looking in all the wrong places," Seth suggested.

It was on the tip of her tongue to ask him where the right places were, but Abbie resisted the impulse. "Maybe," she conceded, and stirred the half-eaten salad with her fork. Absently she glanced at the slim, gold watch around her wrist. Her eyes widened when she saw the time. "It's after one. I have to get back to the office." She laid her napkin alongside the salad plate and reached for the luncheon check the waitress had left, but Seth was quicker. Her hand ended up tangling briefly with his fingers, the contact sending a tingling shock up her arm.

"I'll buy this time," he insisted.

"Please," Abbie protested. "I don't really have time to argue. She opened her purse to take out her money, intending to leave it on the table regardless of what he said.

"You said yourself that you're short on time," Seth reminded her. "If you insist on paying, just put whatever you feel you owe in the collection plate this Sunday."

"I . . . all right." She gave in to his persuasion and refastened the leather flap of her purse.

"Don't forget your father's sandwich." He handed her the paper sack when she started to get up without it.

"Thank you." She gratefully took it from him. It was bad enough being late without her father having to go hungry, too.

"See you Sunday."

The walk to her father's office seemed longer

than it was. Abbie suspected it was because she was late and trying to hurry so she wouldn't be later than she was already. Her father was a tolerant, easygoing man, but he was a stickler for punctuality.

When she walked in, the door to his private office was closed, but she could hear muffled conversation within. His one o'clock appointment had obviously arrived. Abbie hurried to her desk, returning her purse to the lower drawer and setting his sandwich atop her desk. She swiveled her chair to the typewriter and picked up the headset to the dictaphone. Before she had it comfortably adjusted so she could hear, his door opened.

Abbie saw his irritation as he approached her desk. "I left a file on your desk." He picked up a folder from the IN tray.

"Here's your sandwich." She handed him the sack.

"I'm surprised you remembered. What kept you?"

"I had lunch with Reverend Talbot." She knew the judge would mention it if she didn't. Besides, keeping it a secret would only mean there was something to hide. "The time just slipped away."

He harumphed but didn't comment. Instead he opened the sack to peer inside. "Roast beef?"

"Yes."

There was a relenting of his stern expression. "At least you brought back my favorite."

Chapter Four

There were more people at church than Abbie remembered seeing in a long time, especially since it wasn't Easter or Christmas. A lot of it, she guessed, was curiosity about the new minister. Seth made a striking figure standing at the pulpit in his robe while he conducted the services.

He was halfway through his sermon before Abbie realized he wasn't using a microphone, yet his well-modulated voice carried his words effortlessly to the back row. He talked easily, as if he was carrying on a conversation instead of giving a sermon. His gestures were natural rather than dramatic. There were even places where the congregation laughed at a bit of humor that contained a message.

It seemed that Seth had barely begun when he finished. Abbie would have liked him to go on, and it was the first time she could ever remember wishing a sermon had been longer. She stole a glance at her parents sitting in the pew beside her. Her father was looking at his watch with a stunned expression, while her mother continued to give her rapt attention to the man at the pulpit.

A few minutes later, they were following the people filing out of church. The line moved slowly as those ahead of them paused to shake hands with the minister on their way out the door.

Her father leaned sideways to murmur, "Your reverend isn't bad, Abbie."

"He's not *my* reverend, Dad," she corrected in an equally low voice, not liking the insinuation that she was somehow linked to Seth simply because she'd had lunch with him once.

"If you say so." He shrugged, letting her move ahead of him as it became a single-file line to greet Seth.

Abbie waited patiently for her turn, a ripple of anticipation warming her blood while she watched Seth chatting with the couple ahead of her. The black robe seemed to make his hair look darker, more brown than gold, but the trappings of the clergy didn't alter his male appeal.

His glance strayed to her and lingered briefly in recognition. The vivid blue of his eyes darkened with a glow that made her feel special. The look tripped her heartbeat but Abbie refused to flatter herself into believing it held any significance. She was just a familiar face, someone he knew after meeting so many strangers.

The exchange of glances lasted only a few seconds before his attention reverted to the couple. Then they were moving down the steps and it was Abbie's turn. Close up, Seth seemed taller, more commanding in his black robe. His hand reached to take hers in greeting and continued to hold it when Abbie would have withdrawn it.

"What's the verdict?" There was warm, mocking amusement in the downward glance that took in his preaching robes. "Will I pass?" He was teasing her about the way she had criticized him about his dress at lunch that day.

"Yes." The corners of her mouth dimpled with a responding smile. "And you *sounded* like a minister, too, Reverend."

His head was tipped back to release a throaty laugh. Its volume was subdued, but no less genuine. Seth inclined his head to her in mocking acknowledgment. "That's the highest compliment I've received today. I thank you, Miss Scott."

"You're welcome, Reverend." She would have moved on, but his firm grip wouldn't relinquish her hand. There was uncertain confusion in the look she gave him, but his attention had swerved to her parents.

"Is this your father?" Seth inquired in a tone that prompted her to make the introduction.

"Yes. I'd like you to meet him." Only when she spoke to indicate her compliance with his unspoken request did Seth release her hand. "Dad, this is Reverend Talbot. Reverend, my father, Drew Scott. You've met my mother already."

"Yes, I have." He nodded, shaking her hand.

"It's good to see you again, Mrs. Scott. And it's a pleasure to meet your husband. How do you do, Mr. Scott."

"I've been looking forward to meeting you, Reverend," her father admitted. "Enjoyed your sermon."

"I understand you're a fisherman." Seth didn't mention that Abbie had been the source of that information, but her father guessed it. "Maybe you can point me to some good fishing holes around here later on."

"Be happy to," her father agreed, then added a qualification, "as long as you make sure the next time you take my secretary out to lunch, she's not late getting back."

"Daddy." It was a low, impatient protest Abbie made. He made it sound like she was likely to have lunch with Seth again.

But Seth wasn't bothered by the implication. "You have a deal, Mr. Scott."

There were still more people behind them waiting to leave the church. Abbie was relieved when her parents moved past Seth to descend the steps with her. Not all the congregation had dispersed once they left the church. Some were scattered along the wide sidewalk, socializing in small groups. Her parents were too well known to go directly to their car without being stopped by someone. Since Abbie had ridden with them, she was obliged to linger on the fringes each time her father or mother paused to speak to someone.

Her glance invariably wandered back to the

church doors. She recognized Fran Bigsby when she came out with her two small children. There was no sign of her husband as the bleached blonde stopped to talk to Seth. Flirt with him seemed a better description, Abbie thought cattily. There was no sign of Fran's husband but she noticed her younger sister, Marjorie, was with her.

Suddenly, Abbie realized there were a lot of women that had attended the morning service without their husbands, especially those families who weren't regular worshipers. She didn't like the conclusion she was reaching because she had the unkind suspicion they hadn't been drawn there today to welcome their new minister, but rather to meet the handsome bachelor-pastor the whole town was buzzing about.

It made her silent, and more than just a little thoughtful, while she studied her own motives. No matter how she tried, Abbie couldn't ignore the fact that she was strongly attracted to him on a physical level. She was living in a glass house and couldn't very well afford to throw stones at anyone else.

Abbie glanced at the clock as she rolled the finished letter out of the typewriter. It was close to noon, time enough to type an envelope and have the letter ready to mail before she left for lunch. It was Thursday, exactly a week to the day since she'd lunched with Seth.

The knowledge must have been hovering at the back of her mind, because when she heard the street door open, her heart did a little somersault. She turned, expecting to see Seth walking into the office. But Judge Sessions didn't look like him at all. It was difficult to keep her smile from dying.

"Hello, Judge." Abbie forced the cheerfulness into her voice. "Dad's in his office. You can go in, if you want. He doesn't have a client with him."

"Maybe I didn't come to see him," he challenged lightly. "Maybe I'm here to see you."

"It's possible, but I doubt it." Now that she had gotten over her initial disappointment, Abbie could respond more naturally to the judge's teasing remarks.

Her father stepped out of his private office. "I thought I heard you out here, Walter," he accused, and crossed to exchange a back slapping handshake. "What are you doing, you old crook?"

"I came to take my favorite father-daughter pair to lunch," the judge replied, then slid Abbie a glittering look. "That is, if your daughter doesn't have a previous luncheon date?"

"I believe I have a vacancy in my social calendar today," she replied, laughing.

"You could have been saving all your free time for that handsome new reverend," the judge suggested. "When are you going to see him again?"

Abbie was beginning to lose her humor at his probing remarks. "Probably Sunday at church just like everyone else," she retorted with a trace of coolness. "Just because I had lunch with him once, purely by accident, it doesn't mean it's going to become a regular event."

"Drew, I think the girl's sick," the judge declared. "She's trying to claim she's not interested in this fellow."

"I'm not," Abbie protested, and wanted to bite her tongue for telling such an outright lie.

"What makes you different from all the rest of the women in town?" He challenged her with a disbelieving look. "From what I've heard, they're falling all over themselves trying to get his attention."

"Is that a fact?" her father inserted, siding with the judge to gang up on Abbie. "All the gossip manages to get funneled to you, Walter. Why don't you let us in on it?"

"I understand that his cup runneth over. The older ladies are bringing him casseroles, cakes, salads, cookies, homemade bread, and just about anything else you care to mention. There isn't a bare shelf in his refrigerator or cupboard."

"I think that's nice," Abbie insisted in defense of the gifts. "It's the neighborly thing to do when a newcomer moves in."

"But those old ladies are wise." The judge winked slyly. "The way to a man's heart is through his stomach. Haven't you heard?"

"Come to think of it, Alice baked him a green-apple pie just this last Tuesday," Drew recalled. "Maybe I'd better keep a closer eye on my wife. She was at the parsonage for almost an hour."

"Dad, you can't be jealous of the reverend."

Abbie wasn't sure if he was serious or just razzing her.

"I don't mind if she looks . . . as long as that's all she does," he said, then laughed to show he wasn't worried.

"It seems there are a lot of young wives who have suddenly discovered they have marital problems, which came as quite a surprise to their contented husbands . . ." the judge inserted. ". . . and now they're going to the good reverend for his advice and understanding."

Abbie had the uneasy feeling that Fran Bigsby was probably one of them. She saw the point the judge was making. It was all a ruse to get Seth's undivided attention, to try to attract his interest.

"But it's more than his sympathy they're after," her father added, confirming Abbie's private thoughts.

"Women are volunteering right and left to help with anything from typing the church bulletins to doing his housekeeping." The judge gave an exaggerated sigh and looked at her father. "And they say a bachelor's life is a lonely one. One crook of his little finger and half the women in the county would come running. I'll bet the church will be filled to the rafters next Sunday."

"I wouldn't be surprised," her father agreed with this summation.

That's when Abbie made the decision that she wouldn't be one of them. She didn't want Seth to get the impression she was chasing him just like all the other women in town seemed to be. She didn't necessarily attend church every single

Sunday, so it wouldn't be out of the ordinary for her to skip a couple of weeks.

She was very casual about it when she talked to her mother on Saturday and mentioned that she was going to visit Grandmother Klein on Sunday and skip church. Her mother took Abbie's decision at face value. Her father gave her a strange look but said nothing.

On Monday morning, Abbie didn't have a chance to make the first pot of coffee before the street door opened and the two Coltrain sisters came bustling in. They always seemed to wear outfits that clashed with what the other one was wearing. Esther had on a brightly flowered dress, predominantly grape-colored, while Isabel wore a gaudy, fushia-pink dress.

"There you are, Abbie!" Esther declared happily. The fluorescent lights in the office seemed to reflect the grape from her dress and cast a lavender tint on her curling white hair. "We thought we might find you here at your papa's office."

"Yes, I work here during the week," Abbie explained, certain she had told them that before.

But neither of them had ever worked. They had been raised to believe women should stay in the home, married or not. Luckily the inheritance from their parents had left them with substantial annuities so they could.

Isabel opened her enormous black tapestry bag with its bold pink-rose design, and pulled out a stack of loose papers in assorted sizes and colors. A slim rubber band strained to hold them together.

"We were going to give you this yesterday at church but you didn't come," Isabel explained.

"What is it?" Abbie reached for it with a puzzled frown.

"Don't you remember?" Esther looked stricken. "You said you'd type our manuscript for us."

"Do you mean you've written it already?" Abbie looked up from the first piece of paper, filled with scrawly handwriting, to stare incredulously at the two sisters.

"Oh, goodness no!" Isabel laughed merrily at the thought. "We decided it would be easier if we gave you what we had finished as we went along."

"Haven't we gotten a lot done?" Esther asked excitedly. "We worked on it every single day, didn't we, Isabel?"

"It was so much fun, Abbie," Isabel declared, puffing up with proud satisfaction. "I'm so glad the reverend suggested it."

"I can imagine." Abbie couldn't recall when she had seen either sister so animated or so enthused. It was contagious. She felt herself catching their excitement too, and smiling right along with them.

"I do hope you won't have any trouble reading it." Isabel cupped a hand to her mouth to whisper secretively to Abbie. "Esther used to have such beautiful penmanship, but with her arthritis it's sometimes not very legible."

"I don't think I'll have any difficulty. But if I have any questions on a particular part, I'll call and ask," she promised.

"We aren't telling anyone what we're doing." Esther put a protective hand over the uncompleted manuscript Abbie was holding. "You're the only one who knows."

"I won't breathe a word." Abbie crossed her heart in a child's solemn promise. "In fact, I'll put it in the bottom drawer of my desk right now."

"You won't lose it." Isabel looked worried as Abbie walked to her desk to put the handwritten papers away.

"Call us as soon as you have it typed," Esther advised. "We'll have some more ready for you." She took her sister's arm. "Come, Isabel. Let's go home so we can start on the next part."

"Bye!" Abbie called as the two white-haired sisters bustled toward the door. "I'll phone you when I'm through with this."

That evening was the start of what became a nightly routine, with her portable typewriter sitting on the small dining-room table in her apartment and the pages of the manuscript setting out. The Coltrain sisters had used everything from yellow tablet paper to fancy stationery to write on. Abbie quickly discovered that the page numbers on the sheets were not necessarily correct. More often than not, they were out of sequence.

Before she could start typing, she had to decipher the handwriting and read and arrange the pages in their proper order. She had expected the manuscript to be a collection of loosely connected anecdotes of their early years and stories of some of the area's first citizens. Abbie was shocked to realize the sisters had fictionalized it into a story—a rather torrid, period romance set in Eureka Springs around the turn of the century.

Each night, Abbie sat down to the typewriter for three hours, correcting misspelled words, or finding the right one when a sister had fallen victim to malapropism, and inserting the right punctuation where none existed. It was a long, tedious process, made fascinating by the characters and stories she remembered the sisters telling as they became part of the plot. Just when she became used to reading Esther's handwriting and could get some typing speed, the next part would be written by Isabel and she'd have to slow down again.

The typing gave her a perfect excuse to miss church that Sunday, and the sisters had more written when Abbie finished the first installment. She missed the following Sunday's service as well.

The long days, working at the office and in her apartment on the nights and weekends, were beginning to wear on her. Abbie was dragging Monday morning when she arrived at the office. She was leaning on the table, waiting for the coffee to finish dripping. Her father walked out of his office, carrying his cup, just as she was in the middle of a large yawn.

"You can't keep this up, Abbie." He shook his head at her. "You need to get out and have some fun. I hear you hammering away at that typewriter every night."

"I'll take tonight off, Dad," Abbie promised, and tried to swallow another yawn.

"Not just tonight," he advised. "You take a couple or three nights off. Go to a movie—or ask some guy for a date. These are liberated times. You don't have to wait for a Sadie Hawkins' Day."

"Yes, Dad." She smiled wryly, because there wasn't anyone she was interested in asking—except Seth. She shook away that thought. The red light blinked on to indicate the coffee was done. "Coffee's ready."

"I've just got time for a quick cup, then I have to get over to the courthouse," he said with a quick glance at his watch.

By the time her father left, Abbie had drunk her first cup of coffee and felt that at least her eyes were open. She poured a second cup and sat down at her desk to see what dictation had been left for her to type. The more she thought about her father's suggestion, the more convinced she became that he was right. It was to the point where she was typing in her dreams.

When she heard someone enter the office, Abbie tried to summon a suitably cheerful smile to greet him. But the "him" was Seth Talbot.

Her hazel-green eyes widened in surprise, and she was suddenly very much awake.

In the past three weeks, she'd only had occasional glimpses of him behind the wheel of his dark green sports car. But here he was—in the flesh—and her pulse started fluttering crazily. As Seth approached her desk, so tall and lean and flashing her that white smile, Abbie felt weak at the knees. The whiteness of his clergyman's collar contrasted sharply with his darkly tanned neck, but her senses didn't have any respect for his attire. They were all reacting to his raw manliness, his roughly chiseled features, and deeply blue eyes.

"Hello, Reverend." Abbie was amazed that she sounded so calm.

"Good morning." His eyes crinkled at the corners, partially concealing the intensity of his scanning gaze as it swept over her. "How are you?"

"Fine." She nodded. It seemed logical to assume it was her father he came to see, so Abbie explained. "I'm sorry but my father is out of the office just now. I expect him back around noon."

"I'm not here on a legal matter." Seth corrected her thinking. "I came by to see you." He said it so casually, yet her reaction was anything but. A heady kind of excitement tingled through her nerves, while a breathlessness attacked her lungs.

"Oh?" She tipped her head to the side at an inquiring angle, her pale copper hair swinging free.

"I haven't seen you in church lately," he said. "I thought I would stop to see if there was anything wrong."

"Ah." Abbie nodded her head in bitter understanding. "The shepherd is out looking for the sheep that strayed from his flock, is that it?"

There was a slight narrowing of his gaze at the bite in her voice. "Something like that, yes," Seth admitted. "I miss having an honest critic in the congregation. If I say or do something you don't like, I know you'll tell me about it. You aren't the type to flatter my ego."

But he was flattering hers by trying to make her believe it mattered to him whether she was there or not. Except that was his job, to persuade members to attend church regularly.

"I'm sure you know how it is." Abbie shrugged. "A person goes to bed on Saturday night with the best intentions but somehow doesn't make it up in time for church the next day." The wryness in her smile was caused by many things. "I warned you I wasn't one of the truly faithful."

"And I warned you that I'd bring you back into the fold," Seth reminded her with a crooked slant to his mouth.

"So you did. Okay, I promise to be at church this Sunday. Is that good enough?" She didn't want him to do any arm twisting. If she spent too much time in his company, she was afraid he might guess that she was no different from any of the other women in town, attracted to him as a man.

"That was easy." He appeared to regard her quick capitulation with a degree of curiosity.

"'Ask and ye shall receive,'" Abbie quoted.

"That's an offer I'm not going to turn down," Seth replied as the corners of his mouth deepened in a faint smile. "Would you be willing to do some typing for me?"

"I understood you had a lot of volunteers," she countered.

"Ah, but not necessarily volunteers who can type," he explained with a mocking look. "Or maybe I should say—who can type with more than one finger."

"I'd like to help you out but I've already agreed to type a manuscript for—someone else." She kept the Coltrain sisters' authorship to herself, as they had requested. "Between doing that at nights and working here during the day, I don't have time to do any more."

"It sounds like all work and no play."

"It has been hectic," Abbie admitted, but refused to feel sorry for herself. "But I'm treating myself to a night off this evening."

"Do you have a date?"

In a small community like this, there was no point in lying. If she claimed to have a date, she'd have to produce one or be caught out. "No," she answered indifferently to show it didn't matter.

"Good. Then how about having dinner with me?" Seth invited, and leaned both hands on the front of her desk.

It was the last thing Abbie had expected. She

was so tempted to accept but—she shook her head. "Thanks but I was really planning to have a quiet evening and an early night."

"That's no problem. We'll have dinner and I'll bring you straight home so you can have a restful evening," he reasoned. "What do you like? Mexican food? Pizza? Steak?"

It was so hard to refuse. "I don't think you heard me," she said weakly.

"I'll wear my collar tonight—just for you," Seth mocked.

Abbie took a deep breath and held it a second. "You don't understand what it's like living in a small community like this, Reverend." She sighed. "If I had dinner with you tonight, by tomorrow morning, rumor would have it all over town that we're having an affair."

"So?" he challenged.

She wished he wasn't so close. Even with the desk separating them, the way he was leaning on it brought him much nearer. She could even smell the tangy fragrance of his after-shave lotion.

"So—you're a minister." Abbie wondered why she was reminding him. "And a bachelor. You can't afford to have that kind of talk going around."

"Empty talk can't hurt me." He hunched his shoulders in an indifferent shrug without changing his position. "It doesn't bother me, so you shouldn't let it bother you."

Abbie had run out of arguments. "It doesn't."

"Then you'll have dinner with me," Seth concluded.

"Pizza." The atmosphere at a pizza parlor would be more casual, invite less intimacy. Plus there wouldn't be any lingering after the meal. It seemed the safest choice all around.

"I'll pick you up at six-thirty. Is that all right?"

"Yes, that's fine." Abbie nodded, certain that she had lost her senses completely. "Do you know where I live?"

"Yes. Your address is in the membership files," he said, indicating he'd already checked. Deliberately or just as a matter of course, Abbie didn't know.

"It's probably my parents' address that's listed. I live in the apartment above the garage," she explained.

Seth straightened from her desk. "I lived in a garret when I was attending the seminary. My friends and I had some good times there."

"I like it," Abbie murmured in response.

"I won't keep you from your work any longer," he said. "I don't want to get into any more trouble with your father over that." But he was smiling in a way that belied his expression of concern. "I'll see you tonight."

"Yes." Abbie just hoped that she knew what she was doing.

Chapter Five

At ten after five that afternoon, Abbie was clearing her desk to leave. Her father stepped out of his office, a pair of reading glasses sitting low on his nose and a letter in his hand.

"I've changed my mind about the way I want this letter worded, Abbie. I'll need to have you retype it," he said, hardly paying any attention to what she was doing.

"You don't have to have it yet this afternoon, do you?" she asked hopefully. "It's already after five."

He bent his wrist to look at his watch. "I hadn't realized it was that late already. You don't mind staying a few more minutes while I reword this. There's no reason for you to rush home."

"As a matter of fact there is," Abbie admitted. "I have a date."

He took off his glasses to look at her. "Since when?" He was surprised. "Don't tell me you took my advice and asked a man out?"

"No." She wasn't quite *that* liberated. "Reverend Talbot stopped by this morning. He invited me to go out and have a pizza with him tonight."

"Reverend Talbot." He repeated the name with curious emphasis. "My, my."

Abbie knew that tone of voice. It always preceded a cross-examination to determine her degree of interest in a particular date.

"Dad, we're just going out for a pizza," Abbie cautioned him not to blow it out of all proportion. It was good advice for herself as well.

"I guess the letter can wait . . . just as long as you retype it first thing in the morning," he decided, and didn't pursue the discussion of her evening date.

"Thanks." Abbie waved him a kiss as she hurried out of the office to her car.

On the surface, it would have seemed more practical to ride back and forth to work with her father, but he was an early riser, often arriving at the office to work at four or five in the morning, when it was quiet and there were no interruptions. Abbie didn't need to be there until the office opened at nine, so she usually drove Mabel.

Mabel grunted her way through the traffic and grumbled up the winding street to Abbie's home. Abbie only had an hour before Seth arrived, and she used every minute of it. While the bathtub filled with water, she ran a dust cloth over the furniture and picked up the clutter of magazines and newspapers.

A quick bath and Abbie was faced with the

impossible decision of what to wear. Nothing seemed exactly appropriate. Her outfits were either too tight, or possibly too revealing, or too plain. Finally she settled on a pair of white jeans and a velour top in a rich kelly-green. Its V-neckline plunged a little. She'd have to remember to sit up straight.

She was just running a brush through her hair when she heard the roar of the sports car's motor coming up the drive. In her haste, she accidentally hooked the bristles in the gold hoop of her earring, giving her ear a painful tug.

"Ouch!" It was a soft, involuntary cry, interrupted by the sound of footsteps on the stairs.

Hurrying out of the bathroom, Abbie reached the door just as he knocked. She opened it, intending to leave with him immediately, but Seth walked in.

"I'm a couple of minutes early. I hope you don't mind," he said, and turned to look at Abbie still holding the door open.

"No, that's all right. I'm ready." She noticed he was wearing his collar. It just peeped over the light blue of his windbreaker.

"This is nice." His glance made an assessing sweep of her apartment. "I wish I had this and you lived in the parsonage." A frown flickered across her face as Abbie wondered whether a minister should be making such comments. Seth read her look, a smile slanting his masculine mouth. "Don't worry. I'm not breaking any commandments. I don't really covet your garret."

"I—"

"You weren't sure," he insisted.

"No."

"You might want to bring a scarf." His glance ran over the coppered blond of her hair. "I've got the top down on my car. The wind's likely to mess up your hair."

"Good idea." There was a nervous edge to her smile as she backed away toward the apartment's small bedroom. "It'll just take me a minute to get one."

"There's no rush," Seth replied.

But Abbie thought otherwise. In her bedroom, she rummaged hurriedly through the top dresser drawer until she found the sheer silk scarf with the green and gold print. The green wasn't the same shade as her velour top but it was close enough.

When she came out, Seth was standing by the table with her typewriter, looking at the stack of handwritten pages beside it. His fingertips were resting on the top paper as if marking a line. A thread of apprehension ran tightly through her edgy nerves.

"Is this the manuscript you're typing?" Seth asked, looking up as if sensing her presence in the room.

"Yes." Abbie tried to remember where she'd left off and what the next scene was that he was reading. Some parts of the book were rather racy.

"I'm glad the Coltrain sisters took my advice," he said, glancing back at the page.

"How did you know?" Abbie stared in stunned wonderment.

"I recognized the handwriting." A hint of a smile made indentations at the corners of his mouth. "Isabel sent me a note. No one else writes with all these flourishes and curlicues." A dark brown eyebrow was arched in query. "Why? Is their identity supposed to be a secret?"

"They asked me not to tell about the book," Abbie admitted.

"Their secret is safe with me," Seth assured her with easy amusement. He tapped a finger on the paper. "Judging by this passage, I think I know why they don't want it known."

"Which passage?" Abbie moved anxiously toward the table and stopped cold when Seth began reading it.

"'His hand cupped her breast and Sophia thought she would surely swoon with pleasure.'" The audible gasp from Abbie prompted him to pause at the end of the sentence, his glance going to her.

"The book really has a good plot," Abbie insisted. "You really shouldn't judge it by that little bit. The characters are interesting and they've done wonderful things with the background."

"I'm not judging it." Laughter and something else gleamed in his eyes. "Did you think I was offended by what I read? Or shocked?"

She bit at the inside of her lower lip, flustered and unnerved. "I don't know," she murmured.

"It can't be your normal reading." Her glance strayed unconsciously to his collar.

"For pleasure, I read mysteries." There was a mocking gleam in his eyes. "Travis McGee is one of my favorite characters. He's had his share of love scenes."

"Oh." Abbie didn't want to pursue this discussion of love and human passions. Sex was the word she was avoiding. She was too conscious they were alone in her apartment. How long had he been up here? Five minutes? Ten? What if her mother or one of the neighbors had noticed? "Maybe we'd better be going," Abbie suggested, clutching the scarf tightly in her hand.

"Of course," he agreed, but amusement continued to lurk in his expression as he followed her to the door. Abbie was conscious of the blue study of his eyes. "How long has it been since you've had a man in your apartment?" Seth asked, just as they reached the door to the stairwell.

She was startled into turning. "Not since—" Abbie almost said, not since she broke up with Jim, but there wasn't any reason to be so specific. "Not for quite a while," she answered instead, and took the door key from her purse.

"I thought you seemed ill at ease." Seth waited at the top of the steps while she locked the door. "Not many people do that around here," he observed, then explained, "Lock their doors when they leave."

"It's a habit left over from living in the city,"

she admitted as she returned the key to her purse and moved to the stairs to join him.

It was a wide stairwell, wide enough for both of them to descend side by side. The touch of his hand on the back of her waist almost stopped Abbie, not quite ready for such casual familiarity. Its warmth electrified her nerve ends and made her overly conscious of his masculine form, lean, muscled, and tall next to her. He didn't take his hand away when they reached the bottom, remaining to guide her to the passenger side of the car. Then Seth moved ahead to open the car door for her.

"Sometimes the latch is stubborn." He used the inside door handle to open it and waited while she climbed in, then pushed it securely shut.

It was a small car, the bucket seats set closely together and a stick shift on the floorboard between them. The close quarters were made even more so when Seth slid behind the wheel, his shoulder nearly touching hers. Abbie tried to hide her awareness of it by busily tying the scarf under her chin. Seth made no attempt to start the motor until she was finished.

"All set?" he asked. Abbie turned her head to nod affirmatively to him and received the full force of his gaze as he made a thorough study of her face. "Your eyes look more green in that color."

There was a crazy little lurching of her stomach. It was so difficult to keep this friendly outing in perspective that Abbie wished he hadn't noticed the way she looked. Compliments put it on a different level, more personal.

"Thank you . . . Reverend." Abbie needed to establish his profession in her mind and somehow keep it there.

His expression took on a thoughtful quality before he turned his profile to her and started the car. The powerful motor growled instantly to life. His hand closed on the gearshift knob and accidentally brushed her knee when he shifted into reverse.

He laid his arm along the top of her seat back as he partially turned to back the car out of the driveway. His carved features didn't seem to have any expression now. Abbie tried to relax now that all his attention was on driving.

The roar of the engine and the wind generated by the car's motion fairly well negated any attempt at conversation. Abbie kept her eyes to the front and her knees out of the way of his constant gearshifting.

The low-built sports car zipped down the winding, tree-shaded streets that *never* crossed at right angles with another. Throughout the hillside town, there were miles of gray stone walls to terrace and hold the steeply sloping earth. Seth avoided the business route through the historic downtown area and turned east on the main highway.

When they arrived at the pizza parlor, the parking lot was relatively full, but there were two empty tables inside. Seth directed her to the one secluded in a quiet corner. Abbie was undecided whether he had chosen it for the privacy it afforded or to avoid being noticed, aware that there was only a fine difference between the two reasons, but a telling one.

There were four chairs around the red-checkered cloth-topped table. After Abbie was seated, Seth pulled out the chair on her right for himself. Once they had ordered, Seth began talking. Before she knew it, there was an easy flow of conversation between them. She stopped being so self-conscious with him and began responding to his friendly manner.

"You can have the last slice of pizza, Abbie." Seth pushed the cardboard circle toward her but she leaned back from the table, shaking her head in refusal.

"I'm so stuffed I can't eat another bite, Reverend," she insisted. "It was really good, though. Thank you."

"You're welcome." He accepted with a mocking tip of his head. "Would you like anything else, Abbie? Another soft drink?"

"No." She reached for her glass, a third full yet. "I have plenty."

There was a moment of silence as he watched her take a sip of the cola through the plastic straw. His glance slid from her mouth to her eyes when she looked up.

"You don't go out much socially do you, Abbie?" It was in the way of an observation more than a question.

She nervously stirred the ice in her drink with the straw. "As much as I want." Abbie defended her lack of an active social life, quietly insisting it was by choice.

"What about close friends?" he asked.

"I was gone for four years and you sort of lose touch," she admitted. "Most of them are married now, with their own families to look after, or else they've moved away. But I'm not lonely, Reverend." She wanted that clear because she didn't want him feeling sorry for her. "I guess I like my own company." She made light of it with a quick smile.

"Or you're just not ready to commit yourself to a close relationship so soon after breaking up with that man in Kansas City," he suggested.

Abbie went a little white. "How did you know about Jim?"

"I could pretend that I was only guessing you'd been hurt recently by a man," Seth replied with a half-shrug. "I suspected it but—in a small town—you find out anyway. Were you very much in love with him?"

"No. I thought I was." She set the glass on the table, her tension growing. It was something she hadn't discussed with anyone. She wasn't sure if she wanted to tell him about it either. Actually there was very little to tell. "But I got over him too quickly, so I guess it wasn't the 'real' thing."

"What happened?"

"Nothing." Abbie discovered a twisted humor in the very appropriate answer. "I was ready to get serious and he wasn't. It was a relationship that had nowhere to go and nothing to keep it going, so it ended."

"I'm glad there aren't any lasting scars." His look was gentle yet contained a certain strength. Loud, laughing voices came from the front of the pizza parlor where there were young people standing. Seth glanced their way, then back to Abbie. "It's beginning to fill up in here. Maybe we should leave so someone can have our table."

Abbie signaled her agreement by pushing her chair back from the table to stand up. His questions concerning her abortive romance kept buzzing around in her mind as they left the restaurant. She began to suspect that was the reason he had invited her out. She had to know, so she wouldn't foolishly think there was another reason.

"Reverend . . ." Abbie slowed her steps when they neared the car. Impatience flickered in his eyes as he paused to meet her steady look. ". . . did you ask me out tonight because you thought I was suffering from a broken heart and needed some consoling?"

A startled frown crossed his forehead. "That never occurred to me, Abbie," he denied, and she doubted that he could have faked that reaction. She felt immensely better, smiling her thanks when he opened the car door for her. He walked around the back of the car and climbed into the driver's side. "I promised to take you straight home, but it looks like we're going to have a beautiful sunset tonight." Seth nodded to the western sky and the pink glow already tinting the clouds. "Would you like to drive up to the lookout and watch it?"

"Yes, I would." Abbie suddenly wasn't in any hurry to go back to her empty apartment.

They weren't far from the lookout point with its overview of Eureka Springs. Its location on the east end of town provided them with the ideal vantage point to observe the glowing colors of sundown.

Seth stopped the car at the farthest edge, facing the west. Turning the ignition off, he combed his fingers through his wind-rumpled hair to restore it to some semblance of order. The hush of twilight seemed to spill over Abbie, the warmth of a summer breeze softly stirring the air. She untied the scarf and let it slide from her hair, while a purpling pink streaked with red painted the horizon.

"It seems too beautiful to be real, doesn't it?" She half glanced at Seth.

"It can be like that," he agreed, and stretched his arm along her seat back. "If an artist tried to put it on canvas, it would look artificial."

"That's true." Abbie realized that her voice was barely above a murmur and laughed softly. "Why are we talking so quietly?"

"Probably because we're the only ones here." Seth smiled. His glance swept the lookout area. "That probably won't be true once it gets dark. This looks like the ideal place for teenagers to park and make out." He tipped his head at Abbie. "Is this where they come?"

"It . . . used to be the local lovers' lane," Abbie admitted, unsettled by the thought.

"Did you ever come here with your boyfriend?" He was mocking her hint of embarrassment.

"A few times, but that was several years ago, Reverend," she replied.

"Will you stop calling me Reverend every time you turn around?" he declared on a note of amused exasperation. "I do have a name, you know. It's Seth."

"I know, Reverend—" she began, suddenly uncertain.

Her pulse rocketed at the silencing finger he placed on her lips. "Seth," he corrected firmly.

She was so tied up in knots she couldn't breathe. He was leaning toward her, his other hand resting on the curve of her shoulder. She felt drawn into the dark aqua depths of his eyes. When his finger slid across her lips in a near caress, a quiver of longing trembled through her.

"Say it," he ordered huskily.

His gaze shifted to her lips to watch them form his name. "Seth," Abbie whispered.

His head bent toward her and she knew instinctively that he was going to kiss her. The tips of his fingers rested lightly along her jaw and the curve of her throat, holding her motionless with no pressure. Excitement danced through her senses, but Abbie willed them to stay under control.

The first brush of his lips was soft and teasing, but they came back to claim her mouth with warm ease. Abbie was hesitant to respond, unwilling to have him discover how much she wanted this, but he coaxed a response from her.

Her lips were clinging to his by the time he finally drew back a few inches to study the result. Slowly her lashes lifted to show the dazed uncertainty of her eyes. Her lips remained slightly parted, melted into softness by his persuasive mouth. She was motionless, but inside she was straining to be closer to him. Abbie was too unsure of herself—and him—to take the initiative. His heavily lidded gaze noted all this with satisfaction.

"Seth?" The rising inflection of her voice put a question mark at the end of his name.

His mouth curved in a compelling smile that seemed to take her breath away. "You've finally got it right, Abbie," Seth murmured, and started to close the distance between them again.

Her lips were moving to meet him halfway when the moment was shattered by the roar of another car approaching the lookout. Abbie abruptly pulled back to cast an anxious glance over her shoulder. His hand came away from the side of her neck and rested on the softness of her upper arm as if he expected her to bolt from the car. The other vehicle wasn't in sight yet, but the roar of its unmuffled engine was coming steadily closer.

Seth hung his head and cursed under a heavy sigh, "Devil damn." Then he was squaring around to place both hands on the wheel.

"What did you say?" Abbie looked at him, her eyes narrowing in bewilderment.

There was a wryness in the sidelong look he sent her. "Devil damn." One corner of his mouth was pulled up. "I had a grandfather who was Danish. Whenever he was upset or angry, that's the expression he used—devil damn or devil damn it. It's much better than breaking a Commandment and taking the Lord's name in vain."

A tremulous smile touched her mouth, inwardly thrilled that he was upset by the interruption. "Yes, it is," Abbie agreed softly.

He held her gaze for a long second that seemed filled with all sorts of heady promises. With another sigh, he reached to turn the key in the ignition just as a car full of teenagers drove into the lookout area.

"I guess I'd better get you home," he said.

While he backed onto the road, Abbie tied the scarf over her hair once more. She felt so good inside that she felt like singing, which of course she didn't do. More than once during the drive home through the back streets, she was conscious of Seth glancing at her. Maybe because she kept stealing looks at him.

Stopping the car in front of the garage, Seth switched off the engine. Abbie waited until he had walked around the car to open her door. He took her hand to help her climb out of the low car.

"I enjoyed myself this evening. Thanks for asking," Abbie said, letting her hand stay in his grasp a moment longer.

"It was *my* pleasure," Seth replied. "I'll walk you to the door."

"There's no need for you to walk me up that flight of steps," she assured him.

"Suit yourself." He shrugged with a mocking look. "I only suggested it because I thought it might bother you if I kissed you good night here—where your parents or the neighbors might see us." When Abbie released a laughing breath of shock at his statement, Seth chuckled and asked, "Would you like to change your mind?"

"It isn't fair to ask a girl that," Abbie protested, because if she said yes, it meant she wanted him to kiss her, and if she said no, it wouldn't be true, but at least she wouldn't sound so brazen.

"I see." The dimpling corners of his mouth were mocking her as he curved an arm along the back of her waist and guided her in the direction of the roofed stairwell. "A man is supposed to walk the girl to the door and take his chances."

"Something like that," she admitted, slipping off the scarf and absently fluffing the ends of her hair.

Her heart was tripping all over her ribs as they climbed the stairs. She didn't know what any of this meant or where these feelings would lead. It was too soon to know. But she liked this glow she felt when he walked beside her like this.

"Do you have your key?" Seth asked when they reached the top of the stairs.

"Yes." Abbie opened her purse and slipped the scarf inside before taking out her key ring.

When she had produced it, his hands settled onto the rounded bones of her shoulders, so she faced him. The width of his chest was in front of her, his head inclined at an angle toward her while his magnetically blue eyes held her rapt attention.

"What do you think my chances are?" he asked with a sensual curve to his hard, male mouth.

It was so easy to sway toward him, her head automatically tilting upward to provide him with the answer. The pressure of his hands increased to bring her nearer. A second before his mouth moved onto hers, a little voice inside warned Abbie that she was kissing a minister and not to respond too wantonly.

But it wasn't an easy warning to heed, not when the soft curves of her body came in contact with the hard contours of his male form, and she was reminded of the differences between the sexes. Her hands slid tentatively around his lean middle, while the breadth of his hands glided down her spine to hold her firmly.

His mouth did not explore this time, already having discovered the warm softness of her lips. There was more depth to his kiss, more subtle demand, less warmth and more fire. Abbie felt the stirrings of desire coming to life within her and pulled reluctantly away before she shocked him with her behavior.

It was difficult to breathe naturally, especially when his arms continued to encircle her and she could still feel the muscled solidity of his thighs brushing against her legs. The moist warmth of his breath was near her cheekbone. Abbie glanced at his face through the top of her lashes, then lowered it to the white collar showing above the black dickey.

"Thank you again, Rev . . . Seth," Abbie corrected herself.

He slowly brought his hands from around her and let a distance come between them. "Good night, Abbie."

"Good night," she returned the farewell. "I'll see you Sunday."

Seth paused on the first step to add, "If not before."

There was a hint of a promise there, even if it wasn't anything definite. She was smiling as she unlocked the door to her apartment, listening to the sound of his footsteps on the stairs.

Chapter Six

"Well?" Her father leaned against her desk and swung a leg over a corner to half sit on it. Abbie moved her cup of coffee to the side so he wouldn't accidentally knock it over.

"Well, what?" she asked with a frown. "Was there something wrong with that letter I just retyped for you?"

"Not a thing. I'm waiting for you to tell me how your date with Reverend Talbot went last night," he said.

Abbie avoided his gaze and began arranging the papers on her desk in neat stacks. "It wasn't a date exactly. But I had a good time—if that's what you're asking."

"A good time." The corners of his mouth were pulled down. "Funny, I had the man pegged as the kind capable of arousing more of a reaction than just a good time."

"Dad, he's a minister," she protested, knowing full well he was right.

"He's a man—made of flesh and blood, just

like the rest of us. Don't put him on a pedestal, Abbie." He studied her more closely. "Are you going to see him again?"

"I imagine." She nodded, then slid him a twinkling glance. "At church on Sunday."

"You know what I meant, did he ask you out again?" her father chided her for being facetious.

Abbie could answer truthfully, "No."

Her father thought about that for a minute and studied his empty coffee cup. "I guess a minister doesn't have a lot of free evenings, what with church youth groups, choir practices, and the civic functions he's expected to attend. It's bound to limit his social life."

"I hadn't thought about it." There was reassurance in it, though, because it offered a possible explanation why Seth hadn't been more definite about when he would see her again.

"Well." He slapped his leg and pushed off her desk. "Guess I'd better get some coffee and get back to my office so you can get some work done."

On Thursday, Abbie left the office early for lunch so she could stop by the post office and send out some registered mail. When she returned a few minutes before one o'clock, her father stuck his head out the door of his private office.

"Reverend Talbot stopped by to see you," he informed her. "He came shortly after you left."

Frustration clouded her expression. This was

the first indication that he had meant to see her before Sunday—and she had missed him.

"Did he say what he wanted?" she asked, feigning a mild interest.

"I guess he wanted to take you to lunch." Her father appeared to be a little vague on that point. "He did say he'd try to catch you another time."

"Oh." Another indefinite. "Thanks, Dad." Abbie sat down to her desk and stowed her purse in the drawer, trying not to be too disappointed.

Saturday morning, Abbie was up early, gathering up her dirty clothes and linen and driving to the laundromat to do her washing. Her mother had offered to let Abbie use her automatic washer and dryer to do her laundry, but it usually took the better part of a day, washing one load at a time. At the laundromat, it usually took just over an hour. Since she would have insisted on paying her mother for the use of the machines anyway, Abbie preferred the time she saved at the laundromat to the convenience of running next door, as it were.

With the laundry finished, she stopped at the grocery store on her way home and picked up the few items she needed. It was going on eleven when she turned Mabel into the driveway. Abbie stepped out of the car, juggling the sack of groceries while she searched her purse for the door key.

"Abbie!" Her mother called from the back stoop of the house. "You had some phone calls while you were gone. They called here when they didn't get any answer."

"Who called?" she frowned.

"Isabel Coltrain. She didn't say what she wanted, but she seemed very anxious to talk to you." Her mother was consumed with curiosity. "Do you have any idea what she might have wanted?"

To see if Abbie had finished the last stack of manuscript pages the sisters had given her? But Abbie had kept her word to the women. "Maybe it had something to do with typing," she said in a half-truth. "The word has spread that I'm doing typing on the side. I've gotten several calls."

"But what would they want typed?"

"Who knows?" Abbie shrugged to avoid an outright lie, and turned again toward the garage.

The acceleration of a car engine as it turned into the driveway pulled her glance over her shoulder. A dark green sports car zoomed toward her, its racy appearance making it seem to travel faster than it actually was. Excitement leaped along her veins when she recognized the car and the driver, and turned to meet them.

"I forgot to tell you," her mother called belatedly. "Reverend Talbot phoned, too." When he turned off the engine and vaulted out of the car, her mother explained to him, "I was just telling Abbie that you called for her."

"That's all right, Mrs. Scott. Thanks." Seth nodded to the woman, then walked toward Abbie with an easy, rolling stride. He was wearing Levi's again, and a blue chambray shirt opened at the throat—with no collar.

"I just got back." The gladness she was trying to contain shined in the emerald-green flecks of her hazel eyes.

"So I gathered. Here." He reached for the grocery sack. "Let me carry that for you."

Her resistance took only a token form as she relinquished the sack into his arms and walked to the stairway door. "I'm sorry I missed you Thursday, Reverend. Dad said you stopped by."

"Are we going to start that again?" Seth challenged.

"Start what?" Abbie paused on the first step.

"That Reverend business." The dark intensity of his gaze made her blood warm.

"I call 'em as I sees 'em." She mocked him with a provocative glance. Immediately she was attacked by pangs of self-consciousness that she had actually been flirting with him.

"Look, Abbie." He touched the tanned hollow of his throat with his free hand. "No collar. For the rest of the day, you're looking at Seth. So you be sure to call him the way you see him."

"All right—Seth," she agreed, her tone a little more subdued.

"Do you have anything on your day's agenda?" Seth asked as he mounted the stairs one step behind her.

"The Coltrain sisters are getting anxious. I was going to do some more typing on their manuscript," Abbie explained.

"It's a fine August day. What you need is fresh air and sunshine—not more hours in front of a typewriter," he insisted. "I'm here to unchain you from that."

"You are?" Abbie unlocked the door and pushed it open, walking in ahead of Seth. She was alive with pleasure. The realization that he wanted to spend the day with her swelled within her, but she didn't want to appear too eager, too overjoyed.

"Yes, I am." Seth walked to the counter-bar on the kitchen side of the room and set the grocery sack on it.

Abbie moved to the opposite side to begin putting the groceries away. The brilliance of his dark gaze was difficult to meet. There was something possessive about it that started a fire licking along her veins.

"You'll have to give me a few minutes to change clothes after I get these groceries put away," she said.

His eyes made a lazy inspection of the faded blue jeans softly hugging her slim hips and the thin white blouse with its capped sleeves and half-collar. Her auburn-gold hair was pulled back in a ponytail, a white silk scarf tied around it.

"What you're wearing is perfect," Seth insisted.

They were everyday clothes, clean but showing the wear and thinness of many washings. Abbie looked down at them, then back at Seth. If her present clothes were suitable for the occasion, it raised a question. "Where are we going?" She tipped her head to the side.

His strongly shaped mouth slanted in a half-smile. "Heaven."

"What?" Abbie blinked.

"I should have said, heaven on earth," he conceded, with the richness of amusement deepening his voice. "I found a quiet, little spot in the country. It's peaceful, beautiful—the perfect place for a picnic."

"A picnic." She smiled at the initial appeal of the idea, then became serious as she began to think about what food she had in the apartment that she could fix.

Seth appeared to read her thoughts. "I already have a picnic basket filled with more food than we can possibly eat. It's sitting in the back of my car. You don't have to worry about fixing a thing."

"Isn't there anything I can bring?" she asked.

"Just yourself." His gaze claimed her with a vibrancy that made Abbie feel shaky inside.

"All right." Her voice was tinged with a soft breathlessness as she let herself drift under his persuasive spell.

The telephone started ringing, its shrillness making a sharp intrusion between them. Abbie bit her lip in indecision and glanced at the ringing phone.

"That has to be one of the Coltrain sisters," she murmured and wondered what excuse she could give them for not having any more of their manuscript typed.

"I'll answer it." Seth was already moving toward the phone when he spoke.

"Oh, but—" Abbie started to protest, taking a step after him.

But Seth already had his hand on the receiver. He sent her a backward glance over his shoulder. "You get those groceries put away so we can leave," he ordered. "I'll handle the sisters for you."

Abbie gripped the sides of the cardboard milk container she had taken from the sack and watched anxiously as Seth picked up the phone. What would the sisters think when he answered her phone?

"Miss Scott's residence," he said into the mouthpiece and paused. "She's busy at the moment. This is Reverend Talbot. May I help you, Miss Coltrain?" He glanced over his shoulder and noticed Abbie just standing there.

His mouth curved into a wry line as he motioned her to get busy. Without taking her anxious gaze from him, Abbie moved sideways to the refrigerator and opened the door to set the milk inside.

"No, she hasn't finished the typing for you," he said into the phone. "Miss Scott planned to type more today, but I have decided she's been working too hard, so I'm taking her out for the balance of the day." Seth half turned from the waist up to send a smiling look at Abbie and nod in response to the voice on the other end of the line. "I knew you'd understand, Miss Coltrain."

There was another short pause. "Yes, I'll tell her. Good-bye."

Abbie quickly pushed the loaf of bread into the bread drawer as Seth replaced the receiver on its cradle and crossed to the counter. Her glance bounced off his masculine features.

"What did she say?" she murmured.

"Isabel apologized for rushing you about the manuscript and hoped you weren't too exhausted by all the typing you've done for them." Seth relayed the message. "She thought the outing was an excellent idea."

Abbie turned away to put the box of cereal in the cupboard. "But didn't she . . ." She didn't finish the question, concerned that she might be too sensitive and guilty of overreacting.

". . . didn't she think it strange that I answered the phone?" Seth completed the sentence, almost verbatim to what was in her mind. "Why should she?" he countered evenly when Abbie turned with a guilty start. "It's normal for a minister to call on members of his congregation in their homes."

"Yes, but . . ." She couldn't finish that sentence either.

". . . but you are a young and very attractive single woman." Again Seth accurately guessed the rest of it. "And I'm a bachelor."

"Something like that, yes," Abbie admitted.

"As romantically inclined as those two spinster sisters are, I'd guess they're tittering with the possibility a romance is developing between us." A suppressed smile deepened the corners of his mouth as he met her startled look.

"Oh." This small response was all she could manage, since he had confirmed exactly what she had guessed they'd be thinking.

"We lunched together, had pizza one evening, and now we're going on a picnic together," Seth reminded her. "It isn't unlikely that an outsider would jump to that conclusion."

"I know." Abbie nodded.

With calm deliberation, Seth walked around the counter-bar and took the sack of sugar out of her hands, setting it on the countertop. Her protest died when his hands moved over the bareness of her upper arms with caressing ease.

"Why bother to deny it?" Seth challenged softly while he looked deeply into her eyes. A shiver of sensations slivered through her veins. "It's true, isn't it?"

"I—suppose." The whispered admission was hesitant; she was wary of declaring too openly the feelings that were growing stronger with each meeting.

He tipped his head to one side, bronze lights darkening his hair. The expression on his roughly carved features mildly taunted her for her cautious reply, while his hands continued their slow, lazy kneading of her arms.

"You don't sound too sure," he said. "If this isn't the start of a romance, what else would you call it?"

"I don't know," Abbie admitted with an uncertain smile.

"What's the matter?" Seth asked. "Why does it bother you to admit it?"

"I guess I'm not used to being so candid," she suggested, then deliberately tried to side-track the conversation. "How did the Coltrain sisters find out that you knew about their manuscript?"

The faintly mocking glitter in his eyes informed her that Seth knew why she was changing the subject. "They invited me to dinner Tuesday night. I mentioned that we had been together the previous night and that I'd read a couple pages of the manuscript you were typing without revealing that I had recognized their handwriting," he explained. "They were so eager to find out my reaction that they confessed they had written it and asked what I thought." His smile became more pronounced. "So they don't think that you betrayed their secret."

"I wondered," she acknowledged.

"I also promised them I'd write a letter to some friends of mine in the publishing business and see what I could do to help them when it's finished." He let his hands come away from her arms and turned to look in the grocery sack. "Is there anything else in here that's perishable?"

"No, I've already put those items away." There were only some canned goods left.

"Then, let's leave the rest and go on our picnic," he stated.

"Okay." Abbie had the feeling she would agree to almost anything he suggested.

Within minutes after leaving town, Seth turned off the main highway onto a graveled county road that twisted along the ridges and hollows. Abbie was completely lost, having no idea where they were going. She'd never done that much exploring of the countryside to be familiar with all the hill roads.

The August heat had seared the grasses a golden brown to intersperse the thickly forested hills with patches of bright color. Abbie turned her face into the blowing force of the wind generated by the sports car, kicking up plumes of dust on the graveled road.

An azure sky contained a scattering of powder-puff clouds, drifting slowly while the golden sun-ball blazed above the earth with its light. Overhead, a hawk circled, floating effortlessly on the air currents. They were riding on a ridgeback, the Ozark Mountains undulating into the distance like ocean waves.

There was a change in the powerful hum of the engine as Seth eased the pressure on the accelerator slowing the car. A fairly straight stretch of road lay before them with no roads branching off it. All Abbie could see was a short lane leading to the gate of a fenced field, but it appeared to be Seth's destination as he braked the car to a slower speed to make the turn onto it. When the car was stopped, he switched off the engine, removing the sunglasses he'd been wearing.

"This is it," he said with a glance at Abbie while he pushed his door open to step out.

Abbie looked at the gate and the sign tacked on the post that very plainly read: PRIVATE PROPERTY—Trespassers Will Be Prosecuted. "We aren't going into that field, are we?" She climbed out of the passenger side, but eyed Seth with a bewildered frown.

The nearly bald knoll had only a scattering of tall oak trees to shade its yellow grasses. There didn't appear to be any animals grazing in the hill meadow, but the sign on the fence was very definite.

"Wait until you see the view," Seth replied after he had issued an affirmative nod. He reached behind the driver's seat and lifted out a wicker picnic basket. "Do you think you can carry this?"

"But there's a no-trespassing sign on the gate," Abbie pointed out as she took the basket from him and hooked her forearm under the handles. "We can't go in there."

"Yes, we can." Seth removed a Styrofoam cooler from the car's trunk and started walking to the gate. "This land belongs to my family."

"Your family," Abbie repeated with surprise. "I didn't know you had any relation living around here."

"I don't." He stopped at the gate and set the cooler on the ground. There was a padlock on the chain that circled the fence and gatepost. With a key from his pocket, Seth unlocked it and unwrapped the chain to let the gate sag open. "It's a case of absentee ownership, an investment for possible development or resale in the future."

"Oh." But Abbie didn't feel that she knew any more despite the enlightening remark.

"Careful you don't trip on the wire," Seth cautioned as she started to walk through the narrow opening. "I don't want to be responsible for causing a personal injury lawsuit."

It was said in jest but Abbie just wondered all the more. As she went through the gate she was close enough to read the small lettering at the bottom of the sign. The owner was identified as the Tal-bar Corporation. "The Tal-bar Corporation belongs to your family?" she asked when Seth followed her, leaving the gate open behind him.

"Yes. It's a combination of Talbot and Barlow. Barlow was my grandmother's maiden name, and her brother was one of the original partners with my grandfather," he explained. "I thought we'd have our picnic under that oak tree over there." Seth indicated the closest one with a nod of his head.

"Is it a big company?" Abbie suspected it was, since it had landholdings in the Ozarks.

"For a family-owned company, I'd say it's fairly large, but it's certainly not a major national corporation." There was a dry amusement in his tone.

"I guess your family mentioned they owned some land here when you were assigned to our church," Abbie guessed.

"Actually I was here a few years when we originally bought this property, so I was a little familiar with the area before I obtained my transfer."

"You aren't active in your family's company, are you?" Abbie frowned, automatically stopping under the tree when Seth did. She didn't see how it was possible when he was a minister. Yet his remark about looking at the property seemed to indicate otherwise.

"My father insists that I remain on the board of directors to act as their conscience," Seth admitted as he crouched down to set the cooler next to the tree. "There's a small blanket in your basket. We can spread it on the ground."

While she digested the information, Abbie opened the lid of the wicker basket and took out the square blanket lying on top of the plastic dishes. She shook it out and laid it out flat on the grass-stubbled ground. Kneeling on it, she began taking the dishes and utensils out of the basket. "I know it's none of my business . . ." But she couldn't help prying a little more into his personal affairs. ". . . but I have the feeling your father would have preferred that you had joined the company. . . ."

"Instead of becoming a minister?" Seth completed what she had left unsaid. There was a light shrug of his shoulders as he began taking out containers of assorted salads. "In the beginning, he was against the idea—until he was convinced that it was definitely what I wanted. I've had his full support and his blessing for several years now—as well as from the rest of my family."

She was glad that Seth's chosen profession had not created any friction between him and his family, but it sounded too trite to say so. The removal of the napkins and the salt and pepper shakers emptied the picnic basket. Abbie sat in the grass out of the way.

"We have here a private buffet." Seth indicated the various uncovered containers arranged in a semicircle on the blanket. "Macaroni salad, potato salad, ambrosia, tomato aspic, cold roast chicken, ham, fresh fruit, cheese. There's a couple things that I don't know what they're called."

Abbie stared at the array of food. "You don't expect us to eat all this?"

There was a wicked glint in his eye. "To tell you the truth, it was the quickest way to clean out my refrigerator. The ladies in the community have been more than generous about bringing me samples of their cooking."

"Maybe they thought it was the way to win the favor of a bachelor minister," Abbie suggested with a hint of a teasing smile.

"'The way to a man's heart . . .'" Seth followed her thinking and chuckled. "Unfortunately, they couldn't know that I had already been tempted by a copper-haired girl on the road, who gave me fruit." He paused a second to hold Abbie's glance. "There are some who believe that it was the peach, not the apple, Adam and Eve ate in the Garden of Eden."

"Really," she murmured, a little unnerved by the sensuality of his look, so vibrant and alive with his male interest in her.

"Yes, really," he mocked, and turned to reach inside the cooler. "Don't you think you have what it takes to tempt me into sin?"

"Are you sure it's not the other way around?" Abbie countered, matching his sexual banter and not letting him see how much it disturbed her.

There was a heartiness to his throaty chuckle. "I deserved that. You know the right way to put a man in his place, don't you, Abbie?" Seth didn't appear to expect an answer as he took a bottle of chilled wine from the cooler. "Now, this happens to come from my own private stock. It's not a gift from anyone."

Abbie looked at him askance. "Are you allowed to drink wine?"

There was patience in his strong face as he uncorked the bottle and splashed a small portion of wine in two glasses. "In the Book of Matthew, Jesus explains in chapter fifteen that it is not what goes into the mouth that defiles man, but what comes out of his mouth. 'Whatever goes into the mouth passes into the stomach, and so passes on, but what comes out of the mouth proceeds from the heart. . . .'" he paused. "Anything in excess is not good for the body—sweets, fats, or alcohol."

"That's true," she agreed, taking the glass he handed her.

"In biblical times, they drank wine with their meals because the water wasn't potable, for the most part," he added. "It was the fruit of the vine that Jesus gave to his disciples at the Last Supper. That's hardly a justification for the consumption of alcohol. But there's a vast difference between drinking and having an occasional glass of wine with a meal."

"I agree." Abbie swirled the rose-red liquid in her glass. "I wasn't really criticizing you for bringing the wine."

"Weren't you?" It was a mild accusation.

"No, although it probably sounded like it," she admitted with a rueful laugh.

"Sometimes I get the feeling you are more pious than I am," Seth mocked. "No deviating from the straight and narrow."

"I've never been very well acquainted with a minister—on a personal basis." Abbie defended some of her preconceived notions. "So I don't always know what to expect."

"I have noticed." He nodded, a faint smile touching the corners of his mouth. "Right now, you're wondering if I'm going to say a blessing before we eat."

"I was," Abbie admitted on a note of bubbling laughter.

When Seth bowed his head, Abbie did, too. "We thank you, O Lord, for this bounty You have placed before us. And we pray that You will also feed the hunger of our hearts with the Grace of Your Love. Amen."

"Amen," she echoed softly, and lifted her head to glance at him in silent wonder, touched by the simple blessing.

"Shall we dig in?" Seth murmured, arching an eyebrow in her direction, and passed her the small bowl of potato salad.

Chapter Seven

Although Abbie had only taken a small sample of everything, there had been too many dishes. There was still some food left in her plate, but she didn't have room for another bite.

"I think it's a case of my eyes being bigger than my stomach." She sighed and set her fork on the plate.

"There's a lot of wildlife around here that will eat it, so it won't go to waste." Seth rolled to his feet. "If you're finished, I'll scrape your plate on that stump so the scraps won't be attracting the flies around us."

"I am finished." Abbie handed him the plate.

While he walked to the tree stump about twenty yards away, she started putting the lids on the containers and returning them to the cooler so they wouldn't spoil. When Seth came back, he lent a hand, stowing the dishes and silverware in the wicker basket. Once the blanket was cleared and shaken free of any crumbs, Abbie shifted to sit near the middle of it, leaning on her hands and stretching her legs out to ease the fullness of her stomach. Before she could guess his intention, Seth was lying down at right angles to her, with his head resting on her lap.

"Do you mind me using you for a pillow?" Seth looked up at her with deceptively innocent eyes, aware of asking permission after the fact.

"No." But she did find it disturbingly intimate. Her senses were operating on an uneven keel with his head nestled against her thighs. The faded material of her jeans had been worn thin, providing a scant barrier for her sensitive skin.

"Good." Seth closed his eyes and settled more comfortably in place, folding his hands across his chest in a gesture of contentment.

With his eyes shut, Abbie took the liberty of studying the irregular angles and planes of his strong face. There was power in the lift of his cheekbones and steady determination in the clean line of his jaw. His stubby lashes were dark and full, a shade darker than the brown of his eyebrows. There was a slight, crooked break in the line of his nose, and his mouth was well defined, neither too thin nor too full, and definitely masculine.

The dark, rumpled gold of his hair invited the smoothing touch of her fingers. Abbie curled them into the blanket to resist the urge to slide them through his hair. The body heat from his wide shoulders warmed the side of her hip and thigh and spread through the rest of her body. All sorts of dangerous thoughts were running through her mind when she let her glance stray to the even rise and fall of his chest. Starting a conversation seemed the wise thing to do.

"Where does your family live, Seth?" she asked.

A little frown creased his forehead. "Pillows aren't supposed to talk," he grunted.

Abbie laughed softly at that. "Well, this pillow does," she retorted. "Where does your family live?"

He sighed in mock resignation. "My parents live in Denver."

"Is that where the Tal-bar Corporation has its offices, too?"

"Yes."

"How did the company get started?" she asked.

Seth opened one eye. "My, but you are full of questions."

"How else do you learn anything?" Abbie reasoned with a small shrug.

"My grandfather and great-uncle started out as well drillers, then got into the oil and gas business, and backed into cattle ranching."

" 'Backed' into cattle ranching? How do you do that?" Abbie smiled at the phrase, finding it curious.

"My grandfather thought he was acquiring the mineral rights for federal land and found out he had actually obtained grazing rights instead. So he and my great-uncle turned a mistake into a business," Seth explained. "The company also has some mining interest."

"Do you have any brothers or sisters?" she wondered.

"A whole houseful." He sat up unexpectedly, and turned toward Abbie, bracing a hand on the opposite side of her legs. "I have five sisters and three brothers. My parents believed in a large family. Do you like large families?"

"Yes." Her answer was hesitant because she wasn't sure what he meant by the question.

Seth took it a step farther. "How many children do you want when you get married?"

"That's something . . . I'd have to discuss with my husband." She had trouble breathing when he leaned closer. Her heart started fluttering against her ribs.

"What would you say . . ." He tipped his head to kiss the side of her throat. There was a wild, little leap of her pulse. ". . . if your husband wanted . . ." He turned his head to mouth the sensitive cord on the other side of her neck. ". . . a lot of children?"

So many other things were happening in reaction to his nuzzling kisses that Abbie almost forgot the question. "I think . . . I'd like the idea." Tension knotted her throat until she couldn't swallow. A moan trembled somewhere inside her, waiting to be released.

"And if he wanted to adopt some children . . ." His mouth grazed along her cheek, feathering her skin with the warmth of his breath. ". . . in addition to your own?"

"Why not?" she murmured, turning her head to end the tantalizing nearness of his mouth.

It moved onto her lips with a sureness of purpose, claiming them as if it had long been his right to do so. There was no resistance to its commanding pressure. Her lips parted willingly to deepen the kiss as his hand curved itself to her spine. A heady tide of feeling seemed to swamp her, and she reeled at the whirling mist of glorious sensation. She felt drunk with his kiss and wondered if it was the wine.

Then there was no room for thinking, only feeling. Abbie was weightless, floating in a mindless bliss. She wasn't conscious of sinking backward onto the blanket, only that her hands no longer had to support her upright position and were now free to glide around his muscled shoulders and curl into the virile thickness of his hair.

Tiny little moans of pleasure came from her throat when he nibbled sensually at her earlobe and made an intimate study of her neck and throat. The hard contours of his body pressed their male shape onto her flesh while the stroking caress of his hands wandered over her.

Desire seemed a natural extension of all the raw emotion his embrace was disclosing to her. It was the purest form of passion she'd ever know, and the beauty of it swelled her heart until she ached for him. The need inside her strained to be released.

His hand glided smoothly across her ribs, nearing the heated fullness of her breasts. The sensation of skin against skin suddenly shocked her into an awareness of how far out of control she'd gone. Her blouse had fallen loose, the old material stretching to release the lower buttons.

With a stifled moan of panic at what he must be thinking of her, Abbie wiggled from under him and scrambled to her feet. Her breath came thickly as she quickly turned her back to avoid his stunned and frowning look.

"Abbie?" His voice was low and husky.

"I'm sorry." She quickly began stuffing her blouse inside the waistband of her jeans, a task made difficult by her shaking hands. She heard him stand up. "I don't know what got into me," she insisted. "It must have been those two glasses of wine."

His hands closed on her shoulders, the contact momentarily paralyzing. Her blouse was half in and half out, and Abbie couldn't seem to move to finish the job.

"That's not a very flattering thing to say," Seth declared and forced her to turn around. She looked everywhere but into his face, yet the sight of his manly chest, so broad and muscled, hardly hidden at all with his shirt clinging to the heated dampness of his skin, was almost equally unnerving. Abbie kept her hands rigidly tightened into fists so they wouldn't be tempted to touch him.

"I don't know what you mean," she murmured tightly.

"You indicated it was the wine that made you respond to me," he said in a voice that was warm and indulgent. "I was hoping it might have been my kisses."

"It was. I mean . . . I just got carried away because . . . of the wine," Abbie insisted.

Seth crooked a finger under her chin and lifted it to study her face at an angle. "It wasn't because of the wine. You were enjoying being kissed and caressed."

"I was, but . . ." She was close to tears, so anxious for him to think well of her. She had never felt so vulnerable in her life. ". . . I don't want you to think I'm immoral."

"Why should I think that?" Seth questioned with a smiling frown of confusion.

"Because—" Abbie couldn't finish it.

"Because I was touching you? Because I wanted to touch your breasts?" He was even more specific, and his bluntness was more than she could handle. "Or because you wanted me to?"

"Seth." She shut her eyes so he couldn't read how right he was in her look.

"I'm relieved you didn't call me Reverend," he mocked, and gave her a little shake to force her eyes open. "Abbie, I'm a man, not a saint. You are a beautiful woman with a beautiful body. Do you think I don't feel desire when I'm near you?"

"I don't know," she whispered.

"Well, I do." The corners of his mouth deepened with a smile. "Desire isn't necessarily sinful. Promiscuity, infidelity, adultery—those are sinful. Desire is a warm and wonderful thing between two people who care for one another. You don't need to be ashamed of it."

"I wasn't, not really. I just didn't—" She broke

off in midsentence when Seth suddenly began unbuttoning his shirt and pulling it loose from his Levi's. "What are you doing?"

"I'm unbuttoning my shirt. What does it look like I'm doing?" he countered. "You seemed embarrassed because your blouse came unfastened. I thought it might make you feel better if mine was loose, too."

"Seth, that's ridiculous." Abbie couldn't believe he was serious.

His low, throaty laugh vibrated over her. His hands were at her waist to pull her into his arms. That curling sensation started all over again in her stomach as his mouth came down to probe apart the softness of hers. Warmth flooded through her limbs as his molding hands roamed her back and hips to fit her intimately to his hard, male length.

Seth deepened the disruptively sensual embrace with consummate skill, dazzling Abbie with the ecstasy he evoked. Her hands were flattened against his bared chest, absorbing the heat of his body to add to the fire burning inside. She was trembling when he finally lifted his head to trail a butterfly kiss on her closed eyes.

Reluctantly, she started to shift away from him, thinking that he was signaling an end to the embrace, but his arms tightened to keep her fused to the muscled columns of his legs. "Stay here," he murmured, "where you belong."

His hand cupped the back of her head, his fingers tangling with the tendrils of rust-gold hair that had escaped from her ponytail, and firmly directed her head to rest on his shoulder. Of their own volition it seemed, her arms slid around his middle under his loosely hanging shirt. Abbie rested her cheek contentedly against his collarbone, breathing in the heady, male smell of him.

There was a very definite sensation of belonging in his arms. The hard line of his jaw was rubbing against her hair in a sensual caress. With a slight turn of her head, Abbie let her mouth lightly taste the warm flavor of his skin, tanned and tautly stretched across sinew and bone.

Her lips touched the coolness of a gold chain, reminding Abbie of her previous curiosity about it. She shifted slightly in his arms to lift a hand to follow the path of the long chain to where it ended in the center of the springy, silken gold chest hairs. They curled softly against the back of her hand as she held a plain, gold cross between her fingers.

"I wondered what you were wearing around your neck," she admitted softly. The edges were worn, a few scratches dulling the finish. "It looks very old."

"It belonged to my grandfather. He was a very religious man in many ways. And a very passionate man, too." His head tipped slightly downward for a glimpse of her face. "The two can go together."

The sheer naturalness of being held by him had been so overwhelming that it wasn't until his comment that Abbie realized his hand was curved to the underside of her breast, his thumb absently stroking its rising swell. Both her blouse and her cotton brassiere lay between his hand and her flesh, but his touch suddenly seemed to burn through both of them. Abbie stiffened in a delayed attack of modesty.

Guessing the reason, Seth let his hand slide down to the curve of her waist. "I knew what my right hand was doing, so I'm not about to cut it off," he mocked with gentle amusement. "I have the feeling, Abbie, that you are as steeped in Victorian traditions as this town."

Thinking he was ridiculing her for being prudish, Abbie started to pull away, but the bronzed band of his arm stopped her while he cupped his hand to the side of her face and forced her to look at him. There was smoldering pleasure in the darkness of his gaze.

"And I'm glad you are that way," Seth added to assure her that he approved of her keen sense of decorum. "Just remember there will come a time when there is no need to hold back your desires."

"Yes." It seemed very close, too. Abbie hoped, desperately, that she wasn't wrong.

There was a hard, brief kiss before Seth released her from the close contact with his body. "As enjoyable as it would be to idle away the rest of the afternoon kissing you, I think we'd better get our picnic things packed away in the car so we can visit your grandmother."

"Grandmother Klein?" She felt stupid saying

that. She was the only grandmother Abbie had—living that is.

"You usually visit her on the weekend, don't you?" he said. "At the moment, it seems the prudent way to spend the afternoon rather than yielding to the temptation of this blanket and you."

"I think you deliberately try to shock me," Abbie declared, still not quite used to his frankness.

He reached down to scoop up the blanket and begin folding it into a square. His side-glance ran to her, glittering with amusement.

"I have to do something to shatter that sexless image you have of a minister," Seth countered.

"You're succeeding," she admitted, without mentioning that it was something of a revelation.

"It's about time," he replied with a mocking slant to his mouth.

It didn't take long to stow the picnic items in the car. After Abbie had given him a general set of directions to her grandmother's farm, they started out. Less than thirty minutes later, Seth turned the sports car onto the lane leading to the white, clapboard house.

White leghorn chickens squawked and ran from the car with flapping wings when it rolled to a dusty halt in the farmyard. An old gray tomcat sauntered out to inspect the visitors to his territory and meowed an aloof welcome when he recognized Abbie, then eyed Seth with haughty inquiry.

"That's Godfrey." Abbie identified the cat. "He thinks he owns the farm."

"I had the same impression," Seth replied.

"Where's your mistress, Godfrey?" Abbie glanced at the house but there was no sign of life behind the gray-meshed screen door. The cat swished his tail and jumped lithely onto the rear fender of the car to begin cleaning himself, disdaining any notion that he would lower himself to act as guide. "She's probably in the garden," Abbie guessed. "It's around in back."

As Abbie started in that direction, Seth fell into step beside her, his hand fitting itself familiarly to the small of her back. There was something lightly possessive about his touch that made her feel she belonged to him, a sensation she definitely liked.

Just when they entered the fenced yard, a small woman in loose-fitting pants and a flowered blouse came around the corner of the house. The slight stoop to her shoulders was the only visible concession to advanced age. Her short hair was still carrot-red, the result of a regularly applied henna dye. Her sun-leathered complexion was liberally dotted with youthful freckles. She was carrying a five-gallon bucket, loaded full of sweet corn ears, and showing no indication that it was too heavy.

"Hello, Grandmother." Abbie called the greeting.

The woman stopped and waited for them to come to her, but she didn't bother to set the bucket down. Sharp, green eyes made a thorough inspection of Seth, not leaving out a single detail.

"I thought you were probably in the garden," Abbie said. "I wish you wouldn't work out there during the heat of the day."

"I've gotta keep moving at my age," her grandmother insisted, and turned her gaze once more to Seth. "So, you've finally brought a man for me to meet. It's about time." She didn't give either of them a chance to speak as her glance went past them to the dark green sports car. "Is that your car? I always wanted to go tearing down the road in one of those racy convertibles —with my hair flying in the wind. I used to wear it longer, when I was young."

"I'll take you for a ride in it anytime you say, Mrs. Klein," Seth offered with an engaging half-smile. "I'm Seth Talbot."

"I'm pleased to meet you, Seth Talbot," her grandmother replied and looked at Abbie. "You've picked out a strong, virile man. I'll wager he'll have you pregnant a week after you're married."

"Grandmother!" Abbie was aghast. She'd never said things like that before. There had always been the urgings to get married and start a family. Being a farmer's wife, she had always been very casual about the mating habits of animals. Despite this, her grandmother's remark probably wouldn't have struck her as being so scandalous except that—"Seth is a minister."

"So? He's a man, isn't he?" It didn't seem to

make any difference to her grandmother. "He might as well know that I'd like to have a great-grandchild before I die."

"There's plenty of time. You aren't that old," Abbie protested as she sought a tactful way to explain that her grandmother was misreading the situation.

"Considering how long it's taken you to find a suitable man, I wouldn't say there's plenty of time. I was married at seventeen, and had my first baby in my arms when I was eighteen. You're twenty-three years old already, Abbie. You've taken your own sweet time about becoming engaged, let alone married."

"Seth and I aren't engaged, Grandmother," she corrected.

"I thought that's why you brought him out here with you." Her grandmother looked taken aback, and perhaps a little bit embarrassed. "You haven't ever brought a man with you when you've visited me before."

"I was the one who suggested we come here this afternoon," Seth stated, taking the responsibility for the decision. "Abbie had mentioned that she usually visited you on the weekends. Since we had picnicked not far from here, it seemed logical to stop by." He took a step forward, apparently untroubled by the initial conclusion the older woman had reached. "Would you let me carry that sweet corn for you?"

"I can manage it." Her grandmother was a little flustered by her mistake, not liking to appear old and foolish.

"I'm sure you can," Seth agreed easily. "But my father would have my hide if I didn't carry it for you, the way a gentleman should."

Abbie was amazed to see her grandmother surrender the pail of corn to him. Any time she had offered to carry something heavy, her grandmother had impatiently waved her off, insisting she didn't like being fussed over.

"You can set it on the back porch," her grandmother instructed. "Then we'll all go in the house for some cold lemonade."

"These are good-looking roasting ears, Mrs. Klein." Seth complimented her on her garden produce.

"It isn't easy staying one step ahead of the raccoons. Between them and the deer, they play havoc with my garden." She always claimed to have an ongoing battle with the wildlife in the area. "I'll get you a sack, Abbie," she said as they started toward the back door. "So you can take a couple dozen ears of this corn home for you and your folks. You can take some home with you, too, Mr. Talbot. Or should I call you Reverend."

He slid a dryly amused glance at Abbie. "'Seth' will do fine, Mrs. Klein."

When Seth and Abbie walked out of the house more than an hour later, they were each laden with sacks of goods. In addition to the sweet corn, Grandmother Klein had sent along jars of her freshly made tomato preserves and peach butter. She followed them out to the car to bid them good-bye.

"Alice said she was coming out Tuesday to help me put up the corn," Grandmother Klein remarked as Abbie settled into the passenger seat. "Tell her to bring some jar lids."

"I will," Abbie promised.

"Don't forget, Seth, you promised to take me for a ride in this car sometime," her grandmother reminded him.

"How about next Saturday?" Seth suggested, setting a definite time. "You and I can go for a spin while Abbie fixes lunch."

"It sounds like a terrific idea," she agreed in youthful vernacular.

"It's a date." He started the engine and revved it up a few times for the old lady's benefit, then turned the car in a circle in the farmyard to head down the lane. "Your grandmother is quite a woman," he said to Abbie, raising his voice to make himself heard above the noise of the motor.

Abbie responded with an affirmative nod, not attempting to compete with the car or the whipping wind. The noise increased with the acceleration of the engine as they turned onto the state highway and headed for Eureka Springs.

It seemed an exceedingly short ride—and a short day, too, but it was already after five when Seth stopped the car in the driveway. Abbie climbed out of the car and reached for the sack stowed behind the seat.

"I'll carry that up for you," Seth volunteered.

"Thanks, but I'm going to divvy it up with my

parents first," Abbie explained and stood awkwardly, holding the sack in her arms. "And I had a wonderful time, and the picnic was delicious." She remembered the last time he'd taken her home and threatened to kiss her in full view of anyone looking. But she hadn't any excuse for going to her apartment, then coming directly down with the sack. It would be just as obvious to anyone watching.

"I'll see you in church tomorrow," he said and bent his head, lightly brushing her lips with his and drawing away before she could react.

It was only after he'd backed out of the drive that Abbie noticed her laundry still sitting in Mabel's backseat. She could have had Seth carry it upstairs for her. It would have been the perfect excuse. She sighed over the lack of foresight.

Her father came out the back door, carrying the kitchen wastebasket. "That was the reverend that just left, wasn't it?"

"Yes. We were out to Grandmother Klein's." She waited near the back door while he emptied the wastebasket into the garbage can. "There's a bunch of sweet corn here for you and Mom."

"Have you been with the reverend all day?" He took the sack out of her arms. "I thought you were in your apartment typing all this time."

"We went for a picnic, then to Grandmother's," she explained.

"Are those bells I hear?" he teased.

"Dad, you're impossible."

"Why?" he countered lightly. "Is the reverend the type that fools around? I've heard Bible salesmen are notorious philanderers. Maybe ministers are too."

"That isn't funny." She didn't want to think that Seth might just be toying with her.

Chapter Eight

The menu lay unopened on the table in front of
her. Abbie took another sip from her water glass
and glanced at her watch. With the advent of
September and the start of school, there was a
lull in the tourist trade. She hadn't taken it into
account when she left the office early to stop at
the post office before meeting Seth for lunch.
They had agreed to meet at twelve noon, and it
was still five minutes before the hour.

In the last month, she'd seen him on a fairly
regular basis. They usually lunched together
twice a week and went out to dinner or a local
show one evening a week. Unless he was working on his sermon, they usually spent part of
Saturday together, too, sometimes visiting her
grandmother, who was positively mad about his
car.

"George, isn't that the young Reverend Talbot
talking to the judge by the door over there?"

Abbie perked up visibly when she heard the
woman in the next booth mention Seth sotto

voce. She looked around, but she couldn't see him from where she was sitting.

"I think it is," the man in the next booth, obviously George, responded to the woman's low question.

"He isn't wearing his collar again," the woman said in disapproval, and Abbie hid a smile, reaching for the water glass. "His behavior isn't at all proper for a minister."

"You can't very well condemn the man just because he takes his collar off once in a while," George defended him carefully. "It's probably like wearing a tie. When I'm not working, I don't want one around my neck."

"It isn't only that, George," the woman insisted. "It's the way he's carrying on with that Scott girl."

Once she had started eavesdropping, it was impossible for Abbie to stop. She knew the gossip was running rampant because of the frequency of her dates with Seth. It was to be expected.

"Both of them are single. I don't see that there's anything wrong in him dating her," the man said. And Abbie thought, Hooray for George. At least he was sticking up for them against the malicious intonations of his wife, assuming the woman was his wife.

"She doesn't live with her parents, you know, although a lot of people think she does," the woman went on. "She fixed up an apartment for herself in the loft above the garage. It's completely private from the house." The woman's voice lowered to a conspiratorial whisper that Abbie was just barely able to catch. *"They say the reverend has been in her apartment."*

"Really." George's voice was dry with disinterest.

"Don't you think it's strange the way she came back so suddenly from Kansas City? Supposedly she gave up a good job." The remarks were full of malicious innuendos that had Abbie bristling. "If you ask me, there has to be a reason why someone as attractive as the Scott girl hasn't gotten married. I'll bet she's hiding something."

"You have a remarkable talent, Maude, for seeing sin in other people," George muttered.

"I still think he should be dating a nice girl instead. . . . Don't look now, George, but he's coming this way." In a louder voice, the woman issued a sweetly bright greeting. "Hello, Reverend. How are you today?"

"Fine, thank you," Seth's voice replied.

In the next second, he entered Abbie's side vision. She glanced at him briefly, her smile a little stiff. He slid onto the opposite booth seat, a warm light gleaming in his blue eyes for her.

"Hello, Abbie. You're early," he observed. "I thought I'd have to wait for you."

"I had a couple of errands to run." She opened her menu, willing herself not to pay any attention to the idle gossip she'd overheard.

But Seth was too well acquainted with her moods, too able to read her mind. "Is something wrong?" He tipped his head to one side, the thickness of his dark bronze hair showing signs of having been ruffled by the wind and then tamed with combing fingers.

Abbie started to deny that there was anything the matter, then she thought about the woman in the next booth, who must have realized she'd been sitting there all the time. When Abbie spoke, her voice was a little louder than it needed to be.

"I was just thinking about 'sticks and stones,'" she replied. Seth drew back, his gaze narrowing slightly to study her with a considering look. Abbie turned her attention on the menu, missing his glance at the booth behind her. "Meat loaf is the luncheon special today. It sounds good. I think that's what I'll have."

When the waitress came to take their order, Seth echoed her choice. "Might as well make it two luncheon specials." He waited until the waitress had left to ask, "How have you been?" As if it had been awhile since he'd seen her when it was only two days ago.

"Fine. By the way, I finished typing the manuscript," Abbie informed him. "It's safely delivered into the writers' hands already." Abbie was careful not to mention the Coltrain sisters by name, not with the possibility of a big set of ears listening.

"That's good timing," he replied.

It seemed a curious response. "Why is that?" She laughed shortly.

"Because I could use some help typing up some church notices I want to mail out next week. It shouldn't take you more than one evening."

"That sounds as if I've already volunteered," Abbie retorted in amusement.

"I knew you'd agree." Seth mockingly pretended she had. "Is there anything wrong with doing it tonight?"

"I suppose not," she replied, acknowledging that she would do it.

"Why don't you stop by the parsonage a little before seven?" he suggested. Abbie tensed, wondering what the woman in the next booth was making out of her going to the parsonage. "I have to be at the church shortly after seven for a wedding rehearsal," Seth added, and she breathed a silent sigh of relief. "You can have the office all to yourself. I wouldn't want to be accused of disturbing you while you were working."

"I should hope not. Shall I bring my typewriter or do you have one?" she asked.

"A manual."

"I'll bring my portable electric," Abbie stated.

Halfway through their lunch, a member of the church board stopped by the booth and sat down to chat a moment with Seth. Abbie heard the couple in the adjoining booth leave and relaxed a little.

Inevitably the conversation between Seth and the director turned to church matters, which fairly well left Abbie out of it. From church business, there was a natural transition to a discussion of the Bible, and a pointed, but amicable, difference of opinion about the correct interpretation of a particular passage of the Scriptures.

"You settle it, Miss Scott." The board member turned to her for a third opinion. "What do you think it means?"

She felt suddenly trapped, and embarrassed, because she wasn't familiar with the passage they were talking about at all. Seth came to her rescue.

"I think Abbie is going to insist on remaining neutral," he said. "She doesn't profess to be a student of the Bible, so it isn't fair to ask her to referee."

"The reverend is right." Abbie used his title when referring to him in the company of others. "I stay quietly neutral about such matters."

"I imagine you and the reverend have other things to discuss besides the Bible." The man winked.

It was an innocent remark, without any critical intention, yet Abbie wondered if she shouldn't become more familiar with the Bible. Just as this man had, others would expect her to be more knowledgeable about it than she was. The thought continued to prey at the back of her mind through lunch, and the rest of the day as well.

Abbie slowed the car as she neared the parsonage that evening. "I guess we might as well park right out in front, Mabel. The whole town probably knows I'm going to be here tonight anyway," she murmured aloud to the car, and maneuvered the cranky vehicle close to the curb.

With the brake set, she stepped out of the car and walked around to the passenger side where her typewriter was sitting on the seat. The screen door to the parsonage banged shut. Abbie half turned to see Seth running lightly down the steps. He looked so striking, dressed all in black, with only the narrow band of his white collar for contrast.

"Let me carry that typewriter for you," he said as he approached the car.

"It's lightweight." Abbie objected to the notion that she needed any help, but he firmly took it out of her grasp.

"How would it look to the neighbors if I let you carry this into the house when I'm empty-handed?" Seth reasoned with a mocking gleam. "They'd think I didn't have any manners at all."

"And do you?" she challenged, and moved ahead of him to open the door, letting him enter the house first.

It was an old house with typically high ceilings. The screen door opened into a wide foyer with doors leading off from it. A throw rug didn't quite cover the worn patches of the carpet and layers of dark varnish covered the woodwork. The fern-patterned wallpaper probably had once matched the carpet on the floor but it had faded.

"The office is through here." Seth pushed open the door to the right with his foot.

Abbie followed him into the office. There was

an immediate difference. The entryway had created the overall impression of something tired and worn down, but the study had a vibrant warmth to it. A pair of plushly stuffed armchairs were covered in an ocher-gold corduroy, a color carried through in the drapes at the front window. The carpet was a pale cream shade that widened the paneled walls of the room.

"This is where you spend most of your time, isn't it?" Abbie guessed.

Seth placed the typewriter on his desk and turned to lean against the front side of the old walnut desk, letting his gaze sweep around the room before settling on Abbie. "It shows, does it?"

"Yes."

"I had the chairs recovered and bought new drapes and carpeting," he admitted. "The whole house needs something done to it, but I don't know what."

"It has a lot of possibilities."

"Such as?" Seth challenged dryly, and pushed away from the desk to walk to the middle of the room where she was standing.

"As old as this house is, I wouldn't be surprised if there are hardwood floors under that carpeting in the entryway. You could paint the walls a sunny yellow and brighten it up a lot," Abbie said, throwing out ideas off the top of her head.

"Would you like to fix the place up? I'll give you a free hand to do whatever you want," he offered.

It would be a challenge, but Abbie shook her head, expressing skepticism. "I don't think the church would go along with spending that much money on the parsonage. You'd have to go to the board with plans and estimates."

"The board wouldn't care if I paid for it out of my own pocket." Seth dismissed that obstacle. "What do you say? Do you want to do it?"

Again she shook her head. "People are talking now. Can you imagine their reaction if I started redecorating the parsonage?" Abbie eyed him as if he had taken complete leave of his senses.

"'Sticks and stones.'" He used her phrase from lunch that day—deliberately.

"'May break my bones.'" She continued the children's rhyme, but changed the ending to it. "But words can end up hurting you, Seth."

"And what about the words you heard today?" he challenged quietly.

"I don't know what you're talking about," Abbie protested.

"Yes, you do," he insisted, taking her by the arms and pulling her slowly toward him. "You overheard Mrs. Jones saying something before I arrived for lunch today, didn't you?"

"It was nothing. I just considered the source and forgot it. I'm not thin-skinned," she assured him, and spread her hands across the black material covering his chest.

"You have a very sensitive skin," Seth replied, and folded her into his arms to prove it, kissing her throat and the side of her neck.

Little quivers of delight ran along her flesh to

thrill her. His clean-shaven cheeks were smooth against her skin, the tangy fragrance of a male cologne stimulating her senses. It seemed every time he held her in his arms, she experienced this heady rapture that burned deep into her very soul.

"I thought you asked me here to type." The huskiness of her voice revealed how much he was disturbing her.

"Maybe I changed my mind." He burrowed his mouth into the side of her hair.

"What about the wedding rehearsal at the church?" she reminded him, then added to get his attention, *"Reverend?"*

"Now *that* was unkind." He lifted his head while his hands continued to glide up and down her back with lazy interest.

"The bride and groom can't practice without the minister." Her gaze lingered on the strong shape of his mouth, fascinated by the feelings it could evoke.

"But the minister isn't expected for another twenty minutes," Seth informed her. "That's plenty of time for Seth Talbot to—"

"Behave yourself, Seth." Her hands pushed against his chest as she suddenly realized the screen door was unlocked. Anyone could walk in and find them.

"Why?" He allowed her to create a small space between them, but kept his hands linked together behind her back. "Do you think I'm going to lose control of my prurient desires?"

"Don't you think you'd better show me what

you want typed?" Abbie suggested, unable to handle his conversation.

"I suppose." He sighed with mock reluctance. "Come on." He took her by the hand and led her to the desk where he'd set her typewriter. "Here are the envelopes." He pointed to a stack, then to a card file. "And in there are all the addresses of the names on the list."

"Is that it?" Abbie had been under the impression it was more complicated.

"That's it. Do you think you can handle it?" A light danced in his glittering blue eyes.

"It looks simple enough," she conceded. "Any schoolgirl with one semester of typing could do it."

Seth angled his body toward her, that disturbing darkness back in his look. "So you think you're overqualified for the task?" he challenged huskily.

"I didn't say that at all," Abbie denied with a reproving smile.

"Good, because there isn't anyone else I want to do it," Seth declared, then glanced at the wall clock with its swinging pendulum and sighed in regret. "It's time I was getting over to the church. Are you sure you don't have any questions?"

"None," she assured him.

"I don't know how long I'll be." He released her hand. "If anyone calls, they can reach me at the church."

"Okay." Abbie nodded.

His fingers gripped her chin to hold it still

while he pressed a warm kiss on her lips. Then he was drawing away, winking at her as he turned and walked to the door. In just that brief contact, her pulse beat at an irregular rhythm, affected by the possessive quality in his kiss.

The screen door banged shut before Abbie finally moved from where Seth had left her standing. She walked around the desk and found the outlet to plug her typewriter cord into, but her actions were all automatic, not directed by conscious thought. There had been nothing special in this parting, nothing to set it apart from others, yet Abbie had no more doubts about the way she felt toward him. Even without Seth there to disturb her senses and affect her physically, she was in love with him. The knowledge was clear and certain within her, no longer shadowed by question marks that it might be mere infatuation or physical attraction.

A small smile touched her lips as she sat down in his chair. There weren't any bells or lightning bolts, no blinding light—just the pure, warm feeling filling her whole being with the certainty of her emotion. It was a discovery to savor for the moment. Later on, she could wonder whether it was a love that was requited.

She rolled the first envelope into the typewriter and switched on the power, then went over the list of names and addresses to quickly familiarize herself with them before she started. Once she began, more time was spent taking the envelope in and out of the typewriter than typing.

A moth fluttered into the room, drawn to the goose-necked lamp that curved over the typewriter. Abbie let her fingers pause on the keys and arched her back muscles to ease their tension. With satisfaction, she noted that the stack of typed envelopes was taller than the stack of blank ones.

As she typed out the city and zip code to complete the address on the envelope in the carriage, the telephone rang. She picked up the receiver, using her shoulder to cradle it to her ear while she rolled the envelope from the typewriter.

"Parsonage." There was a faintly preoccupied tone to her voice. Silence followed on the other end of the line, drawing her full attention. She gripped the receiver in her hand and glanced at the mouth piece. "Hello?"

"Who is this?" a woman's voice sharply demanded.

"This is Miss Scott." Abbie identified herself, a defensiveness creeping into her words.

"I want to speak to Reverend Talbot. Is he there—with you?" The light emphasis on the last monosyllable made the woman's implication very plain.

"No, he isn't." Abbie made her voice very definite on that point. "Reverend Talbot had a wedding rehearsal this evening. You can reach him at the church."

"I have already tried the church, Miss Scott, and I didn't receive any answer," was the haughty reply. "Are you sure Reverend Talbot isn't there?" The question blatantly implied that Abbie was lying.

"I am very sure," Abbie retorted, just managing to keep her temper. "Perhaps you should try phoning the church again and letting it ring. It's possible Reverend Talbot wasn't able to answer it earlier."

"And it's possible he isn't there," the woman responded. "Do you have any idea what time it is, Miss Scott?"

She had been so busy typing that she hadn't paid any attention to the hour, except to note that it had grown dark outside. She glanced at the wall clock, a little surprised to learn how much time had gone by. "It's eighteen minutes after nine."

"Would you mind telling me what you're doing at the parsonage at this hour, Miss Scott?" the woman challenged.

"The reverend had some typing that needed to be done." If it weren't for the possibility that Seth might suffer the repercussions of her rudeness, Abbie would have informed the woman that it was none of her business.

"How convenient," the woman murmured dryly.

"If the reverend comes back in the next few minutes, may I tell him who called?" Abbie sweetly demanded to know the woman's identity.

But the woman ignored the question. "I'll do as you suggested, Miss Scott, and try the church again." There was a click as the connection was broken, followed by the hum of the dial tone.

Burning with indignant anger, Abbie slammed the receiver down. Her lips were pressed tightly together as she glanced at the window. She hoped the woman had to eat all her nasty little thoughts when Seth answered the phone at the church. A flicker of curiosity ran through her mind and she wondered why he hadn't answered when the woman had supposedly rang the church earlier.

The question impelled her to leave the desk and cross the room to the front window. The outer darkness created mirrorlike reflections in the glass panes, making it difficult for Abbie to see outside. There didn't appear to be any lights burning in the church. A frown narrowed her eyes. If the wedding rehearsal was over, where was Seth? Bewildered, she turned from the window and walked blindly back to the desk. She had to force herself to concentrate on typing the balance of the envelopes.

Forty-five minutes later, she took the last one out of the typewriter. A dull pain was pounding at her temples. She rubbed at it with her fingertips, but it didn't go away. Sighing heavily, Abbie turned in the chair to arrange the typed envelopes in neat stacks. The desk lamp cast a pool of light over her work area but shadows lurked in the rest of the office-study.

"All finished?"

The voice from the shadows made Abbie

jump. She hadn't heard Seth come in. His black-clad form blended with the darkened opening of the entryway. He was leaning a shoulder against the door frame, arms crossed, when she saw him. She had the impression he'd been watching her for some time.

"I didn't hear you come in," Abbie declared after the shock of discovering she wasn't alone had passed.

"Sorry." Seth pushed away from the door, unfolding his arms to lower them to his side as he walked to the desk and into the pool of light. There was something deeply disturbing about the way he was looking at her. Her heart seemed to do crazy, little flip-flops. "I didn't mean to startle you."

"It's all right. Did you just come from the church? I thought it looked dark when I glanced outside earlier," Abbie said.

He sat sideways on the front of the desk, an amused glint in his blue eyes as he surveyed her. "Checking up on me, were you?" Seth chided dryly.

Abbie hadn't meant to give him that impression and rushed to explain. "No, it's just that a woman called here for you and said she hadn't received any answer when she rang the church. I suggested she try again and let it ring. Did you talk to her?"

"No." An absent frown crossed his rugged features. "What time was it?"

"Almost twenty minutes after nine."

"I'd already left the church by then," Seth

admitted, then noticed the questioning look that flickered uncertainly in Abbie's glance. An amused line lifted the edges of his strong mouth. "The groom's parents had a late buffet supper at their house for the wedding party, which I was expected to attend. I put in a brief appearance and left," he explained. "Did the woman leave her name or a message?"

"No. When she didn't call back, I assumed she had probably reached you at the church." Since Seth hadn't been there, Abbie could easily guess what the woman had conjectured from that. She didn't mention the snide comments the woman had made to her.

"Whatever she wanted to speak to me about couldn't have been too important, or she would have called back," Seth concluded, dismissing the matter from the conversation. "Since you're all finished with the typing, how about some coffee?"

If it hadn't been for the woman's phone call, Abbie probably would have accepted the offer. But she was conscious of being alone with him in the parsonage. "It's awfully late. I'd better not." She refused with a shake of her pale auburn hair and leaned down to unplug her typewriter. It was already after ten o'clock, and someone was bound to notice her car was still parked outside.

"In that case . . ." Seth straightened from the desktop when Abbie stood up to wind the cord around the typewriter. ". . . I'll just have to come up with some other reason to persuade you to stay." He moved leisurely around the desk to come up behind her.

"Seth," she protested self-consciously as he slid his hands around to the front of her waist to pull her back against him.

Her entire back was molded to the unmistakable maleness of his solid chest, flat muscled stomach, and thrusting hips. Abbie made a token attempt to push aside the hands circling her rib cage and stopping tantalizingly near the straining swell of her breasts. But she signaled the weakness of her opposition by tilting her head to the side to give his nuzzling mouth access to the bare curve of her neck.

A rising heat flooded through her veins to melt her into pliancy while he nibbled along the sensitive cord near the base of her shoulder. Her eyes drifted closed under the waves of excited sensation. His arms tightened around her, one hand sliding lower onto her stomach and igniting another kind of ache.

The ringing of the telephone was a decidedly unwelcome intrusion, but definitely a timely one, or Abbie might have yielded to Seth's delaying tactics. She felt him stiffen in resistance to the telephone's summons.

Drawing a shaky breath, she insisted, "You'd better answer that."

"I know," he muttered, and reluctantly let her out of his embrace to step toward the desk and pick up the phone. "Reverend Talbot speaking."

Immediately Abbie took advantage of his distraction to lift her portable typewriter into her arms. If she didn't leave now, chances were that it would be much later before she did. Seth sliced her an impatient look when he realized her intention.

"Just a minute," he said to the caller, and lowered the receiver to cover the mouthpiece with his hand. "Abbie, you don't have to leave."

"Yes, I do," she insisted, and moved out of his reach, walking toward the entryway and the front door. "It's late and I have to work tomorrow."

"Abbie—"

"Is that the woman who phoned earlier?" She paused in the shadowed doorway.

"Yes, I think it is but—" It was of no consequence to him; that much was clear in his expression.

"You'd better not keep her waiting," Abbie advised, because it would probably just fuel the woman's imagination. "Bye."

Without waiting for him to respond in kind, Abbie left the office-study and walked with quick, purposeful strides to the screen door. She pushed it open with the side of her arm, her hands carrying the typewriter. As she stepped outside she heard Seth talking on the phone again.

Chapter Nine

A steady rain beat against the panes of her apartment windows. Gray, dismal clouds cast a depressing gloom into the living area. Abbie wandered restlessly from the window and the rain that showed no signs of letting up. She was at a loss for something to do.

There was nothing interesting on television and the radio offered no less passive entertainment. She paused in front of the low shelf of books and glanced over the titles. One seemed to jump out at her, its gold lettering gleaming against its maroon background—Holy Bible. It was the Revised Standard Version of the King James Bible, a gift from the church when she had become a member.

After a brief second's consideration, Abbie slipped it from the shelf and carried it over to the sofa. She curled herself on one corner of the couch with her legs tucked under her and began leafing through the pages. There was a vague thought at the back of her mind that she might accidentally run across the passage Seth had been discussing at lunch the other day.

Since Seth was a minister, the chances were good that there would be more conversations like that one, and her ignorance of the Bible would only become more noticeable. It was something she needed to correct.

A noise made itself heard above the steady patter of rain on the roof. Abbie lifted her head to listen, but she didn't hear anything more. She flipped through a few more pages, then stopped, out of loyalty to her sex, to read the Book of Ruth in the Old Testament. Halfway down the first column, she heard footsteps on the stairs.

The knowledge ran swift and sure within her that it had to be Seth. Even though there hadn't been any definite arrangement for him to see her this Saturday, she had guessed he would come by or call if he was free. She swung her feet to the floor, leaving the Bible lying open on the cushion beside her, and hurried to the door.

There was a knock just before she reached it. Abbie opened the door to see Seth standing outside, rainwater dripping from his jacket. He was wiping the wetness from his face, then shaking it from his hand.

"It's raining," he offered wryly.

"I never would have guessed." Abbie laughed and opened the door wider to let him in. "I'll get you a towel." She walked to the kitchen area to fetch him a hand towel from a cupboard drawer. "Don't you have an umbrella, or did you forget to put the top up on your car?"

"An umbrella, that's what I forgot," Seth mocked as he shrugged out of his jacket.

The rainy autumn weather had brought a damp chill to the air. Abbie noticed Seth was wearing an ivory pullover in a wide-ribbed knit as a concession to the cooler temperatures. It emphasized the width of his shoulders and the solidness of his muscular chest, tapering as it did to his narrow waist and hips. The rain had darkened his hair to a bronze brown, gleaming in the apartment's artificial light.

"Do you have any plans for this afternoon?" he asked when she returned with the towel, giving it to him and taking his jacket.

"Nothing. As a matter of fact I was becoming bored with my own company." She hooked his jacket on an arm of the wooden clothes tree by the door. "Why? Where were you thinking of going?"

"I wasn't thinking of going anywhere, but right here," Seth replied. When Abbie turned to look uncertainly at him, he looped the towel around her neck and held both ends to pull her toward him. There was a heady excitement in the lazy way he looked at her.

"And do what?" she asked, not really meaning to sound provocative.

Bending his head, Seth kissed at her lips. Weak-limbed, Abbie clutched at his forearms for support. "What were you doing when I came?" he murmured between kisses, the heated warmth of his breath mingling with hers. "Whatever it was, that's what we can do—

162

among other things, like this." His mouth closed onto her lips, finally giving her a chance to respond. When he lifted his head, Abbie was contentedly lost in a glorious daze. "Aren't you going to invite me to sit down?" he chided.

"Have a seat." Her hand moved through the air to obligingly second the invitation.

He released one end of the towel and swept it from around her neck, then took her hand to bring her with him as he walked to the sofa. The opened Bible occupied the middle cushion. Seth picked it up to move it so they could sit together, then recognized the holy book. He cocked a curious look at Abbie.

"What's this?" he asked, and glanced at the book it was opened to. "You were reading the Book of Ruth?"

A smile teased her mouth as she remembered his earlier question. "That's what I was doing when you came."

"Any particular reason?" An eyebrow was lifted with speculating interest. "Or are you just trying to impress me?" He sat down on the middle cushion while Abbie bent a knee under her to sit on the end.

"Since I didn't know you were coming, I can't be guilty of trying to impress you," she denied, aware his question had been only half-serious. "I admit I was slightly prejudiced when I picked out the Book of Ruth to read, since it's about a woman. It seemed to be the fair thing to do, to stick up for my sex."

"It's a very logical choice," Seth agreed, leaning against the back rest. "I apologize if I was wrong the other day at lunch when I indicated you weren't well enough acquainted with the Scriptures to offer an opinion."

"You don't need to apologize, because you were right," Abbie admitted with a rueful shrug. "That's why I picked it up to read and learn more about what's in it than the stories they taught me in Sunday school."

"I see," he murmured, absently looking at the opened pages.

"It's a shame there isn't anyone around who could tutor me." She sighed in mock regret, a teasing sparkle in her glance.

"Is that a broad hint that you want to spend the afternoon with me—reading the Bible?" Seth countered with a glittering look that lingered on her mouth, made softer by his kisses.

"You were the one who suggested we could spend the afternoon doing whatever I was doing when you arrived," Abbie reminded him with a small, dimpling smile.

"So I did." His smile was turned down at the corners but no less filled with amusement. "And ministers don't lie, so I guess I'll have to read to you from the Bible." He began turning pages. "Do you have any requests?"

"No." Abbie shook her head. "You choose."

"Let's see." Seth paused, partially closing the book to skip ahead. "What would you like to hear?" It was a rhetorical question, absently murmured aloud. "Something for Abbie. Abra, the namesake of Solomon's favorite. The Song of Solomon." He reopened the Bible to that book of the Old Testament and arched her a glance. "Does that sound appropriate?"

"Very," she agreed, and turned to lean against the sofa's armrest, facing him more squarely.

She watched him turn a couple of pages as if selecting a particular passage, then stop when he found what he was looking for. There was something vaguely enigmatic in the glance that ran over her face.

"From the Song of Solomon," Seth repeated, and began reading in a voice that was vibrant with expression and pitched low.

"How fair and pleasant you are,
    O loved one, delectable maiden!"

The words seemed to send a caressing finger down her spine. It was not what she had expected to hear. The beat of her pulse picked up a little in anticipation, her gaze locking onto his face and watching his mouth form the words when he continued.

"You are stately as a palm tree,
    And your breasts are like its clusters.
I say I will climb the palm tree
    And lay hold of its branches."

Her breathing stopped at the passion and promise in his low voice. A fiery warmth burned through her veins, heating her skin with the things he was saying—the boldness of them, and the beauty of them.

"Oh, may your breasts be like clusters of
   the vine,
And the scent of your breath like
   apples,
And your kisses like the best wine
   that goes down smoothly,
Gliding over lips and teeth."

Seth lifted his gaze from the pages, his deeply blue eyes turning their attention to her. Abbie was helpless to conceal how much the passionate selection had affected her. She was trembling with the desire it had aroused.

Taking the book, he turned it and offered it to her. "Now, it's your turn to read to me." She took it with both hands and glanced dazedly at the page. "Start from here." His fingers pointed out where she was to begin.

Her voice had a husky sound as Abbie began reading the words, and feeling them, too.

"I am my beloved's,
   and his desire is for me
Come, my beloved,
   let us go forth into the fields,
   and lodge in the villages;
Let us go out early to the vineyards,
   and see whether the vines have
   budded,

Whether the grape blossoms have
  opened
And the pomegranates are in
  bloom.
There . . ."

Abbie paused, her voice dropping to a whisper
as she lifted her gaze to Seth. "'. . . I will give
you my love.'"

"Will you?" he murmured and leaned toward
her.

"Yes," she whispered with an aching need to
give to him, seduced by her own undeniable love
for him.

She didn't know he took the Bible from her
hands and laid it aside. She seemed not to be
aware of anything but the pounding of her own
heart and the deeply blue eyes that held her
forever captivated by their fire.

"Then come here, my delectable maiden."
His hands closed firmly on her waist, near her
hipbones, and impelled her to slide toward
him.

Like a willow, she bent under the leaning
force of his body. His mouth was mere inches
from hers as he gently lowered her to the sofa,
the weight of his hard body pressed alongside
hers. It was a moment lost in time, without a
beginning or an end.

It could have been seconds or minutes before
Abbie felt the warmth of his mouth on her lips. It
was a kiss of raw wonder that searched and
explored the boundless limits of pleasure, then

deepened with the insatiable hunger that grew more intense with each taste. Her lips parted under the hungry probe of his tongue to know more of her. Abbie trembled at the fullness that came with the exchange, and the appetite it aroused for still more.

Her legs were tangled with his as her hands roamed over his sweater-covered shoulders, feeling his muscles flex and ripple beneath the ribbed knit material. His mouth rolled over her parted lips while his tongue lightly traced the sensitive inside corners, drawing a moan from her throat.

"Your kisses are like wine, Abra," Seth murmured into her mouth. "Intoxicating and smooth, 'gliding over lips and teeth.'"

And he drank of them again, but Abbie was certain she was the one who was drunk with love for him. It was a shattering experience to be helpless with longing, desperately needing what another person had to give. She strained closer to the raw heat of his body, hard and aroused against her side. His mouth was on her lips, her throat, her ear, her neck, wildly delighting her wherever it touched and tasted.

His fingers were on the buttons of her blouse, deftly slipping them free from the stitched holes, surely working their way downward. Briefly her flesh was exposed to the coolness of the air until his hand warmed it, spreading his heat and making it hers.

Then his head was turning to look at the

feminine beauty he had exposed. Abbie felt no need to conceal her body from his gaze. She loved him and his desire was for her. She wanted him to be pleased with her—with all and everything that made her unique.

"You have lovely breasts, Abra," he declared thickly. "Lovely."

His hand cupped a creamy breast in his palm; his stroking fingers evoked an intimate pleasure so intense it was like pain. His mouth came down to ease the ache and make its own tactile exploration of the hills and valleys and hardened peaks of her breasts. She was a tightly coiled spring inside, wanting to absorb him into her flesh and needing the absolute closeness of love's consummation.

"Love me, Seth," she whispered, her fingers curling into the faint dampness of his hair. It was less a request for physical possession and more a prayer for emotional commitment—that it be as beautiful and meaningful to him as it was to her.

He dragged his mouth roughly across the hollow of her throat, a groan coming from deep inside him. "Abbie, don't ask that of me," he protested.

"But—" The sharp ache of rejection choked her voice, stabbing her with remorse.

"It can't be," he insisted with a trace of hard-jawed anger. "Not for you and me."

His hands pulled her blouse closed, firmly crossing the material. Then he gathered her hard into his arms, flattening her breasts against his chest and burying his face in her hair. The tautness of his long body was pressed into hers, making its male angles intimately felt. It was almost torture to have him so close and know there would be no satisfaction. Abbie wasn't sure why. Her thoughts were too muddled with unfulfilled desires to make anything clear. She clung to him.

"Abbie." Seth released her name in the middle of a long, heavy sigh. "I want you. I'm not pretending to deny that."

"Neither am I," she murmured rawly.

A sound, something like weary laughter, came from him. "What am I going to do with you, Abbie?" The rhetorical question he muttered only confused her more.

The telephone, positioned on the table at the end of the sofa, rang shrilly, almost in her ear. Abbie stiffened with a guilty start, as if the caller could see them locked so intimately in a prone position. There was a moment of indecision while she debated whether to answer it or let it ring. Seth took the decision from her, loosening his arms to let her go.

"You'd better answer it," he advised with husky reluctance. "It could be important."

She moved away from him to sit up shakily, partially turning her back to him. On the fifth ring, she picked up the receiver while the fingers of her free hand fumbled with buttons on her blouse.

"Hello." She heard the breathlessness in her

voice, caused not from exertion but from the softness of love.

"Miss Scott?" a woman's voice demanded.

An icy chill ran down her spine as Abbie recognized the voice as belonging to the same woman who had called the parsonage the other night.

"Yes." She was stiff and wary. "Who is this?"

"This is Mrs. Cones. I'm trying to locate Reverend Talbot. Is he there? It's urgent that I talk to him," the woman stated.

Abbie pressed the receiver to her chest and glanced over her shoulder. Seth was sitting and raking a hand through his hair. "It's a Mrs. Cones," Abbie whispered. "She wants to talk to you."

His head lifted, as if scenting trouble, then a blandness stole over his features as he reached out a hand to take the phone. "I'll talk to her."

"Just a moment," Abbie said into the phone.

"He's there? I thought as much." The woman sniffed in a haughty way.

A scorching heat burned her cheeks at the accuracy of the woman's vile imagination. Abbie avoided looking at Seth as she rose from that end of the sofa and handed him the phone. She moved to the center of the room using both hands to button the rest of her blouse and smooth the dishevelment of her clothes.

"This is Reverend Talbot speaking," she heard Seth say into the phone.

Not wanting to hear even one side of the conversation, Abbie walked to the window to stare at the falling rain. She rested a hot cheek against the coolness of a glass pane and blanked everything from her mind.

When Seth's hand touched her shoulder, she was brought back to a world of awareness. There was a slight movement of her head to acknowledge his presence, but she didn't turn from the window.

"I'm sorry that happened, Abbie," he said.

"It's all right." But the words made her hurt inside, and it was evident in the flatness of her voice.

"Wait a minute." His fingers dug impatiently into her shoulder and forced her to turn at right angles to the window and partially face him. "I'm apologizing for the phone call—not for anything else." Although her expression changed little, the dull green flecks in her hazel eyes brightened visibly. His gaze narrowed on them in satisfaction. "Not for anything else," Seth repeated for emphasis.

"I'm sorry about that phone call, too," Abbie admitted, because it seemed the safest comment to make. There didn't seem to be any point to reiterating her feelings for him. She had already expressed them very explicitly, both by word and deed.

The hand on her shoulder eased its pressure but continued to hold her. "Do you want to know why I chose that particular section from the Bible?"

"Why?" Perhaps his answer would tell her what she wanted to hear.

"Because I wanted you to see it's a book of love and passion, suffering and caring, but mainly it's a book of love," he explained. It was a subject she was intimately familiar with, since its richness filled her. "Don't look at me like that, Abbie." A muscle leaped along his jaw, revealing an inner strain for control.

"Like what?" It seemed no different to Abbie than the way she'd always looked at him.

"Like—" His mouth came down to crush her lips in a fiercely possessive kiss. It took her breath and made a mockery of her normal heartbeat. When he pulled away, his mouth was edged with tautness and his blue eyes glittered with turbulence. His voice fell somewhere between a groan and a curse. "I'm made of flesh the same as you are, Abbie."

"I think I've always known that," Abbie admitted as she leaned back against the coolness of the window to study him. "I just kept letting the collar get in the way."

"You think I haven't known that," Seth murmured dryly, including a slight shake of his head with the reply. His hand moved over her shoulder in a restless caress. "There's a lot we need to talk about, Abbie, but I don't have time now. Mrs. Cones called because her mother is in the hospital, very ill, and her father—the woman's husband—is overwrought. I promised I'd come sit with him for a while so I have to leave."

"I understand," Abbie assured him, smothering her regret that he had to go now.

"Will you wait for me after church tomorrow?

We'll have Sunday dinner together here or at the parsonage. It doesn't matter, just as long as we can have the privacy to talk," he said.

"I don't think the parsonage is a good idea." Neither place was exactly wise but Abbie suggested, "Why don't we eat here? I can put a roast in the oven so dinner can be ready when church is over."

"That's fine." His glance flicked past her to the falling rain outside, then returned to sweep her face. There seemed to be struggle going on inside him. "I have to leave now," Seth stated with grim determination, and kissed her hard before turning away to walk swiftly to the door, as if he thought he might change his mind.

He grabbed his jacket from the hall tree and opened the door, pausing to look over his shoulder at Abbie standing by the window. His mouth twitched with a quick, hard smile, then he was walking out the door, pulling it closed behind him.

Chapter Ten

Abbie followed the line of people shaking hands with Seth as they left the church. When it was her turn, she placed her hand in his and felt his grip tighten in firm possession. There was an added vibrancy in his blue eyes, an interest meant for her alone.

"Good morning, Miss Scott." He faintly drawled the words, as if mocking the formality.

"Good morning, Reverend," she echoed his greeting, a responding smile playing with the corners of her mouth. Abbie was conscious of others listening to their exchange, some critically and some with simple curiosity.

"Your parents aren't with you?" Seth observed with a questioning inflection in his voice.

"No. They went out of town today—to Missouri to visit some friends," she explained.

"I hope you've fixed a good Sunday dinner then."

"I have," Abbie assured him, fully aware that

his comment was a subtle reminder they would be sharing it together. It was written in the way he was looking at her.

Then he was releasing her hand to greet the next ones in line and Abbie moved on. At the base of the steps, she angled to the edge of the sidewalk, removing herself from the flow of people leaving the church. She lingered there to wait for Seth.

The Coltrain sisters spied her as they came down the steps in a glaring mismatch of colors—Isabel dressed in pink and Esther in bright orange. The two sisters were inseparable, yet they seemed determined to establish their own individualities, hence their clashing clothes. Abbie smiled a greeting as the pair converged on her.

"Good morning," she said, noting the excitement in their faces.

"We saw you in church and we were hoping we'd have a chance to speak to you," Isabel rushed.

"Yes." Esther echoed her sister's words and leaned closer to Abbie to whisper conspiratorially, "We mailed the you-know-what to a company in New York."

"The reverend gave us the man's name. He'd already talked to him personally about us and the man wanted to see—what we'd done. Isn't that wonderful?" Isabel nearly giggled like a giddy young girl.

"It certainly is." Abbie didn't have to pretend to be happy for them. She was hardly a judge but she had enjoyed the novel they'd written and felt certain a publisher would like it, too.

"The reverend said it might take two months before we hear what the man thought about—it," Esther explained. "But . . ." She hesitated and glanced at her sister.

"Esther and I have another idea," Isabel spoke up. "But we aren't sure whether we should start on it until we've found out about the first. We could just be wasting our time."

"Yes, and we wanted to ask you what you thought we should do," Esther finished.

"If it were me, I'd go ahead and start working on it," Abbie replied, and their faces lit up.

"Do you hear that Esther?" Isabel declared. "I just knew she'd say that. Didn't I tell you?"

"If we didn't have you and the reverend to talk to about this, I think Isabel and I would bust," Esther insisted, ignoring the "I-told-you-so" challenge from her sister.

"You'll do the typing on this one for us, won't you?" Isabel inquired anxiously.

"Of course, I will." She could hardly refuse.

"You really are a wonderful girl," Esther said, and squeezed Abbie's hand. "And you shouldn't pay any attention to all that talk going around. Those people spreading it are just nasty busybodies who don't have anything better to do." She didn't appear to notice the sudden tension that whitened Abbie's face as she turned to her sister. "We have to get home, Isabel."

"Yes. Now that you've agreed that it's the right thing to do to start on another one, we have a lot of research we need to begin. We don't mean to rush off," Isabel explained. "But you do understand."

"Of course." But it was a somewhat absent response Abbie gave as the two women hurried away.

Abbie had known her relationship with Seth had stirred up a lot of idle gossip. It was to be expected when a local minister was involved. Some of the remarks that had gotten back to her had been unfair and unkind. She had always been more concerned about all the talk affecting Seth's standing in the community rather than her own. But Esther's comment seemed to indicate Abbie was the one being maligned, and she was absolutely helpless to do anything about it. It did little good to tell herself she shouldn't be bothered by vicious gossip, because she suddenly was.

The stream of people coming out of church had ended, although the doors remained open. There was no sign of Seth, but Abbie assumed he had gone to change out of his robes. The church grounds and parking lot were virtually emptied of people and cars. She felt rather conspicuous standing near the bottom of the church steps and decided it would be more discreet if she waited inside the door.

As she entered the church she heard voices coming from the pulpit area. She recognized Seth's among them and was drawn across the small entry area by an inner need to see him. Seth and three other men were standing by the front pew. Abbie noticed he was still wearing his black robe. She had no intention of intruding or even eavesdropping. The three men were members of the governing board, so Seth was obviously discussing some church business with them.

Before she could turn away to wait near the front doors, she heard one of the men mention her name. She was held motionless, frozen by a kind of dread. Against her will, Abbie listened to what they were saying.

"We don't mean to sound critical, Reverend." A bald-headed man was speaking in a stiffly censorious voice that belied his words. "But we have an obligation to ourselves and the church to express our feelings on this matter."

"I'm sure your intentions are above reproach." Seth's murmured response was exceedingly dry. Even from this distance, Abbie could see the coldness in his blue eyes and the attitude of challenge in his stance.

"It isn't that we have anything personal against Miss Scott." A second man hurried to assure Seth of that.

"We freely acknowledge that she comes from a good family. Her parents are respected members of the community and this church," the third man said. "Miss Scott herself is probably a very nice girl."

"However?" Seth prompted the qualification that had only been implied by their tones.

"However . . ." The bald-headed man glanced at his two colleagues. ". . . she doesn't strike us as being a suitable . . . companion"—he paused before selecting the words—"for the minister of our church."

"Since Miss Scott has returned to our town, she hasn't participated actively in church affairs. She didn't even attend church on a frequent basis until you came," the third man explained.

"These are things you couldn't have known about her," the second man inserted. "Which was why we felt we should bring it to your attention."

"I'm sure you understand now why we are advising you to break off your relationship with Miss Scott. It would be in the best interest of everyone concerned," the bald-headed man concluded, with a slightly righteous tilt of his head.

Tears burned the back of her eyes as Abbie heard the final edict. She hadn't dreamed that anything like this might happen. The whole scene took on a nightmarish unreality. Her gaze clung to Seth as the silence stretched over the span of several seconds.

"I fully understand the concern that prompted you to seek me out, so this could be discussed openly." Seth's low-pitched voice was clear and concise. "And I'm in full agreement with you that Miss Scott lacks some of the qualifications that are regarded as essential for a woman to be considered as a minister's marital partner. . . ."

An involuntary gasp of pain was ripped from her throat at this ultimate condemnation from the man she loved. Abbie cupped a hand to her mouth to smother any more sounds, but it was already too late. Seth had seen her.

"Abbie!" He called to her.

But she heard the irritation in his voice and whirled away to run out the door. Tears blurred her vision as she hurried down the steps, breathing in sobs. Her high-heeled shoes restricted her pace to a running walk.

All her illusions were torn asunder. She suddenly realized why Seth had wanted to talk privately to her today. He had intended to break it to her gently that she wouldn't be a suitable wife for him. Love had led her down another dead-end road.

Yesterday, that passionate scene on her apartment sofa had been just that—passion—at least on Seth's part. Now Abbie could see what he had been trying to tell her when he had asserted he was made of flesh. The desires of the flesh—as opposed to the desires of the heart.

She remembered the way he had held her and murmured, "What am I going to do with you, Abbie?" Tears ran hotly down her cheeks as she reached her car in the church lot. It was all very clear now why he had said that. No doubt Seth had guessed that she was in love with him, but marriage was out of the question. What a fool she'd been! What an unmitigated fool!

"Abbie!"

Her glance was jerked in the direction of Seth's voice. He was half running across the lawn toward her, his black robe billowing out behind him. The flutterings of panic went through her. She couldn't face him, not yet—maybe never.

Wiping at the tears running down her cheeks, Abbie yanked open the car door and scrambled behind the wheel. Her shaking hands dived into her purse for the key and fumbled in their first attempt to insert it into the ignition lock. She glanced frantically out the front windshield. Seth was nearly to the car, a forbidding grimness etched into his rugged features.

"Don't fail me now, Mabel," Abbie pleaded with the car as she turned the key in the switch.

The motor grumbled in protest but its slowly turning noises were encouraging. Abbie pumped on the pedal to give it more gas and the grumble became a constant complaint. The gears ground together as she shifted into reverse, but it was too late.

Seth was opening the passenger door and reaching across the seat. Abbie pressed herself against the driver's door to elude him, but he wasn't intending to grab her. He was after the key. By the time she realized it, he had already turned the motor off and extracted the key from the ignition.

Cornered, Abbie squared around to face the front and gripped the steering wheel with both hands. She held herself rigid, refusing to look at him, not wanting to see the pity in his eyes.

"Will you please give me the keys?" she requested stiffly. Her jaw was white with the effort to contain her emotional turmoil.

There was a rustle of material as Seth climbed

into the passenger side and shut the door. Tension screamed through her nerves when he leaned over and inserted the key into the ignition switch.

"There's your key," he challenged.

Her chin started to quiver. Abbie had to grit her teeth to control it. "Will you please get out of my car?" she insisted, still without looking at him.

"We're having Sunday dinner together, remember?" Seth replied evenly.

"The invitation is withdrawn," Abbie retorted wildly, and blinked quickly to keep back the tears.

"That's too bad. I guess I'll just have to sit and watch you eat," he countered. "But we're going to get this misunderstanding straightened out."

"There is nothing to straighten out." She lifted her chin a little higher. "The situation has been made perfectly clear to me, so we have nothing to discuss. I understand completely."

"Do you?" he murmured dryly.

"Yes, I do," Abbie stated. "There's nothing you have to explain."

"Whether you want me to or not, I'm going to do just that," he stated. "You obviously overheard my meeting with the representatives from the church board."

"Obviously," she admitted on a bitter note, and flashed him a brief glance that was almost her undoing. The brooding intensity of his gaze seemed to reach out for her, but she succeeded in avoiding it.

"There are a great many disadvantages to marrying a minister. Your weekends are never free. Come rain, shine, sleet, or hail, you're in church on Sunday mornings. A lot of week-nights, your husband is gone attending church meetings. Everything you do is scrutinized by the good members of the congregation, from the clothes you wear to the way you fix your hair. You're expected to join every charity, every social and church group, and attend every meeting, unless your children are sick. You—"

"Stop it!" Abbie closed her eyes, unable to take anymore. "I'm fully aware I don't qualify for the position, so you don't have to give me a bunch of reasons why I wouldn't want it anyway!"

"You may not be applying for the position, Abbie," Seth said quietly, "but I'm asking you to fill it."

She caught her breath at his words, but refused to believe he meant them. Her eyes were bright with tears when she finally opened them and turned an accusing glance at him. "I heard what you said in there, Seth," she reminded him. "I don't—"

"If you had stayed to hear what else I had to say . . ." Seth interrupted, ". . . you would know I don't care whether you'd make a suitable minister's wife or not. You're the woman I want to marry."

"I . . ." Abbie stared at him incredulously, daring to listen. "Is this a proposal?"

"Yes." A slow smile began to spread across his mouth. "I'd get down on one knee but Mabel has me in cramped quarters." He hitched up his robe to reach in his pants pocket. "I was going to offer you this after dinner."

Dazed, Abbie slowly uncurled her fingers from their death grip on the steering wheel as she caught the sparkle of a diamond ring. When he reached out for her hand, she hesitantly offered him her left. She watched him slip the ring onto her third finger. "It's beautiful," she murmured.

"Does that mean you'll marry me?" Seth mocked.

"Yes . . . if you're sure." Abbie qualified her acceptance.

"I am very sure," he insisted, and proceeded to prove it.

His kiss was ardently possessive and demanding as his arm circled her waist to pull her across the seat to achieve a more satisfactory closeness. There was a wild singing in her ears, a rush of joy that was almost unbearably sweet. When he finally dragged his mouth from hers, she buried her face in the silklike robe covering his chest.

"I never realized I could be so happy." Abbie breathed out the words. "I thought I'd lost you."

"Not a chance." His fingers tunneled into her auburn hair and lifted her head so he could study her love-softened features. "You are going to be my wife . . . Mrs. Seth Talbot."

Hearing it made her tremble with happiness. "I still can't believe that you want to marry me, but I'm glad you do."

"Don't you remember the second time we met,

I told your mother that I hadn't married because I hadn't found anyone who was suitable for me," Seth reminded her. "I was never looking for a suitable minister's wife. I wanted a woman who would be right for me. You are that woman, Abbie."

"I had forgotten you had said that," she admitted.

"Maybe if you had remembered, you wouldn't have run out of the church the way you did." His mouth twisted in a wry line. "If you only knew how frightened I was at that moment—and how angry I was, too, because their unthinking remarks had hurt you."

"It wasn't just what they said, but the remarks *you* made yesterday, too," Abbie explained.

"The remarks I made?" He quirked an eyebrow. "What did I say to give you the wrong impression?"

"It was a lot of little things. When I wanted you to love me, you refused and told me not to ask that of you," she remembered.

"That's simply because I didn't want to anticipate our wedding night," Seth explained, then shook his head in stunned disbelief. "I suppose you thought I was saying that I couldn't love you."

"Not at that moment, I didn't think it—only later when I began piecing things together," Abbie admitted ruefully, because she had gotten the picture all wrong.

"What things?"

"Like when you said you didn't know what you

were going to do with me, I thought you were trying to find a way to break it to me gently that you didn't love me."

"I love you," Seth stated, so there would be no more question of that. "As for that remark, I'm not really sure what I meant other than that I'd been waiting for so long for you to finally recognize I was a man, that I loved you as a man. Because I was a minister you kept trying to put me above such things. Yesterday you nearly made me forget I was a minister, too."

"And I'll learn to be a good minister's wife," Abbie said, tracing her fingers along his jaw and trailing them across the slashing groove to the corner of his mouth.

"That's the other thing I was trying to explain to you yesterday. I don't want you to feel that because of me, it's your duty to know the Bible, or attend church, or anything else. If you want to do it, then let it be for the same reason I have. Do it for the love of God, not because you feel obligated because you are the minister's wife."

"I will," she whispered. "I promise you that."

His arms tightened around her, gathering her against him as his mouth came down to claim her lips. It was a long and passionate kiss that rocked Abbie all the way to her toes. She felt him shudder and bury his mouth in her hair.

"How I love you, Abbie," he muttered thickly.

"Seth." When she opened her eyes, her glance strayed over his shoulder to the walls of the church. "Do you realize we are practically necking in the church parking lot?"

A low chuckle came from him after a second's stillness. He lifted his head, amusement crinkling the corners of his eyes. "Can you think of a better place? I love you. In the eyes of God and the eyes of man, I want you for my wife."

"And I want you for my husband," she whispered, because she couldn't think of a better place to love him either. Then suddenly she remembered something else and pulled back from him. "The roast!"

"What about it?" Seth frowned.

"It's still in the oven." Abbie glanced at her watch. "Dinner is going to be ruined," she groaned.

"There will be plenty of other Sunday dinners," he assured her, and pulled her back into his arms where she belonged.

Love a good story?
So do we!

Don't miss any of these bestselling romance titles from Pocket Books.

The
New York Times
Bestseller!

One Last Look • Linda Lael Miller
Someone wants her next breath to be her last…

Alone in the Dark • Elaine Coffman
A woman discovers she has a long-lost twin…and is plagued by recurring nightmares of her own death.
Is she…**Alone in the Dark**?

Priceless • Mariah Stewart
A man and woman discover that love is the most precious treasure of all.

Paradise • Judith McNaught
Escape to passion. Escape to desire. Escape to…Paradise.

INTIMATE MOMENTS

#1237 SOME MEN'S DREAMS—Kathleen Korbel
Single father Dr. Jack O'Neill could work miracles in the E.R., but he needed help healing his own family, stat. His young daughter was in danger, and only Dr. Genevieve Kendall knew what to do. By revealing a secret from her own past, Gen might be able to save the child's life, but would any amount of love be enough to save the father's frozen heart?

#1238 TRUTH OR LIES—Kylie Brant
The Tremaine Tradition
To catch a criminal, detective Cade Tremaine turned to Dr. Shae O'Riley, the beautiful surgeon who had caught the eye of a suspected drug runner—and the officer on his trail. But neither Cade nor Shae expected the spiraling path of danger and corruption they faced. And they didn't anticipate finding love— love they were terrifyingly close to losing forever....

#1239 FREEFALL—RaeAnne Thayne
When a tragic accident left Sophie Beaumont to care for her sister's children, she was reunited with Thomas Canfield, the children's paternal uncle and her former lover. Soon old passions reached new heights. Sophie feared falling for Tom again, but he was the only man who made her feel safe. Especially once she learned that her sister's death was no accident, but murder....

#1240 RISKING IT ALL—Beverly Bird
How to defend a guilty man? That was the question attorney Grace Simkanian faced with Aidan McKenna, an allegedly crooked cop who claimed he'd been framed. Though mistrustful of men, Grace couldn't deny the crackling chemistry they shared. But could she let go of past prejudices in time to save his career—and her hardened heart?

#1241 HEARTBREAK HERO—Frances Housden
Kiss-and-tell, a sweet-sounding name for a deadly drug. It was up to DEA agent Kell Jellic to track down the woman carrying the formula. But when he unwittingly fell for Ngaire McKay, his prime suspect, he found himself torn between duty and desire. With the world watching, Kell had to prove that she was actually innocent before they both wound up dead.

#1242 NO PLACE TO HIDE—Madalyn Reese
A stalker was hunting Emma Toliver, and the only man who could protect her was Anthony Bracco, the ex-corporate raider who had once tried to steal her company—and her heart. Though she thought Anthony was out of her system, one look into his enigmatic eyes sparked a heat too intense to ignore. Suddenly Emma wondered who the *real* threat was....

SIMCNM0703